George Pellew

In Castle and Cabin

Talks in Ireland in 1887

George Pellew

In Castle and Cabin
Talks in Ireland in 1887

ISBN/EAN: 9783337327668

Printed in Europe, USA, Canada, Australia, Japan

Cover: Foto ©Andreas Hilbeck / pixelio.de

More available books at **www.hansebooks.com**

IN CASTLE AND CABIN

OR

TALKS IN IRELAND IN 1887

BY

GEORGE PELLEW, A.M., LL.B.

OF THE SUFFOLK BAR

————

NEW YORK & LONDON

G. P. PUTNAM'S SONS

The Knickerbocker Press

1888

and at once to solve the group of problems so long unfortunately known as " the Irish question."

To the kindness and interest of the ladies and gentlemen I have mentioned I desire to acknowledge my indebtedness for a most delightful and instructive summer ; and those who were my friends, acquaintances, and hosts in Ireland will well know that, if I do not thank them personally in this place, I am not the less grateful for their kindness and hospitality. Whatever the event of the future, may it bring them nothing but peace and happiness ! ·

GEORGE PELLEW.

ERRATA.

PAGE 43, for Clonmell, *read* Clonmel.
PAGE 158, for Sixth Massachusetts Volunteers, *read* Ninth.

CONTENTS.

iii

PART III.

IN CONNAUGHT.

PART IV.

IN ULSTER.

PREFACE.

It is the general belief that a change in the social and political condition of Ireland must soon be accomplished, a change so fundamental as to be properly called a revolution. The system of "landlordism" is to be superseded, we are told, by "peasant proprietorship," the government of Great Britain by Home Rule. Such changes may, perhaps, be effected without bloodshed, but not, certainly, without intense excitement. The excitement that out of the ruins of the old parties has created two new parties, the Home Rulers and the Unionists, and that in Ireland nicknames the Unionists "traitors" and the Home Rulers "rebels," must, to some degree, blind men's eyes and deafen their ears. The questions about to be solved in Ireland, the necessity or the reverse of landlordism, and the proper limitation of local independence, involve principles that are at the root of all society and government, and claim the interest of serious-minded citizens in any country. Especially do these questions deserve the careful attention of the American people, since Irish politics perpetually exercise no indirect influence on our own, and we cannot help being important factors in Irish affairs. Books upon the subject are so numerous that some excuse seems needed for the publication of another, but, as a rule, the books and articles we read are the controversial statements of professed

partisans, so that place may, perhaps, still be found for
an uncolored record, however incomplete, of thought and
conduct in Ireland at the present time.

Last summer I spent rather over four months in Ireland, from the beginning of July to the early days of
November. Letters of introduction were, with the
greatest kindness, furnished me by W. E. H. Lecky the
Marquis of Sligo, Lady O'Hagan, Mrs. Penrose Fitzger-
ald, Sir Louis Mallet, Sir James Caird, and Sir George
Young, to representative Unionists, and to representative Nationalists by the Hon. W. R. Grace of New
York, John E. Ellis, M. P., Mrs. Green, A. P. Graves,
and Charles E. Mallet of London. In Ireland, the
Honorary Secretary of the Irish National League, Timothy Harrington, M. P., most courteously gave me a cir-
cular-letter which secured me the hospitable and serious
attention of Nationalists from Kerry to Donegal. Every
person I met I tried to draw into conversation upon the
condition of the country, and the reasons that made
them desire Home Rule, or oppose it. Full notes were
taken of every conversation, however apparently unimportant, and, on reading them over, I found that they
contained records of talks with over two hundred people,
including officials, landlords, land agents, priests, farmers,
professional men, merchants, shopkeepers, commercial
travellers, and laborers. Four months is, perhaps, not
long enough to find out much about a country so vari-
ously interesting as Ireland. If I can, however, succeed
in making the reader feel as though he had seen and
heard what passed in my presence during those four
months, this little book may have been worth the reading.
It will, at least, suggest some of the difficulties to be met
by any statesman and by any nation that proposes finally

IN CASTLE AND CABIN.

INTRODUCTION.

THE AGRARIAN AGITATION AND THE LAND ACTS.

In the volume of the "State Papers" for 1557, there is a despatch from the Lord Deputy to Queen Elizabeth, recommending the appointment for Ireland of "Commissioners to settle the rent" to be taken by landlords from their tenants, and also of a "Commission to compound for arrears."[1] That the legislation of the last few years in regard to the tenure of land in Ireland has been along the lines suggested more than three hundred years ago, proves that special and permanent conditions have isolated the Irish people from the general tendency of civilization, a tendency that has invariably been from "status" to "contract," from perpetual state interference to the greatest possible freedom of individual action.

"That condition of society in which the land suitable for tillage can be regarded as a mere commodity, the subject of trade, and can be let to the highest bidder in an open market, has never, except under special circumstances, existed in Ireland."[2] This fact is the reason for the existence of the "Irish Land Question." Under

[1] T. M. Healy : "A Word for Ireland," 1886, p. 7.
[2] "Report of the 'Bessborough' Commission," 1881, p. 4.

the early tribal system the land was owned by the tribe
in common, with the exception of a certain portion that
was held by an elective chief for the time being. No
permanent interest in the land existed under this system,
" tanistry," as it was called, and no people has ever
become civilized till it has been discarded. Such indefi-
niteness of individual rights was abhorrent to English
notions of law and order, and wherever the conquering
power of England extended, the chiefs or their succes-
sors were held to be the owners of the soil, and the people
tenants at will or from year to year. This change, if it
had come about by imperceptible stages and naturally, as
in England, or even if it had been enforced throughout
the whole country and at once, would have been acqui-
esced in and would have made for civilization ; but the
conquest of Ireland was an intermittent and piecemeal
conquest, that for centuries kept the country in confusion. Within the " pale " English law prevailed ; outside, anarchy mitigated by survivals of tribal customs.
Later came the period of " plantations." Under Elizabeth the vast property of the Desmonds was confiscated.
In the times of the first Stuarts, Ulster was planted. By
the " Act of Settlement," in 1653, Ireland was again dis-
tributed among adventurers and soldiers, and the natives
were removed beyond the Shannon. Under William III.
over a million acres were escheated, and " when he died
there did not remain in the hands of Catholics one sixth
of the lands which their grandfathers held " after the
passing of the Act of Settlement. During all these centuries it is clear that the tenure of land was not regu-
lated by contract. When the original occupiers were
allowed to remain, they remained as serfs rather than as
tenants, and when they were replaced by others the new

settlers were selected for special reasons, military, religious, or political.

To this long continuance of social confusion are due the facts that especially characterize the "Irish Land Question" : the low standard of living among the peasantry ; the absence of improvements by the landlords ; and the limitation of industry to agriculture. The "potato," introduced in the early part of the seventeenth century, soon became the popular crop of the country, for "it was easily raised, the yield was great, and the produce was too bulky to be carried away by plunderers." Improvements by a landlord are the result of agreement or contract, and as the tenants came in only by custom or favor they were naturally neither expected nor demanded. Moreover, in the tribal period the chiefs certainly made no "improvements," building no fences for their people, for the people were too little civilized to need more than they could do themselves ; and in the later period the new landlords made no "improvements," for they were often needy adventurers, and even a rich man would be beggared by building houses and fences for a tenantry so numerous and with such small holdings. Manufactures were naturally slow to arise in such a society. Even in England, manufactures were confined chiefly to the northern counties, to the neighborhood of the large coal fields, and in Ireland coal of a good quality is not to be found. Two manufactures only attained prosperity, those of linen and of wool, for the climate and soil of Ulster were peculiarly suited to the growth of flax, and the wool of the Irish sheep was unusually fine ; but the woollen industry was practically destroyed by Act of Parliament under the influence of the mistaken political economy of the eighteenth century.

4 IN CASTLE AND CABIN.

During the French and the Peninsular wars farming became exceptionally profitable, and under the protective tariff the Irish farmers enjoyed almost a monopoly, at artificial prices, in supplying English markets. Between 1780 and 1846 flour mills sprang up like magic wherever there was water-power, and great quantities of wheat and wheaten flour were exported. In the south of Ireland the grass-lands were broken up and planted with this lucrative crop.

In 1795 the franchise was extended to Catholics, with freeholds of the value of forty shillings a year, and as the restrictions on the holding of land by Catholics had been before this time repealed, all restraints on subdivision were cast aside, and an enormous number of small hold-ings replaced the comparatively large farms of earlier times. For a while all went well. Meadow-land, and even bog moor, was found capable of producing excel-lent crops of the best wheat and the largest potatoes. "But how were these enormous crops grown? By precipitating or rendering soluble the phosphates. How was this done? By skimming off and burning into ashes the whole of the upper two inches of the surface of the ancient grass lands, the very cream and marrow of the land, where for years, and in many cases for centu-ries, lay the accumulated vegetable matter of the soil." [1] Land was let for this purpose for two or three guineas per rood by the season, and at a merely nominal outlay a crop was produced that would realize from £8 to £11 per acre. [2] Mountain bogs were prepared for potato planting with equal simplicity; the land was limed, ploughed, and sown, and then all covered with guano and clay. The gain was enormous, and the harvest left

[1] William Pilkington : " Help for Ireland," 1887, p. 4.   [2] *Id.*

the land, "which had hitherto been scarcely worth one shilling per acre, in excellent order for sowing corn crops or grass seeds, and permanently worth at least £1 per acre."[1] The practice of land burning extended over Ireland. "Three fourths of the arable land in the provinces of Munster, Leinster, and Connaught have been treated in this destructive manner." Life was easy, and early marriages became the rule. In 1847 the population had risen to nine millions, having more than doubled in fifty years, while at the same time the food-producing power of the land had decreased. The neglect to use fresh seed predisposed the potatoes to disease. Partial famines occurred every few years during the first half of the century, and in 1847 the potato crop was a total failure. In 1851 the population of Ireland was six millions and a half.

A condition suitable for freedom of contract in respect to land, it was clear, had not yet been reached in Ireland, for the farmers were ignorant and short-sighted, paying fancy prices, fines, and bonuses gladly for the possession of land as for a share in a lottery, and the landlords had complete control of the only means of subsistence.

In 1843 a commission, the "Devon" Commission, was appointed to inquire "into the state of the law and practice in respect to the occupation of land in Ireland," and in 1845 its report was presented to Parliament. The Ulster custom of "Tenant Right" was fully described, by which a tenant is allowed to "obtain from his successor a sum of money, partly in remuneration of his expenditure and partly as a price paid for the possession of land which the new tenant would have no other means of acquiring." On the 9th of June, 1845, Lord

[1] Trench : "Realities of Irish Life," London, ch. vii.

Stanley introduced a bill "for the purpose of providing compensation to tenants in Ireland, in certain cases, on being dispossessed of their holdings, for such improvements as they may have made during their tenancy," and immediately afterwards Mr. Sharman Crawford moved for leave to bring in a "Tenant Right Bill," but both were rejected. The "famine" was followed by a series of evictions on an enormous scale, and in 1850 there was organized "The Tenant League," to establish the principles that "a fair valuation of rent be made between landlord and tenant in Ireland"; that "the tenant should not be disturbed in his possession so long as he paid such rent"; and that "the tenant should have a right to sell his interest, with all its incidents, at the highest market value." [1]

In 1848 the "Encumbered Estates Act" was passed to facilitate the sale of estates heavily charged with indebtedness on the petition of owner or creditor, giving the purchaser a simple and indefeasible form of title. The properties of many old Irish families were sacrificed under the Act, and purchased by business men, for the most part Irish men, as an investment, who for the first time dealt with the tenants upon principles of rigid contract. "Although not blind to the hardships which often attend this greater strictness," wrote Mr. Sullivan, "I consider the new system has introduced few more valuable reforms than this, which enforces method, punctuality, and precision in the half-yearly settlements between landlord and tenant in Ireland." [2]

In 1870 an Act was passed giving tenants, in case of capricious eviction, compensation for the disturbance, and on leaving their holdings voluntarily or upon notice

---

[1] A. M. Sullivan : "New Ireland," ch. xiii.   [2] *Id.*, ch. xii.

from the landlord, compensation for improvements. By the so-called " Bright clauses " the creation of a peasant proprietary was encouraged by the loan of the Board of Works of two thirds of the purchase money. For the next five or six years the price of cattle was high, and the competition for farms so great that rents rose enormously, but were paid generally without complaint. In 1877 a series of bad seasons began, culminating with a partial famine in 1879. The farmers were impoverished by forced sales upon a falling market, and in the autumn the Land League was formed by Michael Davitt. The Land Act had given the tenants compensation on eviction, but what they wanted was " fixity of tenure " at a " fair rent." The Land Act provided for " the conversion of occupiers into owners by the slow process of individual agreement " with the landlord, but the occupiers wanted to become owners at once. The League then proposed the compulsory sale to the tenants of any estate upon the tender of a sum equal to twenty years' purchase of its " Poor Law " valuation, and meantime urged every member to take no farm from which a tenant had been evicted, to offer to pay a " fair rent " only, equal to the " Poor Law " valuation, and if that was refused, to pay no rent at all. The " valuation " referred to was begun in 1858 by Mr. Richard Griffith, as a basis for the assessment of local rates. It varied greatly in different parts of the country, and was considered at the time to be, except in Ulster, twenty-five per cent. below a fair letting value.

In 1881 the " Bessborough " Commission reported to Parliament these important conclusions : " The farmer bargains with his landlord, under sentence of losing his living if the bargain goes off. . . . We grant that it would

be inexpedient to interfere with freedom of contract between landlord and tenant, if freedom of contract really
existed, but freedom of contract, in the case of the majority
of Irish tenants, large or small, does not really exist.[1]
. . . The farmer should no longer be liable to the dis-
placement of his interest in his holding, either directly
by ejectment, or indirectly by the raising of his rent at
the discretion of the landlord.   The landlord's right to
eject should, we think, be limited to certain stated cases,
and some way should be provided for the determination
of the fair amount of rent to be paid in cases of dispute."[2]
A Land Act was at once passed in accordance with these
views.   "A great and noble measure," said Mr. Sullivan,
"a charter of freedom for the long-oppressed tenantry of
Ireland."[3]

The Act created a Board of Land Commissioners with
power to fix a fair rent in the case of agricultural ten-
ancies, with certain exceptions, on the application of
either landlord or tenant, the rent then to remain unchanged for a period of fifteen years.   So long as the
tenant paid his rent and observed the covenants of his
lease he was not to be evicted, and he was allowed to
sell his tenant right, subject to the option of the landlord
to buy it at a price to be decided by the commissioners.
Still larger advances than before were also allowed to
tenants purchasing their holdings.   These provisions involved, in the words of the "Bessborough" Commission,
"a certain loss to the landlord, namely, that of his legal
reversion, considered as a piece of substantial property.
His greatest loss, however," is "that of sentiment—of the
sentiment of ownership."[4]   This beneficent measure got

---

[1] Report, p. 21.   [2] *Id.*, p. 19.   [3] "New Ireland : A Sequel" ch. iv.
[4] Report, p. 20.

no fair play from the Land League. "Not merely was it decried, denounced, and scorned, but its contents or provisions were shamefully misrepresented. To say a good word for it was rank heresy in the popular ranks. To call it a mockery and a fraud was the orthodox profession of faith."[1] Yet, "as a rule, the reductions given under the Act averaged twenty per cent."[2]

At Tyrone Mr. Parnell announced the doctrine that the landlords were justly entitled only to the "prairie value" of the land, its value as it was in an uncultivated condition, as the logical deduction from the "Land Act," founding himself on a declaration by John Bright that "if the land of Ireland were stripped of the improvements made upon it by the labor of the occupier, the face of the country would be as bare and naked as an American prairie."

The smallness of the reductions at first given by the Land Commissioners and the frequent appeals made by the landlords, grievously disappointed the hopes of the farmers. The creation of a new salable interest in the "tenant right" was soon found to be a mixed blessing. The "tenant right" was at once used as a convenient method for raising money, and this money was spent not so much in "improvements" as in more expensive living. The combination of "free sale" with "fair rent" was found to be impracticable. The "land hunger" was given freer play than ever before, with the difference that the competitive price for a farm was given to the out-going tenant instead of to the landlord, and the only persons benefited were the tenants in occupation when the Act was passed. Enormous prices were often paid for the

[1] A. M. Sullivan : "New Ireland : A Sequel," ch. iii., p. 458.
[2] T. P. O'Connor : "The Parnell Movement," p. 135.

tenant right. On the property of Captain Hill in Donegal, in 1883, £60 were paid for the tenant right of a farm
rented for ten shillings a year, 120 times the rent—or, as
the phrase is, 120 years' purchase of the rent. Out of a
hundred cases of such sales that have been tabulated, in
forty-six, over twenty years' purchase was paid ; in thirteen, over thirty years' ; in ten, over forty years' ; and
in six, over fifty years' purchase was paid.   In all cases
where over twenty-five years' purchase is paid for the
"tenant right," the practical result is more than to
double the rent of the new tenant, if the money could
have been invested at 4 per cent.   Sales of tenant right
were accordingly promptly denounced by the League
as " land-grabbing."   Boycotting and outrages prevailed
throughout the country, and in October after the passing
of the Land Act the Land League was suppressed, and
was at once succeeded by the "Irish National League."

In 1882, by the "Arrears Act," any tenant whose
rent did not exceed £30 a year was allowed to appeal to
the Land Commissioners for an extension of the time
within which to pay the arrears, and in hard cases the
landlord was compelled to wipe out the arrears upon
payment of one year's rent by the tenant and of another
by the government.

Since 1881 the prices of agricultural produce have
fallen continuously, with the exception of a sudden but
short-lived rise in cattle in 1883, in consequence of the
increasing severity of American competition.   The Land
Commissioners gave larger and larger reductions in the
rent as time went by, but failed to satisfy the farmers.
" There was an average fall of 22.3 per cent. in the
prices of the nine chief articles of produce in 1885, com-
pared with the prices of the same articles in the six

years ending 1878, while the judicial rents fixed up to August, 1885, are only 19.4 per cent. lower than the old rents."[1] Leaseholders who were not entitled to go into the land courts, and farmers whose rents were fixed in the early days of the Act, when prices were high, were bitterly discontented when they noticed the reductions awarded to their luckier neighbors. By the end of August, 1886, 176,800 "fair rents" had been fixed by the Land Commissioners, but by that time there was open rebellion against the rents fixed prior to 1885. In October of 1886 the " Plan of Campaign," so called, was formulated by Mr. Dillon at Woodford, on the property of Lord Clanricarde. The "plan" itself was widely cir- culated in the form of a broadside, and was briefly described in *United Ireland* for October 23d as follows : " The tenantry on any one estate were advised to assemble under the presidency either of the priest or any intelli- gent and sturdy member of their body, in order to con- sult, and, after consulting, decide by resolution on the amount of abatement they would demand. Every one present was to pledge himself to abide by the decision of the majority, to hold no communication with the land- lord or any of his agents, except in presence of the body of the tenantry, and to accept no settlement for himself which was not given to every tenant on the estate. Should the agent decline the abated rent offered, it was to be deposited with a managing committee, to be placed by them with a secretary, trustee, or trustees. This money was then called the Estate Fund, and was 'absolutely at the disposal of the managing committee for the purpose of the fight.' The employment of the

[1] Pierce Mahony, M. P., and John J. Clancy, M. P.: " The Land Crisis," London, 1886.

fund was to depend on the course the landlord would pursue, but it was recommended that it should in general be devoted to the support of the tenants who were dispossessed either by sale or ejectment. Dependence was placed on the National League to take care, in the event of loss of any deposited money through individual dishonesty, or in the event of the demands upon it outrunning the fund, the grants would be continued to struggling tenants from funds otherwise obtained. There were other details as to procedure in case of ejectment, sale, distress, or bankruptcy proceedings of less interest, and one paragraph stated 'that no landlord should get one penny rent anywhere on any part of his estate, wherever situated, so long as he has one tenant unjustly evicted.'"

Nor was a "Purchase Act," generally known as Lord Ashbourne's Act, given a fair trial, though it provided for the advance of purchase money to tenants on easier terms than ever before. The "Plan of Campaign" was conducted by Mr. Dillon and Mr. O'Brien, M. P., on their personal responsibility, but the opposition to "purchase" was warmly instigated by the National League. "The National League," said Mr. Dillon to the Ballyhaunis tenantry, "intended to lay down a law, wherever it had power, that no estate shall be bought on which tenants have been evicted, until every tenant evicted since 1879 had been put back again in his holding. . . . On estates where the rents were rack-rents, they should allow no man to sell his interest; for the man who sold his interest on a rack-rented estate, and allowed a man of means, a man of trade, to come in, was one of the tenants' greatest enemies. The man of means would be the first to go in by the back door and betray his fellow-ten-

ants whenever they stood out for a reduction in their
rents." [1]

The "Plan of Campaign" was at once adopted on the
properties of Lord Clanricarde in County Galway, of the
Marquis of Lansdowne at Luggacurran, in County Meath ;
of Mr. Brooke at Coolgreany, in County Wexford ; of
Colonel O'Callaghan at Bodyke, in County Clare ; of
Mr. Ponsonby at Youghal, and Lady Kingston at Mitchelstown, in County Cork ; and of the O'Grady at Herbartstown in County Limerick. The landlords generally
felt themselves aggrieved by the compulsory reductions
of their rent, and held the more firmly by the rights they
thought still left to them. An all-round reduction, even
in the case of non-judicial rents—rents not fixed by the
courts,—seemed to them unjust, and often ruinous. The
result of the " Plan " was a series of attempts at eviction,
more or less successful, by the landlords, and a cessation
of all payment of rent by the tenants on the estates
involved.

The " National League " itself disclaimed any responsibility for the " Plan," but adopted practically the agrarian theories of the " Land League." The Land Law
Reform it proposed was thus stated in its Constitution :

" The creation of an occupying ownership or Peasant
Proprietary by an amendment of the Purchase Clauses
of the Land Act of 1881, so as to secure the advance by
the State of the whole of the purchase money, and the
extension of the period of repayment over sixty-three
years.

" The transfer, by compulsory purchase, to county
boards, of the land not cultivated by the owners, and not
in the occupation of tenants, for re-sale or re-letting to

[1] *Freeman's Journal,* Nov 15, 1886.

laborers and small farmers in plots of grazing common-
ages.

"The protection from the imposition of rent on improvements made by the tenant or his predecessors in
title, to be effected by an amendment of the Healy clause
of the Land Act of 1881.

"The admission of leaseholders and other excluded
classes to all the benefits of the Land Act. . . .

"The levying of taxes (now raised off all farming
lands) upon grass lands, and the graduation of such
taxes, so as to place the greater part of the burden on
large farms.

"The breaking of all covenants compelling tenants not
to till their holdings."

In the meantime fresh interest was added to the discussion of the "Land Question" by a letter by Sir James
Caird to the *Times.*[1] "The land in Ireland," he said,
"is held by two distinct classes of tenants : the small
farmers who pay rent from £1 to £20, and the comparatively large farmers who pay rent from £20 upwards.
Of the first class there are 538,000 holdings, averaging
£6 each ; of the second class, 121,000 holdings, averaging £56 each. . . . If the present price of agricultural produce continue, I should fear that from the land
held by the large body of poor farmers in Ireland any
economical rent has for the present disappeared." In
the autumn Sir James Caird was appointed a member of
the "Cowper" Commission, to inquire into the reason
for the failure of the Land Acts, and its report the following year was immediately followed by a new Act,
under which, throughout Ireland, the "judicial rents"
that were to remain untouched for fifteen years have been

[1] March, 1886.

reduced, on an average, fifteen per cent., and which admitted leaseholders to have their leases broken and their rents re-settled.

At the present time in Ireland the only tenants still bound by their contracts with their landlords are tenants of holdings not agricultural nor pastoral in character ; tenants of *demesne* land, that is, land held by the owner in connection with the mansion house or home farm and let temporarily ; tenants of "town parks," that is, land used in part for the accommodation of a town ; tenants of land let mainly for pasture, of a valuation of £50 or over ; tenants who hold their land as laborers or servants ; or who hold their land in *conacre*,[1] or for temporary grazing, or for a particular temporary purpose ; tenants of cottage allotments, of not over half an acre ; and "ecclesiastical persons" occupying glebe lands. Every one else may serve a notice on his landlord to have a fair rent fixed by the Land Court, and in fixing the rent no rent is charged on improvements, by him or his predecessors. "Improvements" is taken to include tillage, manure, etc., the benefit of which is unexhausted, and any work which is suitable to the holding, and which adds to its letting value. The presumption is taken to be that the improvements were made by the tenants if made since 1870, or within twenty years before. Finally, in making reductions, reference is to be had to the fall in prices since the lease was made or the rent fixed.[2]

The tenant may have paid nothing to anybody on coming into possession of his farm, but he has now, so long as he pays rent, an interest almost amounting to a

---

[1] " A letting in conacre is merely the sale of a crop, with a license to enter on the land for the purpose of planting, tilling, and taking it away." [2] Healy : " The Land Act of 1887."

joint-tenancy with the landlord, in perpetuity, which he can sell for all it will fetch in open market.

It is, moreover, to be remembered that the rents usual in Ireland, even before the Land Acts, were not, as a rule, the full commercial rents, as were the rents demanded for similar land in England and Scotland. Such is expressly stated in the Report of the " Bessborough Commission." It is also to be remembered that the prices of agricultural produce, though falling steadily, are still higher than they were on the average in 1858.

If, then, after having his rent reduced a tenant wishes to buy his farm, and can agree with his landlord as to the price, the government will advance him the whole of the purchase money, which he can repay with interest at $3\frac{1}{8}$ per cent., by annual instalments of 4 per cent. a year, becoming the owner of the farm at the end of forty-nine years. These yearly payments will seldom amount to more than three quarters of the rent he would otherwise pay. The average price paid in such cases has been a little over eighteen years' purchase of the rent, that is, if the rent is £100 a year, the price agreed on would be £1,800, 4 per cent. on which with interest would be £74. The government, then, pays the landlord £1,800 and charges the tenant £74 a year for forty-nine years ; at the end of that time the tenant owns the farm.

In addition to these special benefits, the condition of the tenant has been considerably improved in other respects during the present century. Since 1838, the tithes, and later the rent charges which took their place, have been assessed directly on the landlord instead of on the tenant ; since 1870, half the county cess, the chief tax in the country, has been paid by the landlord, who also has to pay in respect of holdings of over £4 valuation half the poor rates, the only remaining general tax, and in respect of all other holdings, the whole of the poor rates.

The Irish farmer, it was hoped by the landlords, would be now contented. The "three F's," the nickname applied to the "Free Sale, Fair Rents, and Fixity of Tenure," that had been the limit of the demands of the Tenant Right League, had now been granted, the judicial rents had been reduced, and the holders of leases expiring within ninety-nine years from 1881, had been given the privileges allowed tenants from year to year, and they had been the chief supporters of the "Plan of Campaign." Four hundred tenants on the "Kingston estate," and five hundred on the "Ponsonby estate," went into the court, and the latter received the other day 22 per cent. reduction, instead of the 25 per cent. they demanded, and their demands were finally granted in full by the landlord.

As early as October last the opinion of the popular leaders was expressed by Mr. O'Brien at Mallow,[1] that the "Plan" had been a success, and had been justified. "Only 140 men were evicted out of the 30,000 tenants," he declared, "who, to my own knowledge, lodged their money under the Plan of Campaign in Ireland. . . . But that is not all, because I can state to you from facts within my own knowledge that, within the last ten days, we have received offers upon three or four of the great estates, offers to reinstate one hundred and fifteen of the one hundred and forty tenants, to reinstate every one of them upon terms that the tenants would have jumped at twelve months ago, but they are in no hurry to jump at them now. . . . I find the universal feeling prevailing through the country that fifty per cent. of the rents is

[1] *Freeman's Journal,* October 31, 1887.

the very utmost that can be wrung this winter out of the unfortunate tenants by swords—or by bayonets, for that matter. . . . We clung to the new Land Act as long as there was a shadow of hope of adequate redress for our poor people under it. . . . They mauled it and they mangled it to please the House of Lords, and now . . . they have turned it into a downright curse and a downright mockery by appointing a lot of broken-down rackrenters and bumbailiffs to administer it." Nothing, he concluded, remained save to continue the "Plan." And in respect to the "purchase clauses," the Act is also condemned. "The people," said Mr. Conybeare,[1] M. P., at Westport, in County Mayo, September last, "the people must not buy the land ; they will get it for nothing from an Irish Parliament. The man who told them to give the landlord the price of their own improvements was their enemy. He was a wolf in sheep's clothing." The *Nation* of August 27th, finally, gives this positive advice to the people : "We have no hesitation in declaring now that the farmer who pays a rent that his land has not realized over and above all the cost of production and family maintenance, is a fool, and that whoever would assist him to pay it is no friend of Ireland."

This slight introduction is, perhaps, sufficient to make intelligible the following conversations, which do not represent, it is true, the relative number of the different opinions I heard, but which do express with considerable accuracy the various arguments and illustrations.

[1] "The Western People." Ballina, October 1, 1887.

PART I.—IN LEINSTER.

A MEETING OF A CLUB IN DUBLIN.

THE club was invited to meet one of the most distinguished of Irish patriots. Besides the guest of the evening there were present a distinguished professor of Trinity College, a well-known political economist, an Irish representative of a large English woollen firm, an Englishman intimate with the leaders of the Unionist party in Parliament, several young members of the Protestant Home Rule Association, some American visitors, and twenty or thirty others. The subjects of discussion were Gladstone's Home Rule Bill, and the settlement of the Land Question. The guest of the evening, with his bright eyes twinkling under a finely wrinkled brow, was speaking slowly in a strained voice as I entered. The Irish Parliament should, so soon as it was established, buy out the landlords by an annuity of three per cent. on a sum equal to twenty-one years' purchase of their rentals. "This," said he, "would be only fair, and it would keep with us a body of men, an educated class, that the nation cannot afford to be without." "That would be well enough," cried some one, "if we could force the landlords to live here." Another objected that, in competition with America, the country could not afford the extra tax.

"American competition is exaggerated," suggested the commercial traveller. "The American soil is decreasing yearly in fertility, while the Irish land is perennially fertile. The substitution of a small charge for the present rents would be an immediate boon to the farmer. With the sense of security thrift would increase. Ireland is now but half cultivated, and the present produce of almost every farmer might be easily doubled. The burden will be lighter every year, and in a generation it will cease for ever."

An American observed that it was true the fertility of the Western prairies was soon exhausted. The farmer there usually purchased with borrowed money or on mortgage, and so had often heavy annual charges. The cost of transportation had reached its lowest point. Prices had fallen as low as they ever would.

" Do you call that just," cried out a sharp-voiced professor, " when prices are temporarily low to deprive the landlords of their estates at the depressed value ? I call that robbery. How can you expect to raise a great nation on a foundation of robbery and petty fraud ?" The remonstrance was received with a smile.

The farmers, it was admitted, would for some years have to struggle with low prices ; but our guest suggested that such a great revolution as was proposed could not be accomplished without sacrifice and privation, and that by the method he proposed the privation would be only temporary.

Some one argued that the new tenant proprietors would become landlords in their turn, and would let at extortionate rents. "There is a great difference," was the reply, "between landlords and landlordism. The evils of landlordism consist in the existence of an alien and absentee class who take the whole, or as nearly as possible the whole, of the produce of the soil from the farmer, and whenever the harvest is below the average, turn him out to starve. These evils are due chiefly to the accumulation of property in the hands of a few through primogeniture ; to the unjust laws that let the tenant be deprived of the value of his improvements ; and to the difficulty of getting new holdings through the expensiveness of conveyancing. Under the new system we should have native landlords in sympathy with their tenants ; primogeniture should be abolished by one of the first acts of the new Parliament, which should also enforce fixity of tenure at a fair rental."

"If you allowed 'free sale,'" exclaimed another, "you would certainly bring back landlordism."

"Why so ? " asked a professor ; "in France land is bought and sold as freely as any other commodity, and yet, though there are landlords in France, there is no landlordism. Abolished by the French Revolution, the popular sentiment and the testamentary laws have prevented its revival. May not such a great social revolution as ours have the same result ? "

Our guest summed up the matter with a judicial air : "So long as human nature remains the same there unquestionably will be landlords, and in spite of any laws that may be devised, it will be possible for excessive rent to be exacted from improvident or unwise tenants that will reduce them to starvation. But with the extension of education and the gradual rising of the standard of living, there will be naturally developed intelligent habits of self-protection that will prevent tenants generally from making bargains absurdly opposed to their own interests."

A member asked what was thought of the exclusion of the Irish members from Westminster. "It is said," was the answer, "that Ireland will lose her voice in the government of the colonies ; but that is of no consequence, for Parliament does not now govern the colonies. It is said that Ireland will be deprived of all power in determining the imperial policy for war or peace, but no great question of foreign policy has yet been determined by the votes of the Irish members. We are losing nothing of value. On the contrary, we shall need all our best talent for the next few years in our Irish Parliament, and cannot spare a hundred able and experienced Irishmen for Westminster."

Some one suggested that the retention of the Irish members was prompted by a latent wish to keep Ireland within the taxable area of the empire. "If we are represented there, they will tax us ; if we are not, they will not dare to."

"Lord Salisbury and Lord Hartington," said the Englishman, in answer to a question, "are as sincerely anxious as Gladstone to provide a measure conciliatory to Ireland." "The difference between them, "exclaimed an Irishman, "is that Gladstone wants a Home-Rule bill that will satisfy the Irish members, and his opponents want a bill that will not satisfy them." "Chamberlain," said a professor, "has had to surrender his local-board scheme for that very reason. I was at that great representative meeting in the Rotunda in 1879, that asked for a Parliament for local affairs substantially similar to Gladstone's Parliament. The only evidence we have is that that is what the Irish people want, and that has been accepted by the whole Parnellite party."

Criticism was made of the anomaly proposed by Gladstone of a house with two orders instead of two houses. "Instead of a system that has been tried with fair success throughout the world," said our guest, "Gladstone has substituted one that no one has ever tried anywhere." "It existed in Scotland," said the professor. "The most corrupt Parliament that ever was," was the retort. "Also in the Irish Disestablished Church," he continued. "That is not much in its favor."

The chairman suggested that the most important question was as to the powers of the Parliament, though that might seem a matter of detail.

"No sooner shall we have a Parliament on College Green," said a professor, "than there will arise more and more serious questions between the two countries than ever before. The Irish Parliament will insist on exceeding its powers, by laws protecting trade and Romanizing education, that will be vetoed by England. That will increase national hatred. As for the home measures, they will be absurd. For my part, let an Irish Parliament rule India, and discuss the defences of Afghanistan, but let them keep their hands off my and my friends' business at home. Any thing but that." Everybody smiled as the professor sat down and another professor rose. "You must remember," said he, "that sovereignty is single and absolute : you cannot give it and retain it ; you cannot retain it and give it. If Mr. Gladstone's bill amounts to any thing, it means that as to Irish affairs the Irish Parliament is to have the sovereign power, and no other body. Otherwise the bill gives merely a nominal sovereignty and will satisfy nobody." "Why do you wish for a change of government?" retorted his unabashed opponent. "A hundred years ago unjust and barbarous laws were common everywhere, and Ireland has been no worse off than any other country. England has governed Ireland as well as she has governed her-

self." " Your argument," was the answer, " seems to be
that since England has been unable to govern herself
well, she should continue to govern Ireland. The trouble
lies in this, that one country can never govern another
well." The hour was getting late, and the discussion
became informal and general when I departed, marvelling
at the extraordinary amiability with which these old
friends debated so frankly and clearly questions of such
exceeding importance.

THE LORD MAYOR.

" A good and useful land bill," said the Lord Mayor
of Dublin " would not be opposed by the Nationalists
simply from the idea that it would injure the cause of
Home Rule, though we would not postpone Home Rule
for any thing. The land question is difficult and dangerous and many say it would be unfair to establish an
Irish Parliament until it is settled. It is very fortunate,
for instance, that the question of disestablishment has
been disposed of. But that is not my feeling. We
would face the question manfully and, I believe, wisely;
and I would not postpone Home Rule for any thing.

" What guaranties could be given for the payment of
purchase money? A great cry was raised against the
imperial guaranty proposed by Gladstone, and it is
hard to see how the Conservatives can take it up again.
As to local guaranties, neither the grand juries nor the
unions could be made guaranteeing bodies. The grand
juries are a doomed institution and, instead of having
their powers enlarged, should be deprived of those they
have. The unions are absolutely unsuited for such a
purpose. If the landlords, the ex-officio guardians, vote
on the question, it will be considered unfair ; and if the

elected guardians alone vote, no guaranty will ever be given. There is no institution in the country capable of guaranteeing the purchase money. A special body might be constituted by the government, but there would be great difficulties in so doing. No Castle board could give a guaranty worth any thing ; and any board capable of guaranteeing would have to have legislative power, and power to impose and collect taxes and to issue debentures. However, one thing is certain, no matter what boards are chosen or constituted, only the land actually put into the court can or ought to be available as a guaranty for the payment of the money for the landlord's interest in that particular property. A native Parliament ought to be able to do something more than that, and it alone could give a real guaranty.

" With regard to the suggestion that demesne lands be sold : we are fighting for a principle and can yield in all such non-essentials. That is a theory, and may be modified. The theory, moreover, would mean no invasion of private rights. The clause in the National programme is not to be construed literally. There will be landlords here to the end of time. The old landlord class was, however, a hostile class. The landlords were not only spendthrifts, but were, till lately, debauchees. They speak now against lawlessness, but it was they who used to make the sheriffs swallow their *latitats.* Nature herself now seems to have come to our relief, and put an end to landlordism ; for the time has come when the land will no longer support two classes of people.

" An Irish Parliament would give substantial justice to all parties, for it would want peace, and it would be the public interest that all classes should be represented and reconciled. An extreme party could not carry

through any wild project, for there would have to be
there representatives of the gentry and the merchants
It is often supposed that an Irish Parliament would consist of the present Parnellite M. P.'s, and men of no
property. The Parnellite members are sent, however, to
Westminster not to legislate but to fight. In our Parliament the men who fought and won the battle will be
present, but the other classes will be there too. We are
a combative party in the Imperial Parliament, but in our
own we would want representative men of a different
type, men with practical experience of trade and commerce. We should have to get the element of stability
there ; and the first thing Parnell would do, if he had
the choosing of the members, would be to pick out and
put in just such men.

"Do you remember how the legislature was constituted
in Gladstone's bill ? In one house there were to be
twenty-eight Irish peers, and seventy-five members having each a personal qualification of £200 *per annum,*
elected for a period of ten years, and by electors rated at
£25 *per annum.* This would be a very conservative
house. Then in the other house, the present sixteen
Unionists from the north of Ireland would be doubled ;
and these, with the Upper House, would make, in joint
debate, nearly one half of the whole Irish Parliament.
How is it possible that injustice should be committed by
such a body ?

"Now, although this particular bill has fallen through,
any scheme that will be entertained will and must provide for the inclusion in the Irish Parliament of a class
of people who are not now active in the National movement, even were the scheme devised by the present Irish
members themselves.

"Would a constitution like that of an American State be accepted, with its bill of rights and conservative limitations? Certainly. We should be fools not to accept such a constitution. Give us the engine and you may put on what brakes you like. The Irish people would not accept a purely administrative body, but would accept any fair measure of Home Rule."

A UNIONIST.

A gentleman who has filled many important public positions, who is untiring in his efforts to promote every plan for the improvement of education or the development of Irish industries, is a strong Unionist. Yet a leading Catholic Nationalist described him to me as being, though a Protestant, "one of our most useful citizens." The opinions of such a man deserve attention.

" The poverty of the Irish farmer," he said, " is largely due to himself; he sleeps all the winter, without doing a stroke of work. He and his family do not knit socks, make flannel cloth, or weave flax as they used to ; he does n't drain the fields or improve the roads. A Swiss farmer in his place would grow and work osiers, make straw hats, or do wood-carving. Suppose a man with five or six acres gets £50 worth of produce. He sows worthless seed, for the people eat the good potatoes and sow the bad, instead of sowing the best. His method of farming is so wasteful and negligent that his farm produces only half what it might. Remove the rent altogether, in a family of five or six that would only save a pound apiece. That would not help matters. It is far more a question of diligence and restraint.

" They neglect the means of money-making at their

hand. Irish butter, for instance, might always command wholesale a price of a shilling a pound, instead of six-pence, the usual price. The Irish farmer with few cows churns twice a week ; with many cows, every day. The churn is very small. The churnings make successive layers in the firkin ; this is over-salted from ignorance of the market, water is added to make weight, and the churns are seldom clean. The result is that the butter, when it comes to market, is half rancid and is classed as third-rate. The National Board of Education and the papers are always urging the farmers to change their methods. They might have coöperative butter factories as in Belgium and Holland. Some have been started and are successful ; but usually the farmers are too suspicious of one another to work together. Or the land-lord might start a factory, buying the cream from the farmers and selling the butter. But many such factories have been boycotted by the League, and the landlords won't risk the necessary capital. With a better system, the farmers of Ireland could make several million pounds a year extra out of butter.

"The case is the same with other industries. The Roman Catholic Archbishop of Ross said, in a recent circular : 'Apart from the training necessary to handle a boat, there remains the utter want of knowledge and manufacture of the necessary appliances. Take nets as an example. . . . There is not at present one machine for making nets in the whole of Ireland, while in the small town of Peel, in the Isle of Man, there are three large net factories, worked by machinery, affording em-ployment for hundreds of men, women, and children. There is scarcely one, in over a hundred miles of the adjacent coast, competent to make a sail or rope for one of their fishing boats. As for fish-curing, one instance will suffice. There is but one pilchard curing establishment in Ireland, and that is situated at Baltimore.' Some good will be done by the new Piscatorial School at Baltimore.

" The Nationalists always endeavor to conceal the fact that the motive of religion is at the bottom of the Home-Rule agitation. The enmity to the Queen is largely due to the fact that she is a Protestant. The landlords are Protestants, Saxons, and Conservatives, while the tenants are Catholics, Celts, and Nationalists, so that party, race, and creed all combine to set class against class. In the schools the patrons are either Protestant or Catholic, and as a rule the teachers and pupils are either all Protestant or all Catholic.

" However, the power of the ecclesiastics will continue only so long as they advance with the political sentiments of the people. When Home Rule is granted, the priests will all side with the Conservative faction of which Parnell will be the head. The party of disorder will work heaven and earth to get the priests on their side, but will fail, for a priest can go only a certain length. The priests will not be able to save the country, for they have lost enormously with the people since they have shown that their morality has become the morality of a politician and not that of a man of God.

" We should have nothing to fear from a Grattan's Parliament, but every thing to fear from a Parliament of men chosen from the riff-raff of the people for the sole purpose of annoying England in every way in their power. The M. P.'s are clever, but so is every Irishman ; and the best of them are such men as Tim Healey, who is animated by a perfectly sincere hatred of the Saxon.

"What Ireland needs more than any thing else is more general, thorough, and technical education. Half the misery of the people comes from ignorance. At the present time £800,000 is paid by the Imperial government for education in Ireland. Proper scientific and artistic instruction would require £200,000 more for elementary education alone. The revenues of Ireland were estimated by Gladstone at four millions a year. Could a Home-Rule government afford to pay a million for education ?

"The financial question is worth considering. The police cost a million pounds. People say most of that would be saved, as we shall not need so many police. If, however, we abolish the Irish Constabulary, we shall have to pay more for others to perform the many and various duties, besides the police duties, of the Constabulary. They are, for instance, revenue officers, preventing fraudulent distillation, etc. They are officers of the Registrar General, collecting the statistics of the country. They put in operation the regulations under the Contagious Diseases Act. Under fifty or more other Acts of Parliament they are the acting agents. When, for instance, the question of compulsory education was discussed, it was decided that such a measure would have to be carried out by the Constabulary.

"The whole of the civil-service charges of the country would probably come to at least another million. There are some four thousand officials in Dublin. Many new departments would be necessary to take over business now transacted in London, such as, a Treasury and an Audit Department, a Home Office, a Board of Trade, and, pretty certainly, a Portfolio of Agriculture and Commerce. Besides all these there would be the salaries of the Judiciary, and of J. P.'s, and other magistrates who now act gratuitously.

" What would be cut down and saved in one way would be more than counterbalanced by additional expenses.

" Home Rule, besides being dangerous, would be expensive.

" But as much local government as is possessed by Scotland would be beneficial to Ireland. Irish industries and trade should also be especially encouraged by the government. The absence of wood is a great injury to the country. There might then be a moderate bounty paid for every acre planted with certain timber on certain specified conditions ; for in planting timber one can get no profit for the first thirty years, though afterwards it is one of the most profitable crops.

" I believe in protection for a limited time.

" The official liquidator in the Court of Bankruptcy says that almost universally Irish tradesmen and shopkeepers are so indebted to English manufacturers that they dare not give orders to rising Irish firms. The account is always carried forward, £80 or £100, from year to year at about the same amount, showing that the English manufacturers are interested in keeping Irish firms in debt. The Irish manufacturers might assume the debts, but that would require a large capital and a spirit of enterprise not often seen in Ireland.

" The power to levy duties was omitted in Gladstone's bill, in order to secure the votes of the Lancashire towns, Manchester and Birmingham,—but Gladstone's bill is withdrawn.

" Any country that has not got superior facilities for producing a sufficient number of articles cheaper than any other country, will cease to exist under free trade as a commercial community, because it can produce nothing to exchange. Ireland is in that position, or nearly so ; it has no external facilities, it is badly off for minerals, and even as a grazing or agricultural country it is undersold by America. There is only a limited amount of finishing grazing land in Ireland, chiefly in Meath and Dublin ; most of the grass land would produce only inferior cattle. The cultivation of grain for export has almost ceased. Nothing but protection can save us from American grain.

"Manufactures require coal and iron, and having to import them raises the cost of production here. Coal is perhaps as cheap here as it is in Kent, but then Kent is not a manufacturing county.

"Finally, Irish labor is not cheap labor, because the people drink and are lazy.

"The one thing that might make up for these disadvantages would be a superior technical education, as in parts of Switzerland, Germany, and France.

"Five times more carriage-makers, twenty times more cabinet-makers than now were employed here fifty years ago. The tanning trade was once enormous, it is now dying out. Has Ireland derived any corresponding benefit from getting cheaper furniture and cheaper carriages?"

"If you had had protection, would you not have had a more serious famine here in 1879 ?" I suggested.

"We can form a fair idea in October," he answered, "of the corn grown that year, and there is always in the country a supply of corn for a year ahead. We should have six months then to prepare for a famine, and that would be time enough. Then, too, the only parts of the country where famine threatened in 1879 were where there was no corn and the people lived on potatoes. As our industries increase and the standard of living rises, the danger of famine will decrease."

A DUBLIN BUSINESS MAN.

If great business ability and unusual shrewdness in judging human nature give value to the opinions of a private citizen on public matters, these opinions should be specially valuable.

" The whole question is one of £. *s. d.*, of the almighty dollar, and to call it a question of politics or of political economy is all nonsense.

" I remember when a shilling, thirteen pence, and even fourteen pence was paid for a quartern loaf in the days before the corn laws. Then when the duty on corn was taken off, the landlord class expected to be ruined. There was less to be divided among the different sharers in the produce, so the landlords lost part of their plunder.

" The farmers afterwards took up cattle, and for a time 'growing meat' seemed to be an industry eternally profitable. But the introduction of the refrigerating process in transportation has completely revolutionized this business. Prices may be expected to fall still lower in the future, for until now, in cattle at least, home stock has been superior in quality to the imported ; but of late years the high-cost home breeds have been exported and domesticated in America and New Zealand, and cattle are now being imported identical with the best domestic cattle. Under free trade there has been gradually brought about an equalization in prices throughout the world for articles of the same quality, now there is coming about an equalization in their quality. The profit has gone from the produce of the land and therefore from the land itself, and the question now is between the landlords and the farmers as to who shall be the sufferers.

" These two classes, the landlords and the farmers, are fighting for the control of the government. In the past the grand jury may be said to have been the government of the country. The grand jury is something of the nature of a shire parliament—the equivalent, in some ways, of the town meeting. It represents the landlord class, passes all rates, and has the powers generally which in England are divided among the grand Jury, the vestry, and various other local boards.

" Ireland and England were once in much the same condition. England has fought her way out of this oligarchical system, but Ireland remains unchanged. Why? On account of her religion.

" While the governing classes of England were gradually persuaded to yield more power to the people, because they were of the same religion and could have confidence in them, it was not so here. Here there existed an hereditary warfare between the classes, on account largely of their being of different religions ; one or other it was felt must be uppermost, and the one which got on top wished to keep there. The bulk of the landlords were Protestants, and always took on themselves the office of holding the country for the British crown. It is the interest of the landlords to make themselves the medium for advising the government in Irish questions, and they have done so with a view to their own profit. It is the interest of the priests that their people should share in the government and should have sufficient worldly wealth. There has been a regular fight between the priests and the landlords.

" The election for Parliament was, till within two years, so arranged as to give the Protestant interests predominance. Only for a short interval in O'Connell's time was there an Irish party of any importance in Parliament, and they gained Catholic emancipation.

" Under the last Reform Bill eighty-nine Nationalist M. P.'s were returned, and it is hard to see how any compromise can be effected with them short of Home Rule. Gladstone has formulated a possible bill which, in case of his death, will be a rallying point.

" The great difficulty consists in an unascertainable factor, the control the Catholic clergy can exercise over a Home-Rule Parliament. If they exert much influence, the result will be bad, because clerical domination is always bad for a country, and Catholic clerical domination worst of all. The Protestants have effaced themselves, and made of their clergy simply paid professional teachers, but this is not yet true of the Catholics.

" The Catholic priests have followed the popular movement, but in order to get control of it, though some are still rather conservative. All Archbishop Walsh's predecessors were conservative in the sense of being opposed to agitation, but the bishops now, like Croke and Duggan, have taken the popular side vehemently.

" I have asked many Protestants whether, if all the Irish were Protestants, they would object to Home Rule. Most of them would welcome Home Rule in that case. The Protestant Irishman does not object to govern himself, but he does object to being swamped by a Catholic majority. That is the difficulty in a nutshell. The poorest are uneducated, and the uneducated are Catholics. Gladstone tried to secure the country against this danger by the provision that one third of the legislature could hang up a bill for three years, as the Protestants could probably return a minority of one third.

" It is an Irish trait to try to get a thing no matter who suffers. Before the last rising, it was said the Fenians had settled by lot among themselves what property each should have. There is a feeling abroad now among the uneducated classes that a revolution would be the occasion for a resharing of property.

" It is easy for Parnell to be in opposition ; but when his party comes to govern and keep order, the section that looks for spoils by the change will have to be dealt with. The American phrase has been adopted here, ' To the victors belong the spoils.' There will have to be a readjustment of social order, and control of the managing priests —this will be the first work of the Home-Rule Parliament.

" The goal the country has set its mind upon is self-government and a legislative Parliament. That would satisfy them. The educated Catholics all realize that to continue part of the British Empire would be more to their advantage in a civil sense than to be an independent republic.

" Those who cry for the green flag and for an Irish nation are in the van. But you must have a van to any movement, and you must make a bid in advance of what you expect to get, in order to get any thing. Men ignorant of politics and the science of government are infatuated with the zeal of nationality, and seek the exhibition of its maximum development. These are the tail of the party, that will have to be beaten back when civil order comes to be established.

" As to protection : the question is too broad to discuss, but two facts often overlooked need to be remembered.

"With Home Rule and a peasant proprietary for a long time there will be no surplus agricultural produce to export, because the people will live better and will not require to sell so much of their produce to pay rent. What is now a surplus they will consume themselves. Take the rent roll of the country, the wealth of the people will in time be increased by that sum, and they will be in a position to be large purchasers. The increment of the landlord will become the purchasing power of the peasant proprietor.

"Then too our home industries depend very largely on imported material. It is not generally known but is a fact, that the wool of the Irish sheep is too coarse to make any cloth but frieze ; and it is an every-day occurrence for wool to be imported from Australia *via* London, or the Yorkshire district, to mix with Irish wool to make fine tweeds.[1] The linen trade, too, could not exist without free importation of foreign flax."

A FENIAN.

"I am not a Democrat," he began to my surprise, "nor a believer in universal suffrage. It has amazed me that the English Conservatives should not have fought to the end against the last Reform Bill. There was no demand for it. Nothing has happened yet, for the newly enfranchised millions have n't learnt their power, but when they do learn it, there is no change that they may not make.

"I can understand the position of the Unionists. What I blame the government for is, not for coercing,

---

[1] "An unmitigated lie," said a farmer when I read him this sentence : "This thick blue serge I am now wearing was made entirely from the wool of my own sheep. And Blarney tweeds are the finest in the world."

but for coercing foolishly. They must either concede or coerce. The English have not governed Ireland at all for the last three or four years. It is the National League that has governed Ireland. If England wishes to govern Ireland again, it must then first destroy the League. The new Coercion Act, like all previous ones, is bound to fail. It does n't coerce enough. There can be no efficient half-way measure. The only logical thing for the Unionists to do, is to govern this country as a crown colony and to exclude our men from Parliament.

"I am not in sympathy with the agrarian movement. The tenants' party is unreasonable and unjust, and the landlords are fools. Walsh is a very influential man, and might have helped them to checkmate the other side, if they had accepted his suggestion for a conference. At such a meeting landlords and tenants might have got to appreciate each other's position in a way impossible by any number of letters. Even if no agreement were had, the conference would do some good. If a spirit of yielding is shown, something is shown that is good, and mutual understanding often leads to eventual agreement.

" The land question is inferior to the other, but it may save us trouble if it is settled first. The one important thing is separation as complete as possible, for perfect separation is impossible owing to the numerical superiority of England and to our geographical situation. No one ever thought of fighting England without foreign aid. In case, however, of war between England and America or Russia, ninety-nine out of a hundred of us would be on the side of America or of Russia or of the Devil himself if it would only injure or cripple England.

"Home Rule is what we want. The English know

nothing about Irish affairs. Even Gladstone does not really know any thing about Ireland. John Bright is the only English public man who ever did know any thing about us, and he has now turned against us. In the same way the English can't understand the Americans, nor you the English, although you have the same customs and speak the same language. The whole trouble rises from one country governing another. That is opposed to all justice and to all the teaching of history. No country ever governed another well. If Ireland were a part of England as Yorkshire is, would the Irish people have been allowed to die of starvation during the famine by hundreds of thousands?

" Our party is now not a transacting party. Parnell is the leader of the Irish people. All the various conflicting parties rely on him. His death would be almost as fatal to our cause as the death of Gladstone, for if Parnell died to-morrow the man would lead who is the most unfit to do so—Dillon. Dillon is a narrow fanatic and could never lead Davitt. In talking with Parnell the first thing I noticed was that he was a first-rate listener, and the second thing was that every thing he said led to action, to something to be done. He has will, a frightful will. O'Brien's position is Dillon's. They have the Plan of Campaign business, and O'Brien's power is very great with the people from a sympathetic point of view, but if Parnell put down his foot he would yield at once. Whether Dillon would I do not know. Davitt's following is very big among the farmers, ten times bigger than Dillon's or O'Brien's. He is the only power in Ireland independent of Parnell. As for us, we are non-transacting at present, but complications might arise in which we would again be a power.

"Home Rule is what we want. Even after it is granted, hatred of England will not die out at once, but in the course of a generation it will cease from want of nourishment. The Imperial Parliament may give us a Parliament in words subject to itself, but if the Home-Rule Parliament is a subject Parliament in fact, it will be no cure at all for the discontent of Ireland. In the case of Home Rule following or coincident with peasant proprietorship, we shall of course suffer two great losses. The landlords would take their money ; they would also take themselves, and that would be a very serious loss, since they are the only cultivated class.

"It is said that if we had Home Rule we should persecute the Protestant minority. We would not, and the guaranties are : first, that the Protestants are a million and a half out of five millions, and they have most of the property and the best education ; secondly, that of the Catholics many are only nominally Catholics, they were born so, but have ceased to feel strong interest in religion ; and, thirdly, that there are many Catholics who, though sincerely religious, are more or less conservative in politics. All these classes would make together about two millions and a half, or half the Irish people, who would be opposed to any thing like persecution.

"Education, again, would prevent the Irish from blindly following the priest. The average Irishman now only listens to the priest on matters about which he does n't know or care much. Then, too, the priests have taken part in this movement from sympathy with the farmer rather than as priests. Ninety-nine out of a hundred are sons of tenant farmers. Sons of gentlemen, or of professional men, become Jesuits but not priests.

"Emigration would do Ireland no good. Home Rule

would greatly check emigration. Emigration means to take the able-bodied and the best and to leave in the country only the weakest and the least courageous. Emigration should be encouraged only from a surplus population, and Ireland is at present only half-culti-vated.

"Under Home Rule the Irish instead of being a wholly agricultural people might be induced to take up many domestic manufactures. Ireland may never be-come a manufacturing country like England, since it has no coal, but it might well become manufacturing to the extent that France is.

"As for us, we are happier now than we ever hoped to be. For the first time a great English party has taken up our cause and offers us practically what we wish. The-orists must be sensible, and no honest man would for an ideal end run the risk of a war."

A CATHOLIC PROFESSOR.

The Professor is a foreigner who has lived in Dublin for more than twenty years, taking no part in politics, but watching with the keen interest of a student of his-tory and a teacher of religion the kaleidoscope of Irish agitation.

"The secret of the agrarian distress," he said, "is a violation of the principles of political economy, aris-ing from the sentimental Celtic attachment to the soil which leads the people to disregard their obvious inter-ests. In County Tipperary there is little agrarian agita-tion, because the farms are large and the land good. But the Irish have the same peculiar race sentiments that still make Brittany the most backward part of

France. The peasants there will refuse the most lucrative positions in a town for the sake of keeping before their eyes till they die the gray stones around which as children they pastured their sheep.

"If Brittany were an island it would give the French government the same trouble that Ireland gives to the English government. The same is true of the Welsh. The poorer the soil, the more the Celts seem to be attached to it. Their poverty arises from their insisting on living on farms too small to support them comfortably. This would not be cured by peasant proprietorship, nor even by the systematic division of all the land in Ireland among the farmers, for even then each man would not have land enough to yield him at the present rate of prices more than the bare means of subsistence. A comparison with France is misleading, for land there is exceptionally good, and the people are the most industrious and frugal in the world.

"The spirit of nationalism should not be encouraged simply because it is national. Races are formed in the beginning like species of animals or plants, by localization. For a long time in the course of civilization it is necessary that special social qualities should be developed, for adaptation to the purely material environment of the country is essential. As time goes on the horizon of a people broadens. The influences of soil and climate become relatively less important. It is no longer a question of the survival of the fittest among a few tribes in a small district, but of the survival of the fittest among the nations of the world. The highest civilization then requires the reunion in one nation of many local qualities. One should prune off from the trunk of nationality those offshoots that have ceased to be productive,

not because they are national, but because they disqual-
ify for the battle of modern life ; and those offshoots
only should be encouraged that are productive, not
because they are national, but because they qualify for
that battle. It is deplorable then that such things as
the Celtic language and the Celtic love of the soil should
be fostered, as is now done by so many able and honest
priests and statesmen. They are disqualifications for the
battle of life. The glorification of the Celtic race as such
is equally vain. As Sir John Lubbock has shown, it is
almost absurd to talk of a pure Celtic race. The English and Irish are mixtures in different proportions of the
same races. Even the study of early Irish history, largely
legendary, is of little practical service to-day.

"The question of Home Rule, so far as it means more
than local self-government applicable to the whole of
Great Britain, becomes then, comparatively simple. It
is desired for the sake of perpetuating national qualities
simply because they are national ; and for the purpose
of isolating a community that is too much isolated and
peculiar already. Moreover, what is to be done now-a-
days in the world cannot best be done by a small nation.
In dealing with other nations unity is necessary. In
domestic matters large means and an absence of local
prejudice are necessary to advance wisely the civilization
of the people. Finally, how can a Home-Rule government sustain itself with benefit to Ireland without money
and without credit ?

"Of the social confusion of the day, I could say much.
It is enough that I knew of children not long ago dying
in Clonmell of scarlatina, because the father was boycotted, and the apothecaries did not dare to put up the
doctor's prescriptions."

A PESSIMISTIC FARMER.

"I am a tenant farmer," he began, "but for a dozen years I was manager of a country bank. This agricultural crisis would have come on long ago if it had not been for the action of the banks. I was dining with a landlord in 1879, who was boasting of how well his rents were paid; at that moment I knew that my bank had advanced money to practically all his tenants. At last the banks suddenly stopped giving the farmers credit, and that helped to bring on the crisis.

"No matter what reductions the tenants may get, so long as these bills are hanging over their heads, the reductions will do them no good. Until the banks compound with these poor wretches they will get no relief.

"The farmers don't want peasant proprietorship, because then they will have to pay all the rates themselves— the large holders all the county cess instead of half, and the small holders all instead of none. They are in debt and without capital, and unless the government comes to their aid they cannot work their farms to advantage even when they own them. It is true there is more money in the country than there ever was, and that in the National Bank alone there are deposited eight million pounds, but it is not in circulation in Ireland.

"The whole number of agricultural tenants in Ireland is about five hundred thousand; of these one third have holdings of under £4 valuation, and another third have holdings of under £10 valuation. It is preposterous to make these men proprietors. They would starve.

"Gladstone's Purchase Bill would simply have left the landlords for twenty-five years to squabble over the distribution of the purchase money among the chargees on the property. It was utterly impracticable. You **must** remember too that there is some injustice in any scheme of compulsory land purchase. What do you say to the not infrequent case where a man had land in his own possession ten years ago and has since let it to tenants?

" English rule is hated in.this country, and I am not surprised. Look at the Under Secretaryship just vacant. Why should the government put in a military officer with no knowledge of the country—a man from India, when hundreds of able Irishmen are available, men like Sir Thomas Butler, if you want a landlord? Even if a Land Purchase Bill is passed, the agitation for Home Rule will still continue."

A PROSPEROUS FARMER.

Not far from Dublin is a low, one-story, rambling, thatched farm-house. About the house stretch on every side extensive level fields. Crops that are the wonder and pride of the whole country-side yearly rejoice the heart and overflow the barns of the sturdy, thrifty farmer of this rich alluvial land. He was standing in front of the creeper-grown porch, with his daughter's St. Bernard beside him, when I first met him—a massive man, dressed in thick blue serge of the wool of his own sheep, with a magnificent Landor-like forehead towering over a face that was one large smile.

In the morning we walked over the farm. The large cattle-sheds were built in an original manner, the windows sloping upwards through the thick walls and widening towards the inside, so as to avoid draughts and secure ventilation. The cows had their horns all cut out, to keep them from always "pucking and punting" one another.

We turned across the fields. "Beautiful land is the

Irish land," he said. "On an average neither England
nor Scotland can compare with the land of Ireland.
Their first-class land is far inferior to our first-class land ;
and our second-class land is equal to their first. Cali-
fornia wheats don't have the same amount of gluten as
our dark-colored Irish wheat. We are not afraid of any
other country under the sun.

"I never had finer crops of wheat or potatoes in spite
of the drought. We get three tons of straw to the acre.

"Look at that crop of wheat ; " he cried, "it is as thick
as grass in a field. The land is teeming with it ; it could
hold no more of it."

On his land he usually has in succession, four white
crops, one green crop heavily manured, and two hay
crops. "Off that field, since breaking up the lea, I have
had one crop of wheat, which was too rank and long ;
three crops of oats to reduce the land, the first of which
was too long, the second too light, and the third excellent ; then one crop of potatoes ; one crop of wheat—a
magnificent crop, so strong and heavy that it strained the
self-binder; and the crop of oats we are now looking at."
From another field in two years he took a crop of potatoes which realized thirty pounds an acre, one of cabbages of the same value, and one of wheat which brought
in twenty-three pounds an acre. One twelve-acre field
grew five crops of grass in one year. He raises forty or
forty-five tons of turnips to the acre, and has not an acre
of land under tillage from which he does not expect to
realize twenty pounds over the cost of cultivation.
Ninety acres he has let at different times for five pounds
an acre, and there is plenty of land in the neighborhood
for which four or five pounds is paid willingly.

I asked him what rent he paid. "Here 's a piece of

one hundred and eighty acres. In 1827 it was let for £100 a year, when the landlord took it up and relet all but forty acres to my people for £128. The lease terminated last year, when the landlord reduced the rent to £82, and agreed to pay half the cess, thus practically reducing the rent to £73 or £74."

A farmer so prosperous and so intelligent might naturally be expected to have little cause of complaint with the government. He is, however, a strong Nationalist. Why, may be best explained in his own words :

"We cannot compete on the whole with American products ; we must then be protected by a duty. The agricultural classes cannot be permitted to die out. They recruit all the other classes. We were nine millions, we are now five millions, and have lost those four million laborers and their products. Every laborer sent away takes a pound a week, and that is gained by America. The laborer is also a consumer of domestic industries, and, by his removal, another pound a week may be said to be lost by England and gained by America.

" The protected nation succeeds best. For this reason the Germans and not the English supply the colonies with most of their imports of manufactures, and America supplies England with more than two thirds of the breadstuffs it consumes.

" Reciprocal trade is the great thing, prices will not rise till then.

" I want Home Rule, in the first place because it would mean a policy of protection."

We took a delightful drive through the valley, and back along the Wicklow hills. Here and there the lofty walls of some gentleman's demesne cut off the view ; again we clattered along the ill-paved streets of a little village, and near every village were the ruins of deserted mills and melancholy rows of cottages, with broken window-panes, of long-forgotten mill-hands. " There were fourteen or fifteen paper-mills here," he murmured, " in my boyhood ; now they are all obliterated, simply because the great thinkers of the world decided that there should be no tax upon knowledge, and so news-papers were sold for a penny instead of sixpence. All this looks well, but it does n't work. . . . There were, even up to three years ago, ten or twelve flour-mills in the neighborhood in operation ; but now all are ruined by American competition."

In the good old times things were very different, and I half forgot the jolting of the car, as he slowly recalled some of the familiar figures of the past. " My grand-father, C., was a farmer with plenty of land. He sup-plemented his farm work by dealing in timber. He would buy twenty or thirty acres of oak wood and strip the bark, dry it, and sell it in Dublin. Of the timber he would select what was good enough for ship-building, and the débris he made into charcoal. He had two sons and five daughters. He and his two sons were weavers, and all his daughters carders, and the family wove and carded the wool of their own sheep and sold the flannel and dressed themselves in it—coats, jackets, and trousers were all home-made. They had plenty of money to spare for every thing. Now there is not a weaver in Wicklow.

" My great-grandfather, K., was also a farmer in Wick-low with a hundred acres, but he was a hatter besides, and kept fifty men at work supplying woollen hat frames for the English army. I remember him well, and he re-membered when the O'Tooles held Wicklow.

" Nothing at that time was imported but tea and sugar. This state of things Home Rule would bring again."

In the porch of the farm-house we sat talking till late. A sincere Catholic, he is not bigoted. We had driven in the morning through a miserable little village, with the ruins of an old church and a bishop's palace, and he exclaimed : " Wherever the church predominates, the wealth of the country ceases to exist." His opinion about the disestablishment of the Irish Church is then, perhaps, fairly impartial. " I never knew any thing more farcical. After the disestablishment, the tithing charges were absolutely enforced by the commissioners, while previously they had been discretionary with the incumbents. As to the actual payment of the tithes, which was what we complained of, they have not been abolished, but are merely paid to different persons. The clergy, too, came off very well. A man, ninety years old, with a stipend of £4,000 a year, receiving twenty-two years' purchase of the £4,000, and his successor getting nothing—that was one of the ludicrous sights I saw. I wonder the clergymen of England don't at once get disestablished, and put their money in their breeches' pockets and walk away with it."

Curiously bitter he was against the landlords. " They are vampires and parasites, feeding on the blood, bones, and sweat of the people." In spite of the vampires he has flourished, but the cause of his hatred is not personal. " One third of the produce of the country," he said, " passes annually into the hands of the landlords and is spent in England ; and if the land comes into the hands of the people, it will be more than twice as productive."

" The subserviency of the Catholics and the intolerance of the aristocrats, will be slow to pass away, but

I see the people becoming more self-reliant and independent every day.

"The Catholics of Ireland do not wish to be separated from England. What we want is to rid ourselves of the monopoly of England, the centralization of England. We want to keep the fruits of our own industry to benefit our own country, and not have them spent elsewhere. I should be very sorry, indeed, to see Ireland separated from England. Indeed, its position forbids it.

"The Parnellite party has not always used unobjectionable methods, but remember, you cannot make war with rose-water. There are some extremists; they exist, however, in all countries, and not merely in Ireland— people who wish to get up a scramble. The government of the people by the people will exert more influence than the British government ever can, and the Irish will then become the most loyal people in the empire."

A very sweet Irish voice interrupted us. "The Catholic Church," she suggested, "is the greatest friend to England in this country, for the clergy are horribly afraid of republicanism and of any thing unknown."

"Yes," said her father, "and the Irish race is by nature conservative and aristocratic. Their leaders in the past were all gentlemen, and that is one reason for Parnell's success. They would never pay so much respect to one of themselves. Finally, I firmly believe that an Irish Parliament would insist on just compensation to the landlords. It might be difficult to constitute the proper machinery, but it would be done."

TALKS IN WEST MEATH.

Of the smaller towns in Ireland none has in the stranger's eyes such an air of prosperity as Athlone. The rea-

son is not far to seek : it is one of the few manufacturing
towns outside of Ulster. "Here there is very little poverty," said the parish priest, Father McKeogh, "because
there is a fine factory here, Gleeson and Smith's Tweed
Manufactory, which employs five or six hundred hands ;
and then in the suburbs the people make a fair living by
selling vegetables. Six or seven miles off, there are
grazing farms extending for miles, and at present the
graziers are not very well off.

"Home Rule," he continued, "will benefit Athlone,
because an Irish Parliament will establish woollen factories with government money and thus utilize the magnificent water power of Shannon.

"I think if the land question were settled, Home
Rule, however, would become of less importance, and
the farmers would not be so enthusiastic about it. Home
Rule to-morrow, with the land question still unsettled,
would be a very serious matter. A fair Land Purchase
Act would be taken up by the farmers."

"Why did they not take advantage of Lord Ashbourne's Act ?" I asked.

"Many think," he replied," that if they got Home Rule
they would get the land on their own terms.

"The temperance question is one of the most important matters to-day. If we can make the people temperate, that will be so much money in their pocket, and
they will be the more fit for Home Rule." The good
father then showed me the rooms of the League of the
Cross. The society has only been started for two or
three years, and already numbers two or three hundred
members in Athlone and hundreds more in Galway,
Castlebar, Ballinasloe, and other towns throughout the
country. A skittle alley, a billiard-room, and a band-

room belong to the League, and the cartoons of the
Weekly Freeman and *United Ireland* that cover the walls
sufficiently attest the political preferences of the young
men of Athlone.

Over one of the great woollen-mills I was shown by a
partner. Coal from Wales is used, and not the water-
power of the Shannon that flows past it. There are
ninety-two looms and four hundred workmen. The wool
is taken just as it comes from the farmers, cleaned, dyed,
spun into thread, and woven into cloth. The average
output is eleven thousand yards a week, at a cost price
of a halfpenny a yard.

"The government," said he, "in the past let the exac-
tions of the landlords run on till the bulk of the tenants
were stripped. Farmers of under a hundred acres now
I don't think have much on their backs. In West Meath
they are fairly prosperous, and in Roscommon ; but I have
watched them growing poorer year by year. The landlords about here have had the name of being moderate,
and some are resident : but even the moderate men have
not been fair. The tenants, or their forefathers, have
reclaimed the land. I have known land not worth a
shilling an acre reclaimed and drained, the stones picked
or blasted out, and the walls, barns, and outhouses built,
all by the tenants, and then their rent raised from one
shilling to thirty shillings an acre.

"The Irish nation will be more generous, I think, to
the landlords than an English Parliament. If they think
the British taxpayers will pay them a guaranty in any
contingency, I fear they are mistaken ; but the question
will probably not be left to an English Parliament to
settle.

"The first thing for a Home-Rule Parliament to do

will be to secure a better system of education, technical
and industrial education. The tenants have never learnt
any thing but agriculture : the landlords, who were drawing all the surplus capital from the country, gave nothing
in return ; they should have taught the people by founding schools and starting factories. I would have industrial schools. England has not the same need of them,
for every manufactory is a technical school in itself.

"English competition, it is true, would destroy any
rising industry here, unless we had exceptional oppor-
tunities for education. Protection, I do not believe in.
It is preposterous to have any thing that would raise the
price of food ; though a small tax on flour might be permitted. As to duties on manufactured articles, I don't
believe in that at all. Without protection, we here in
Athlone have the world at our command ; with protection, we should be shut up in Ireland.

"There can be no great manufacturing centres here as
in England, but in every village or town there is surplus
labor that can be got for very little and only needs to be
utilized. All our own wool ought to be manufactured on
the spot, and all kinds of hosiery, flannels, and carpets.
It can be done perfectly well ; I am doing it myself ; and
if we could make as much more we could sell it all. We
sell as much out of Ireland as in it ; in England, Scotland, and America ; and we have been busier than ever
since the Home-Rule movement began and the Dublin
Exhibition was held.

"This mill was started in 1859 by an Englishman and
an Irishman, who lost all they had by it. The failure
was due to the lack of technically educated hands ; but
some few did get educated and formed the nucleus for
another start which ended in a second failure.

"I learnt the business in a mill that has since failed for £50,000, and left a mill that is now in Chancery to come here in 1870. Both failures were due to lack of education. Here after a hard struggle we forged ahead.

"There is enough capital in Ireland to start industries, and nothing is needed from the government but the collection of information and the diffusion of technical education. The means of transit also need improving. Such matters cannot be attended to by an English Parliament. There is no use in tinkering with local bodies. I am, therefore, a Home Ruler.

"The Roman Catholic Church would be a guaranty against socialism, and I say this though I am a Presbyterian. The Irish people are essentially a most conservative people, and that is a fortunate thing, for there has been enough to justify a revolution. Our market is England, and must always be on account of our want of coal, and separation, therefore, would be ruin. That is a false cry."

It was a great change from the neatness and bustle of Athlone to the dirt and sluggishness of Mullingar. Few people seemed moving in the streets except an occasional half-drunken soldier. At the hotel a drummer could not restrain his lamentations. "An hotel like this," he shouted, "ought to be thronged on Saturday night; now we two are the only people in the place. I remember when during the few weeks before Christmas there were thousands of country people in Dublin buying, six hundred where you find one now. Only fifteen years ago, I remember when the ships were ranged along the Liffey, with their prows out in the river; now they lie there alongside the shore. Commercials now are few, and there are none now at places where I used to meet six or a dozen. I don't believe my employers make any thing above my travelling expenses, and how they manage to keep me going I don't see.

"These things make me feel the need of Home Rule. I used to oppose it, but was converted by this argument of a merchant in the North : ' The people of Ireland are quite upset now, and their trade is gone in consequence. There is no plan suggested that will settle them but Home Rule. Therefore, Home Rule is absolutely necessary.' "

There was a shouting outside and the tramping of many men on the pavement. Hayden, the editor of the *West Meath Examiner*, was being taken to prison for having obstructed the police at an eviction. The people cheered and dispersed gradually as he was rapidly driven away.

"This arrest," said the Secretary of the League, as he stood at the door of his bakery, "is the most exciting thing that has happened here for months. There is no political excitement here nor outrages, and there have been few, if any, evictions in the neighborhood."

The president of the League, Father O'Reilley, described the county as entirely a grazing county. "This town exists," he continued, "solely by supplying the graziers and farmers who come to the fairs and markets.

"Here and there you find little strips of civilization in this country, where there is some manufacturing, but such is not the case in West Meath. The trouble is that under free trade manufacturers have been driven out by the English and Americans.

"The holdings of the graziers in this county average probably two hundred or two hundred and fifty acres, and those of the farmers about thirty acres. These

graziers are chiefly Catholics, but I don't think they are
very earnest in the cause of Home Rule. They adopt
that cry from fear of offending their neighbors, for really
we have as much objection to them as to the landlords.
They are all practically land-grabbers. Some own four
or five hundred acres ; and many are sons of poor farmers, who have gradually bid in from the landlords farm
after farm of their neighbors, and then have turned the
whole into pasture land. I don't think they are genuine
Home Rulers."

"The question of Land Purchase here, then," I suggested, "would have rather special and undesirable
effects."

"Yes," he answered, "but these matters are too hard
to discuss. You should wait and see the Bishop."

IN A SMOKING-ROOM IN COUNTY CARLOW.

From the windows we looked out over a broad vel-
vety lawn that sloped down to a large deer park, and in
the distance was a steep mountain-side, down which was
falling in the humid air a column of smoke, like a water-
fall, from a peat bog and plantation lately fired by an
incendiary. Few men in Ireland can boast of a more
ancient, or more purely Irish descent than the owner of
this vast demesne, which his ancestors have held since
prehistoric times. A few years ago he was the idol of
the people, to him they used to come to decide their dis-
putes and to make matches for their children ; now he
is hated for his open defiance of the National League.
Yet the rents on the estate are the old customary rents of
the last century. A neighboring secretary of the League,
whose father had been a tenant of his called him a generous landlord ; and a car-driver in Kilkenny who had

been born on his property repeated: "A good landlord
he was; I knew that in bad years he often gave the tenants receipts for their rents in full." Many years ago he
used to be spoken of as "the tenants' friend," and was
one of the first to advocate in Parliament compensation
for disturbance by the landlord. Why should such a
man be pursued with curses and hatred by the whole
Nationalist press? The reason, perhaps, was given me
by the man most competent in Ireland to give a reason,
one now in jail.

"In contests between parties," he said, "individuals
must suffer. If this gentleman were a good landlord and
not a tyrannous one as I believe, he would still have to
lose in this contest. It is enough that he belongs to a
landlords' association."

"Why should you blame the landlords for doing in
self-defence exactly what you are doing?" I enquired.

"Well, let them," was the answer. "If they do there
must be war between the two organizations, and we 'll see
which will win. We are fighting landlordism to the death."

And yet this landlord is resident, native, benevolent,
and public-spirited. Outside the demesne gates the
neatest and most comfortable laborers' cottages line the
roadside. "But for the good lady at the great house,"
said a laborer's wife to me, "I could not have got through
the winter"; and the same good lady draws herself the
most delicate designs for the lace-work of the tenants'
daughters.

In the smoking-room a little company sat talking late
into the night.

"I have eight hundred tenants," our host was saying.
"The average size of a farm on my estate is about fourteen acres. Many of the tenants go away as laborers in

the autumn, and some have plots of only two or three
acres.

" The only practicable scheme of land-purchase would
be to give the landlord an option to sell under the act,
and then, on his consenting to sell, to make purchase
obligatory on the part of the tenants. Otherwise the
tenants will hold off in the hope of something better
turning up.

" How far such a scheme would be taken advantage of
by the landlords would depend on the amount of the
purchase price. A fair price cannot be calculated by
reference solely to the rent or to the value of the tenant
right. The tenant right is no evidence of the value of
the land, for a small holding fetches more in proportion
than a large one, because there are more who want it and
who could work it. And, as to the rent, obviously a
rack-renter ought not to get so many years' purchase of
his rental as a generous landlord.

" A purchase act, however general, will be, I fear, of
but temporary benefit, for the landlords of fifty years
hence will differ from the present landlords only in being
of peasant extraction and of inferior education. Native
landlords, will not, probably, be better than the present
ones ; for almost all the worst cases of rack-renting have
been on properties held by middlemen, themselves farmers. Immense quantities of land, too, will in fifty years
have passed into the hands of money-lenders, 'gombeen
men.' A gentleman I knew, fifty years ago let a townland to five or six tenants at £2 1s. 2d. an acre. A year
or so ago only one of the original tenants was represented
in that townland. All the rest of the property was held
by a money-lender, and the other fifth or sixth had been
divided between the five children of the original tenant.

"In order then to effect any good, a purchase bill must contain a clause forfeiting the land to the creditor, and forfeiting all previously paid instalments, in case of subletting before the purchase money has been paid completely.

"Some years ago a tenant of mine, Mrs. C——, sublet a plot of land to a carpenter, who proceeded to build a house on it. At once she took steps to evict him and let the house and land to another. The carpenter began to take up the flooring and carried some of the planks away, but was stopped by the caretaker. The carpenter assaulted the caretaker and was arrested, and so the case came to my notice. That is the way the farmers will treat one another."

"The present movement," said a landlord from the neighborhood, "is largely a socialistic one for the division of our property among the people. I heard of evidence some time ago that some estates had been raffled for." "Yes," said a distinguished ecclesiastic, "we knew it in 1867. In Cork there are said to be representatives of every property in the south of Ireland, who are recognized as descendants of the original owners, and are impatiently waiting for the revolution. I frequently meet the man who is to get my glebe."

"I know the name of the fellow who is to get my property," interrupted our host. "He was in the Fenian movement. I should not mind so much if I knew he would keep the place up."

"During election time we can hardly show our faces," said a clergyman, "they insult us and the ladies of the family in such indescribably indecent language."

"The President of the League in —— always balances up against my dog-cart in drunken friendliness on

fair day," said a landlord, "yet he has called me a nar-
row-minded and bigoted magistrate. 'G——,' I said
once, 'why do you tell such lies about me?' 'Shure,'
said he, 'every thing's fair in political times.' 'But you
know it's untrue.' 'Ah, shure your Honor, they did n't
believe it, they knew the difference.' Then they go and
elect as doctors for the dispensaries the greatest black-
guards, who have n't even a diploma."

"Look at the number of bankrupt Nationalist Unions,"
cried out the clergyman ; "they can't even manage their
own local affairs."

"They are very ignorant and priest-ridden," said our
host. "When I was canvassing for ——, I went to
the house of a farmer to ask him to vote for me. His
wife came to the door and with tears in her eyes said :
"For ——, your Honor, don't ask Ned to vote for
you. Father —— says if he does my baby will be born
with horns on its head.' It is chiefly through the women
that the priests work ; and then the priests stand by the
polls and mark each man as he goes past. Take any
parish, take this, and how many liberal-minded Catholics would you find here ? Not five. In West Meath not
fifty. A few in Dublin, fewer in Cork, and very few in
Belfast. Be sure that Home Rule when it comes will
mean the rule of Archbishop Walsh."

"During the Franco-Russian war," said another,
"while France was supposed to be succeeding, our
lives we thought not worth a moment's purchase : but
Sedan settled the Irish question for many years. Home
Rule means civil war. Only the soldiers keep Belfast
down. The Scotch would pour into the north and
the Irish-Americans into the south. It would be a case
of the Kilkenny cats," said the landlord ; "before two

years were over there would not be a tail left in Ireland.
England would have to come in, and whichever side
England took would win. Why begin the fray? The
London Companies are already leaving the north of
Ireland, depriving the people of vast sums they spent in
charities. I greatly fear the exodus has begun."

A COUNTY CARLOW LANDLORD.

From the hospitable house where we happened to be
staying I made many little trips in County Carlow with a
descendant of one of those ancient Norman families that
were said three centuries ago to have become more Irish
than the Irish. He is seldom out of Ireland, for his duties on agricultural societies, local boards, the union,
grand jury, and the bench are enough with his home
farm to keep him busy from January to December. His
popularity with all the people was delightful to see.
" Good luck to your Honor ! " " Fine day, your Honor ! "
the farmers shouted as they jolted past us, and for every
one he had a kind word and a good-natured joke.

" I own six thousand acres," he said, " and have had
no evictions for six years, except in the case of a man
who settled, and I allowed him to sell out, which he did
for £180.

" It cost me £1,500 some time ago to take up a farm
of 192 Irish acres, and four years ago I paid £1,050
to take up a farm of a hundred acres all in grass.

" There's H., a schoolmaster, his rent is £11 10s. for
11 acres. His brother had the farm, but died in debt.
I took it up and was going to sell it to a neighbor. H.
wrote to ask me to take him on and I did so. He proceeded to build an expensive house on it, far too good,
and now he owes me £23 rent. The other day he

served me with a notice to go into court and have the rent fixed. Now that rent has not been raised since 1820, and no one knows for how long before.

"I went over my rent roll a short time ago. I had complete rent rolls of 1841 and 1881, and I found the rental had increased only seven and a half per cent. since 1841.

" The tenants' improvements are much talked about. It is usual here for the tenants to make improvements that in England are made by the landlord, but there is no injustice in this, for rents in Ireland are much lower than they are in England. Virtually we pay for the improvements through asking less than the commercial rent of the land.

"As a rule, when a tenant builds a house, he draws the slates and does the labor, and we pay for the timber and the slates. Bills for timber and slates are taken by many of us as cash.

"All rent is now called rack-rent. Between 1850 and 1857, under the Encumbered Estates Act, many speculators bought Irish land, with the intention of selling again. Adair, of Glenveigh, was one of that class ; he began with only £2,000, and went on buying land, raising the rents, and selling again at an enormous advance. But land owned by old families is invariably let at a rate much less than the market price. It is the jobbers who have rack-rented. I have never let at the highest market price."

Soon we came to the farm, chiefly pasture, with a low, neat house not far from the road. " This, a hundred and one acres, the rent of which was £178, and the valuation £127, I took up in 1883 from a tenant for £1,050. It came down to me from father and son through ten generations. I then borrowed money from the Board of Works and rebuilt the house on the old foundations. The farm was very much run down when I took it, so I spent £300 in draining it, and have spent more than I have made so far. In October last I bought fifty yearling bullocks for £286. They have had nothing but hay and grass, and I expect to sell them in October for £500 or £550. The only farm hands I keep are a steward and a herd, each of whom gets 10s. a week, grass for a cow and donkey, and three roods. I sold some fifteen months' colts the other day for £37 10s. Meadowing hay I sell for from 50s. to 70s. an acre. Altogether, I have three hundred Irish acres of grass and tillage, and four hundred of wood and waste, and I make from it a little more than I should if I let it.

"Not half of my rents are falling in. The May and June rents, which I have usually had paid by this time, have n't been paid.

"We retrench as much as we can. I have had to discharge a carpenter and a mason I had in constant employment for twenty-five years, as well as two hands in the garden and four on the farm. There are many like myself, who have n't a common copper except what comes from the land, and we never know whether we shall have any thing in a year's time. Why should we be put in this pinch simply because of an exigency of the government?

"Free sale, of course, operates as a second rent on the purchasing tenant, but the tenants don't think of it as such, because they never look on money as a fund; they never think of investing money for the sake of interest. The League soon saw that the tenants selling and getting high prices for their tenant right prevented the courts from reducing the rents, so they denounced sale as land-grabbing. It is their interest to keep a broken man in possession of a farm, in order to depreciate its value. I know lots of men who are in difficulty, who would gladly sell and invest their money in a smaller farm, much to the benefit of everybody, but they are not allowed to.

" The land question is taken up by the priests and Parnellites for different purposes, and by both as a means to an end : by the former, in order to expropriate the minority who now own the land, who are Protestants ; and by the latter, in order to secure a Home-Rule Parliament. The young and more rabid priests are leading the movement, and the older and better educated are following, so as to keep on the crest of the wave.

" In a system of land purchase, county guaranties will only be good if the country continues under the imperial government."

" Who will leave the country if a peasant proprietary is established ?" I asked.

" I and many others like me," he said, " would not go away, and many would go with regret only because they could not afford to keep their places. The smaller proprietors would be unable to remain. There are an enormous number of small landlords who purchased Irish land as a good investment, and a great many of them will have to go, since they have often retained no land at all in their own hands, except one house each and a garden plot. The large landlords have great demesne which they can cultivate, and their grand houses and demesne they would be loath to leave and unable to abandon, for they certainly could not sell them. Those who have no residence here do not live here now, and as to them there will be no change. Those who have residences here now and live in them will remain if they possibly can."

"Even peasant proprietorship will not cure all agrarian distress. The careful man will purchase from the improvident, and the government can never keep a sharp enough look-out on the individual farmer to prevent him from subletting.

"The people also are extremely illogical. This summer on the Board of Guardians every one wanted to keep the rates down, as it was going to be a very hard year. I warned them that in a hard year more paupers would come upon the Union than in a good year, and that that contingency must be provided for. Now, outdoor relief has increased enormously, and the Union is in debt over £200.

"If we are to have Home Rule, it will not do to trust the present electorate, but one must provide for the presence of representatives of capital and commerce, of the legal and medical professions, on important boards and committees. The merchants of Dublin could be trusted, but they are so few in proportion as to be practically disfranchised.

"I would n't trust the people with the administration of the criminal law, for at present they are too demoralized to have regard for law, and if they could, would remove a judge who did not decide according to their notions.

"I would n't trust them with what might be called the incidence of taxation, but only with its collection ; for if they could, they would throw the burden on unpopular persons and classes.

"The people, I think, are not at heart disloyal when

they are let alone. The O'Connell movement was aided
by the desire for Catholic emancipation, which no one
with a sense of justice could oppose ; and the Nationalist movement is aided by the agrarian agitation.

"The leaders of the agitation, however, go to dangerous lengths. This is from a letter written to me by a
tanner, a prominent leaguer : 'We like our nobility and
gentry when they promote employment and add to the
general prosperity of the country, and we desire to have
them always living in our midst, feeling themselves—as
they are—quite as secure as if they were surrounded by
all the armed forces of the British dominions ; taking
their proper places, not at the tail of an English oligarchy,
but at the head of the Irish people ; the nobility of an
Irish self-sustaining, independent nation, and bound to
England only by the golden link of the crown and by
ties of affection and affinity.' Home Rule is opposed by
most on religious grounds. My gardener and steward are
Protestants, and they are more afraid of Catholic ascendancy than I am ; they think their lives would not be
safe.

"You ask me what changes in the laws are most
needed. I am in favor of a duty on flour, dead meat,
and manufactured articles. Law costs in the Land
Courts should be reduced. They are absurdly high. On
January 9, 1882, there were nineteen cases on trial before
the subcommissioners at Mayo ; six cases were dismissed.
Of the remaining thirteen, the original rent was £107
18s., the reduction £40 16s. 6d. The total of the solici-
tors' charges was £32 10s. : and of the fees to counsel,
£19 19s.

"The poor-rate is assessed unfairly. It has always
been assessed on land only, but why should it not be

assessed on income? A farmer living in a house worth £30, and making £100 a year, ought not to pay, as he does, the same poor-rate as a trader living in a similar house, and making £1,000 a year."

A MILLER.

Throughout Ireland one sees by every river-side deserted, ruined mills ; but in County Carlow some giant water-wheels are turning still. In one of the largest of these mills the machinery is elaborate and of the newest designs, chiefly of American invention and manufacture. The wheat used is American and Black Sea, only ten per cent. being Irish. The output is a thousand sacks a week, and is all sold within a radius of fifty miles ; for it does n't pay to send flour to the seaboard. "I am not a landlord," said the miller, "and the farmers speak frankly before me. In their hearts they don't want Home Rule, and are sick of the National League. Unless a man wants to get a slap at a neighbor, he would rather be rid of the League. The only people who gain by it are particular shop-keepers who are secretaries or treasurers of the local branches.

"A majority of the people are for Gladstone's bill, but a good system of local self-government twenty years ago would have saved us all this trouble. In the union the Nationalists are a majority, and they obstruct business and take every opportunity of insulting us. 'The voice of the people is against landlords and Protestants, and I go with the voice,' said my gardener to me when I was a candidate for office.

"There would be protection here in a moment, if there was the power, for nine tenths of all classes favor it. You do meet an odd free-trader now and then, but I

rarely come across one. All manufactured articles, I
think, should be taxed,—flour, for instance, but not
wheat.

"I don't believe in Home Rule. An Irish government would be practically bankrupt; it could n't borrow
money even at twelve per cent. There would also be
much petty persecution of the Protestants. The Irish
are less religious than they were, but they are more
bigoted; their antipathy to Protestants rests on the idea
that every Protestant is a friend of England, while they
wish to get rid of England altogether. The motives of
the leaders are largely selfish. Is n't it much pleasanter
for ——— to get three hundred pounds a year to go to
Westminster and bait Lord Hartington, than to earn
twelve shillings a week as a stone cleaver?

" It is human nature to wish to get every thing as cheap
as possible, and that is the case with the farmers and the
land. The Irish farmers have found out that the Land
Commissioners will reduce the rent enormously on an
uncultivated farm in bad order, and they act accordingly.
Still every one knows that the last five years have been
very bad, and this is the worst of all. As to coercion,
what the papers say is all nonsense. The matter with
Ireland is that we have license here instead of liberty."

A NATIONALIST LEADER IN COUNTY KILKENNY.

My companion was a self-made man in an old sleepy
town. We walked up and down the long promenade by
the river's side, fringed with trees, and crowded with
young men and girls strolling in their Sunday clothes.
As soon as we could find a comfortable bench a little
apart from the line of people, who were perpetually
saluting us, my companion composed himself to talk.

"Look at that weed-grown ditch," he said, pointing to an old embankment at our feet. "That was to have been a canal, leading to the sea, to bring provisions to the town. £25,000 was spent on it, but it was never finished. The canal was planned by the Irish Parliament a hundred years ago. Now it is a ditch full of rushes.

"There used to be a manufactory of blankets here; there were a thousand hand-looms; there were hatters, boot-makers and glove-makers here. These have all vanished off the face of the earth, before English competition. It is like the large shop crippling the smaller shops. Home Rule would have kept these industries alive by wise enouragement. As it is, the agitation for home manufactures has at last created a demand for Irish woollens, and the woollen factory has recently been restored.

"It is natural to think that protection would help to restore our industries, but there are other means.

"At present there is great need of technical education. That ruined flour-mill below us I should like to turn into a paper-mill, but I don't know how to make paper. We are not a travelling people and know nothing about the trade and the methods of manufacture in use by the rest of the world. We depend solely on the produce of the land. I would have a technical school in each province, to teach chemistry, political economy, etc., and also to be a centre of commercial information about the needs of different markets and the current prices.

"The Protestants fear Catholic oppression. There is, however, little bigotry here. Sir J. Gray, M.P. for Kilkenny six years ago, was a Protestant. ———, who has been town clerk of ——— for fifty years, is a Protest-

ant, appointed by the old Catholic corporation, at a time
when a Catholic would not be tolerated in office in
a Protestant town. A few months ago he was retired
on pension by a Catholic board. A Protestant was
appointed sessional clerk for the county. I believe
that, so far from a Home-Rule government being a government by ecclesiastics, after Home Rule has been
granted the power of the priests will begin to wane.
When the people have got the power into their own
hands and have acquired the habit of thinking for themselves, they will ignore the priest in politics,—and though
the majority of the Nationalist party at present are co-
operating with the priests in this agitation, still, they are
not men who will allow the priests to govern them.
They are using the priests for their own purposes. It
was the tyranny of the English government that gave the
priests their power in the past, for the people had only
the priests to look to for guidance. Take away the
English government and let the people govern themselves, and the priests will at once lose their political
power. The best proof of this is that in all countries
where the priests have once had political influence, they
have lost it, as in France and Italy.

"I pledge my word, though a good Catholic, that I
think there would be more chance, if there were any
chance, of making Ireland Protestant, by granting Home
Rule than by leaving things as they are. The priests, I
don't think, care a halfpenny ticket about Home Rule,
but they have to follow the agitation. Religious bigotry
will decline. Beyond a doubt, in the event of Home
Rule, this place will be very much Americanized, and
America is certainly not a priest-ridden country.

"There is intimidation in the country at present, but

a Home-Rule government could put down intimidation in three days, not so much by putting people in jail as by creating a popular sentiment against it.

"There is not much socialism in Ireland, for it is opposed by the Church, and the farmers so soon as they get the land will become conservative. Men will always try to improve their position, and the laborers individually may try to get land, but that they will agitate generally against the farmers, I don't believe. It is quite possible that the farmers might not be so keen about Home Rule if they got the land first ; but the traders in the towns will have still to be reckoned with.

"Absenteeism works great evils in County Kilkenny. Lord Ormond draws some £20,000 a year from the county and spends it elsewhere, and yet he has never asked a favor from his town that has not been granted, in one case a grant of land, and at another time riparian rights. Now, however, the object of the agitation is, of course, to make the life here disagreeable to the land-lords.

"The Land Acts have not finally settled the land question. The courts at first gave miserably small reductions. The costs of the courts are excessive. On one property, the Shea estate, it will take five years for the reductions to pay off the costs.

" To-day the crops are poor even where land is good. Oats and barley are a quarter crop. Fifty per cent. reduction is necessary this year.

" The evils of absenteeism and the evils of landlordism can be got rid of only by a comprehensive system of land purchase, and that is possible only by Home Rule.

" A bill has been suggested making the purchase compulsory on the tenants of any estate on the option of the landlord, the purchase money to be guaranteed by county boards. Such a bill would be ridiculous. The *onus* of cultivation is now the landlord ; for a landlord has either to cultivate the land himself or to get some one else to cultivate it for him. Such an *onus* in a bad year is a burden, and ought not to be transferred to the tenant without his voluntary consent.

"Again, any such guaranty would be absurd. Suppose the price fixed be exorbitant ; is it just that the county should be liable ? Those on whose shoulders the taxes are to be imposed ought to have a voice in fixing the amount of the taxes. If a county board is to be taxed as a guaranteeing board, it ought to have the power of determining the amount of the guaranty, or tax, or price of purchase. A special elective board would have to be created for the purpose, for a grand jury is neither elective nor representative.

"The only alternative, if the government pass a Purchase Bill and determine by officials the amount to be paid, is for them to give an imperial guaranty. The very meaning of 'guaranty' is that the guarantor has a fund over and above the sum guaranteed, something besides the actual thing guaranteed. If the imperial government pay too much for the land, they have other resources ; but a county board would have nothing over and above the land of the county, and the value of that, or a possibly exorbitant price for that, is what it is proposed to guaranty. How can you get a guaranty out of impoverished land in Connemara, so much rushes, bog, and rock ?

"Why should the government exact a county guaranty ? Why not make six counties the unit of guaranty, for the larger the area the stronger and the less onerous would be the guaranty ?

"Again, the imperial government confiscated my ancestors' property, and gave it to others. Now that they
restore it to me, why should they make me assume a
heavy obligation ?

"The only other kind of guaranty I can think of besides an imperial guaranty is a guaranty by a Home-
Rule Parliament. If an imperial guaranty is impossible,
the land question can be settled only by an Irish
Parliament.

"It might be made a condition of granting Home
Rule that the Home-Rule Parliament will settle the land
question and guaranty to the landlords a certain yearly
percentage equal to the current price of money on the
value of their property, according to a valuation previously made, until such time as the purchase money has been
paid in full. That would be a fair plan, and the only
practicable one ; and I don't believe there is any probability that a Home-Rule Parliament would ever break a
condition of such a sort precedent to Home Rule itself.

"We have come round again to Home Rule. Gladstone's bill is open to criticism. I am certainly in favor
of keeping our representatives in Parliament. It will be
better for the imperial government for us to have a voice
in imperial affairs ; it will give Irishmen a chance to
work and speak in England, and will tend to preserve
amity. The obstruction which was, I admit, vicious in
the past will cease when the causes of it are removed.

"Then, no matter how parties may change and shift in
Ireland under Home Rule, it will make no difference to
England so long as hatred of England does not increase ;
and that, I believe, will not be the case, for Home Rule
is not an opening wedge for separation. That, indeed,
would be impossible, for a few men with sticks in their
hands are not an army and cannot make a revolution."

A KILKENNY MANUFACTURER.

This is a man of great energy of character, which has built up a large and prosperous business, and won him the admiration and love of the people. Although a Protestant and not active in public life, he has been publicly honored by a Nationalist and Catholic corporation. Every one speaks well of him. How does such a man regard the political and social questions of the day? As we strolled through his long green-houses, he tried to describe to me his state of mind,—one that seems to be characteristic of the more thoughtful, serious, and conscientious business men throughout Ireland.

"Home Rule," he said, "means throwing the entire political power of the country into the hands of the Catholic priests. The lower orders will do exactly what the priests tell them. The influence of the priests in politics is, however, not so great as it will be. In a movement like this, the great political feeling that is excited for the moment excludes all others, and the religious feeling is suppressed ; but so soon as the political question is settled, the religious feeling, which is now only latent, will predominate. I regret this, not so much because it will be injurious to the Protestants, as because it will be fatal to the country, for no country can be properly governed by a body of ecclesiastics.

"An infallible church, however, must be a persecuting church : it can allow nothing to stand up against it. They might take our churches from us, but they might do infinitely more serious damage by petty persecution. It would be quite possible to make the country too hot for a Protestant to live in it. There are many liberal Catholics, but in the practical working of Home Rule would not they be thrust aside? Archbishop Walsh said

once that it was infamous that in the Catholic city of
Dublin the finest site should be occupied by a Protestant
university."

I referred to the popular discontent, and the apparent
inefficacy of the land acts to check it. "They are all
mere stop-gaps," said he. "What other remedy is there
but Home Rule? I cannot suggest any. Gladstone's
speech was an able argument, but I have been and am of
the opinion that Home Rule is not workable ; that things
would come either to a separation, for the people are
more or less in favor of separation, or to the restoration
of the present conditions ; and meantime the country
would be kept in hot water, by which I mean that there
would be no place for a business man in it. I would, however, certainly be a Home Ruler, if I could convince
myself that the country would settle down under it.

"I am afraid that Irish discontent is a permanent evil.
In 1782 the Irish Parliament became practically independent, the country may have prospered, but ten years
afterwards it was in a state of rebellion, and the rebellion
would have effected a revolution, if it had not been sub-
dued by force of arms.

"If the bulk of the people were agreed on this subject
as they are in the South and West, there might be some
hope ; but the better and more energetic classes of the
North are against it to a man.

"It is true that business will never prosper till the
political question is settled. What chiefly affects business is confidence or the want of it. Would the country
at large have sufficient confidence in a Home-Rule government? The whole thing is a gigantic experiment,
and it is very difficult to know beforehand how it will
turn out.

"The welfare of England is largely our welfare. If England were reduced to a third-rate power to-morrow and its wealth dispersed, we should seriously suffer here. But whether a Home-Rule Parliament might not interfere with English success at a critical moment, I really cannot decide.

"Peasant proprietorship would be beneficial to business, for there would then be no absentees, and all the money got from the land, after the purchase money was paid, would be spent in the country. I don't think nationalization of the land will take place under Home Rule, because of the influence of the Catholic clergy, and of the land hunger, which is as great as ever it was. The insecurity of tenure was what specially impoverished the country, and if the people would only settle down peaceably, without Home Rule, the country would prosper, but that they will not do.

"The proclamation of the League was unwise. It ought to have been suppressed at first. It is the nature of things to culminate, and then to decline, and the League was beginning to decline. The best way of treating it would have been to despise it. The League has never been in violent opposition to the law. The people here were never very enthusiastic about it; those most so were some workingmen who had been out in the Fenian movement. As to Home Rule, however, the people almost to a man are in favor of it. The franchise is now almost manhood suffrage, and men of the lower classes always like to do things in a flock; they don't like to be on the losing side, and always vote for the man they expect to win. It would require the Duke of Wellington and the whole English army to put this movement down. The English government here is now only nominal, and Home Rule is safe to come sooner or later.

"Some advantages may come with it. There is a great deal of capital lying idle here, that a bounty system could make operative, besides tempting more. Protection, generally, however, would be impracticable on account of the laborers who would be unwilling to pay more for food or clothing. The falling off in business, however, I do not attribute wholly to the agitation, but partly to the general depression. The telegraph and railways, again, would make rebellion very difficult.

"But, in spite of this, I must say that it is my firm conviction that we shall get Home Rule; that in ten, twenty, or more years, there will be either such anarchy here or so general a rebellion for complete separation that the English government must interfere and put us back where we are now, and that this series of movements and counter-movements will be continued *ad infinitum.* Of the Land Acts I have little more hope, for, as I have said before, they are mere stop-gaps,—and, besides, the Irish land-hunger and thriftlessness will create a new class of landlords, who again will have to be expropriated."

"You seem painfully pessimistic," I could not help remarking as I shook hands.

"1 wish I could be otherwise," he replied, "but I am simply stating, as frankly as possible, my honest thoughts, so far as I know them. And in spite of all, there will be no unreasonable opposition to Home Rule here; we will give it a fair trial. Mr. Jones in New Ross recently transferred a large factory for dressing skins to England, but I don't think I would transfer my business even if I could, as I could n't."

A YOUNG solicitor at the office of the League I asked about the alleged excesses caused by the Plan of Campaign. "The tenant farmers," he said, "have enormous respect for the word 'rent.' A money-lender here told me the other day that they raise money at extraordinary rates to meet their rent.

"'No rent' is not the meaning of the people, though the cry might not be so unjust as it seems to be. The judicial reduction of rents is in some sort a measure of what the landlords have taken in excess of their just dues. The excess that the tenants have thus been shown to have paid would at a moderate compensation amount to ten years' purchase of their farms. So we might argue that no more rent is due. Thousands of pounds, moreover, is now owing to shopkeepers, and those debts are as just obligations as the rent. The farmers, however, would be glad to settle. Many of them purchased under Lord Ashbourne's Act at prices far in excess of the value of the land.

"Cork County is free from crime. The East Riding is quite free and the West Riding nearly so. At the last assizes in the city only four petty bills were presented by the grand jury. There are only four or five places where there is any outrage or boycotting, and that is where the landlords are fighting the Plan of Campaign. There are

outrages at Millstreet, but there is the only priest in the
county who speaks against the League. It is a bad thing
when the priest is not in sympathy with the people, for then
he cannot restrain them. If the League is suppressed, a
great deterrent of crime will cease to operate, for the people will then be acting for themselves, without their leaders
and priests working with them and directing them."

"Is the Plan of Campaign just," I asked, "in insisting
on all the tenants being given the same reduction, no
matter how different their circumstances?"

"While twenty can pay their rents," was the answer,
"forty often cannot. If the twenty, who perhaps have
large means, pay, the forty small tenants are evicted, at
the mercy of the landlord. It then is an act of charity
on the part of the twenty to throw in their lot with their
neighbors. On the Luggacurran estate one tenant had
an estate rated at £900 a year, and another at £1,400.
They were the first to suffer. They were able to pay, not
out of their profits, but out of capital which the rest did n't
have.

"Free trade is not worth discussing, but there used to
be any number of mills about Cork which have long
ceased to exist. When these mills were burnt down it
was not worth while to rebuild them. One was burnt
lately here, and another two years ago at Middleton.
Neither has been rebuilt. Only two mills are now operating here. Forty years ago my father was a great buyer
of wheat here for export to Glasgow, now American flour
is delivered here almost cheaper than the domestic grain.

"There used to be a great export trade in provisions
here. Now it is gone, except the export of butter. The
leather trade is also failing, and there are only two or
three tanneries where there used to be fifty.

" To some extent, perhaps, this loss of trade is due to the decline in population.

" What particular benefits do I expect from Home Rule ? The Irish Parliament would foster the fisheries by grants more wisely and energetically than the English government. For instance, small protection harbors and piers are needed along the coast. Now we cannot compete with English, Scotch, or French fishermen.

''There would be a body of clever men anxiously studying and encouraging Irish industries. So much intelligence applied to one object would be sure to have some influence for good. Judicious bounties would start manufactures. There would be a great saving in the expense of private legislation. The increased economy and the wise encouragement of trade might fairly be expected to bring back some of the prosperity Ireland enjoyed under the old Parliament, when all the finer public buildings in Dublin were erected."

I asked whether it might not be dangerous to have the judges appointed by a Dublin Parliament in view of the violence of local prejudice. " On the contrary," said he, " the fair administration of justice would then be the interest of everybody."

A BOYCOTTED FARMER IN COUNTY CORK.

In the list of boycotted persons published by the Cork Defence Union my attention was caught by the case of J. McCarthy, for the cause assigned for the boycotting was that he "took a neighboring farm which had been vacant for two years previously." One fine morning I drove out to see him, in the townland of Barracharang, fifteen Irish miles from Cork. His house, a square, low wooden building, is at the end of a long muddy lane, surrounded by a morass of sodden manure. A man with goatee and lean cheeks like a typical Yankee, with an honest voice and keen, clear eyes, John McCarthy welcomed us with the enthusiastic warmth of one who seldom sees a friendly face.

"When we took this farm last April four years," he began, "there was no boycotting. The farm was not considered an 'evicted' farm, for the tenants had gone to law with one another and had reduced themselves to nothing when Mrs. Longfield evicted them. The lawsuit began in 1872, and every one from here to Cork knows that the farm was vacant for years before we took it. Six or eight of the neighbors bid for the farm, but I was preferred as I had been a tenant of Mrs. Longfield's son. For many months the people were friendly. Then Callaghan, one of the former tenants, complained that he would have got the farm if we had n't interfered. Then a great meeeting was held at Donoughmore; they had two M. P.'s down here, J. C. Flynn and Dr. Tanner, who told them lots of lies, told them that we were land-grabbers. Mr. Flynn called on every one to boycott us, and not to speak to us. Dr. Tanner, who admitted to me that this was not a 'grabbed farm,' did nothing but denounce land-grabbing. The people made up an effigy of me, painted it, put a pipe in its mouth, set it on a donkey, marched it up and down the village at the time of the meeting, and then threw it down and battered it to bits. They called us traitors.

"In August I offered for sale a lot of meadowing. Suddenly notices were put up warning people not to buy it, and I did n't sell a pound of the forty acres. On August 7th one of the two smiths in Donoughmore refused to work for me, and the other was threatened and soon boycotted me too. All the local tradesmen boycotted me. The next year the League pressed my men to leave me. They were hooted and threatened. June 13th they left me, and for some weeks we had no help at all. In September I hired a neighbor's boy for twelve months, and before two weeks were out shots were fired into the windows of this room, the bedroom, and the kitchen. The bullets made these holes in the shutters. No one was arrested, though we could give a strong guess at the parties. The day after I let the boy go. That day, a Sunday, I was hooted at mass, and stones were fired at me as I left the chapel. The Sunday after my wife was bedaubed with rotten eggs in the chapel-yard. The next Sunday my brother and his wife were bedaubed with rotten eggs and hit with stones, and neither she nor this woman have been to chapel since.

"In October or November I went to Macroom fair with some cattle. I sold them, and the purchaser after paying a deposit drove them into a yard. Two fellows warned the man the cattle were boycotted, and they were at once turned out of the yard. They were returned to me and I brought them home again. From that day to this we have sold no cattle at any fair or market. On a Patrick's day I sent a lot of pigs to Kanturk. At midnight four men, one the secretary of the League, and another one of the committeemen, started from here and got to Kanturk before my boys did. The boys thought they had better bring the pigs back.

" For a time we were in a great hobble, for my butter was boycotted. I cannot get a tailor, carpenter, or blacksmith nearer than Cork, and even in Cork tradespeople who used to give us credit now refuse it. Our letters have to be left at the police barracks, for no one dared to

bring us letters from the place the post-boy leaves them.
Laborers I can get only through the Cork Defence Union.
Our neighbors visit us only on the sly, at night and in dis-
guise ; for if they were seen speaking to us they say they
would be called before the League.

"Those two young chaps were confirmed last July.
They were often assaulted on their way to chapel, and on
the day of the Bishop's visitation one was brutally beaten,
and his face cut with a stone. I presented him next
morning to the Bishop, and he threatened to excommu-
nicate any one who molested people in their religious
duties.

"We have suffered as much as any persons in County
Cork. Boycotting is worse than the plague. We would
have given up the farm before but we hoped the League
would be suppressed, and we believed that in twelve
months after that we would have quiet again. To this
day half the people say and think that we are wronged,
but no one dares to speak to us openly for fear of the
League. This June two years, I went to the League
rooms in Donoughmore, before the committee, and offered to give up the farm if they would let me have the
laborers to save the crops. The chairman said that the
rule was that I must give up the farm presently and without conditions ; that was the order of the central board.
But for the Defence Union and that little party of landlords I and my family would be in the workhouse.

"There is a good deal of boycotting in the neighborhood. The police of Donoughmore are boycotted. Notices boycotting them were pasted even on the donkeys'
backs. The young women are forbidden to speak to a
policeman—if a girl does so, she is boycotted. The Catholic curate about a year ago denounced a young man

for throwing eggs at a respectable farmer. The people said that the farmer's daughter had held a policeman's head while he was having a tooth drawn ; and the curate was boycotted. The priests get turf, hay, and oats from the farmers, and they all refused to give him any. Two or three years ago the parish priest was boycotted because he would n't join the League. One day he took two loads of corn to a farmer's hay-yard to be threshed, and in the evening the neighbors carted it all back to him, just as it was. They generally refused to go to his stations too.

" Timothy Harlehy, who has a farm next mine of some sixty acres, was evicted May last by his landlord, Mr. French. For several nights he slept out-of-doors and his wife at a neighbor's. He then was put back as caretaker. The people then boycotted Harlehy, because I suppose he did n't care to go on sleeping for ever in the open air. They burnt his hay rick. They broke his mowing machine by spiking the meadow with bits of iron. His brother-in-law took off a cartload of Harlehy's corn to his barn to thresh. Two or three nights afterwards two shots were fired into the bedroom of the laborer who carted the corn. The man explained that the corn had been taken in payment of a debt, and even then there was a great fight in the League about taking his boycott off. Another man, Barratt, helped Harlehy in threshing. Barratt's corn happened to be stacked in the field, and the next day the bindings were cut and the corn scattered.

" We have been under police protection ever since our house was fired into—two policemen sleep here every night, and we feel uneasy if they are late. People don't care if they kill a man about here, for they know nothing will happen to them if they do.

" Some six years ago I joined the League. A threshing machine was promised me by the owner, and he refused to let me have it unless I joined. I was afraid, and
I went in with another farmer, also under compulsion.

" Half the people have been coerced into joining the
League. The respectable farmers don't attend the
League meetings here, and the parish priest does not
control it. If one of the members has a spite against
you, there is no doubt but that you will be boycotted for
one reason or another. The farmers are getting cool
about the League. It has been necessary, but is necessary no longer now that the Land Acts have been
passed.

" The land is very poor in this townland. The crops
are miserable. Nothing is good here but Champions.
Rent is too high here. I am paying fourteen shillings
an acre. Some of the land is boggy and not worth four
shillings an acre, but some of the arable land would stand
you over a pound. I don't believe there is a man who
can make his present rent. But the landlord is a good
man and does not press us. We were given 25 per cent.
last gale day, but that is not enough. If we were pressed
every man would be evicted. There is not a tenant but
owes from two to three or four years' rent ; yet the landlord is popular. He came down here yesterday, and the
village band turned out to meet him, and the people drew
his carriage down to Donoughmore Cross.

" There are talking against the landlords a good many
Land Leaguers who if they were in their places would be
much worse. A little while ago, before Captain Stokes, R.
M., one D——, a National Leaguer, sued a laborer for
thirteen shillings, arrears of rent, and settled the case in
court for half his manure, which he took and laid out on
his own farm. They will exact the last farthing.

"There are two sides to every question. What do farmers give to the poor? How many laborers do they employ? Will they, when they become proprietors, give as much and employ as many as the large landlords? This country at any rate will never be without landlords. These may be hunted out, but there will be new ones and worse. If this property were owned by one of our neighboring farmers, more people would be evicted than are now. The farmers are sharp about money matters. Croften here, who was the secretary of the League and is now the postmaster, owed seven years' rent when the Arrears Act was passed. He went into court and had the arrears wiped off, and has n't paid a halfpenny since.

"Bad as they are here," said McCarthy, as I turned to go, "they are much worse elsewhere. I don't even condemn boycotting absolutely. A man who goes behind another's back and takes his farm, might be fairly boycotted; but then the people ought to make sure of the facts."

Something that Mrs. McCarthy said showed that she had some opinions of her own about the reason for their being so persistently boycotted. Her eyes twinkled when I asked her to tell me what she thought about it. "Well," she said, with a little hesitation, "the leaders of the League here are the poorest and lowest of the people. Chief among them are some young men belonging to a wrangling family named B——. Their father had a lawsuit with a neighbor sixteen or seventeen years ago, and, when the suit went against him, hung himself. A friendly farmer told us that one of the B—— boys said we had called them the hangman's sons. We would never have said such a thing, and we would n't say so now. But there was a boy in our house who might have said something of the sort. Then, when Callaghan said he would have got the land if we had n't taken it, the B——s were glad to turn his talk against us, and boycotted us out of spite."

I drove on to Donoughmore, a wretched little village, and called on Father Murphy, the Catholic curate. "I know nothing about the merits of McCarthy's case," said he, "and wonder how you came to hear of it. This movement began with the tenants pledging themselves not to take a farm from which another had been evicted unjustly. Then the principle was extended to all evictions. This may explain why McCarthy was not boycotted at first. The principle was not definitely formulated for some time.

"I know he has been boycotted very hard. His brother and his brother's wife, as well as his personal family, were not allowed to come to church, and have since been annoyed coming and going. Other members of the congregation were not allowed to sit in the gallery with them, and some who did so were insulted. McCarthy was reputed a good, honest man till he took the farm.

" No clergyman is permitted to attend a political meeting without the permission of the parish priest, and in this parish the clergy take no part in the League.

" In the matter of boycotting, I distinguish between active and passive boycotting, and discountenance active boycotting only.

" Home Rule we all want, because the Irish are a nation, and a nation ought to govern itself. Moreover, the imperial Parliament has been drawing the money out of the country. A home Parliament would develop our industries by advancing money and by giving bonuses."

I then tried to find Bat Callaghan's public-house. We had to ask the way. At one house the driver got down and knocked at the door. A woman opened it, and, at sight of a tall man in a long, rough coat, ran back, shrieking hysterically in great terror. Finally I found Callaghan, an old man, with drooping lip and shaking hand. "I bought the land," he said slowly, "from a woman who had no right to sell her son's part, but I knew nothing of it. The son sued me, and went from post to pillar. At last, I was only entitled to one third of the farm, though I kept possession of the whole of it."

"My father," the daughter explained, "had paid no rent for the ten years when he was in possession, and the others paid nothing. Then the landlord evicted them all, and got the whole into his hand. We were evicted several times, and put back again. It was twelve months from the last eviction when McCarthy took the farm. My mother acted as caretaker for a time, living here and going over there once in a while. For a year or two there were no crops on the place. For some years we let the neighbors feed their cattle off it."

"The landlord," said Callaghan, "asked me to bid for the farm, and I offered £60, three pounds less than the old rent. I am glad I did not get it, for I could n't have paid the money, nor could the cousin who was going to take the farm in my name. McCarthy offered the old rent."

"They are boycotted!" shrieked Mrs. Callaghan gleefully. "When they went to mass they were pelted with stones and eggs. No one will speak to them or sit in the same gallery with them. Oh, they are boycotted! As for us, we are as much after the old farm as we were the day we left."

" McCarthy came here," suggested the daughter, "and offered us money for my father's good-will, but we would n't take it."

" Did you see the place," asked the old man, "covered with stumps of trees? The landlord gave McCarthy and a few others leave to cut wood there. Then all the neighbors went in, and every man had his tree, the whole country-side, and all the trees were cut down in one night." In a few minutes the ruined wood, with the trees sawn off four or five feet from the ground, loomed weirdly before us in the moonlight as my car galloped on to Cork.

A PLAN OF CAMPAIGN ESTATE.

Half-way from Fermoy to Mitchelstown we caught the first glimpse of the gleaming white towers of Mitchelstown Castle. "Ha! ha!" shouted the driver, "we 'll soon have the green flag floating there, with the harp without the crown." Soon we were in the little town, a town celebrated in the old posting days, but now decadent and wellnigh lifeless. The post-car stops in a square, where on the broad green a gayly dressed party are playing tennis. The old ladies from the " College " opposite, where, by the generosity of an old Lord Kingston, twenty-six ladies in reduced circumstances enjoy half a house each and a pound a week, are sunning themselves near the tennis nets. A tennis tournament in " a plan of campaign " town. What a contrast ! Upon the green open the great gates of the demesne, and the broad road leads slowly up to the castle, more splendid than many a palace, with its Gothic entrance flanked by lofty towers, with its gallery a hundred and fifty feet long, and eighty bedrooms. On the gravel-walk peacocks are jauntily strutting.

The estate is, as is well known, one of the most heavily indebted in Ireland. The building of the castle cost fabulous sums in the first quarter of the century, and the hospitality of Lord Kingston, the friend of George IV., was magnificent but ruinous. In 1845 or 1846 the mortgage on the property was foreclosed, and the story of the seizure and the fortnight's siege of the castle is one of the most romantic episodes in the romance of "New Ireland." In 1850 the estate was sold under the Encumbered Estates Act, and for a time controlled by a land company. Some years ago the mortgages were consolidated into a single mortgage of some £240,000 to the Representative Body of the Church of Ireland, and the interest, a little less than £9,500, consumes yearly three quarters of the entire rental. The rents are in the main identical with those in force at the beginning of the century, and average less than those fixed by the agent of the Court of Chancery in 1845-6.

Such was the state of affairs when in November, 1886, the tenants combined to demand an all-round reduction of 25 per cent., a reduction which if granted would have swept away the entire surplus above the mortgage interest. Lady Kingston, acting in the absence of her husband, offered to give reductions of from 10 to 30 per cent., according to individual necessities,—and the plan of campaign was adopted.

Early in the spring a public auction was held of all the cattle on the estate. The object, of course, was to leave nothing for the landlord to distrain. A violent speech was made by Mr. Mandeville, M. P., threatening those tenants who still held aloof from the combination. From that time on severe boycotting prevailed. The night of February 5th placards were posted throughout

the country-side. This is what they said : "Boycott!
Boycott!! Boycott!!! Fellow-countrymen, be not de-
ceived, boycotting is not done away with. Disregard
the language of cowardice, no matter by whom uttered.
Stand firmly by your homes, by your wives, and little
ones. Strike at your tyrants! All your hopes and fortunes are centred in this fight. Strike 'now or never,
now and forever,' at every one who assists Anna Kingston, Lady Kingston, to recover oppressive rents, or who
pays them. Boycott that disgrace to her sex—Anna
Kingston, the grass widow, the hard-hearted. Boycott
Frend, the agent, the pig-headed representative of the
Church Body, who dismissed the laborers. Boycott
Bulldog Maria O'Grady, solicitor, who betrayed every
client who had the misfortune to be associated with him.
Boycott Benson, the insolent whelp, whose insolence
and extortion all of you have experienced. Strike at the
outposts of the castle ; you know who they are. Boycott Jim Neill, the hangman, and family ; Neddy Kelly,
the ex-farmer ; Dicky FitzGibbon, Clerk of the Union,
the only land-grabber in the district, and his brood of
upstarts ; gombeen-man Coache, and his apostate wife,
the only associate of Benson, and all bailiffs on the
estate,—shun them. Let others, too, take warning and
beware of their fate, or their turn will surely come. By
order of the Vigilance Committee. N. B.—John Cough-
lan, of Hemingstown, has paid his rent. Boycott him and
his shorthorns, and dairy farms. Dairymen, beware!"

The shopkeepers in town, who had been chiefly supported by the castle, wrote humble letters begging to be
excused from filling the orders of Lady Kingston. So
many were the boycotted people, that opposite the green
a shop was opened by Lady Kingston for their benefit ;

every thing was kept there, from pork to pepper, soda to stockings, and young ladies ran in and out with a most amusing air of proprietorship. " Bulldog Maria O'Grady " was boycotted. " The reason I have n't been to my office lately," he said, "is that my servant has been sent off to America, and I have no one to tidy it up. In January the Leaguers announced that they would n't let me, my clerk, servants, or their children go to the parish church, and the priest, through Father Sexton, re-quested me not to go for the sake of peace. Two old clients of mine, one a shopkeeper and the other a seeds-man, have been punished by fine and boycotting for em-ploying me. They threatened to boycott O'Brien, a magistrate, for employing me, and he, for business rea-sons, purchased his peace with them." Benson, "the in-solvent whelp," was boycotted. "They broke the skull of the bailiff with an iron hammer, making a fearful wound. The sheriff swore he saw a certain man strike him, and the man was tried but acquitted." Dicky Fitz-Gibbon and his "brood of upstarts " were boycotted. "His daughter, a pretty girl, fifteen or sixteen years old, on her way to church, was pursued by a hooting mob, and when she took refuge in a shop the shopkeeper put her out. All his servants have left him, and his children are not allowed to go to school."

" The tenant right on the estate brings as high a price as ever. For instance, February 11, 1885, James Moore sold to his son on his marriage thirty-four statute acres, the rent of which was £21, for £275, and a covenant to support him ; January 29, 1885, Mary M. sold to Patrick Clifford, ten acres and two roods, rented for seven guineas, for £150 ; in 1886, a small house, held under lease, paying 10s. a year ground rent, was sold for £500 ;

April 22d, Thornton sold to Roach, a small cottage and nine acres, held under lease, and paying £5 a year rent, for £365 and costs, £10 ; June 1, 1887, John Quinlan sold to Daniel Wallace, a small plot of half an acre, paying 10s. rent, for £200 and costs, £12." The amount of the costs surprised me. "What the landlord and tenant," said Mr. O'Grady, " used to settle between themselves is now, owing to the recent legislation, transacted through the lawyers and the court. So that now the costs amount to pounds instead of shillings. £5 is the usual charge for drawing an instrument ; the fees are about £5 ; and £2 for my perusal, on account of the landlord. The office never charges for drawing such instruments, so by boycotting me the tenants double their costs.

" The people are demoralized. They dodge their own priests if they can. Near Fermoy they nailed up the chapel every Sunday for five or six months. The priests lose money hand over hand, for the people are becoming independent of them through the influence of returning American Irish.

" Home Rule is a hollow sham. Six hundred thousand farmers support it because of the land agitation, and the needy classes because they have nothing to lose, and see before them a magnificent prize—the revenues of Ireland. Under Home Rule there will be ten years of chaos and terrorism, and then decent men will gradually come to the front again.

"There is enormous distress here, but it does not touch the farming class, but only the laborers and the servants. The laborers are very badly off. Several hundred used to find employment on this one estate. The landlords to-morrow, with £200 or £300, could get hundreds of laborers to tear the roofs off the farmers' heads."

With Canon O'Regan I had some talk about the state of affairs. "Suppose the Kingstons cannot afford to grant reductions that richer landlords give, why should the people suffer? That great palace there was built out of the earnings of the farmers. Why should the people starve to enable Lady Kingston to live there? Money was squandered recklessly in the past, it is just that the present should pay for it." Yet there is something touching in the thought of that gentle, sad-voiced lady in that noble castle, for the last time perhaps, watching the peacocks strutting on the gravel, or for the last time strolling through the vast conservatories.

In the village the people speak with curious hatred of the Kingstons, for whom even A. M. Sullivan felt compassion. They repeat dreadful traditions of impossible cruelties in the eighteenth century, and refer vaguely to a curse that the estate shall never pass from father to son for more than two generations, a curse that at least is verified by the facts.

It seemed strange to carry these thoughts to a brilliant ball, and even then they could not be forgotten, for our hostess had herself her own troubles with her tenants, who had only just consented to an arrangement; and many ladies were present who had been reduced to genteel beggary by the failure of family charges that were expected to endure forever. As the party broke up in the early morning, a report spread suddenly that a bailiff had been shot, and a policeman wounded; and as we walked home we passed a burning hay-rick, surrounded by a crowd of jeering rowdies, that no one tried to save. It was said to belong to a widow who had brought back her cows from the place where they had been concealed by order of the League. On arriving at the castle, we found that all the windows had been smashed in the beautiful house of an absentee neighbor, and that a successful raid had been made by the Kingston bailiff, who had driven sixty-two of the tenants' cattle into the demesne. The next day we sat up half the night in the long billiard-room, with all the arms that could be mustered, expecting an attack to recover the cattle. " The poor, deluded tenants ! " said a lady ; " it is necessary to seize their cows to give them an opportunity to pay their rents with safety." Such are some of the excitements of life on a " Plan of Campaign " estate ; they recalled the border warfare of the days of " Marmion " and the " Lady of the Lake."

A few weeks later and a great meeting of Galtee farmers, with blackthorns in their hands, refused to be dispersed by the police, drove them to the barracks, and left two young men dying in the streets. Gladstone wrote the telegram : " Remember Mitchelstown ! " and William O'Brien, in a fortified farmer's house, entered by a ladder, pointed his own moral of that famous aphorism : " I say, God bless you and guard you, and more power to your strong arms. . . . Before that watchword the walls of Dublin Castle and the walls of Mitchelstown Castle will go down and crumble in the dust." [1]

A few more months and the Land Commissioners granted a general reduction of twenty-two per cent. on the rents of the Mitchelstown tenants under judicial leases fixed in 1881 and 1882 ; and, on the tenants still holding out, their demands were finally acceded to ; evicted tenants were reinstated, and the proprietors announced their intention to offer the estate for sale. This is the final consummation, so long delayed, of " the ruin

[1] September 24, 1887.

of that noble house, the wreck of that princely fortune, once the boast of Southern Ireland." [1] These landlords were not rack-renters, they were not absentees, they made the town of Mitchelstown beautiful, and their own estate they were perpetually improving ; they built almshouses and a church, and a town-hall, and yet they are driven from the country with execrations.

A GENTLEMAN FARMER IN COUNTY CORK.

A handsome sunburnt, athletic man appeared one day at luncheon. The owner of an estate of some five thousand acres, he has but few tenants and is trying to farm most of it himself. It is a dairy district, and the profits seem to be reasonably remunerative. " Take," he said, " a farm of twenty acres. That will support at a low valuation eight cows (wet and dry, *i. e.*, winter and summer) on hay and grass. Those cows ought to produce three firkins of butter each, three and a half would be usual. That is worth, at 50*s.*, 10*s.* less than has been refused by some of my tenants this year—£7 10*s.* If you allow a calf to each cow, the farmer would make a further sum at present prices of £3 each. Two pigs at least can be kept for each cow, selling for 30*s.* each, after being fed on buttermilk and potatoes. The gross receipts would then be £108. In addition to this there would be potatoes grown for family use and a little oats for straw to make manure, which I don't charge for. The rent of the farm would probably be, with the present reduction, £20, a pound an acre. The taxes would be half the rates at 1*s.* in the pound, or £2. So the net income of the farmer would be about £85 or £86.

" The farmers spend too much money on funerals,

---

[1] A. M. Sullivan : " New Ireland," Chap. XII.

fairs, meetings, drink, and shop goods. Much harm is also caused by their peculiar marriage customs. If my son were to marry a daughter of yours, for instance, I should have to give my son a farm, twenty acres and ten cows, perhaps, and you would give with your daughter an equivalent in money—£200. But that money, instead of going into the bride's pocket or her husband's, goes to me as the father-in-law. The father gets the marriage portion of the girl. In seven years hence, when the son is probably the father of seven children, they are all dependent on the farm and ten cows, and the rent has to be met all the same. The result is too often bankruptcy without any fault on the part of the landlord.

"Then the priest tax is heavy. It is not unusual to hear the farmer saying after a priest has left the parish ; ' He was a devil of a fellow, and knocked the heart out of us.' They get about ten per cent. of the girl's marriage portion, and are paid large fees at christenings and funerals. 'That was a great funeral,' said a farmer to me one day, 'four priests at £3 a head.' All the tenants on an estate are apt to be related to one another. The priests encourage their parishioners to marry among themselves, for they get a percentage on both fortunes.

"I have given reductions in the last three years, even on judicial rents, whenever it seemed necessary. There is no mistake about it, some of the judicial rents are too high. I have seen the rents upheld on farms where the tenant was thriving with hard labor on poor land, and reduced on farms where the tenant was improvident on better land. Some of the land was valued in June and some in December, but it is impossible to judge the value of land in winter. That was the case with my property. Land should be valued in summer when the crops are growing. The result has been great inequality in the fairness of judicial rents.

"Eviction, of course, is sometimes necessary. I explain my reasons as clearly as possible to my tenants. 'If I let this man have his land for nothing, I tell them, 'I can't make you pay.' The dangerous man to evict is the man who has nothing ; the man who has money does not care to risk his neck. It is bad policy to turn out the poor.

"The national movement is led by a body of very clever men, but they have countenanced outrages because their object is to make things so uncomfortable for us that we must either join in or be crushed. When the tenants are made proprietors, the owners of the large estates will have to leave the country, but men like myself will remain. I am half farmer, half landlord, and succeeding, so I cannot be hurt much."

AN ESTATE IN COUNTY WATERFORD.

For miles in every direction the land is the Duke's. The beautiful castle that overpeers the Blackwater is vacant, but the evils of absenteeism are averted by a wise and almost princely generosity. The railroad from Fermoy to Lismore was built by the Duke, and he gave to the people the long, graceful Lismore bridge.

With one thoroughly familiar with the estate I spent a day in driving over it. " John D—— lives there," he said. " The rent is £26 2s. for two small holdings, and last Lady-day his arrears were £178. We have had a decree against him for twelve months past. He has paid only one year's rent in six years, and that on threat of eviction. I visited him personally to induce him to join the landlord in having his arrears wiped off under the

Arrears Act, and he promised, but did not.   A nationalist guardian said they were anxious to have an eviction
on the Duke's property, and had a League hut all ready
to put up for him.

" Here 's a farm that belonged to Michael Flynn, who
paid about £340 for 352 acres in two farms.   He paid
punctually and made money, dying thirteen or fourteen
years ago.   His grandson inherited it and a good sum of
money ; drank, gambled, soon ran up £600 arrears, and
sold off his stock.   As he was impoverishing the property, doing no good to any one, the Duke evicted him,
let the arrears go, and gave him about £100 to emigrate.
For three years the farm was then worked from the
office.   Expensive improvements were made, laborers'
cottages were built and fences.   A steward was hired
to work it.   One year the old rent above expenses was
cleared ; the next year £102 was carried forward, and
the third year there was no balance.   Three years ago a
woman took it in excellent condition for £300.   In three
months she married Gallagher, and died with her first
child.   The first half-year's rent she paid, and he paid
the second.   He was given twenty per cent. reduction.
Then he put up his stock at auction to avoid paying the
third half-year's rent when it was long due.   We had had
a judgment against him for a long time, and distrained
the morning of the auction.   He paid then out of deposit receipts amounting to over twice the rent, and the
same day auctioned off all the stock, and has bought
none since.   The place is now ruined.   The laborers'
cottages have the windows broken and the doors off their
hinges.   The fences are down ; he has ploughed up
three fields without sowing any seed in them.   He is a
tough customer."

I spoke to a laborer in one of the fields.

" The place is in a worse state now," he said, " than when young Flynn left it."

" On the Duke's property," continued my companion, "the buildings and drainage are fully half paid for by the landlord. There has not, however, been much reclamation of land in Tipperary and the south—none worth speaking of since the famine."

We passed a Land League hut thirty feet by fourteen, with two rooms and one window, built of corrugated iron sheathing lined partly with wood. Here lives vigorous, voluble, aged Mrs. M—— and her decrepit husband. " I had those 315 acres," she said. " The valuation was £272 10s. I sunk £1,400 my father left me in the farm, and was evicted for £500, though there was not a year's rent due. Six illegitimate daughters own it, and evicted me on July 1st, when there were a hundred acres of corn on it.

" I have nine children, one in Scotland, one in France, three in America. They support me, for I can't do any thing for myself.

" We stay here near the farm in the hope of getting it again, and we shall stay here till we do. One of my sons will buy it for us at a fair valuation.

" The Duke's agent is our best friend and has helped us."

I rejoined my kind host and companion, who, as we drove on, spoke frankly from his practical experience of many years.

" There's a farm on the estate that has a characteristic history. It was let to the widow Fenton for £13 a year. The rent was reduced to £11 10s. ; and the valuation was £11. She sold her tenant-right to Willoughby of

Wicklow for £125. The interest on this sum practically raised the new tenant's rent to £16 10s. The neighbors threatened him, and he forfeited his instalment of the purchase money and went away. The farm was put up again and was bought by Mrs. Brien, a widow, for £110. She lived there for a while, but was threatened ; and after being annoyed persistently by ghosts, she sold it to a neighbor for £95. There were other changes, but it finally passed into the hands of a neighbor, who probably had had his eye on it all along. Every farm could be sold, if free sale were really allowed by the people themselves ; but Parnell makes a great point of boycotting free sale. £11 an acre could be got for almost any farm after the passing of the Act of 1881.

"As to land purchase, I think things will come to such a pass between landlords and tenants that if the landlords can get passably fair terms, or even any terms not amounting to absolute confiscation, it may be for their benefit ; but even then it may not be for the good of the country. The loss of the landlord's expenditure may be a serious blow. In congested districts such a transfer of property would only perpetuate poverty.

" The Nationalists have set themselves to bring about the extermination of the landlords and the sale of the land for its prairie value ; that is, on confiscation terms. With this view they hindered the success of Lord Ashbourne's Act ; otherwise many would have purchased who would have been worthy proprietors. The inducements were great, for by paying twenty or thirty per cent. less than his present rent, a man could own the land in forty-nine years. There has, however, been dangled before the farmers the notion that in time they will get the land for nothing. Now no good can be done by making an insolvent tenant a proprietor against his will. A bad or thriftless tenant is apt to make a bad or thriftless owner. The ownership of land should be the reward of a man's own industry. Land purchase is unquestionably no remedy for the distressed districts and a very doubtful benefit for the others. A large addition to the number of proprietors would certainly be a great advantage, but it ought not to be indiscriminate.

" It is rather a strong argument against Home Rule, or even any extension of local self-government, that the Nationalists don't use well half the time what power they have.

" The —— Union is run by the Nationalists, and is not very efficient. One division has mortgaged itself as far as it can for erecting laborers' cottages, and the object in most cases is merely to spite the landlord or to annoy a farmer who is not a member of the League. One of the last votes, overruled by the Local Government Board, was to put three cottages, taking up an acre and a half, on the plot of land belonging to the bailiff, who has only four acres altogether, and those within the town limits, though the object of the act was to prevent the influx of laborers into the towns.

" The Duke always used to give seventy-five per cent. of the cost of building laborers' cottages, though the rule was generally here to contribute only half towards other improvements. The farmers could hardly be induced to put up cottages or any thing they did not need for themselves.

" The Unions also get into debt to the banks, because they insist on keeping the rates too low to meet their liabilities. They say the people cannot pay the necessary rates ; but it seems to me that if you incur a debt

you should pay it. They are also very lax in the matter
of out-door relief. They say : ' Oh, he 's very poor, and
if he comes into the house it will cost more than to give
him a small sum and keep him out.' The fact is, that
coming into the house acts as a test of a man's poverty ;
no one would object to taking public money and living
as he is accustomed to live. The pittances, too, are often
so small as not to keep a worthy but proud person from
starvation.

" I should, however, favor a very liberal scheme of
local self-government. It is a substantial grievance that
we cannot establish railroads without the expense of a
journey to London and a hearing before a parliamentary
committee, though the Nationalists make no outcry
about this. The Board of Trade can give temporary
orders, under a recent act for the establishment of tramways, etc. This power should be enlarged to cover
railroads.

" The grand-jury system should be made representative.

" The preservation of the Union is, however, essential
to the prosperity of England and Ireland ; and it is
essential to the preservation of the Union that the imperial government should have the appointment and
control of the magistrates, the judges, and the police ; in
a word, of the executive of the country. The brutality
of the people is greater than that of any other civilized
people, for here only is public sympathy given to criminals. On the Sunday morning here, when the news
came that Carey had given information about the Phœnix
Park murderers, each man's face was as black as a
thunder-cloud, as though a great public calamity had
happened ; and when it was moved in the Board of

Guardians to adjourn out of sympathy with the Duke's bereavement, Mr. ——, a Nationalist, spoke against it, saying that the Duke had not shown any sympathy for him when he was arrested as a suspect, and he did not see why he should show any sympathy for the Duke for the murder of Lord Frederick Cavendish.

" My belief is so strong in the tenacity and back-bone of the North that I am convinced of their power, in the event of Home Rule, to hold their own, if not to conquer the rest of the island."

" I can see nothing that can come from Home Rule," interrupted a friend, " but utter fiscal smash and a row. Behind the farmers are a vast army of laborers and loaf-ers, who outnumber the farmers, and the probability is that they will agitate against the farmers when the latter become proprietors, as the farmers have done against their landlords, for land which they will be very loath to give them."

" On this estate for the present," continued the other, " all is quiet. There has been no combination against rent, but there is great carelessness and indifference as to whether they pay or not, and an absence of the exer-tion to work they made in former years. Within a year, however, the agent met X. Y., of B——, near the bank. ' I have n't been to the office,' he said, ' because they are dogging me to see if I do go ; but I have paid the rent to —— to pay you.' "

Ten or twelve fields I passed of fair land, but yellow with weeds. " Premiums were offered," I was told, on making some comment, " for autumn cleaning of the fields ; but only two or three farmers could be induced to do so ; though the horses are idle in the autumn, and though in spring there is no time for cleaning before the early crops are planted. It is also impossible to make the farmers get their crops in early enough. When it 's fair, they think it will stay fair forever; and when it rains, they think the rain will never stop."

A WATERFORD FARMER.

The farm-house was a comfortable two-story building, and the dining-room in which we sat was neat and well furnished. The farmer spoke slowly and impressively between long puffs at his short pipe. "I own a hundred and four acres," he said. "The poor-law valuation is £126, and the rent is £132, less twenty-five per cent.

"Twenty-four acres are in oats, six in turnips, four or five in potatoes, and the rest chiefly grass. The oats are very light this year, and so short that they are hard to cut with a machine. The turnips are a total failure; the potatoes very bad; the mangels not half a crop; and the hay rather over half. I keep sixteen or seventeen dairy cows, three horses, and occasionally sheep.

"I used to buy cattle and exchange them after feeding, but cannot this year. Sheep used to pay fairly, but I cannot venture on them this year; the grass is so short, and hand-feeding so expensive. I used to make a good profit on calves in the spring, but cannot this year on account of the poor crops of turnips and oats. I send my milk to the creamery at Tallow, getting back the buttermilk, and payment according to the prices in the English market. Last year I made about £5 a cow for the butter, gross receipts. Now there seems to be no feeding quality in the grass, and I don't see how to carry my cows through the winter.

"I keep careful accounts of income and expenses. I have two servants whom I pay £10 in cash and board.

I work with three hands generally. By the year I pay a laborer £13 and perquisites, coals, potatoes, etc., and board. Extra labor during harvest, etc., probably comes to £15 more. Before the last two years, 1 used to spend a good deal of money in fencing, ditching, and other improvements. This year I put out about £2 an acre of potatoes and turnips for artificial manure. Seed corn we usually grow ourselves, but other seed costs me £5 a year, or about 10*s.* an acre. The county cess and poor-rates come to about £15 a year, and the priest tax is some £5 or £6. I have five children, and I and my wife live very economically. I come straight home from fairs, and am very slow in changing a pound. If the times were good, people could make a living as they used to ; but this year I am sure I shall lose something very large. Fifty per cent. reduction would not be sufficient to carry me through. Twenty per cent. is the average given here. The Duke is also very good in allowing for improvements and for losses of cattle. I should like to live off the land as an industrious working man wishing to improve his farm. I don't understand Home Rule or Land Purchase well enough to give an opinion, but I should think that if they came about we would be in a better position for improving our land. What is ruining the country now is the absence of capital."

TIPPERARY FARMERS.

A farmer, who is to some degree employed by a landlord, but who seemed more than usually honest and capable, I beguiled one morning into saying what he thought about peasant proprietorship. The amount of land needed to support a family in comfort seemed an inquiry worth making.

"You need," he said, "fifty or sixty acres about here to get a comfortable living out of the land, about a hundred English acres ; but even with that one would be worse off without capital than with capital and less land. Ten pounds an acre is needed for good farming, or at least £5.

"The opinions of the neighboring farmers I know well. What they want is to get their land cheap, if possible for next to nothing. They don't want any reasonable purchase scheme, for, as a tenant farmer told me, whom I urged to buy under Lord Ashbourne's Act, as he had plenty of money—'I would have been delighted to buy the place at higher terms twenty years ago, but now we hope to get it for much less by waiting. Besides, it would be like paying the rates—we would have to pay; and if we got behind, the government would make no allowance, as Mr. —— would.' Yes, they would always prefer a good landlord to the government for their creditor. The real trouble in the past has been that so many landlords were not accessible.

"In a few months after peasant proprietorship has become established, I am afraid the farmers will be shooting each other, and in six months they will be in the hands of the Jews. In the struggle for land they would buy from one another at enormous prices, and would borrow the money at very high rates. Of late years there has been more shooting of tenant farmers than of landlords. If they want a piece of land and cannot get it, they will coerce the owner to sell at their own terms, by force if necessary. Despotism, tempered by assassination, will be the result in no little time of peasant proprietorship."

Another farmer, an old man of Scotch birth, was talking one evening to me and a journalist. " There were two farms held by two brothers," the journalist was saying, "on Lord Bantry's property, at C——, on the shores of Bantry Bay, a wild, mountainous region. Their name was Harrington, or Sullivan, I forget which. The rental was originally about £27. One brother improved and spent a lot of money in fencing and draining, and his rent was raised gradually to £40. The other brother made no improvements ; and when asked a short time ago why he did not follow his brother's example, 'Shure, I shall be fined if I improve,' said he. ' Pat pays £40, but I am still paying only £27.'"

"It was much the same thing in Scotland," interrupted the farmer. " I have seen the farmers there slowly working up the side of a mountain. So soon as one bit was cultivated, the rent would be raised, until they were driven up to the very top.

"The Purchase Acts are much talked of, but to my knowledge tenants have been forced to purchase at exorbitant prices, just as they used to be forced to take leases. On the Marquis of Waterford's property, near Carrick on Suir, in this county, the tenants have been forced to buy at twenty years' purchase. Most of them were in arrears and were writted, and then, three months ago, they were given the alternative of purchasing. What have those men to fall back on ? The average rent was 30s. an acre, but I don't believe much of the land was worth 10s. The rest of the tenants have joined the Plan of Campaign ; and perhaps the others may be able to break their agreements.

"Free-trade in breadstuffs is what has ruined the country.

"Cattle have gone down fifty per cent. What is the

good of landlords offering reductions of ten or twenty per cent. ? The country is all burnt up this year, and what are we to do ? "

One afternoon, while driving, I stopped and entered the tiny house, or rather hut, of a farmer near Cahir. He told me he had eleven acres ; one acre and a half in potatoes, another acre and a half in oats, three in hay, and he keeps two cows. He has made no profit on milk this year, because of the drought. Oats are not bad, but the price is very low. The rent is £11 18s., and was settled by agreement out of court some five years ago, and no reduction has been made since then. "We have neglected the shopkeepers to pay our rent. We have five children," said he ; and his wife added, from a dingy corner : "My husband lost four years out of his health, and I had to sell the horse at Clonmell fair for £20, and we have gone without a horse ever since."

By the roadside one day I noticed a little wooden box of a house, like a toy house. It was one of the laborers' cottages, built under the recent act. There were two rooms below, and a trap-door leading to a garret by a ladder. The laborer's wife was in. She had her seven young children with her, and said her husband got usually one shilling a day, sometimes as little as four shillings a week, and sometimes as much as eight shillings.

When I asked the car-driver about laborers' wages, he said : "Ordinary laborers get usually 6s. or 8s. a week ; and last year, for the two weeks' season of potato digging they got 2s. 6d. a day. A ploughman gets from £12 to £13 a year."

A TIPPERARY LAND AGENT.

"The Plan of Campaign," he said, "is a widespread scheme to ruin the landlords as a class. In the case of a good but weak landlord, or one who is encumbered, or averse to a row, the leaders have no mercy on him. Even at this late day the landlords and tenants would come to terms if they were allowed to fight the question out without the interference of third parties ; but, as a rule, pressure is brought to bear by the tenant organizations on the tenants, or in special cases on the landlord by a landlord association, as by the Cork Defence Union at Youghal. Landlord and tenant are like two boys fighting, both wanting to run away but neither daring to. Whenever the tenants show a disposition to give way, a big meeting is called, and swells come from Dublin to start the excitement again. A few days ago Lady Kingston made some seizures, and a few tenants paid their rent. Instantly a big meeting was held, and down came William O'Brien by express. Condon, M. P., is kept there all the time, watching the estate as a cat does a mouse.

" There is great intimidation practised on any one who is lukewarm in joining the League. A popular form of punishment is for the Union to put a laborer's cottage on a man's farm. On —— property cottages were erected on the holdings of many tenants for which there was no other possible reason. As a rule the larger farmers should be selected ; here they picked out only small farmers.

" I have had a few cases, but not many, of payment in secret. The tenants go much together, and are loath to act independently. One tenant, after paying me, came back and asked me, when the ejectment cases came on in court, to have his name called with the rest, and so I did.

" There is a property belonging to an estate in chancery of which I have charge. A tenant was paying £300 a year for a farm there on which he had nothing but a herd's hut, as he lived on another farm forty miles off. I evicted him for non-payment of rent, and there was no sympathy for him, as he was very litigious ; but the farm is boycotted to this day, and the grass withering on it. I made two attempts to sell it at auction, and two to sell at private sale. No one will bid, though hay is scarce. One or two offers were made privately, but withdrawn. We have lost over £800 by this transaction, and without the slightest fault on our part.

"As a large landowner in Somersetshire said to me, ' I suppose, if I were to call my tenants together, and ask them if it was their wish I should continue to own the land, they would vote no, and would vote to divide it among themselves.' That would be the condition of the Irish landlords before a Home-Rule Parliament. Life and property would be insecure under Home Rule. They might succeed here in time, but there would be chaos meanwhile. The land question is blocking the way of Home Rule.

"Land purchase on any large scale is impossible without an imperial guaranty. The grand jury, of which I am a member, recently voted to guarantee the interest, at four per cent., on a few thousand pounds to build a light railroad, the government making some contribution. We cannot raise a single pound now, and many of the counties are probably in a similar fix. Much less would any land bonds be taken without an imperial guaranty.

"Another difficulty in the working of a local board to purchase through is the want of courage and public support to enable it to evict, if necessary, in order to secure payment.

"The various Land Acts would have succeeded in pacifying the farmers, if they had been given an honest trial, but that the League prevented. No evictions would have happened if the League had allowed free sale of the tenant right. Not sticking to that one clause of free sale has been the end of every thing. The League wants to keep up evictions. Meanwhile, the land is occupied by vagabonds, who are exhausting it, as well as paying no rent.

"Finally, I am in favor of greater local self-government. The associated cess payers on the grand jury should be made elective. Otherwise the grand-jury system is a great anomaly."

DRIVING WITH A MAGISTRATE IN TIPPERARY.

Early in the morning the magistrate called for me to drive with him sixteen Irish miles to petty sessions at Mullamahone. He himself is the ideal of a country magistrate—a bluff, hearty, earnest, sensible gentleman, of an old Norman family that has lived in Ireland for over five hundred years ; intensely honorable, hating nothing more than deceit or falsehood.

A broad valley stretched on each side of the road, and in the distance towered the gloomy masses of Slievenaman. The farms we passed seemed but poorly cultivated, but here and there a steam reaping-machine puffing by the roadside showed that modern methods were being slowly introduced. These machines are generally used in Tipperary, and are hired out by the richer farmers to their neighbors at 10s. a day.

The country was full of reminiscences to my companion. "We drove over a hundred head of cattle once from that field into Clonmell." "In that field, three or four years ago, we seized twenty milch cows." And he explained : "It used to be a part of our duty to be present, when required, at distraints for rent, but is so no longer."

Soon we were changing horses in the decayed little town of Fethard, where, in one short street, I counted fifteen ruined cottages.

Passing out of Fethard, we saw a large, apparently deserted farm. "One Meagher used to live there as tenant of some four hundred acres. Six years ago he was evicted with great violence. A number of neighbors joined him in resisting the officers, and eighteen out of twenty-three were convicted. For some time the farm lay vacant, then a stranger took it who was boycotted so severely that he had to go, and now it is leased for a nominal sum to the Land Corporation."

Mullamahone is a poor little village with two long streets, famous, if at all, for being the scene of a rising in 1848. The court-room was in the upper story of a rickety barn-like building. Three magistrates were on the bench. The cases were chiefly liquor cases and unimportant. Two men were on trial for drunkenness, and an excuse was pleaded that startled the court : that in the spring there had been a terrible outbreak of contagious fever, and so frightened were the people that no one could be found for a long time to bury one poor girl who died of it. These men volunteered, after first making themselves drunk from fear of the infection, and then left the coffin lying for several hours at the church-door. "Discharged." Another case I noticed was of malicious cutting of a tree by a tenant with a hand-saw. "My grandfather planted those trees," said the tenant, while the bailiff, an old man, swore that the trees were ornamental ash trees along the road. "Four shillings compensation, 10*s.* fine, and 3*s.* costs, or seven days," was the order of the court.

As we drove back : " In South Tipperary," said he, " intemperance has decidedly decreased. The fines have diminished seventy-five per cent. in a few years. In Clogheen there is usually but one 'drunk' where there used to be thirty, and at the last session at Cahir there was not one. This reform is due to the efforts of individual priests."

One landlord in the neighborhood I heard everywhere spoken of with great enthusiasm, Lord Lismore. "He's a man," cried the driver, " who can walk from one end of Ireland to the other without a stick." "He has made enormous reductions," said the magistrate, "but the tenants are most ungrateful, and are not paying him a cent. He did every thing to improve the horn-stock and pigs in the neighborhood. Indeed, the excellence of the breed of pigs throughout the south of Ireland is due to him."

" Four years ago, for about eighteen months, there was great disturbance on Lord Lismore's property for some eighteen months, and we had to bring the cavalry out day and night to encourage the well-affected. Cogherty's house here was set fire to twice, four years ago, and two other tenants of Lord Lismore have had their houses fired, all good rent-payers.

" Irish officials are accused of every crime, but they do their duty according to their lights, usually according to common-sense.

" The government is blamed for not having tried to settle the land question sooner ; but what really held back the land question was the question of disestablishment of the Irish Church, a great anomaly. Now matters

are come to such a pass that peasant proprietorship is
inevitable. Gladstone created the dual ownership : that
is on all sides held to be impracticable, and the only way
to get out of it is to deprive one dual owner of his property. The landlord is asked to go to the wall : the government has taken half his property, and now is going to
take the other half.

" The landlords are reviled now, but they have generally been kind and even generous. Lady Margaret
Charteris spent £3,000 in building an aqueduct for the
town of Cahír. Lord Sligo did the same at Westport.
It was a rule of Lord Sligo's that whatever the people
subscribed towards a public improvement he would
double. Most Irish landlords always gave the land for
chapels free, and sometimes for convents. Railroads
here are very expensive, partly from the great wear and
tear of the cattle traffic, and to them the landlords have
subscribed largely out of public spirit. Many thousand
pounds have been spent in this way by my own relations,
and the Duke of Devonshire gave over £100,000 towards
building the Lismore and Fermoy R. R.

" In Ireland the people never combine voluntarily to
make any public improvement ; they are always afraid of
some getting more good from it than the rest.

" Old Lord Waterpark had a hobby for improving his
property, and sank an enormous amount of money in it.
This is not taken into account now, and though the
father lived in the most economical way for years to save
the property, his son is now almost bankrupt.

" Many cases even of apparently cruel rent-raising are
probably not as they seem to be. On Lord Sligo's estate,
during the famine year, a large farm was given up in a
very impoverished condition. The rent had been £80.

He let it to a tenant on condition that he should pay 1*s.* the first year, £40 the second year, £60 the third year, and after that the full rental. The parish priest brought the tenant before the Bessborough Commission, and remained in the room while he swore his rent had been raised four times in seven years.

"All good feeling between landlord and tenant has now been swept away, and it will never recover.

"The parish priest here is a brother of one tenant and the uncle of another, and so with most of the clergy ; and they are all tenants themselves, so you cannot expect them to oppose the people in this movement.

"The Irish are not independent by nature : the landlords were the masters, and they usually used to keep a tenant going in an irregular, unbusiness-like way, and he in return used to give at least one vote to his landlord. Then the priests struggled with the landlords for the vote and got it, becoming the masters in their turn. Now the priests have been succeeded by the agitators, who are the hardest and most exacting masters of all, and the most expensive, but the League dues are now being objected to, and the agitation would cease but for American money."

"You don't fear persecution under Home Rule?" I asked. "That depends on what you mean by persecution," he replied. "We never get justice in any lawsuit as it is, and even under the present government we never get any appointment except by competitive examination. What will become of us at the mercy of people so bigoted that the law cannot be enforced against a priest, and a woman in this town refused to sue the parish priest for her wages—'If I do that,' said she, 'he 'll curse me and I 'll rot.'

"What is needed is more industry. In Wexford, Carlow, and even here, eggs are sold in large numbers to eggers for the English market. If a better breed of fowls were kept, the profits would be enormously increased. Butter from the Cahir creamery sold for 1s. 2d. a pound in Manchester during May, instead of 6d., which is all the farmers usually get. These creameries might be indefinitely increased, and profitably to all concerned, for we pay nearly seven per cent. interest."

A TIPPERARY LANDLORD.

For some days my host was one of the most genial, witty, and popular of Irish landlords. He is a learned man, a student and writer ; he has sat in Parliament, as did his father before him ; he is a conscientious magistrate ; he is perpetually improving his large property. His house is like the ideal English country-house, with a broad lawn sloping gradually towards the banks of the loveliest of Irish rivers. Pictures by old masters and family portaits lean from the walls. The library is crammed with old and rare books. His active, clever wife teaches the tenants' daughters to work embroidery, designs the patterns, and gets the work, when finished, sold. To the younger children she offers prizes for flowers and collections of every sort, and her influence for good was proved by the happy faces of the neatly dressed children who gathered round the long tables in the garden at the annual flower show. The shadow of impending fate rests lightly here, but it is not absent.

"Shall we have to leave our pleasant homes we love so well—this house, this garden ? We shall try to get the land near us into our own hands and farm it ourselves. Then we are told our friends and neighbors will be

forced to go away, and soon we shall be left alone and
be unable to live here in peace. I am glad that we ourselves are comparatively young. For the old, you have
no idea how sad these changes are. My grandfather began to build a beautiful house in a small country town.
When my father took the property he had little money
and spent all he had for years in finishing and furnishing
the house. The rest of his life he has passed on the
estate, devoting himself to improving the neighborhood.
He built almshouses, and started an agricultural society
to encourage a knowledge of scientific farming. When
this agitation began the Land Leaguers tried to make
trouble between him and his tenants; they called him
a tyrant and insulted him in the town council. Now the
poor old man is quite heart-broken."

One of the most beautiful and distinguished of Irish-
women was the centre of a little group of courtiers on
the afternoon of the flower show, speaking with charming
animation. What are they saying?

"The people about here say I lost so much by that
field, when they mean 'I laid out so much on it.'"
"Lord V——, when on the Land Commission, was so
disgusted by the absurd demands of one farmer that he
cried out, 'I want to know if you expect to be compen-
sated for the damage done by Noah's flood.'" "Did
you hear Morris' retort to Lady Aberdeen when she
said, 'I supposed you were all Home Rulers here.'
'There 's not one in the room, except your ladyship and
maybe one or two of the waiters.'" "My mother found
a cottage on the place where all the family and the calf
lived in one room. She built them a second room, and
in a few weeks found the calf in the new room and the
rest huddled together in the other one as before."

"Home Rule is an absolute experiment, with an off chance of doing some good and a great probability of absolutely ruining every one." "Wellington said : ' People good at making excuses are good for nothing else ! ' It is so with the Irish. With them it is always the government, the weather, or the soil." "The farmers openly rejoice that Providence has again interfered to prevent them from paying their rents. They are glad it is a bad year."

The last words I heard were spoken by a beautiful and distinguished lady, a true Irishwoman, of large possessions and high position.

"Is it right," said she, "that we who have always been loyal to the government should be handed over to the tender mercies of these men ? They are Catholics, and no doubt many have preached to them what was said by a priest at Waterford : ' The portion of the landlords is dynamite in this world and hell fire in the next.' If Home Rule comes, we shall be driven from our homes like the Huguenots ; but we shall not go to England. We shall cherish till death an unrelenting hatred of England, a country that we once trusted and served, and that sacrificed us."

The many talks I had with my kind host and friend were so interesting that it may be well to group them in a single statement.

"The Nationalists," he said one day, "often base the claims of the tenants on their descent from the original owners of the soil. There is no such historical continuity. The greater part of the tenants on my estate (I have about three hundred) are not Tipperary men, but are descendants of families brought here by my ancestors from other parts of Ireland. Murphy, for instance, is a common name on my estate, and the Murphys all came from Wexford. That dairymaid is a Devereux, a Norman and a Wexford family. The tenants represent only to a limited extent the old state of affairs. The landlord's title is often far older than theirs. What they do represent is the religion of the past. It would be quite exceptional for the tenant to be the descendant of the original inhabitants of the land, and who the original inhabitants were in any barony or parish we know almost to a man.

" This is the not uncommon, indeed is the typical, history of an Irish estate, especially of an estate in Tipperary. About 1780, a year of great change in the south of Ireland, the land was growing out of a pastoral into an agricultural state, on account of the high price of wheat. A Tipperary landlord had a lot of grass land and found it would pay him to break up the pasture. He brought men from a distance and settled them on it. The land, we will say, paid 10*s.* an acre as grazing land. A man offered 15*s.*, and was accepted. He set to work, built a farm-house, made fences, grubbed up the furze-bushes, and, in rare cases, dug drains. Twenty years later, during the Peninsular war, prices rose greatly and the competition for land was intense. A man could now pay 25*s.* as easily as he could pay 10*s.* in the earlier period. The landlord in the meantime had done nothing, but was neither grasping nor unkind. After a while this farm comes into the hands of a man who does n't want to work it for some reason, and is anxious to get out of it. He feels he cannot go out without any thing. He comes now to the landlord and says : ' Your Honor, I don't feel up to the work, and I would be greatly obliged to your Honor if you would let my sister's cousin take the

land.' 'Willing to oblige you, Pat, you scoundrel,' re-
plies his Honor, 'and what will your sister's cousin pay
me?' 'Thirty shillings,' says Pat. The cousin comes
in and under the rose gives Pat some money. With the
rising prices the new tenant would be as well off as the
original .tenant at 10s. And so on to the famine time.

" In this way 'tenant right' sprang up. It implies
that the landlord made no outlay, and the custom became gradually acknowledged as a just one. On certain
estates that sort of thing was put down as much as possible, for the landlord could always bring in a stranger,
but the people lived in a comfortable way together, and
where there was any relationship between the outgoing
and the incoming tenant the custom existed. It was
spreading, as every one who knows will admit, before
1870.

" The real reason for the over-renting was the immense
competition. It was made a frightful grievance if you
did not over-rent and give the land to the highest bidder.

" This state of things made the people false as well as
poor. The Celt is naturally imaginative, but he got into
the habit of promising every thing in the world to get
possession of the land, and it was very difficult to get
him out when once in.

" My estate is a fair example of an Irish property. We
have never altered our rents ; they are the old customary
rents, and the tenants have always been allowed to sell
their interests. Before 1870 from five to ten years' purchase was commonly paid by the new tenant for the good-
will, and a much larger amount for a small farm, because
there is greater competition for small farms and less
money is required to work them."

A returned Australian whom I met accidentally had

complained bitterly of my host as a tyrant who had destroyed a flourishing village at the demesne gate. One
day at dinner I mentioned the story. "There was once,"
said he, "a large distillery here, which created around it
a little village of operatives. The property had been let
to the distillers in the last century under a hundred years'
lease. The small tenants used to pay a head rent to me,
but they were only laborers in the distillery. Thirty
years ago the distillery was removed to Dublin, and ten
years ago the lease fell in. By that time, out of the two
thousand people all but two hundred had disappeared,
and those who remained were simply paupers with pig-
sties, unable to pay any rent to any one, and doing
nothing when I got rid of them   If you can find any injustice there I am willing to argue the question.

"In the last few years I have evicted only one man.
The tenant of a farm near my house had his rent fixed
by the court in 1881 at £112 and his tenant right at £650.
Last spring he owed a year's rent. On Lady-day he said:
'Forgive me the year's rent ; pay me £650, and I will go
out.' I was advised that it would not be safe for me to
take up the farm without an eviction, for the tenant right
might be still liable for the man's debts. Then I went
through the form of an eviction. He removed most of
his goods and furniture himself, and helped the officer to
turn out the rest. I bought all the produce on the land,
hay, and manure, for £100, my steward's valuation. If he
had sold his interest I don't believe it would have fetched
£400, and out of that I should have had a claim for
£112. And yet the League denounced this proceeding
and called me a tyrant.

"The only reason why the present national movement
has greater success than the old movements, is that now

the leaders are working the agrarian question. O'Connell dared not do so, and Fenianism failed because it did
not. It was, however, boldly taken up by Parnell in 1878,
and he has admitted that he would never have 'taken off
his coat' for the tenants except as a means to an end."

"The continuance of the stream of Nationalism in Ireland is due to Romanism simply. The people remain as
a body Catholics ; and Catholics never can be loyal to a
Protestant government. Romanism is an *imperium in im-
perio.* The spirit of Nationalism has died out in Scotland, because Scotland is Protestant ; and its religion
was the chief cause of Russia's difficulty in assimilating
Poland. If Ireland had a peasant proprietary it would
be quieter, but not loyal. Ireland will never be loyal in
the sense in which England is loyal.

"Mill says the difficulty is that Ireland is big enough
to wish for nationality, but not big enough to be a
nation. Such special attachment to Ireland is not in
itself a bad thing, and it would never have caused
serious difficulty if it had not been accentuated by the
desire to rob.

"I believe that if the land question were settled, the
local sentiment would be satisfied by a very moderate
scheme of Home Rule. Farmers have said to me hundreds of times : 'What do we care for Home Rule ?
What we want is to get land for the value'; by which
expression they mean 'for a very small rent.' Local
feeling may be satisfied by a great many things, however,
but national feeling can be satisfied only by independence. It might be willing to have the same queen as
England, but it would never admit of the slightest exercise of power in Ireland by the imperial Parliament.
The national sentiment, however, may be reduced to so

small a factor that it may be disregarded, and that I think is both possible and practicable.

"Before the famine Ireland gained by protection, by a high duty on corn ; for Ireland produced more than she consumed, while England consumed more than she produced. The people now want protection, which means bread dearer for Irishmen and not a whit dearer for any one else. As for a duty on manufactures that is unnecessary, for the chief market for Blarney tweeds is America in spite of a duty of sixty per cent. What an Irishman sees is that under protection forty years ago he got a bounty ; but what he does not see is that now protection would simply make him eat his own guts. What the people apparently want is to have a separate Ireland and to have the advantage of protection throughout Great Britain as well.

"Three quarters of Ireland is much more like England than it is like Connaught. The specially bad part is about an eighth of the country, the western fringe of it. In my mind's eye the western fringe is brown, rock and heather. Then there is another eighth a little less infertile.

"Irish land is more valuable than is often supposed. It is unjust to compare an Irish farm with particular farms in England that are now vacant. It is the heavy wheat lands in the east of England which will produce nothing but wheat, and are expensive to cultivate, usually chalk lands, that don't pay now. Their history is curious. They used to be sheep lands, and then when the price of wheat was high at the time of the French wars they were cultivated and paid well as long as wheat was high, now you cannot get back the good fine grass which was the product of centuries.

"Prime grass lands in Ireland fetch now almost as much as ever. I let much of my land on grazing leases for nearly £4 an acre. There is a great future for grass land. Prime cattle will always pay. The present depression in the meat market is only temporary. It is not the foreign competition that is the cause of the depression, for the consumption in England is so enormous that the foreign importation bears but a small proportion to the whole. The trouble is that times are bad, and the people are out of employment and cannot afford meat. For the same reason the inferior parts of the meat are not brought to market, and so the profit is further lessened. The people who would eat the worse parts cannot afford to eat any. American meat does not compete with fine domestic joints, but only with the inferior. Meat will always pay, but it must be made the chief thing, and other business abandoned. For instance, every bit of grain I grow 1 consume. I give oats to the horses, barley to the cattle, and if I grew wheat I would give that also to the cattle. Irish graziers have not conducted their business wisely. The Irish farmer never fattens a beast, but sells it when it is only a year or two old. Just as he ceases to be a burden on the land, he is sold, and is fattened in England. The result has been a progressive deterioration of the grass land. It needs to be restored by top dressing, or by feeding on imported food such as oil cake. With wise management the land will soon improve.

"The just price for good land under any compulsory bill should be about twenty years' purchase of a fairly high rent, calculated at twenty per cent. off, and payable in a lump sum. But no fair price is likely to satisfy the Irish leaders. They are only satisfied when they are robbing, and then at the moment of robbery. When it is done, they are sorry they did not take more.

"Land purchase, I think, should be compulsory at the instance of the landlord on the entire body of tenants on his estate. The estate should then be valued by a court, taking into account not merely the rental but all the circumstances, at a capital sum, say £100,000. All the chargees and mortgagees of the property should be made parties to the proceeding. Stock of the face value of £100,000 should then be issued by a local body, the grand jury of the county, or a special board, and guaranteed by the government, negotiable and bearing interest. This stock should then be divided proportionally between all the parties in interest. The only parties then left to be dealt with would be the local authorities, the imperial government, and the new proprietors. The local authorities would collect the yearly instalments of the purchase money in the same way and by the same officers as the local rates are now collected, and thus meet the interest on the stock, and with the surplus form a sinking fund for its redemption. On default in the payment of the interest the imperial government should have the power to levy on any of the local rates or other county property in the same way as they now levy on account of unpaid instalments of county loans."

"What objection do you have to Home Rule?" I asked one day.

"Only the objection a man has to being robbed and murdered," he replied. "I want some reasonable guaranty for the protection of our property and for the integrity of our throats. This is not due to any exaggerated fear. These men are a set of scoundrels, and they, the leaders of the League, would be our rulers,—the League

which bases its power on midnight outrages and terrorism as great as ever was in France under the Reign of
Terror. The men who won the battle would have the
power, and would use it without scruple, to crush all
classes and individuals opposed to them. Home Rule
would probably result in civil war in the north, and then
there would be retaliation upon us in the south, who are
too few to fight. There is, of course, bluster on both
sides, but the north would then have something to fight
for. In a revolution the extremists always have things
for a time their own way. We know the party, and know
that under Home Rule they would repeat every mistake
that has been made from the time of Abraham down, at
vast expense. If this country were farther off from
England, there might be more to be said for autonomy,
but now it is and can be only a farm for England. How
can it be improved as a farm, is the question. The Nationalists wish to reclaim more wild land. What I want
is to have the land already under tillage ploughed two
inches deeper all over. But the people are too lazy to
do this."

A UNIONIST PRIEST.

" For some years after I came here in 1872," said the
priest, " when I went about asking the people about their
relations with the landlords, I heard very few complaints.
The rents were usually raised here by the tenants themselves, who would go behind a neighbor's back to the
agent and offer a larger rent. The landlords were human, and could not help saying : ' You must pay me more,'
for I am offered more by your neighbor.' I interfered
on many occasions, and told the agent that the old tenant had made the improvements that justified the in-

crease, so that to charge him more, or let the farm to another, was to rob the old tenant of his improvements.

"Two years before the agitation began butter was often as high as 160*s.* a hundredweight ; cows were exceedingly valuable, selling for £18 or £20 a head, while they sell now, and used to sell previously, for £12. Fancy prices were put on grazing land ; and even shop-keepers speculated in farms.

"That property over there, for instance, used to belong to a Captain L——, who was hurt in a hunting accident, and died of blood poisoning, leaving a widow and three little children. The trustees put the estate into chancery, and the court had it offered for sale in lots. A number of people came to bid. Many offered any rent the agent might fix, and some even offered 5*s.* an acre more than any one else should offer. Proposals were required in writing, and I gave many who asked me for certificates of solvency letters to the agent. The agent, an official of the court, met the farmers one day in this house, and told them he had to receive all the offers made and forward them to the court, but that the rent offered was, in his opinion, absurdly high, and more than the land was worth. I said I had already told every one that the land was originally bog mountain that Captain L—— had improved at great expense ; but the farmers assured me they could make the rent and a good profit as well. In two years prices tumbled, and I spoke to the agent myself and got a reduction of twenty-five or thirty per cent., and since then fifteen per cent. more has been allowed.

"In 1878 and 1879, a cry was raised to pay no more than Griffith's valuation. Young fellows went about from house to house dressed up as bashi-bazouks, by preconcerted arrangement, to coerce the people in fun to adopt

Griffith's valuation. Many farmers got their own children to write notices warning them to pay at their peril no more than the valuation, signed with a skull and cross-bones. Then the farmers would go to the agent and say : 'I would willingly pay more, but I don't dare to.'

"At that time and before five policemen were enough to keep order in the town. Soon these young fellows who went round masquerading were impressed by the secret societies and became regular moonlighters. The League was started, and I believe that all the secret society men are Leaguers, though all the Leaguers are not secret-society men. The oath of the secret societies is, as I know, to take up arms, when called on, for the Irish Republic. Soon after the League was established two bailiffs were murdered near the town, many more were wounded, cattle were injured, and hay ricks were burned. Then a great terror began to prevail throughout the country. A company of soldiers was drafted here, and the police increased to eighty or a hundred.

"Tenants anxious to pay would often pay the landlord through third persons and would refuse to take receipts. Fifty or sixty times since 1881 or 1882 farmers have paid me the rent to my own cheek, asking me to pay over to the landlord the full rent, if necessary, and to get them what abatement I could. This was to avoid the vengeance of the League. You can have no idea of the degree of terrorism created by the League. I could never sanction the League, as a priest.

"The agitation has caused much indirect loss to the country. In 1875 there were some 60,000 visitors at Killarney ; now there are very few. Shooting, fishing, and hunting are boycotted, and yet such sports brought into Limerick £25,000 or more a year.

"The landlords are evidently blamed before the world, many of them justly. The chief rack-renters were purchasers under the Encumbered Estates Act. They had often borrowed the purchase money and had to raise the rents to meet the interest. Fines of £100 or £200 were also sometimes exacted on marriages, transfers, or giving leases. In North Kerry, take the Locke estate for example: the last of the family to hold it was a Miss Locke, who married an Italian count. The land had been let at a very low figure, and the tenants refused to take leases when they could, as happened also on Lord Kenmare's property. The property was bought under the Encumbered Estates Act by various country gentlemen in Kerry who had saved money, and they soon quadrupled the rents.

"Yet the old landlords usually dealt fairly with their tenants, for they had large properties and were not crippled. On the Kenmare estate, before the Land Act, £700 of arrears were cleared off in one year by a stroke of the pen. The kindest men have come off worst, for they had most arrears. Lord Kenmare's mere labor bill was sometimes £300 a week. Up to the time of the agitation he had spent £60,000 in improvements for which he had never demanded a penny, and yet he has been treated as badly as any one.

"A striking thing in Kerry is the apparent anomaly that the cheaper a man gets his land the more idle he is apt to be. There is one townland in this parish let at 2s. 6d. an Irish acre to one man for ninety-nine years. He divided it between his five or six children, and so far as I can see no improvement has been made by the tenants, and they are about the poorest in the parish. There are others who pay heavier rents who work harder and are much better off.

"There is a great want of practical knowledge among the farmers. They keep no accounts and never know how they stand. The women might make good butter if they took pains; but it is carelessly made, and the farmers often keep the butter during the summer for the price to rise, and by the time they sell it it has deteriorated.

"In 1872 the potatoes were not worth taking out of the ground. I had to send to Killarney for potatoes fit to eat, and when I inquired about the seed, I found they had been growing potatoes from the same seed for twenty years. I got seed from Dublin and raised excellent potatoes; but when I told the people that they should change the soil and change the seed every two or three years, they would n't understand, and said I managed the land better than they did. One year I took a field on the road to the station. The year before it had n't paid. I took it for a smart rent, to raise a good oat crop, for the oats are as bad here as the potatoes, for the same reason. I got oats from Cork, and the oats I raised were better than the seed. The field was by the road, where every one could see it, and I drew the people's attention to it. Then they began to think I was a little touched in my head on the subject of seed. In 1879 the potatoes failed. I got champions for seed, and planted champions and some of the old potatoes in the same field. The champions alone survived; but then it was too late.

"It is important to dispel the ignorance of the farmers. I would have agricultural teachers, to travel about and teach something of practical farming. There should be an agricultural school, where farmers' sons could go, in a central place. Glasnevin is not central enough.

What teaching there is now is too theoretical.   Attach an acre or two to every national school.

"A small duty on flour would answer all the Irish need of protection.   This would start the flour mills.   Beyond this I would not interfere with free trade, for if there had been free trade in 1848 there would have been nothing like a famine.

"Peasant proprietorship would satisfy the people. The farmers would then cease to agitate for Home Rule. I would have a measure of compulsory sale and pur-chase, and in estimating the value of the land, I would look neither at the valuation nor the rent, but simply at the condition of the land, allowing for unexhausted im-provements.

"Finally, let the government help the people along the coast to make nets and build boats.   Then the sea would be their farm."

NATIONAL LEAGUERS AT KILLARNY.

The secretary of the League at Killarney is a respect-able auctioneer, and he invited me at once to a commit-tee meeting in the evening.   The room was like a lodge room, but there was no secrecy or formality about the proceedings.   The only business was the distribution of some money subscribed by the central board for eleven laborers discharged by Lord Kenmare for refusing to work on the farm of an evicted tenant.   Five members were present, earnest, quiet-looking men of the type of the average Odd-Fellows in a Massachusetts country town.   Their meetings, they said, were in no sense secret and they had no pass-words or grips.   They were essen-tially not what the government was trying to make of them, a secret society.   They neither did nor thought any thing that might not be published in a newspaper. They wished to win national autonomy and worked for it all they could. The local branches had no initiative, but whenever there was any doubt about the propriety of any action, they referred the matter to the central board. Their part was to foster every spark of independence among the people.

The outrages in Kerry were the doing of persons who acted on their own behalf, and the League now condemned them, though when moonlighting first began it was difficult not to sympathize with some outrages that were excited by injustice. It was essential that the tenants should join in refusing to pay exorbitant rents. There were some years ago a number of old-fashioned farmers who believed that landlordism was part of the system of the universe, and that rents must be paid at any sacrifice. Some young farmers' sons, more liberally educated than their fathers, found that these old men could only be influenced by terror, and then they organized these moonlight excursions. Individually Leaguers sympathized at first with these young fellows, but now they are absolutely opposed to any outrage, as they feel sure of getting their ends by legal methods.

Only a few days before, the League had been proclaimed, and my companions felt some curiosity to know what the proclamation meant. "We may be imprisoned," they said, "but we will meet as long as we are free."

KERRY OUTRAGES.

About Killarney "moonlighting" still continues. "Near here," said a gentleman who fortunately finds scholarship more lucrative than his small property, "Fleming wanted a farm that a widow had given up.

When he applied at the office, they told him it had been given to Murphy. A day or two later some relations of Fleming met Mrs. Murphy and said : ' Well, he has the land, perhaps he wont enjoy it long.' Within a week Murphy was shot.

"Sheehan, a Leaguer, with one brother a priest and another at Stonyhurst, bought an interest in a farm. A neighbor envied it and offered more, and finally got a band of moonlighters and fired into Sheehan's house ; but the man still sticks on, and is protected by police.

" About this time last year, Cornelius Murphy bought an interest in a farm from Moynihan, near Kantuck, in County Cork. The deed was drawn and signed in the presence of the P. P. of Banteen ; the money was paid, the farm stocked and ploughed. The end of January, Moynihan summoned Murphy to give the farm up, as some one else had offered more for it. I asked the priest if there was any thing in the deed to justify such a claim. He replied : ' Nothing in the world.' On March 13th, masked men called on Murphy, late at night, turned him and his wife out of bed, and made him swear, with three pistols pointed at his head, to give the farm up the next day. A few weeks afterwards I got a letter from one Cahill, a returned American, asking to be recognized as tenant, since Moynihan had surrendered the farm. Murphy also wrote me, April 11th, saying : ' I wish to inform your honor that I gave up Moynihan farm as the Rev. Father Mowery has settled the matter. It did not pay me, but I thought better to get out of danger—there is nothing so good as a quite life, and so long as I would hold that place I would not have much pace of mind and dealing with these people.' "

A professional man in Kerry illustrated the prevailing

terrorism when he said : " It would be, I believe, a matter of life and death with me if I told you now the whole
truth about the country. Before 1879, you could n't
with £100 have bribed a Kerryman born at home to assassinate any one ; but the other day I said to an intelligent P. P., in his Bishop's presence : ' Now one could
probably find a dozen men within ten miles who would
assassinate any one for half a crown.' ' I fear,' said he,
' that is absolutely true.'

" The law now is not equal to the punishment of the
graver offences. If six moonlighters were seen crossing
a field in open daylight, not a man would dare for any
money to tell the police.

" I asked a man the other day, What is it Murphy did
that made them shoot him ? ' ' Well,' said he, glancing
cautiously around, ' I think it was pure blackguardism ;
the Divil got hold of them.' ' Is there any sympathy for
him ? ' ' Shure, your honor, there is, but if I met a
neighbor I could n't trust him, and would say, if he asked
me, the Divil meant him.'

" After the imprisonment of Parnell, and the no-rent
manifesto, many men were visited at night and asked to
produce their pass-books. Then, if they were found to
have paid any rent, they were ordered to stand up with
their faces to the wall, and their legs were peppered with
shot. Sometimes their calves were shot away, and many
were crippled for life.

" Murphy was killed by having his leg shot off above
the ankle.

" Leahy, for outbidding another for a farm of Lord
Kenmare's was shot and frightfully bayonetted before
his wife's face. No evidence was given at the trial.

" Donaghue, within a mile of Killarney, was shot in the

legs, four years ago, for buying out a broken-down tenant farmer, part of the money going to pay for arrears of rent.

" Rehilly was murdered near the workhouse in Killarney, on his way home, in December, 1885, about five o'clock in the afternoon, because he had been the caretaker of an evicted farm.

" Brown, a farmer near here, purchased his own and a neighboring farm, which he sublet. His neighbor did n't pay, and Brown threatened to eject him. A few days later Brown was shot while working in a field in the middle of the day. His two brothers in Mollahiffe are to this day not allowed to see or help the widow.

" Curtin was a personal friend of mine. He was a cultivated man, and had been educated by the Jesuits. In 1848 he lived in Limerick, and harbored O'Gorman after the rising. At the time of the celebrated Blennerhasset election he was a tenant of Lord Kenmare's, and was the only one of the tenants who refrained from voting for the landlord's man. He was always generous to his neighbors, lending money and machines. In the autumn of 1875, Curtin, then a member of the League here, headed a deputation of tenants to Lord Kenmare to ask for a reduction. Lord Kenmare referred them to the trustees in whose hands the property was, and the trustees said that, since the Land Act, they could only make a reduction on the order of a Land Court. Curtin then was one of the first to pay rent. Soon after he was visited by masked men who demanded arms. He refused, ordered them to go, shot and killed one, Casey, a neighbor's son, and was shot himself. The next Sunday Casey was buried near Muckross Abbey, and Curtin, the same day, at Mollahiffe. Scarcely a man went to Curtin's funeral, while the whole country-side attended Casey's, and the curate who officiated there told me the whole congregation rose to leave the church the minute he began to regret the death of Curtin, and to avoid a scandal he turned back to the altar and went on with the service. All over Castleisland that Sunday placards were posted warning the people not to pay rent if they would escape the fate of Curtin of Mollahiffe. Mrs. Curtin and her daughters prosecuted, and a brother of Casey was convicted at Christmas. Meantime I often heard the people cursing : ' May the Lord sweep them off the face of the earth for attacking the poor moonlighters ! '

" If Curtin had done like Mr. Kilbride of Luggacurran, who, though a rich man, allowed himself to be evicted at a loss of six or seven thousand pounds, he would be alive to-day."

Through a boggy country, with the fields separated by trenches cleanly cut like gashes in new cheese, past thatched huts with great piles of peat silhouetted intensely black against their whitewashed walls, I drove to Mollahiffe. Girls on the road hooded their faces with their arms, and hooted when we asked the way to Mrs. Curtin's. By the large iron gateway a policeman was pacing, and a few yards within was the house, comfortable to look at, densely ivy-grown.

" I can never live here in peace," said Mrs. Curtin, " but they won't let me go. I tried to sell it at auction, but notices were posted that any purchaser would get the same treatment as old Curtin.

" Laborers will not work for us ; one we engaged last year went off, saying he had been brought before the League and forbidden to stay. The smith won't work for me, nor the carpenter ; they say they would be glad

to, but are afraid of the 'night-boys.' For doing a few
jobs for us, as it was, the smith had his windows broken.
The baker still supplies us, but his house has been fired,
his windows smashed, and his gates unhinged. The
neighbors won't buy of us ; they say they would only be
buying trouble for themselves. In June I bought some
cattle in Milltown, but the farmer who sold them has
been accused by a cobbler, the president of the League.
A fortnight ago an outhouse was burned, uninsured, *for
no company will insure us.* Some months ago Mr. Spring,
a neighbor, bought a calf from me. Tuesday last it was
found by the roadside with its throat slit. He borrowed
a turf 'rail' from us about the same time. Ten days ago,
at night, it was broken up and the pieces thrown into the
river. Three or four weeks ago, near the church, my
driver, a faithful servant, was beaten and left for dead
on the road. The other night the house next door was
fired into ; and the next Sunday notices were posted
warning the woman there not to let her daughter talk to
our policemen.

" Our servants are asked sometimes whether they got
any of the blood-money, and often, going to chapel, they
have the door banged in their faces.

" Whenever the backs of the police are turned, the
people thrust out their tongues at us and spit at us.

" We have had to hear mass in the sacristy ever since
the murder. The people broke up our bench in the
church. Father Pat got us a new one in Cork, for no
one would make it nearer. The driver who brought it
out was beaten, and finally forced to go to America ; and
the new pew was torn from its place and broken to bits
in the churchyard.

" The reason for all this was our prosecuting my husband's murderers. If I had n't happened to recognize some of them, I should never have suspected them to be neighbors. I thought no one who knew him would hurt him. I had made him join the League, for they said they would boycott any one who did n't. The last words he said, as he lay in the doorway, were : 'Go home, boys, now!'"

In the centre of a large untidy farmyard is the high thatched hut of Mrs. Casey. She looked like an old chieftain, with pale delicate face surrounded by the stiff frill of her white cap, as she sat by the peat-fire watching the bubbles rising in an immense iron pot hanging from the crane.

"For the death of Curtin," she said in a clear, strong voice, "three Sullivans, two Caseys, Darley, Spring, MacMahon, Clifford, and others were arrested. The Curtins swore black, brown, and white against Darley and my sons, and laid low one of widow Sullivan's.

"Curtin's people had got blood-money before : his grandfather in '98 was an informer.

"If those boys did that thing, they merely went for arms ; a foolish thing, but it has been done throughout Ireland, and is done to-day.

"As long as I am alive, and my children, and their children live, will we try to root the Curtins out of the land. Now, I will, I will do it. Was n't a young man more than equal to that old codger ?

"Yet I am better off than she is. I can go out to-day, and I won't have peelers about me, and I won't be hooted and booed.

"My oldest boy went insane and I am sick, so, as long as I live, the Curtins shall have my good wishes.

"The Land Acts are no good to us. What 's the

good of going into court, when, if you get a reasonable
reduction, the landlord can appeal ?

" We pay the same for that gravel pit there as for any
thing else.   My landlord has made over £600 out of it.

" The rates, the county cess, and the peeler-tax are
are now more than the rent.   A firkin of butter is selling for half price, and there 's no price for any thing.   I
hope I won't die till I 've seen some good sights."

A NATIONALIST EDITOR IN KERRY.

Mr. D. Harrington is a brother of the member of Parliament and the Secretary of the League, and is the
popular editor of the *Kerry Sentinel*, a man of considerable force of character.

" There have been outrages committed in·Tralee and
Castleisland.   Miss Thompson of Feenit was obliged
to have police protection, and an agent of Lord Kenmare's was murdered not many years ago ; but over
the fellows who commit the outrages the League has
no control, though a few of them may be Leaguers.
Each town has its own set of rowdies, but there is
no connection between them.   Most of the outrages
are due to private motives.   For instance, some of the
landlords are very immoral men.   Wives and daughters
are sometimes sent with the rent to the great house
for reasons that are not generally known.   When Mr.
Stead was here I gave him copies of some of this evidence.   Every thing, however, is twisted into an agrarian
crime.   I have just paid as a rate-payer the last instalment granted the widow of a man who, I believe, was
killed in a street brawl.

" This county is purely agricultural, and the poverty
of the tenant farmers causes general distress.   The

tradespeople suffer as much as the landlords. Our books show £1,400 of debts, of which we shall scarcely get one pound. Of course, for the time, no improvements are being made, and the land is deteriorating. The farmers are waiting till the land question is settled. They would be very glad to settle it, but the movement has gone so far that they won't be satisfied with any but a proper settlement. The terms under Lord Ashbourne's Act were usually made too high. I advised the tenants to be very careful about going in under it. Before they purchase they should have a fair rent fixed as a basis. The courts are doing that very reasonably, and no new machinery is needed. The reductions given by the courts have been generally greater than those demanded under the Plan of Campaign. The Plan has not been adopted on a single property here, and we have paid for not adopting it.

"The flatlands in Kerry are in the hands of graziers, and are turned into sheep walks, while the people are scratching the sides of the mountains. If all were thrown into agricultural land and implements were given the people, we could compete with America. The last resource is a duty on American corn and flour."

"But isn't it wrong," I asked, "for a man to refuse either to pay rent or to give up his farm?"

"Not if half of the land is his," replied Mr. Harrington. "To evict a man and to burn his house is a crime for which a landlord should be prosecuted, for he has destroyed the property of another.

"Home rule will come, there's no doubt about that. Wouldn't it be wiser for the landlords even now to throw in their lot with the people and not talk about taking their money and leaving the country? If they stayed

with us, they would soon become leaders of the people
instead of men like my brothers. But they are blind
and deaf, and persist in raising dishonest cries about
persecution of the Protestants. As to Catholic oppression. H——, a Protestant and Conservative, is Clerk
of the Crown and Peace here. His son Richard is Solicitor to the Board of Guardians, which is Nationalist to
a man. His second son is Deputy Sheriff. The Deputy Sub-sheriff is also of the same party. The Secretary
of the Grand Jury is a brother of the Knight of Kerry.
He makes probably £900 a year. Such men do not
want Home Rule. Yet there are a hundred thousand
men like myself, who would not care for Home Rule,
and would not welcome it, if it meant the oppression of
our Protestant fellow-countrymen.

"It is the English manufacturers who are the chief
opponents of Home Rule, because they are afraid of the
development of Irish manufactures. Parnell said at one
time that we would want protection for two or three
years. Free trade unquestionably is a great evil. But
one great benefit Home Rule would bring, would be that
wealthy Irishmen would return from America and Australia, and settle down here and start industries as they
never would except under Home Rule. It is true we
have no coal-fields ; but I can get coal here in Tralee
cheaper than I could in Kent.

"This 'physical force' business is the merest folly.
We have had the greatest difficulty in restraining the
more violent men. I would go so far as this that if
pushed to the wall I would sell my life as dearly as possible ; but I believe we shall win all we want without
shedding one drop of blood. Davitt is a brave man and
self-sacrificing, but this movement needs a cool head like

Parnell's. It is easy for Americans to talk of fighting, for they have nothing to lose."

A KERRY LAND AGENT.

One of the best-hated men in Ireland was my host for a night, in a police-protected country house on the romantic coast of Kerry. As I watched him laughing merrily, as his daughter sang the magnificent mock-heroic chorus of " The Ballyhooly Horse," it was startling to reflect that this apparently amiable, scholarly gentleman was nearly blown up by dynamite in his own house not many years ago, and that his name is a by-word and a curse throughout the county.

"Gladstone's Land Bill," he said, " is the cause of the present hopeless confusion. By that act the letting of land ceased to be a commercial transaction, and now the motto of the people is ' work as you like, you are bound to live.' In Kerry there never was any custom like the Ulster Tenant Right before, though the landlord often allowed a tenant to nominate his successor, but that was a very different thing, for the landlord then could make sure of the accession of an improving, industrious man.

"The agitation is purely agrarian and communistic. It is spreading all over Europe, but in France is checked by the number of small proprietors, always a conservative body. It is the result of distress, and the distress is due to over-population. In Kenmare a man had a farm paying £10 a year. He wished to divide it between his two sons. I told him that was against the rules of the estate, and, besides, would impoverish his sons. He insisted. To test him, I said he would have to pay me £7 down for the privilege. ' Certainly,' he replied ; but of course I did n't allow it. Another tenant of mine got a judicial rent fixed at £30. The penalty for subdivision was a heavy forfeit. He came to me and said : 'For God's sake, let me keep my two sons.' The best-farmed land in Great Britain is East Lothian. Five sixths of that is in tillage, and yet the population is less per acre than several counties in Ireland that are wholly grass land.

"The dishonesty of the Parnellites was shown by their opposition to a clause proposed by Gladstone in the Land Bill of 1881, granting a million pounds for assisting emigration. Parnell wants the people at home in order to force the hand of the government. What would be thought of a popular leader in New York who refused the offer of a philanthropist to give poor people tickets to New Mexico, where there is plenty of work and grub? My son goes to New Mexico to farm, why should my tenant object to having his son go there ?

"Applicants for government aid for emigration are required to present a certificate of their respectability from the parish priest. A Protestant clergyman asked me the other day if he might sign such certificates, as the parish priest had given out that he would not sign any.

"Another reason for Irish distress is their bad farming. In Scotland there are about a million acres devoted to agriculture, to four million in Ireland, and yet Scotland produces more cereals. In Scotland a pair of horses to sixty acres of tillage is the usual allowance. Here on a farm I own, of fifty-three acres, there are fifteen horses. What the farmer does with them I can't imagine.

"The distress is increased by the farmers squandering their money on drink. One railroad company brought to Tralee, in 1886, sixty thousand dollars' worth of whiskey, and the two companies together about a hundred thousand dollars' worth. Whiskey used to be six shillings a gallon, but now more is drunk when it is ten shillings.

"It is now the shirts against the shirtless; and if a general Land Purchase Bill were passed, the question of Home Rule would be dropped, for then most of the voters would have something to lose.

"Nothing could be more advantageous to the tenant than the purchase clauses of Lord Ashbourne's Act. Suppose a man is paying £100 a year; he could usually buy his farm for £1,800, the interest on which, at four per cent., is £72, a reduction at once of about thirty per cent. He should be willing to have those clauses extended and to have the rents fixed as a basis for purchase by the present land courts. The landlords in general have paid twenty-one years' purchase for their property. I did, and that to the government, under the Encumbered Estates Act. We should expect to be paid at least eighteen years' purchase. The Nationalists say: 'You bought a stone horse, and should take the consesequences'; but the government said to me when I bought: 'We are selling in order to simplify titles.' They might recompense me. What right has the government to give me over to the rabble? They should at least buy my property first before giving me over; for if I stayed here, within a year my throat would be cut. When they tried to blow up my house with dynamite, there were sixteen people in the house, yet all those lives were to be sacrificed; and not a single priest, when I met them, except Father John, of my own parish, expressed any disapproval.

"The melancholy thing about the present agitation is that it strikes at the good as well as the bad landlords,

and at the best most severely, since they are the most
yielding. Mr. Oliver and Lord Cork have the two cheap-
est-let properties in Kerry, and yet one was shot at and
the other has to have police protection. In six years,
during which I was Lord Kenmare's agent, he spent
more money in improving his Kerry property than he
took out of it. An estate under my charge in 1840 was
subject to a rental of £2,376, which was well and punctually paid. At that time there was no railroad within a
hundred and fifty miles of it. Now it has a railroad
station on it; and although the landlord has expended
considerable sums on improving it, the rental has been
reduced by the Land Commissioners to £1,892. During
the same period the rental of Orkney has increased from
£19,332 to £56,850, or 194 per cent.; and yet, the
present M. P. for Orkney has complained about Irish
rack-rents. The landlords will turn at last, for twelve
years' purchase will leave them nothing above their
charges; and their charges, including mortgages, family
charges, duties to the government, tithes, and interest on
drainage loans, are undiminished. I invested £50,000
in Irish land; now if any one will offer me £30,000, I
will take it and be off.

" It is said that the tenants are weighed down by arrears hanging over them from the famine times; but by
the Arrears Act of 1882 a tenant could come into court,
and on the payment of one year's rent, all arrears prior
to the judicial rent fixed for the current year were wiped
off, the government paying the landlord a second year's
rent. For this purpose a million pounds were granted.
In many cases I took one year's rent from the government, and forgave the tenant every thing.

" My plan for meeting the Home-Rule agitators is this:

'You want Home Rule, do you ? Then pay your share
of the national debt ; pay off any loyalists who wish to
leave the country ; appoint the President of the United
States and the Emperor of Germany commissioners to
value the property of the loyalists, and then pay them
and let them go.' Let every one who refuses to agree to
this be disfranchised.

" In every thing Ireland is the poorest country in the
world, and England the richest. Should these countries
be kept apart and by themselves ? No ; jumble them
up, toss them up together as you would a pancake.
There are twelve thousand police in Ireland, all Irishmen. I would establish them in England, and have
twelve thousand Englishmen as policemen here. I would
send all the dispensary doctors to England, and have all
English doctors here ; and I would have the courts amal-
gamated, Irish judges sitting in England and English
judges here.

" One change in the direction of local self-government
I should approve of : Judges or Commissioners of Public Works should be appointed to go on circuit through
the counties, in order to save the expense of our going
to London. In many ways less centralization would be
a good thing, for the typical Irishman gives his soul to
the priest and his body to the government to take care
of."

AFTER EVICTION.—HERBARTSTOWN AND BODYKE.

At the end of August several evictions took place on
the property of the O'Grady at Herbartstown, in County
Limerick. The excitement was intense. The defenders
of one house poured hot water and tar on the officers, and
tried to hook them with a hot iron rod. " The resistance

offered on that occasion," urged the counsel for those who were arrested, "was not offered from the point of view of its being a legal defence, but its aim and object was to attract public attention to what was going on, and to make a protest against what those people might consider an unjust eviction."[1]   An aged, bedridden woman, Mrs. Moloney, it was reported, was cruelly turned out of her home and had to be carried a mile or more through the bitter weather.   A few days afterwards, an Irish member referred in Parliament to her death from the exposure, and arraigned the government for permitting such brutality.   The effect of these evictions on English opinion was said to be greater than that of all the speeches of Mr. Gladstone.   The week following I drove there from Limerick.

The road from Herbartstown passes through excellent lands.   Luxuriant hedges prove the richness of the soil. Here and there a " boycotted " farm breaks the succession of emerald fields, with its patch of black rag-weeds and white thistles.   It is market day at Hospital, and a cartful of pigs jolts past us, closely followed by a company of pig-jobbers in a covered car.   By the side of the road that leads up to the village of Herbartstown is a field that seemed one mass of weeds.   Whose farm is that ? I asked of a neighbor standing in a doorway. " Tom Moroney's," he answered.   " It was one of the best in the town."

McGuire, a blacksmith, the secretary of the League, took me to see Mrs. Moroney, whose husband was in prison for contempt of court.   Her house is the finest in the village, a large double stone house, one half of it a spirit-grocery.   All the furniture had been moved away,

---

[1] *Cork Herald*, September 8, 1887.

except a few chairs and tables. The front door was fortified with a mass of large iron weights, and with an
enormous log of wood that was leaning against it with
one end on the stairs.

"The state of affairs can be put in a few words," said
McGuire. "Three years ago the landlord agreed to
revalue the property, and persuaded the tenants to accept
his own valuer. Moroney and two small tenants refused ;
and one of them went into court and got a much larger
reduction than that allowed by the valuer. For some
years the tenants were allowed fifteen and twenty per
cent. off, but a year ago the agent said he had no authority to continue the reduction. Subsequently he offered
fifteen per cent. all round, and finally fifteen to judicial
lease-holders and twenty-five per cent. to the others.
The tenants demanded thirty and forty per cent. respec-
tively, and adopted the ' Plan.'

"O'Grady served every one with writs, and drove
Moroney into bankruptcy. It was difficult to find out
Moroney's assets, for after the ' Plan ' was adopted all
the tenants sold off their cattle and put the money into
the 'Campaign fund.' Moroney and Father Ryan refused to testify about this ' fund,' and were imprisoned
for contempt of court. This house was sold at auction
by the court to a Mr. Bullen for £50, and Mrs. Moroney
is now holding it only as a caretaker, expecting to be
evicted at any moment.

"O'Grady made successive offers to the people up to
the day of the evictions, but we were pledged not to pay
a penny of costs, no matter what abatements were given.
They went to Mrs. Ryan, and said : ' Won't you make
some settlement if Mrs. Hogan does ?' ' No, I won't,
not a penny,' she said. It was a matter of principle.

O'Grady offered even to take payment by instalments, at first of £5 a year, and then of £1 a year, but nobody listened to him.

"There were thirteen people to be evicted, most of them in the village, but all except the six actually evicted were protected by the new Land Act. Every one believes that if the town people had been attacked, there would have been murder done, for every house is barricaded.

"Moroney has twenty acres, this house, and five small houses, besides the fair ground. The rent is £85. The fair ground used to be rented for £40, and now is rented for £25 ; and Moroney takes the tolls. This house was built by Moroney nine years ago, at a cost of over £600, and all that O'Grady gave towards it was £18. The other houses are very old, and were probably built by Moroney's ancestors. This rent is enormous, but the farmers, if they are to stand at all, need to pay no rent.

"The evictions were brutal. Poor old Mrs. Moloney was taken from her bed and carried to her step-brother's house, at the risk of her life."

"She need only have been lifted for a minute over the threshold," I suggested, "for did n't O'Grady offer to take her back as caretaker?" "Why," explained McGuire, "if she had gone back she would only have cost O'Grady a penny a week, now he has to pay emergency men one or two pounds a week, and last week there were hundreds of cattle going through these farms, for they don't really take care of any thing. Our object, when the landlord goes against us, is to put him to as much expense as possible. It is necessary to punish him. Besides, we are afraid of a caretaker coming to terms with the agent."

The prospects of the campaign seem decidedly bright for the tenants. Not a penny will they pay until their terms are granted, and Moroney and the evicted people reinstated. It is difficult to put Moroney back, for his house has been sold to another man. "That's O'Grady's look-out," cried McGuire, gleefully. "Now we have him at our mercy. He is in a box. But he'll get no rent from any tenant till Moroney is back."

"Then the property is mortgaged for nearly fifty thousand pounds. O'Grady handled only £5 or £6 out of all the rental of Herbartstown. The encumbrancers will have to foreclose, and then put the estate up for sale, and there will be no one to buy it but the tenants."

"The result will be," I hinted, "that you will buy the land yourselves pretty cheaply?"

"Yes, that is what we all expect."

In an inner room of a cottage larger than usual I found Mrs. Moloney, a very aged woman, covered with a patchwork counterpane. "I am well enough to-day," she whispered. "That was a dreadful day. I did n't know what was happening; and now I can't see the old home. I tried to make the rent. Perhaps it would have been better to have gone back as caretaker. I am quite comfortable here. They do every thing for me." As the old lady is now in the house where she was born, and where she can be better taken care of than before, her removal the distance of a single field was not perhaps an act of extraordinary cruelty.

The saddest thing to see was the rank growth of weeds in the fields. The thistles, some three or four feet high, were seeding, and the rag-weeds were like a miniature forest. "Why do you let the land get in such a state?"

I asked of a young fellow. " Ever since we sold off all
our cattle last November," he said, "it has not been
worth while to do any thing."

Twenty miles from Limerick, on the side opposite to
Herbartstown, is Bodyke.   For some distance fine trees
overarch the road, and as soon as the woods are passed
the country opens up flat and boggy.   " A great place,"
said my boy driver, "for catching linnets, finches, and
rabbits " ; and a moment afterwards we met a bird-
catcher with three cages full.   Here and there small
thatched huts are almost hidden behind ricks of hay and
straw and long piles of peat.   Around us are low, long-
rolling hills, flecked with every color from orange to
bluish black, closely spotted with gray heaps of stone
and chequered with bare stone walls ; beyond rise
higher hills, golden brown against a silvery sky ; and in
the valley are long peat dikes and one tiny patch of
emerald grass, with two cows and a few solitary sheep.
Each successive amphitheatre of hills is more barren and
more stony than the last.   Stones lie on every side as
thick as in an ancient graveyard or a glacier moraine, and
where the stones are fewer there is bog.   At last we
swing suddenly to the left, and are in Bodyke, with its
four two-storied, thatched spirit-groceries, and the white
police barracks with its tiled roof.

The feelings of the striking tenants were perhaps expressed most intelligently by a bright-looking, middle-
aged woman, as she sat in the cosy kitchen of a neat cottage, Mrs. Dogherty, a teacher in the National School.
" We have two farms," she said, " and this house in the
village.   One of the farms belongs to Colonel O'Callaghan,—a farm of five and a half acres, of which two
acres are snipe bog, and the rest arable land.   The rent

used to be £12, which we got reduced by the court three years ago to £7 10s. Two years ago we all asked for 25 per cent. reduction, which was refused, and then we joined the 'Plan.' I and my husband could pay the rent, but we are bound in honor to our neighbors to pay nothing till the Colonel gives in. A year ago we were served with ejectment papers, and random evictions were made, but we were not touched. Lately we have been writted again.

"Landlords could do any thing they chose till evictions became difficult. The worst that has been said of the Colonel is not bad enough. Every word of Mr. Norman's pamphlet about Bodyke is true. The greater part of this parish was starving in order to pay their rents, and but for the Plan of Campaign many of the tenants would not be living now. Eighteen or twenty could have paid their exorbitant rents, but the rest could n't make the rent out of the land, and got along only by going out as laborers and teamsters.

"As it is, the Colonel will have to give in to our demands, grant us our abatement of 25 per cent., restore the evicted tenants, and refund enough to make good all losses caused by the evictions."

Eviction used to be spoken of as "a sentence of death." It is so no longer. "The evicted tenants have continued to occupy their farms ever since the evictions, but the police are watching them, and they fear being turned out again. They have got in some crops, and are supported by the 'Campaign Fund,' by regular allowances from the League, and by public subscriptions. The poorer tenants," the good lady continued, "are certainly better off than they ever were before."

It is perhaps worth while noting that even in Bodyke

there is no general strike against paying rent. "Mr. Stackpole, a son-in-law of the Colonel, is a large landowner here, and he has settled with his tenants for a reduction of 15 per cent." Mrs. Dogherty holds a farm of fifteen or sixteen acres from Dr. Collinan, of Ennis, and the house she lives in belongs to the Colonel's sister, and she is paying rent to both.

The suppression of the League in Bodyke was said to have stimulated outrages. A week before my visit a baker was found shot dead under his cart, and the night before two hundred feet of turf was burned to the ground, the woman who owned it being suspected of supplying the emergency men.

As we drove back through the rain the car-boy sang unending mournful songs in a low voice, "to kape the baste in good humor." The streaming road shone like silver in the diffused misty moonlight, and a man marching moodily by his heavily laden "assen car" loomed up like a peasant caught by Millet against a shaft of sunset light.

PART III.—IN CONNAUGHT.

WHY GALWAY WANTS HOME RULE.

IN the town of Galway, the first thing that struck me was that there was no longer there a branch of the League. "There is no League in this part of the country," said a leading Nationalist, a stout, round-faced publican, "for the people are so poor they cannot pay their subscriptions. They were willing but unable to pay. Most of the people in the town," he added significantly, "are Liberal-Unionists."

At the Bridge Mills the proprietor, Mr. Lynch, was sitting in the flour-sprinkled little office, surrounded by a little company of enthusiastic Nationalists. "This is a wool-growing country," he said, "with the greatest water power in the United Kingdom. Independently of Home Rule, factories would start up here of their own accord, if our people were only energetic ; under Home Rule they certainly would.

"Centralization is a great evil. The bill to construct tramways in Galway had to be passed in London. To build a bridge across the little river over which you are sitting, we had to go to London and spend some fifty pounds there. If we had Home Rule we should improve hourly. Galway is the natural port of the country for ships sailing to the United States, and a Home Rule Parliament would build it up as a shipping and steamer station. A few years ago the mail packet subsidy was taken away from us, and hundreds have been starving ever since. Parliament, too, has never given us the pier and breakwater we were promised. Heretofore we would rather have been under a government of Thugs than of the English.

" As to the land question. The Irish Americans, unfortunately, have done much to raise the price of land in Ireland, for they have come back and bought land at any price from sentimental notions. Many of the farmers are in great distress. I know a man named Curran who lives six miles from Clifden, who has fifty or sixty acres, half bog. On this holding the rent was twenty pounds in 1849, and has been raised successively to twenty-seven pounds, forty-five pounds, fifty pounds, and sixty pounds, and was lately reduced by the court to thirty pounds.

" The Land Act of 1881 was necessary, for the land was exhausted by frequent cropping to meet exorbitant rents, and improvements were prevented by the insecurity of tenure. We admit that a great deal of our poverty is our own fault, as we don't cultivate wisely or enough ; but to this we were really forced by the custom of raising the rents for every improvement. Of course, too, over-population is the cause of much of the evil, but how can that be avoided ?

" The establishment of a peasant proprietary would keep money in the country that is now spent abroad. Lord Clanricarde takes out of the country about thirty thousand pounds a year, not a penny of which ever comes back.

" The landlords, moreover, have not quite so strong a claim to compensation as they try to make out. If a merchant buys a certain cargo, he cannot be insured a certain price for it. Why should a buyer of land be better off ? "

I referred to the apparent lack of independence in the people, as shown by their yielding such blind obedience to their leaders. "We have had," he replied, "so much experience of disunion and political treachery in Ireland, that, for the time, we have decided all to yield to Mr. Parnell. Even if we don't approve of his choice of a candidate, we submit for the sake of union. This was strikingly shown at the last election here. We would not have it said that Galway caused a split in the party. Many of our M. P.'s are able men but unscrupulous, and with patriotism only skin-deep, but if Mr. Parnell sent one of them down here we would elect him because he would serve our purpose."

"Would the Protestant minority have fair play under Home Rule?"

"The influence of the priests, you must remember, is not what it was. Except Dr. Croke and Dr. Nulty, who sided with the people, the bishops and almost all the priests held out against the National movement until they saw there was danger of the people falling away from them [" Politically," interjected Sullivan]; then they fell in, and are now to the front again."

"They have been of marvellous service to the cause," Sullivan remarked again.

"Yes," continued Lynch, "but these facts show how independent the people have become, for in old times the priests used to drive the people before them to the polls.

"In Galway again, there are about sixteen Catholics to one of any other denomination; yet of the twenty-four members of the corporation ten are Protestants, and the chairman is a Protestant. On the Harbor Board the majority of the members and the chairman are Protes-

tants.   On the Poor-Law Board the chairman is Catholic,
but three or four of the elected members are Protestants.
The Poor-Rate Collector is a Protestant, though elected
by Catholics, and so are the Engineer of the Harbor
Board, the Town Steward, and the Engineer for the
Town. A majority of the grand jury are Catholics, for the
landlords here are Catholics.

"In fine, I believe that if we had Home Rule to-
morrow, as I pray God we may, any bishop or priest who
stood up for ascendancy would have short shrift."

The opinion of a clockmaker in Galway may be worth
quoting :

"I firmly believe," he said, "that Home Rule would
injure me at first, but that in twenty, fifty, or a hundred
years my business would be benefited. Within a few
years a farmer in the west of Ireland was afraid to have
a clock in his house, because if the agent came round
and saw it, he would probably raise the rent."

WALKING IN CONNEMARA.

From Galway I walked along the coast to Clifden. A
few miles from Galway is Barna, a row of a dozen houses,
huts with thatched roofs, and three two-story, slated
houses by the side of the road. In one of the latter
lived James Hickey, whose story seemed to explain the
violence of so many Irish patriots. Hickey went to
America and enlisted at the breaking out of the civil
war. He was twice wounded, but not mustered out till
the war was over. His regiment was the Sixth Massachusetts Volunteers, the "Irish Brigade"; and with several
other old comrades he took part in the Canadian rising,
and being in the first detachment that crossed Niagara, was
taken, and spent many years in Dartmouth Prison.

" My father rented this strip of land of Lord Campbell and Stratheden, and built these three stone houses,
each with eight rooms, and well slated. Nine or ten
years ago the price of cattle fell, and my father was then
evicted out of one house, but kept this and the next one,
which he let as a barracks to the constabulary. If it had
not been for my wife and children, I would then have
gone to America. As it was I went to London to see
the landlord, but he was never at home to me. I found
myself alone in London, without five shillings in my
pocket ; it was a blue look-out, but I found a friend in
T. P. O'Connor, M. P. for Galway, whom I had helped
in his election ; for I have considerable influence with
the people here, as I speak equally well English and
Irish. T. P. O'Connor got me a situation in London,
and there I stayed till I heard of my father's death. I
came back at once, knowing little of my father's affairs.
He used to keep things in a slovenly way, and it was only
from the agent that I found out he owed two and a half
years' rent. I had no money in the house at the time,
and went to see the agent. I stood outside the rail in
his office and told him ' it can be paid, but I want time.'
' Pooh, pooh !' he said ; ' the landlord can't give you any
time ; he must get the money.' ' See here,' said I, ' the
old times are gone. There 's no dark spot now but a
strong light can be thrown on it as never before, and if
you squeeze me I 'll squeal.' ' When will you pay me ?'
he asked. ' I expect to sell this and that,' I said. ' I 'll
sell every stick I have till I get out of this mess ' ; and
I gave him £38 7s. It was then November, 1883, and
that exhausted my resources. I paid him a pound later,
and £10 more in 1886, and then was at the end of my
tether. I now owe £42, about two and a half years' rent.

"I went to him and said : 'I have no money now, but I own the police barracks, for which I get £12 a year. At twelve years' purchase that is worth nearly £150. Let me mortgage that to you as security, and redeem when I can.' He paused a bit, and then said: 'You have no lease for it,' he said. 'Whose fault is that?' cried I. 'The land the barracks is on is Lord Campbell's, but the building itself is mine. If I can turn over the barracks to him so that he can secure his £42 off it, what 's the harm?' Legally, perhaps, he is owner and I am tenant at will, but my father built the houses. Lord Campbell never gave a shovel of sand towards building it, nor a stick of timber, nor a single slate. Let him mortgage it and hold it as security only. I will redeem it.' The clerk then drew up a paper, which I signed ; and the next day the mean fellow collected a year's rent then due on the barracks, and immediately evicted me out of it, the constables being all turned out and at once put back again.

"He evicted me out of every thing except the house I am now in, and did not leave me land enough 'to sod a lark in,' and in that land there I have invested three times its fee-simple value.

"The landlord now has possession of the barracks and the land, though I could redeem it with only £42, and I am left with only this house and a few potato patches,—and even for these I am writted for evict-ment. While I was away, too, and the old man was sick, every thing fell into disrepair, and it would take £20 to put things in order again. As to the houses themselves, they are solid granite, as solid as Hell Gate in New York Sound before they blew it up.

"Here the rent is not the grievance, though the time

will come, please God, when we shall pay no rent. In
fact we pay the rent now with as good grace as we can,
though we think it an injustice.

"The land acts have done some good, but your improvements you sacrifice even now if you go out for non-
payment of rent, and if you let six months pass after an
eviction without paying, you lose all claim on the land.
When I could n't hold the land, how could I redeem it in
six months, after being still further impoverished? The
period of redemption should obviously be extended."

Hickey led me out into a field behind the house, a
long, green field sloping to the sea. Here and there are
heaps of broken blocks of granite, like the débris of a
glacier moraine. A curving granite pier jutted out into
the blue water and made a tiny harbor. Drawn up on
the beach were ten or a dozen "corraghs," canoes made
of tarred sail-cloth nailed over a bare wooden frame, and
beyond the pier were five or six more. Hickey seemed
strongly moved, and his eyes filled with tears. "About
1859," he said gently, "the place we are walking on was
a prosperous fishing village, named Barna, in the county
and town of Galway. You are now treading on ruined
hearth-stones. There were then thirty-five or forty fish-
ing-boats in this little harbor, instead of three. Barna,
as it was, had nearly six hundred inhabitants. These
people lived here in a rude way, well in good times, and
bearing hard times bravely,—a typical fishing community.

"Where we are now standing there was a solid block
of houses. The present village was only the first row of
the old Barna, and from that to the beach were other
rows, with little lanes leading down to the water's edge.
The rent ranged from 15s. to 30s. a house, and there were
over forty houses.

"The Lord Campbell of that day thought it would be a good idea to have bathing-houses here, and an open way to the sea. He ruthlessly exterminated the whole community, and spent enormous sums in turning the village into the field you see.

"There were little gardens to the houses, surrounded by stone walls : they took the earth from the gardens, and filled in the hollows with the ruins of the houses and the garden walls, and then covered all snugly over with the soil. Do you see those brown spots? The grass does n't grow there, for just beneath the surface is one of the sunken stones of the buried village.

"The Czar of Russia gives subsistence to those he transports to Siberia, but the children and the infirm and the old people of Barna were sent into the workhouse, and the rest wandered here and there over the earth. God knows where some of them went to, for I don't. In Second and Third streets, and in Athens Street, South Boston, there used to be a little colony of these people. Perhaps some of them may be there still.

"The rental of the old village was forty pounds or more a year. After all those expensive operations this field was let for £2 a year. Now it is divided between two tenants who pay altogether about £8. Assign what motive you like to this action of Lord Campbell's, there is something diabolical about it. I used to amuse myself by observing the conduct in Parliament of the present Lord Campbell, who is persecuting me. Whenever he opened his mouth—he has n't now for some time—it was to speak about the misery of the people under the Turks. He might have found, I used to think, some misery nearer home."

With such an experience ever in his heart, it is only

natural that Hickey should feel strongly, but the modera-
tion with which he considers practical questions is significant. Let me recall one conversation as we walked
along the Galway road: "In case of war between England and any other power, Ireland would say to England:
'Give us Home Rule, or —— ' A large measure of
Home Rule, that would satisfy the majority of my coun-
trymen, I would take as a finality, and not, in any sense,
as an instalment merely or an entering wedge. Then, if
it ever came in my power to effect separation, so long as
the government took no unfair advantage and kept the
agreement, I would not break it myself, though personally
I might wish for better terms.

"I should be willing to have all bills of an imperial
complexion settled finally at Westminster, but all other
bills relating to Ireland should be dealt with by a Parliament at Dublin. The Irish Parliament should send over
to England what consideration is settled on as Ireland's
share of the imperial expenses, and the rest of the revenue they should collect and expend as they think best
for the interests of Ireland.

"One *crux* will be the disposition of the Irish constabulary. They are picked men. I don't believe you can
find their match in the world. But they are the tools of
the government; they are spies, taking note of your going out and your coming in, and are looked upon by
their fellow-countrymen as renegades. If we had Home
Rule, and these men remained under imperial control,
they would be a wedge through the heart of Ireland for
England to strike. We should have our enemies at our
doors and be unable to dismiss them. Such a state of
things would be intolerable in any country.

"I would suggest turning them into militia, each

county having a regiment, to supplement the imperial army if called upon.

"As policemen the constabulary are not needed. Their numbers are absurd. In Barna, a policeman, unless he is drunk, does n't lay his hands on a man's shoulder from one year's end to another. There has never been a rape here, and not a murder in my recollection. I never knew a row here, and there has n't been a theft for years. I never lock my back door, and my front door very seldom. I don't believe there are three locks in the village. And yet in Barna there is one barracks and five constables; at Salthill, in the immediate neighborhood, another; in Spiddal, five miles to the west, a third, with an inspector, two sergeants, and eighteen or twenty rank and file; at Moycullen, six miles to the northwest, a fourth; a fifth, two miles and a half off along another road; a sixth, five miles off in a different direction; and at intermediate places there are iron huts, which are occupied by details from different barracks ' on detached service,' as I used to say. This shows the network of police in Ireland. What do we want with so many?

"At first, even with Home Rule, all will not be satisfied. Underlying all there will be a discontented mass of laborers; but the rent saved will soon become a fund for their employment. Till then with the laborers it will be a case of 'Live horse to get grass,' but they will soon be benefited by the reduction of rents. I am paying twenty-three pounds odd for rent. If on my way to Galway I got the news to-morrow that I was absolved from all rent *in sæcula sæculorum*, I should say : ' Now I will turn that field there to better use, and I will improve my house. Here Mick, I want you to go right out with

Pat and Murphy, and get to work at my house and garden.'

"Many laborers will be employed at once, and in nine
or ten years, when some capital has accumulated, there
will be room for all the present laborers and for many
more from America, for even now, every spring and
every harvest the farmers have to wait for laborers."

Of boycotting he said : "It is often the only defence
left the people, and, if used with proper discrimination,
is effective. It may be abused, but what is there that
is n't ?"

We came into the townland of Furbough. "All this,"
said Hickey, "is the property of Colonel John A. Daly,
whose family name was Blake. Here even, after the
passage of the first Land Act, the tenants were most grievously oppressed. They not only paid rack-rents, poor-
rates, and taxes, but also tithes, and in addition they had
to give eight or nine days' labor about the Great House at
sixpence a day in winter, and eightpence a day in summer. There was also a certain amount of 'duty work'
required of them, a survival from the feudal times.
Moreover, every house had to cut a day's turf.

"Some five years ago, on this same estate, there was a
man, Peter Kelly, now living in Galway,—a good fellow
he was, but if you ride on his back, don't spur him, or
he 'll throw you. The bailiff summoned him to cut turf
the next day. He told the bailiff to come some other
day, as he was busy. Some 'drivers,' other bailiffs, so-
called from their occupation, went down and seized his
cow to impound it the very next day, and drove it so
carelessly that it fell and broke its legs. Kelly told me
the cow was worth fifteen pounds, and he never got any
compensation. If he had said much more to the bailiff,
he would have lost his house as well."

In a few minutes a man came driving along the road from Galway in an "assen car." It was this very same Peter Kelly. "Eight days' duty work I had," said he when I asked him. "Divil a copper he paid me for my cow."

"There was another rule on the estates about here," said Hickey, "a harsh one, you will admit. During the famine time and the subsequent years when a large number of tenants were evicted, the other tenants were strictly forbidden to harbor or give any shelter to the evicted people. The reason was that the landlord paid half the poor-rate, and he was afraid that if these poor people stayed here they would come on the Union."

To the left of the road I noticed a little memorial chapel, a sort of mausoleum. "An uncle of Mr. Daly acted as his agent here. One day some one put daylight through him, near Loughrea, and now he lies there in that kennel. He was so detested that one tenant only went to the funeral, and he went from motives of policy. I met the procession on its way here, and, as it passed by, I did not touch my hat."

On either side of the road are little holdings. The country is so rocky and stony that there is scarcely an acre not surrounded by a rude stone wall. When you look at a gradually sloping hillside you see no green, but one wall seems to rise on top of another, so as to present the appearance of a continuous mass of stones. The walls of the little huts are built as loosely as the walls by the roadside, and at a first glance are hardly distinguishable. Now and then I knocked at a door and, with Hickey acting as interpreter, for the people generally speak nothing but Irish, asked a few questions, which were promptly and amiably answered. Anthony Concannon is a tenant of Mr. Marcus Lynch. He has twenty-four acres, four of which he used to sow with potatoes, but cannot now for want of money to buy seed. The rent is £22, having been reduced in 1881 from £26. The day before he had gone to the office to pay some arrears, and looked in vain for a reduction. He has another farm of two acres or so, which he holds from the same landlord on a grazing lease, for three pounds and ten shillings. The rent has not been reduced for twenty years, and the holding is not within the Land Act. For a third plot he pays eight pounds, which has been reduced from eleven. Part of the home farm is often flooded by the tide, and after the passage of the Land Act the landlord for the first time claimed the black-weed, which grows between high- and low-water mark, as well as what washes against the sea wall. " I keep three cows and four or five calves," he said, " besides a mare and a foal. I grow turnips, potatoes, and mangels. The potatoes are below the average, and the turnips and mangels have failed entirely. I am sure I won't make any rent this year." The black-weed, according to Hickey, had always been considered the property of the tenant ; and the drift-weed, which the landlords have generally claimed, Hickey argued was really public property. The way the landlords deprive the tenants of the sea-weed is by closing the roads to the shore. " The land-lords have so many ways of getting round any law, they will outflank you," he sighed, " in spite of the Devil."

Here is Edward Toole's holding. He has ten acres. The rent has been reduced by agreement out of court from fourteen to twelve pounds. The poor-rate is thirty shillings, and the taxes eighteen shillings, due twice a year. The house, a two-storied granite house, was built by Costello, Mrs. Toole's father. A little bit of land a quarter of an acre, they were manuring with sea-weed for a potato patch, but in the whole field there did not seem to be four square yards free from large stones or rock.

We were now passing the Furbough National School, a neat stone building like all the frequent schoolhouses in this part of the country, and there we took up John R. Curtin, the schoolmaster. "Generally," he said, "the children in Ireland leave school about the lower-fifth form, and many in the country from the third and fourth forms, when they are thirteen or fourteen years old. What they know then is not much, and is soon forgotten. The attendance in the country is not apt to be continuous after the age of seven. The busy seasons are spring, summer, and early autumn, for there's turf-cutting in summer, sea-weed gathering in spring, and then the harvest, and at these times all except the very young children are off.

"We schoolmasters want to get 'compulsory education,' but this is barred by the religious difficulty.

"If the children could be kept at school till they had passed through the senior grade of the sixth form, they would be competent to fill a clerical position anywhere. But even the standard of the lower fifth is high enough for practical purposes. In English, they have to be familiar with the fifth-standard reader, though in an Irish-speaking community like ours this hope is seldom realized ; in book-keeping, they go as far as double entry, cash accounts, and personal accounts ; in geography, they have to know well the geography of Ireland, the map of Europe, and the outlines of the continents ; in agriculture, which is taught in the rural schools, we study the natures of the crops, the mode of cultivation, and something about the chemistry of the soil. If we only had a little garden attached to the schoolhouse, for purposes of practical illustration, this course would be of the greatest value.'

As twilight came on, these newly found friends left me, after quoting to my amusement a Celtic curse, common among the people, who, many of them, still believe in the "evil eye": "May the eye of an evil man never rest on you, nor the eye of the dearly beloved Son of God!"

A few miles beyond Spiddal, a squalid little fishing village, I called on the parish priest, Father Hosty. "That wretched land," said he, pointing to a neighboring field, "is measured without counting the stones, and, till lately, was paying thirty shillings an acre. It is now held under judicial leases for from ten to twenty shillings. One reason for the high rent is, that the right to the sea-weed is included.

"Oats are a perfect failure this year, but, fortunately, the potatoes are fair. There is nothing between the people and a famine but those little bulbs.

"I would n't call this place of mine 'a congested district,' because there is plenty of room, and the people could live well enough by fishing. There is, however, no fishing here at all, for there are no boats, and no nets. The fish in the bay are caught chiefly by a company which sends them direct to Dublin.

"These houses are very poor-looking, but the people are quite contented, and are willing enough to go on living on potatoes. They don't care to go to America. though we never say a word to dissuade them."

He took me into the school near by, and I heard the barefooted children, boys and girls, but the girls best, read beautifully, and parse well. "Along this road," continued the good father, "you will find as fine schools as there are anywhere. The younger generation are better educated and more independent than the old, and can take their place with any people in the world."

Near Castlerea, the keeper of the public-house, one Taylor, joined me and piloted me across a boggy mountain to the main road. "I have been many years in America," he said, "and find nowhere more liberty than here. The rent is not the main thing ; the rent is not so much, the taxes will soon be more, and, since this agitation began, the taxes have risen enormously.

"I have a piece of land for which no rent has been paid for seven years. The previous tenant went to America, and then a man came in who sublet half to me. I paid him one year's rent, and won't pay him any more till he pays the landlord.

"The League, in my opinion, has ruined twenty to one whom it has benefited. How many has it driven away who might have been in their little houses to-day? If we are once put out of a place we cannot get another, and cannot get the smallest room in a village without paying rent for it.

"I see as much privilege and liberty in Ireland as ever I saw anywhere, and I have been sixteen years in America. The League may have done some good in other parts of the country, but they have done none in Galway.

"I tell you the farmers will always have to work themselves and cannot employ many laborers, but I knew landlords who used to employ as many as fifty or a hundred laborers, carpenters, blacksmiths, and harness-makers, but they cannot afford to do so now.

"The poorest people, the laborers, are the sufferers by

the agitation, and even under Home Rule the rich will be the best off, but the poorest will be just as poor."

Miles and miles the road continued bounded by bogs on either side ; not a soul, not a beast was to be seen. Not even a dwelling of any sort was visible, till Scrieb Lodge came in sight, a fishing lodge,—a deserted-looking square white house by the side of a wide, straggling morass, dotted with peaty islands, and encircled by low brown hills, with the jagged Connemara " Twelve Pins " in the distance. It recalled the dismal horrors of the " Fall of the House of Usher," and I hurried on as the evening was closing in quickly.

From time to time I knocked at a cottage, to ask leave to spend the night, but I was either refused or unable to make myself understood ; in two of the cottages the cows were in the kitchen. At last I found an inn, where a couple of constables sat and talked till midnight. "We don't trouble ourselves about Home Rule," they remarked, " for we shall then be surely pensioned off. As to the poverty of the people, that is greatly exaggerated. You often see a man living in a hut like a cow-shed, and find that he has two or three hundred pounds in the bank. These habits have come down from earlier times."

The next day a barefooted man, in a red-knitted cap, started me on the road to Cashel. He has a small farm. " The rent is fair, the oats is all dried up, but the potatoes are good, and that 's the main thing."

Two men, a woman, and a boy passed me, carrying enormous bales of hay on their backs, and, later, the cart of a Galway trader, who furnishes the people with groceries, taking eggs in payment. Near a tiny hamlet a couple of laborers, sitting smoking on a rock, asked for news, saying there was a report that a head constable had been shot at Lisdoonvarna. In a cottage on a mountain side at Shanadonel, I got some milk and eggs. Joyce, his mother, and four children were in the kitchen, all barefooted, occasionally tickling with their toes the pigs that were playing with " a little cur dog " and two cats on the earthen floor. The only furniture consisted of a rough wooden table, a couple of home-made chairs, and two pictures on the wall, supplements of old Christmas *Graphics.* Joyce owns a hundred or more acres, how many he does n't know, and pays twelve pounds for it. This is too much, he thought. " If we had a good land bill," said he, " we would not care about Home Rule. Our people ask for much more than they expect to get."

Along a path invisible to my eyes, he led me across several miles of bogs. A stone here, a footprint there were all the signs of travel. We sank frequently ankle-deep, but Joyce, like a satyr, leaped on before, and with his bare toes seizing the bog, shook the mountain side while he shouted : " Don't fear ; it is quite firm and strong." Along this path he has driven cattle to Galway fair, more than forty miles' distance. Such are some of the inconveniences of life in central Galway.

The village of Cashel seemed to consist of a barracks, a national school, and a public-house. The keeper of the latter is Mr. J. J. O'Loghlen, a poor-law guardian. This is in the notorious Clifden Union, one of the six bankrupt unions which Mr. Morley, when in office, tried to relieve by a grant of money, and succeeded only in plunging into deeper debt. " The poor-rate here," said O'Loghlen, " is very high—four shillings in the pound. My valuation is ninety pounds, and I pay twenty pounds' poor-rate. One reason is, that so many of our people have gone to America, leaving behind them the poor old people, who stick to their homes long after they have ceased to make them pay.

" Two old men died here a few days ago who had been for several years receiving out-door relief, and the Union had to pay ten shillings for each funeral. One, Colroy, had a son who was a captain of one of the Black Ball ships, sailing to Australia, which was lost at sea a few years ago with all on board. The other old man saw his children go away to all parts of the world, and they never sent him back a penny.

" There are too many doctors employed by the Unions, five here where two would do, and we have to keep a doctor in Innisbofin Island, which owes us now over five hundred pounds, for we cannot collect any rates from the people.

" In the matter of rents we are not so badly off as many places, and there is here no disturbance ; but the land is not worth a farthing an acre. Payment is made for the land by the holding and not by the acreage. So I don't know how much I have.

" The landlord, Mr. R. Berridge, lives in London, and leaves every thing to the discretion of his agent, Robinson, who has a bad name but is not a bad man. Many people have been evicted at different times, but they are all living on their holdings as caretakers."

" It is through the shopkeepers giving credit to the people that the landlords are able to get in their rents. But for the system of credit there would be no one in this part of the country. I often have out £2,000 in one year, but I get no credit myself from the merchants. I have been owed some £1,400 for the last six or seven years, and if I can get half that I shall be happy, and would take any thing they can give me, a horse, a cow, a pig, or any thing.

"The people are also largely supported by American money. About Christmas time I have often had given me to cash a hundred checks on Boston and New York.

"If we had employment," was his conclusion, "that would be the only kind of Home Rule we should want."

In the evening I found myself still far from Clifden in a heavy rain, so I asked at a little cabin by the roadside for hospitality, and was welcomed cordially. There was only a kitchen and one room. In the kitchen were a cow, a calf, a dog, three or four hens and a cock fluttering noisily about, and in a corner a coop full of chickens. Here I slept on the ground near the ashes of the glowing peat fire ; and in the other room slept the family—father and mother, two girls, and a boy. The silence of the night was broken from time to time by the thud and splash of dung on the mud floor, and the crowing and clatter of the fowls woke me early. There was one chair, one bench, and several boxes to sit on, but no table ; and some rude harness hanging from pegs on the wall was the only ornament. "Michael, rise up !" shouted a man's voice, about seven o'clock, and a boot, as it seemed, struck violently against the wooden partition. Michael lounged in and rekindled the peat fire from the dying embers. In a few minutes in came his mother, and milked the cow in front of the fire into a series of dirty-looking little tin pots, that reminded me of old tomato cans. She then fed the calf on some milk and raw potatoes, and in a little time gave me a cup of excellent tea and a piece of potato bread.

WHAT THEY SAY AT CLIFDEN.

Clifden is a town of some seven hundred inhabitants on an inlet of the sea. A graceful bridge spans a watercourse yellow-brown with sea-weed, famous for salmon, and along the hillside beyond it are two streets of thatched houses.

There is but one small industry in Clifden—the carving of the beautiful Connemara marble, by Alexander McDonnell and his son. The intelligent, kindly old Scotchman expressed in a word the cause of the people's discontent when he said : " We are shut up here as in a prison, and the wealth of the country is, as it were, locked up behind iron bars. Sometimes for weeks we are without meal, for it is too expensive to cart it from Galway, and the little boats are apt to be detained by bad weather. The kelp the people gather a few miles off they send by cart twenty miles to an agent at Cashel, who ships it to Galway. On Saturday, at the fish-market, the fish had to be salted to keep it, and all but two small baskets of fine lobsters had to be thrown into the sea. There are hundreds of millions of tons of the best marble in the world in the Twelve .Pins, but the people cannot get at it.

" I want Home Rule, because an Irish Parliament would spend public money wisely and without so much waste. We need a railroad from Galway to Clifden to open up the country. Then Clifden would double in a year or two, and the people would not have to run away to Scotland or England to earn a little money to keep their homesteads. The people have not the gear nor the boats for fishing. Money for this purpose should be lent by the government. The imperial Parliament mismanages such matters. The government is now spending some £10,000 on a quay a few miles away, and they might just as well throw the money into the sea. They advanced money to the Unions, but charity and distribution of relief only demoralize the people."

The catholic curate, Father Biggins, was not an enthusiastic Home Ruler. " It is hard to see," he said, " how Home Rule could improve the condition of this part of the country, for under any form of government the people cannot be well off so long as they depend on their little holdings. The rent is very little, £4 or £5, and if you made them a present of it, it would n't make them a bit more comfortable. They have n't land enough. All the best land is in the hands of graziers and large farmers. Divide the grazing lands among the dwellers on little patches on the coast ; they would pay more than the graziers do, and that is the one thing that would do them any good.

" The chief benefit Home Rule could do would be to encourage the fisheries and to open up the country. It costs a jobber too much to come here to buy, and a man cannot drive cattle to a railroad forty or fifty miles off and have them in good condition.

" The tenants have not generally got the benefit of the Land Act, partly because of their subletting, and partly because so many accepted the landlords' terms. Mr. Robinson's offer of four shillings in the pound to Mr. Berridge's tenants was generally taken, and the people were at first delighted, but those who went into court got often as much as ten shillings in the pound.

" The rents have been paid about here as well as ever. Hazell, the agent of a Scotch company, living at Cashel, has paid eight thousand pounds for kelp this year. That helps the people a lot and pays the rent.

" The bankruptcy of the Union is due to the low rating. Then, when the forty thousand pounds were given last year for the relief of distress, the local guardians lost their heads and said to themselves : ' If we don't give some relief at once the money will be all spent.' So this year the rates will be eight shillings in the pound, including special rates to meet the surplus expended in excess of the government's grant. The only remedy is to amalgamate two or three Unions with a single common staff."

Father Linsky, the parish priest, is a man of wonderful energy. " I got from Mr. Kendall," he said, "five shillings in the pound reduction on all rents not judicial and three shillings on judicial rents, and this through no agitation except my personal efforts, though I have the National League here in my hand.

" In this parish I urged the tenants to go into court, and I filled in the notices myself and appeared in court for many of them who were too poor to pay costs. On an average I got six shillings and eight pence reduction in the pound.

" So far as it goes, the new Land Act is of great value. What is of particular benefit is that the commissioners will adjudicate the rents on the basis of prices without expense to landlord or tenant.

. " As a rule, rents settled out of court are not settled fairly. At Beeleek and Fahy, on Mrs. Suffield's property, the rents were settled out of court at a very small reduction. The tenants protested, but paid, with my consent, for I found them too poor to fight, so poor that they don't care to come to church on Sunday because of their ragged clothes. There are only some twenty tenants, and so heavily is the estate encumbered that the landlord's interest does n't exceed sixty or seventy pounds.

" The people here are simple-minded. Captain Thompson's tenants agreed to buy their holdings at twenty years' purchase, but the sale fell through, because one man refused, on the recommendation of the parish priest, who thought the land worth not over eight years' purchase. When the tenants were asked by the priest why they agreed to give such an extraordinary sum, 'Well,' they said, 'we thought we would serve Captain Thompson without doing ourselves any harm.'"

In the large beautiful church a series of missionary services was being held. Thousands listened with awe to a lurid sermon on hell by a Dominican friar. "Every sinner makes his bed at the gates of hell." "One spark of hell fire would turn the ocean to steam." These sentences rang out clearly in the intense silence of the hushed congregation. The same voice sounded much sweeter in Father Linsky's dining-room, where we assembled in the evening to discuss peasant proprietorship. "A peasant proprietary," it was said, "would be a success. In France, Belgium, Prussia, and a large part of Russia a similar measure had worked well and not ended in a restoration of landlordism. Why should Ireland prove an exception?

"Land scrip, with a local guaranty, would be depreciated at once, as all paper is which is not secured by property easily realizable. Let the imperial government advance the purchase money, in the same way as it now makes loans to fishermen. Ireland can never be separated from England, and whatever our local government may be, the imperial government will always be able to exact repayment. The government must come in, for the landlords, after they cease to be landlords, can never collect payments, and no one else will be in a position to do so for them. Will the action of the government be resented? Not at all. The collectors of taxes and

other government officials are not odious. Indeed, the
gentleman here who is collecting from the fishermen
repayments of government money is very popular. There
are just men here. Under the Glebe Loan Act not £500
out of £250,000 are outstanding as bad debts. The
payments of the fishery loan and under Lord Ashbourne's
Act tell the same story. Those who wish to keep the
land for nothing are madmen.

" Subdivision has been frequent in the west, largely
because the landlords were needy and got something for
the subdivision,—an increased rent or a fine,—an obolus
of some sort.

" Finally, it is said that a few pounds' rent remitted to
a small tenant would not help him. Suppose I get a reduction of four pounds ; I buy pigs ; half an acre of
turnips out of my six or seven acres will feed them ; the
pigs cost me a pound apiece, and at the end of six months
they sell for four pounds. The rent saved will be a little
capital, and will soon multiply itself."

I visited Mr. King, a farmer at Fahy, who acts as Mrs.
Suffield's agent. He has five acres, for which he pays
four pounds sixteen shillings. He has also commonage
of a mountain and "a strip of the weed" on the shore,
which he uses for manure. His house was built by his
father. He has one acre in potatoes, one in oats, and the
rest grazing. He has no horse now and only one cow.
" I am not in arrears," he said, "but should be if I had
not the agency of the property. My rent is a fair sample
of the others. We all settled outside the court for 25 per
cent. reduction, and thought that reasonable enough at the
time. But prices have been growing steadily worse since
then, and I don't think the land is now worth the rent.
The farmers here don't expect to get the land for noth-

ing, they only want a fair price. They are all for Home Rule, but don't know much about it. They think it will mean employment and the circulation of money, but how no one knows. There used to be a local branch of the League here, but it has died out.

"After a Land-Purchase Act what the farmers need most is loans of money on easy terms. Perhaps, the imperial Parliament would have more money to loan than a Home-Rule Parliament.

"The farmers are very poor and much in debt. They have gone security for one another to the banks, borrowing eight or ten pounds, on which there is charged two shillings a pound interest, and renewing their notes every three months. The shopkeepers in Clifden have given a great deal of credit and won't get much of it back. They also give them 'loan money' for which they charge twenty per cent. interest."

It happened to be market day in Clifden, and in Casey's drapery and spirit shop a little circle of farmers sat and talked. Every one agreed that the crops were exceptionably poor. "The potato crop is very good, hay is very light, turnips are a complete failure, and oats have never been known to be so bad in Connemara."

James Casey, a grazier, came in. He has a tillage farm of about a hundred and twenty acres, which he holds under a perpetuity lease for twenty pounds a year. "Some of it is bog, not worth sixpence an acre, and for some I would n't take three pounds an acre. I have also some two thousand acres of land, one farm at a pound and another at sixteen shillings an acre. These are not within the 'Land Act,' and for some I have to pay in advance.

"I have been four years fighting with this depression, and am now giving up, as I am losing money. A few weeks ago I brought forty or fifty bullocks and heifers to a large fair near here. I have got twelve and thirteen pounds for worse stock, and was not offered a shilling for one of them.

"I belonged to the National League at first, but as soon as it seemed to be turning into an anti-rent movement I dropped out, for it would n't do for me to run the risk of losing my farms."

"The people ought to emigrate," said another. "I have circumnavigated the globe, but the people here think there 's no world beyond Clifden."

The master of the workhouse came in. "I was an anti-Home Ruler till lately, but now believe in it.

"Its principal benefit would be to encourage our native industries. We could put a duty on English shoddy. In Westport, next door to where I went to school, there used to be a distillery, and near by rope walks, and four tan yards at full work. All are gone now.

"If capital is needed for this, there 's the Irish National Bank with two millions of Irish savings in its vaults.

"We would do away with all but a thousand of the fourteen thousand Irish Constabulary and save nearly a million pounds in this single item ; and safely too, for satisfied with our own laws, we could become our own policemen.

"The workhouses should be got rid of. Children under fifteen should be boarded out, and old people left with their friends and given an allowance."

I asked whether the Clifden Union had not been ruined by excessive out-door relief. "The people," he said "were demoralized by relief. Some years ago there was 'Jumperism.' People from England started 'Jumper Schools' in behalf of the Irish Church mission, and all

who attended got so much a week. In 1879 and 1880
there was a cry of destitution when there was but little,
and the government came to the people's relief. In 1886
there was another cry, and Morley got a large grant
passed, which was shamefully abused." (All present
assented.) " This was the fault of the local authorities,
who gave money to people not destitute, and neglected
any remunerative labor test. The money would have
relieved the distress, and yet now we are over four thousand pounds in debt.

" Peasant proprietorship I believe in, and don't think
the evils of the present will recur. I am my own landlord now and have two children. I shall not divide my
land between them, but will act like a Massachusetts
farmer and send one or both of them away from home.
Others will do likewise."

There was a noise outside, and we joined a delighted
crowd that surrounded a juggler, in bright-red tights,
who devoured hot pokers and let the farmers crack
enormous stones on his chest. He took up a collection
that amounted to nearly three pounds !

In the hotel, a somewhat mysterious stranger appeared
in the commercial room, whom I took to be a land
agent.

" These Nationalist Unions," he began, " are miserably mismanaged ; I know more than I care to tell about
the Tulla Union in County Clare. The *ex-officio* guardians have lost control of the management and the chairman is a small farmer holding some twenty acres. The
property of the Union has been seized for debt. The
number of laborers' cottages there is enormous, most of
them built only to spite the landlords.

" Here in Clifden the people have been accustomed to

hand-to-mouth relief, and that has not improved their morals.

"The rents may seem excessive, but these men along the coast who complain so bitterly don't pay more than an ordinary laborer pays in this very village, a shilling a week at most ; and for that they have three or four acres, pigs, corn and potatoes, a right to cut as much fuel as they want, and often sea-weed for manure free. But this, of course, won't support a man with nine or ten children. These people, too, are merely laborers. In Mayo and Donegal they go every year to England and Scotland as harvesters. In Galway and here they are fishermen. In Carrarhoe the principal means of subsistence is making *poteen* whiskey.

"No land legislation can materially help such people. I know well an estate now in chancery, where the tenants have paid no rent for seven or eight years. They are the poorest people in the neighborhood. If they owned the farms it might make them more prudent, but I doubt it, for there are no natural habits of thrift among the people.

"Home Rule I cannot believe in, for the doings of the Tulla Union show me that the people cannot yet be trusted."

CONNAUGHT LANDLEAGUERS.

County Mayo was the birthplace of the Land League, and in Westport a somewhat extreme position was rather concisely stated by a leader of the early movement. "The rights of the landlords are not to be acknowledged, for their titles are bad. The grants to the planters of the north of Ireland required them to provide so many soldiers each. When a standing army was established

these deeds became void.   The land belongs to the people, and can be taken up by them whenever it is expedi-
ent, with or without compensation.   The property of the
landlords was confiscated in part by the Land Act of
1881, which gave leases for a period of fifteen years at
rents fixed by a court, and took from the landlords their
right of resumption.   That principle can be indefinitely
extended.

" It is a question of expediency, not of justice. Justice
is a vague word, an eighteenth-century theory, and appeals to you as a Bostonian and a reader of Herbert
Spencer."

I suggested that the American Constitution prohibited
the taking of private property for public use without
compensation, and that a written constitution with such
a clause might be wisely accepted by Irish Nationalists.
His answer was a surprise.   "America had three million
inhabitants when the Constitution was adopted ; it has
now fifty million.   Is it just that fifty millions should be
governed by three millions, and those of a deceased generation ?   It is unwise to tie the hands of posterity.   It
was so decided at the institution of the present French
Republic.   I should oppose a written constitution for
Ireland.

" If the Irish in America," he said again, " had joined
the Republican party, the Irish question would have
already become an international question.   Egan could
not turn them at the last election, but never will they
vote again for an anti-Irish friend of England, such
as Cleveland."   It was perhaps characteristic of some
phases of Irish thought that the gentleman characterized
Sir William Harcourt as " a—useful scoundrel."

Similar opinions were expressed in Sligo by P. A.

M'Hugh, editor of the *Sligo Sentinel* and president of the local branch of the League.

" There is a great lack of bitterness here, due as much to the character of the landlords as to the apathy of the people. The landlords here have been exceptionally lenient.

" Mr. Phibbs is fighting the 'plan' with success, for the leaders and the clergy have found it impossible to prevent many of the tenants from paying their rent. So many of these cowards were there that no attempt has been made to boycott them. But a few farms on the estate from which tenants have been evicted have been kept vacant for several years, and if Phibbs tried to stock them, injury would probably be inflicted on the cattle and their caretakers. To keep an ' evicted ' farm vacant is one of the strongest arguments we can use, and any one who takes such a farm is regarded as a common enemy and cut off from all communication with the people. The *Times* has reprinted with comments some of the boy-cotting resolutions printed in my paper, and we admit the charge of intimidation and intending to intimidate. We say this is the only efficient instrument left to the League.

" Michael Coffey, in Gurteen, took a farm from which a Mr. McDermott had been evicted. He has been boy-cotted for two years and his business, that of a spirit-grocery, ruined. His children have not been allowed to attend school. No man speaks to them. He is think-ing of removing. For using intimidatory language against Coffey I was prosecuted at Petty Sessions, but the bench was equally divided. The local magistrates were against me, but two of the judges were personal friends of my own, and one, Mr. Tigh, went down from this town to sit there to prevent my conviction.

" Personally, I don't think any eviction could be just, for I don't recognize the landlord's title at all.

" As to Land Purchase, the people are not prepared to adopt such a scheme till advised to do so by their leaders. The price of land is going down steadily; the longer the farmers hold off, the better it will be for them, and the worse for the landlords. That is shown by the willingness of the landlords to adopt Archbishop Walsh's plan of a 'round-table conference.' The suggestion was a mistake. It would be an unnecessary admission of a right. Until the Irish land question can be settled by an Irish Parliament, no other plan should be adopted for getting justice from the landlords save the 'plan of campaign.' If, again, the landlords wait till the English democracy settle the Irish land question, they will be worse off than ever, for the opinion is daily growing stronger that the landlords have no claim to rent or to compensation for the loss of it, and that a free ticket to Holyhead is the most that any of them deserves.

" There is practical unanimity in favor of Home Rule in this part of the country, except among the Conservatives, and the difference between Nationalist and Conservative here is practically the difference between Catholic and Protestant.

" Home Rule will come soon, and I think a little more 'physical force' will hasten it, like that of the blackthorns at Mitchelstown or of something stronger."

Mr. M'Hugh, according, to the statement of a Protestant and conservative tradesman in Sligo, is "an educated and influential man ; he is the mouthpiece of thousands, and there is no other prominent spokesman here of the Nationalist party."

JOTTINGS IN WESTPORT AND SLIGO.

The parish priest at Westport, Father Begley, was a man of moderate but decided views. "There is a great lack of money in this part of the country. But for the collection made a year ago by Mr. Tuke for seed, there would have been great distress here. I gave seed to over five hundred people in this parish.

"The landlords, this year, did not look after the people. In this parish Lord Sligo forgave the rent to many poor people, but made no general reduction. Lord Lucan and Sir Roger Palmer did nothing for us.

"Potatoes are good this year, and there is no danger of starvation ; but there is no sale for cattle and corn, and I don't see how rents are to be paid.

"Home Rule would help us, for the different localities would be represented by men who know their needs. Here you have congested districts and a vast amount of unreclaimed lands. Lord Lucan on one estate has some fifteen hundred acres, nominally grazing or demesne land, all uncultivated. If this and similar land were divided among the small farmers so as to give them fifty acres apiece instead of ten, they will be more prosperous and the shops will prosper and Westport will become twice the town it is. A Home-Rule Parliament would promote migration and distribution of land.

"It would also encourage factories."

There used to be home industries, I remarked, which have now died out.

"Yes," he replied, "clothes they used to make at home, but now it is cheaper for them to buy at the shops. Protection," he added, "I do not believe in."

A landlord, a most liberal-minded man, suggested some points that are often not considered.

"The country may be purely agricultural, but the inhabitants need not be, for they may share in all the mercantile work of England. You can go from Westport to Manchester for eight shillings and sixpence, and from Sligo by sailing vessel for four shillings. It is as easy to go from here to Yorkshire as it is from Kent. Some years ago I had a man here whom I employed with a horse and cart during the winter, while during the summer he used to work in England. I helped him off to Scotland with his people. In two years he was back again. He said he had to pay so much for lodging, board, and coals, that he found himself better off here earning seven shillings a week than in Scotland at fourteen shillings, and that he made more going there every summer than staying there all the time.

"You speak of the condition of Ireland as peculiar; that the tenants have no resources but the land, and cannot protect themselves in any bargain with the landlords. That may be so, but how does that apply to the large farmers, who must have a large working capital? These men are shrewd and as able to take care of themselves as any people in the world, yet the government fixes their rents. One of the earliest cases in court was that of a man in the centre of Ireland who was paying £800 a year, and he got his rent reduced to a little over £600.

"Under the Land Acts a tenant now can do what he likes. A place called Thornhill, between Westport and Lewisburg, was let by Lord Sligo to a friend, a Mr. Garvey, in the Board of Guardians. The property was let for £55 a year, the valuation being £91, and under a twenty-one-year lease. On its expiration the widow of Garvey went into court and got a fair rent fixed at £67 10s. Lord Sligo appealed, and though their valuer valued the land at £90, the Commissioners fixed the rent at £75. No claims were made for improvements. For many years Mr. Garvey was unable to stock the farm, and farmed it only by *conacreing* it and by taking in grazing cattle. A farm has seldom been so ill-treated. Mrs. Garvey again got into arrears, and finally gave up the farm to Lord Sligo. It is now let to two solvent tenants in common for £100, and they pay and prosper.

" There is no trade or profession in the world, but some people break down in it ; *a fortiori*, there must be many break-downs where the people are poor and dependent on the changes of a cold, northerly climate. Since 1879, a bad year, the evictions have been few in comparison with the number of broken-down tenants. Before that, when a tenant broke down, the landlord often gave him some assistance to go, and allowed him, as a very general indulgence, to sell the good-will of his holding. The neighbors, who generally bought, were better off, and the evicted tenant got on well in America when he could n't here. These broken-down tenants are now accumulating ; and the League does not let them sell.

" If there were no question of eviction, the broken-down men would remain, without paying any rent, without selling, and in poverty ; so if they are to go and try to mend themselves in another business or on a smaller farm, the first move must be made by the landlord.

" Things have come to such a pass now that peasant proprietorship is to be desired. It is, however, a question of great intricacy. What is the price to be ? How is it to be paid, in cash, or notes, or a promise with security, or a promise that will never be kept ? If you speak of a county or local guaranty, I should refuse to sell, for I have some chance of getting a little money if I hold the land, but I shall certainly get nothing from the county. You have no right to force a landlord to sell, unless he is to get cash, for otherwise you in no respect improve his condition. For a purchase scheme an advance of money by the imperial government is essential ; and a county guaranty, which to an individual would be worthless, would be effective when given to the government. It would require only an extension of methods already in practical use. In the case of loans for county buildings the government has the first claim on the rates before any officer receives his salary. Where money is borrowed for the purchase of seed, the local government board can impound the money wherever they find it. There is a system known as 'imperative presentments,' to secure the repayment of loans for the support of extra police. If there is any failure on the part of the local authorities to put on a levy to cover the charges, the judge of assize is bound to do so on the mere production of a government certificate that the amount is due.

"A Land Purchase bill ought to precede a Home Rule bill, for it would interest the people in the maintenance of law and order. In my opinion that would be the only possibility of Home Rule succeeding.

" The effect of any Land Purchase Bill will certainly be to ruin half in number, but not in valuation, of the present proprietors. In the case of small properties the owners' interests will be extinguished, for they are more deeply encumbered even than the large landlords.

" Land Purchase is, however, necessary, for the Land Acts involve most of its disadvantages and few of its benefits. When property had its rights, it had its duties.

Now that the rights are abolished, the duties go with them. Lord Sligo will never come here again. He has shut up his stables and his garden. Few people of means live here now, for they cannot get the little enjoyments they used to."

Mr. Richard Powell, Lord Sligo's agent, was little less emphatic.

"Almost universally the landlords will clear out, for the income from the purchase money will not keep up their places. I know many who would be ruined by twelve or even fourteen years' purchase. Only men like Lord Sligo, who have other resources, will be able to live here. The others will have to strike out for themselves in a new country ; and the old, the feeble, and the women will be very badly off.

"It will be hard to raise money for 'land purchase.' Any local guaranty would probably have to be worked from the Unions, where you already have a clerk and a staff ; many of them are bankrupt now and ought to refuse to guarantee any thing except under compulsion. As a poor-law guardian myself, I should certainly refuse to sanction any guaranty."

"Does n't this conclusion bring the whole matter to a deadlock ? " I asked in some perplexity.

"Certainly," he replied. "That is what has staggered all the statesmen.

"After a Land Purchase Act, something further would be required to stop the agitation for Home Rule.

"Many people expect to get 'protection' under Home Rule, but the English people will not give Ireland Home Rule if they think the result will be the boycotting of their own goods.

"If Home Rule, like Gladstone's, were granted, I am

convinced it would be followed by a movement for separation, and that by a repeal of Home Rule and a return
to the present condition of things.

" My relations with the tenants are friendly. I keep
up a correspondence with many of them in America,
and they tell me how they are getting on and ask for
news.

" From November to June last, there were more evictions in this neighborhood than I remember before in the
same time, chiefly because on Colonel Clive's property at
Ballycran there was a general strike against rent, but
after the eviction they all paid up. In my own case from
all I had ejectments against I took, as I always do, one
half the rent due and gave a clear receipt, as all I want is
to get them squared up.   All but two are now in as caretakers.   We leave them in as caretakers till they have
saved their crops, and then, in three or four months,
they have to go, but in the meantime a great many pay.
I give the others then a few pounds and let them go.

" I seldom have trouble with the people, but they are
sometimes singular.   I have known men with money
enough to pay the rent, let themselves be evicted, and
put up shanties by the side of the road and stick there.

" Colonel O'Callaghan was a great exception to the
general run of landlords, and I think that both he and
Lord Clanricarde might have been juster and wiser if
they had given a good reduction at first.   The fact is
that you cannot deal with the Irish people on business
terms but must use considerable diplomacy."

On the car between Ballina and Sligo, part of the way
I sat next a gentleman who turned out to be a Methodist
minister, born and bred in Ballina—an elderly man, with
a quick, decisive manner.   " The first thing the people

have set before themselves is getting rid of the landlords, and the second is complete separation from England.

"When the Land League was started, there were great positive grievances, though they were largely due to the great competition for land during the good times (1865 to 1878) when men would offer the landlord or his agent double or treble the value of a farm even before it was vacant, and to refuse such offers would have been more than human. Now, there is no excuse for the agitation. It continues, however, and to-day throughout the great part of Ireland there is no liberty. I know many who have been coerced into joining the League, but they would be afraid to have their names known.

"Look at the conduct of the trial of the police at Mitchelstown. Mr. Harrington called one witness a 'murderer,' and forced him to state where he lived, in order, as he said, that the place where a murderer lived might be known to the public. And Mr. Harrington is one of the leaders of the party into whose hands I am asked to entrust my life, my liberty, and my character, and that of my family."

"Will there be civil war," I asked, "if Home Rule is granted?"

"There will be no civil war—that is an exaggeration,—but great discontent."

We were passing one of those enormous stone workhouses, that so often disfigure the most charming Irish landscapes. "That is now three quarters empty," was his comment. "These buildings were erected on a great scale throughout the country between the years 1845 and 1850. The houses and the official staffs remain as large and expensive as ever, and eighty per cent. of the rates go to support them and not the poor. This is a fair ground for complaint."

The minister got off at Temple Bar, and his place was soon taken by a stone-mason, a native of Colloony, a neighboring town. "I don't think Home Rule will do much good" said he. "There has been no employment for us since the agitation began. The landlords who used to give us work have no money, and the other party will never give us any. Sligo is full of workmen and trades-people who say the same thing, and yet Sligo is the best county in Ireland, and there is much harmony here be-tween landlords and tenants, and no crime."

In the town the first shop I entered was a stationer's to buy a newspaper. The shopkeeper was a keen-eyed and sharp tongued old fellow. When very young he had been employed in Kerry on the coast survey, and had afterwards been for many years in the constabulary; a Protestant but not an Orangeman. "I know very many persons," he said, "who would never have joined the League if they were free subjects; they were afraid of injury to their cattle or themselves.

"The old farmers did not believe that the landlords could be forced to reduce their rents, and refused at first to join either the League or the 'Plan.'

"I heard Sexton a few years ago address a meeting here, but it was only tall talk. The landlords, accord-ing to Sexton, had confiscated the property of the ten-ants; their right to get any rent at all was very question-able, and, in any case, the rents had already amounted to the purchase value of the whole land; in equity, then, the farmers might justly refuse to pay any rent and not excessive rents only. All this stuff went right down the throats of an uneducated and gullible people.

"In talking about land purchase, I have often said that the purchase money would be advanced by the

government, and have been answered, even by intelligent
people, 'Ah, but it has been paid long ago.'

"In 1882 I went down to County Leitrim on business.
A widow there, Mrs. Moore, whose second husband had
just died without children, wished to sell her farm,
and join her only son in Boston. She had nine acres of
very wet land. The poor-law valuation was £10, and
the rent had been reduced from £13 to £10 10s. The
tenant right of the farm brought £240, after deducting
five per cent. for the auctioneer's fees and £10 for a
year's rent then due on it.

"By the Land Act I think it must be admitted that
the whole of Ireland has been thrown into a state of
hocus-pocus confusion.

"A majority of the people are in favor of Home Rule,
and a very large majority of the shopkeepers, who are
three quarters of them Catholics. There is, however, more
toleration here than in most places, and we have a Protestant mayor and a Catholic majority in the corporation.

"In the harbor there is a fair run of shipping, and
steamers from Glasgow and Liverpool, for we supply the
counties of Sligo, Roscommon, and Leitrim. A grant
was given for a quay some time ago, but the money was
lavished and the quay is left unfinished."

A DAY WITH A POPULAR LAND AGENT.

The property of Lord Clancarty comprises some twenty-
five thousand acres in and around Ballinasloe. The town
itself is neat and thriving, with about five thousand inhabitants. Here there are no manufactures, but the
annual fair of Ballinasloe is the most famous in Ireland.
In the fat years of the seventies, in the early days of
November, ninety thousand sheep and twenty thousand

oxen were often penned in the extensive fair grounds. Now the opening of Connaught by the railroad, and the multiplication of fairs, has reduced the number to a third, but still the farmers swarm here from all parts of the country and for a week every bed in the town is taken at a pound a night.

The late Lord Clancarty was a well-known philanthropist. His son is obliged by ill health to spend much time on the Continent, but is generally in residence from October to February. In his absence the tenants are not neglected ; the labor bill never falls below fifty pounds a week, and the agent, Mr. Edward Fowler, represents the landlord on the Grand Jury, the Board of Guardians, the Board of the Asylum, and the Agricultural Society. Mr. Fowler was once a railroad engineer, and afterwards studied land agency under Mr. Trench. A tall, sturdy, handsome country gentleman, his frankness, impartiality, and fairness have won him the general respect of the people, and enabled him last year to defeat with ease the attempt to start the 'plan of campaign' on the property near Loughrea. The tenants are now all paying their rents as well as ever, except, he said, " the bad lot under the influence of the agitators, and they won't pay even 'judicial' rents."

A long drive with Mr. Fowler over the estate let me see the country as it looks through the spectacles of a land agent. For a few moments, perhaps, I can lend them to the reader.

"There 's a substantial, two-story slated house. The man who lives there has only seven or eight acres ; it is fair land, but besides paying the rent he has been able to pay interest on £150 he borrowed from the Board of Works to build the house.

"This piece of land used to belong to an old Irish family. The last of the race walked out of the window in a fit of D. T., and the property was bought by Lord Clancarty. The tenants were given places elsewhere ; the land was thrown together, levelled, subsoiled, drained on high Scotch farming principles, and let to a Scotch grazier. The rent was lately reduced by the court to £120, on the ground that the buildings were too large for the property, and the tenants ought not to be charged full value for them.

"This farm I let to an English tenant on English principles, building and mending myself, and I wish I could get more tenants of the same sort on the same terms.

"These are the best tenants about here. They are mostly Scotch or north of Ireland men, who came here when the weaving trade was brought into this part of the country during the last century."

A young fellow passed us. "That is Armstrong, a fellow from Fermanagh. He and his father I brought here myself, as I wanted them to teach the others how to farm.

"All that flat valley was, for months in the year, a lake, and at other times too wet to shoot snipe in. Now the larger part has been drained by Lord Clancarty and let to that Fermanagh man. We made him an English tenant, slating his house for him and making other improvements, and now he has the place in splendid cultivation, and is going to break up more land next year.

"Where those haycocks are was once a lake, marked on the ordnance maps ; the water is now six or seven feet below them, and the drainage was all done by me.

"Six thousand five hundred pounds were borrowed by Lord Clancarty from the Board of Works for main drain-

age and roads, exclusively for the benefit of the tenants ;
and nearly all these tenants whose lands we improved
have gone into court and got from ten to fifteen per
cent. reduction.   As it is we are paying over £300 a year
interest and don't get a penny of it from the tenants.
Indeed, on about five farms the rents have been reduced
to below what they were before we drained them.   Practically, the result of the Land Acts has been to stop all improvements by the landlords, and in future every thing
will have to be done by the tenants and will not be done
as well.   Then, too, till 1881 we commonly gave the
tenants timber and slate for building ; but that also we
had to stop so soon as the government began legislating
our property away from us.   If we could have foreseen
what has happened, our best plan would have been to
take up the land from the tenants twenty years ago, improve it ourselves and let it now on judicial leases.

" This is the Manor Mill.   It was let with twenty
acres on lease at thirty-seven pounds a year.   When the
lease fell in, the rent was not raised, although meanwhile
we had deepened the stream and drained the neighborhood at an expense of £600, besides making a new dam
and altering the wheel from an overshot wheel to a low-
breast one.   The miller died before signing an agreement, as he had promised, authorizing us to make these
changes for a consideration of £150, the average profits
for the time the mill had to be closed.   His niece, Mrs.
Sellors, refused our terms and brought an action against
Lord Clancarty for £2,000 damages for injury done to
the mill and the watercourses, which experts swore were
vastly improved.   She swore she had nothing but the
mill to live by, but got only £150 and costs.   The year
after, she went into court about the land, and swore she

lived by the land only, and the mill was worth nothing; the sub-commissioners reduced the rent to £27. I appealed and got the rent reinstated at £37, and last winter the mill did more work than for twenty years past.

"Shanvolly, here, went into court with my permission. I thought he was too highly rented, but wished the reduction to be legally made.

"In the neighborhood of this farm we spent £1,500; that sum has been almost a total loss. No interest was allowed the landlord by the court; the rent was reduced from £42 3s. 8d. to £38 10s.; the value of the tenant right was fixed at £100; and the farm was sold at that with all our improvements."

We came now to the farm of James Ryan, which Mr. Foster had come to revalue by request of the tenant. The sheds were dilapidated, with a tumble-down roof, and the house had most of the window panes broken and seemed deserted. At last Ryan appeared—a middle-aged man, with a pleasant, open face. "This farm," he said, "was taken in the bad times of '48 and '49, at £16 a year. Then £8 was put on on account of the drainage undertaken by the landlord, and a lease for two lives was given to my father, who succeeded his uncle; in due time he built this house," a substantial two-storied building, "and died over ninety years old." With another little farm Ryan has a hundred and forty acres. His father in his day made money and was able to buy land for his other children, but Ryan claims to have lost "some £1,000 since the bad times began in 1879." He keeps very little stock—only four milch cows, two yearlings, and three calves; and so far as I could see, he was a very indifferent farmer. The thistles looked as though they were cultivated intentionally, so thick were they, and so tall and stout. "Sometimes," he said, "I cut them, but most times not. When the cows get them in the hay they eat them just as greedily." The potato field was full of weeds, a sort of wild buckwheat. But, most characteristic of all, were the gates. A cart, with one wheel off, and some loose sticks, like an extem-tempore barricade, formed the gate of the road to the house, and a pile of stones surmounted by a branch of a tree, with bundles of furze stuffed in the interspaces, the gate to the field opposite.

While Mr. Fowler was pacing the land, from time to time consulting his map, and prodding the earth with his stick, Ryan lingered and chatted.

"Lord Clanricarde's property at Loughrea," said he, "is fair land, and I don't much believe in the Plan of Campaign there or anywhere. The best thing is for each man to make his own 'plan' for himself. As to Lord Clancarty's property, in spite of the low prices, I would sooner put money into it than take it out.

"If we are to have 'Land Purchase,' I believe in pay-ing a fair price for it. It is, however, very hard to de-termine the value of land. It is chiefly guesswork. If the purchase money is advanced by the government, they ought to charge us not more than two and a half per cent. interest, or it will be as hard for us to pay as the rent. Such a loan cannot be absolutely secured, for if the farmers don't pay and force is used, there will be a regular revolution."

We drove back to Ballinasloe by a circuitous road, passing through one townland where no one has paid any rent for two years. Here lives a widow, Biddy Dolan. Her husband had been found many years ago in occupa-tion of a little hut on a strip of bog, two miles off. He was, probably, a squatter ; and as no holding was wanted there and the hut was an eyesore to the tidy agent, a high rent, £3 9s. was imposed on the five Irish acres, to drive the man out.

"I want the woman to give the place up," said Fowler, "as I don't care to have such a wretched spot on the estate ; it is tumbling down, and not occupied for any purpose ; no rent has been paid for over two years and none ever will be."

"Biddy," he called out, "Biddy, come here ! I want you to let me take up that place of yours down in the bog, and then Lord Clancarty will forgive you the arrears on it. Over eight pounds you owe us, and you know you can't pay it."

"Shure, your Honor, I 'll keep it till I die, for half the rent."

"I don't think it would be wise for you to keep it for that."

"Shure, your Honor," the son joined in, "the money all went for nothing. It was not able to produce enough to keep the house thatched."

"I know it."

"Give it to me for what your Honor thinks it is worth," cried Biddy.

"I don't want any such tenancy on the property ; it is no ornament to the estate, and no benefit to you."

"Lord Clancarty has had a lot of money for the place," said the son, "and it is not worth sixpence an acre."

"I honestly don't believe it is," the agent admitted.

"My man had it ; and I won't give it up till the Lord calls me."

"You will never make a pound off it."

"I know I won't, but I am tight for land here, and shure I might feed a little baste on it."

"You don't live on it," shouted the agent as a parting shot. "You do nothing with it; it would n't feed a rat; it is a mere strip of snipe bog, and the roof has fallen in. But if you are unreasonable the sheriff will have to see to it."

"It would cost us £2 10s.," he continued, turning to me, "to get a decree, and it would n't be worth that. I shall let it alone now, and report the matter : I don't want a person who does n't live on the estate keeping a claim there for the purpose sometime of raising a flame. I shall probably get a decree at Petty Sessions, and then, if she ever does put 'a little beast' there I can seize it and bring her to terms."

Half a mile farther on we passed a neat little house and farm. "Here is where Kelly lives, a very different sort of person from his next-door neighbor. An industrious man, he pays as much rent as the others, and is never behindhand, and yet has made money enough to buy more land. Killeen, the neighbor, has n't paid any thing for two years.

"In the house opposite, there lives a great, big, brawling fellow. He paid no rent, and in his cups used to say that if ever I came near him he would do something for me." The day I heard it, I went there. He came towards me with a reaping hook in his hand. I sat down on the side of the ditch and began to talk to him. Finally I said : 'Now throw that thing down and shake hands.' He did so, said I was n't a bad fellow, promised to pay up, and kept his promise."

Nearer Ballinasloe is a fine property of some three hundred acres, which Lord Clancarty purchased just

before the Land Act of 1881, at the large price of
£11,000, about thirty years' purchase of the existing
rental. "If he were selling this to the government to-
day," said Mr. Foster, "he would probably not get over
eighteen years' purchase at a pound an acre. See what
utter ruin the government is bringing on the landlords.
I have spent £100 in levelling the fences and making a
new drain on this land, and we wont let it to tenants except in conacre so as to keep it out of the Land Act."

We were thus naturally led on to talk about Land
Purchase. Lord Clancarty will in any event be a large
proprietor. The mansion, the demesne with its thousand
acres, the estate we were looking at, the town and its
appurtenances, will remain his property to keep or sell
as he likes, and the rest the tenants will, probably, be
forced to purchase. A general valuation of the whole
country Mr. Fowler thought necessary. "I, with assist-
ants, could value Lord Clancarty's twenty-five thousand
acres," he suggested, "in six months." The present
commissioners he thought incompetent. "They are, as
a rule, impecunious men of the farmer class, of no standing or experience." No light was thrown on the vexed
question of payment. "Greenbacks on the security of
Irish land, the interest to be paid by the farmers, would
be worthless." In general he seemed pessimistic. "The
expropriation of the landlords," he said, "will be ruin to
shopkeepers. The country will go back a century. I
thought of going away this year."

A DAY AND A NIGHT WITH NATIONALISTS AT BAL-
LINASLOE.

Purtil, the President of the League, I found in his
grocery, an amiable man who prides himself on his mod-

eration. "Lord Clancarty," he admitted, "we don't call a bad landlord. The rents have come down as they are from generations. Here and there we find people who have been tenants so long that they are unwilling to go into court, but think they will soon.

"Mr. Fowler is not a bad man, but he wont take advice. I think he would like to see the tenants well off, if he could get at the right way of going about it. I believe there have been some evictions, but not near Ballinasloe. I know no cases of extreme hardship here.

"We find great difficulty in getting Lord Clancarty's tenants to be active in our movement. One reason is they get so much employment from Lord Clancarty, and they are afraid it may cease if they join us. However, they are getting more independent.

"Last January six shillings in the pound were given for that half year, and four shillings for the half year preceding.

"A few tenants went into court when the first Land Act passed and got little reduction. Then when Mr. Fowler was giving as much as thirty per cent., he refused to consider these cases, on the ground that people who went to law should abide the consequences.

"Any Purchase Act from the present government would be badly received. The people think that 'Coercion' will rob a 'Purchase' bill of many of its merits. The farmers, too, will not avail themselves of any act not given as a final settlement. They will wait for something better to turn up. They would rather take a larger reduction now and wait for a final settlement. They remember that the men who went into the land courts early did not get as good reductions as those who waited till later. It does fall in with the views of a great many that there will be no settlement of the land question till Home Rule is granted, but the people will accept a good Purchase Act first, and then will go in straight for Home Rule.

" The townspeople mostly are in favor of Home Rule, and think it would revive trade wonderfully, but the farmers are slow and have to be educated up to it.

" *They* have too much to do *beyond* to look into our local affairs here. That ought to be done by County Boards, but the national desire for a Parliament would lead to further agitation, even if the scheme of County Boards worked well.

" In this town we have plenty of water power, a splendid river running idly by, and if we had a woollen factory here, which I have no doubt would spring up under a Home Rule Parliament, the young people would be employed, and all would be benefited. When things settle down under Home Rule, capitalists will be willing to invest, and then bounties, duties, and exhibitions will encourage manufactures.

" It may be a government by ecclesiastics. What of that? The clergy of this country have ever been faithful guides of the people, temporally as well as spiritually. In no country in the world do they enter into the welfare and happiness of the people so much as here. A priest will do all he can for a parishioner in trouble, and then it will be the man's own fault if he is not lifted. Both priest and bishop are sprung from the people, and there is no reason why they should not lead them right. Their influence is great, bnt the reason is that it has always been used for our good, and to-day the body of the clergy are as true-hearted and able as ever. Not three people in a hundred in Ireland will disagree with me here."

The secretary of the League is Father Costello. His words were strong. "From here to Banagher," he said, "you pass through Pollock's estate, where he evicted seven hundred families; and four miles to the north, in County Roscommon, he evicted fourteen hundred more. East of this, again, another Scotchman, Mathers, evicted five hundred families. North, south and east there extends a decimated plain. Midway between here and Birr, from a little hill that overlooks the whole country-side, you will see not a house except a herd's hut.

"Lords Clancarty and Clanbrook are the best landlords in County Galway. Lord Clancarty never raised the rents, and never exacted the highest rent for a farm when it became vacant: but the Land Commissioners have taken off forty or fifty per cent. in some cases, and his agent has appealed.

"Lord Clancarty has improved the property fairly, or rather this town, where he has erected many fine buildings. His draining operations I don't believe are very considerable. He gets £16,000 a year, and is most of the time abroad. Where are the factories he might have started?

"Sir Henry Burke's father was a good man, he was a good landlord in his way, not exacting the highest penny for his land, and yet as much as forty and fifty per cent. has been struck off his rents in some cases.

"There is a difference of opinion as to the priority of the land question and Home Rule. As a priest, as the government has conceded the principle of 'dual ownership,' I would not question the title of the landlords. That is the Irish moral opinion. Still the English Parliament is not competent to settle the question of compensation; it has not legislated so often for the good of Ireland.

" For a hundred years we have been governed by England. What has she done for us ? We were nine millions ; potatoes and meal would have supported us, and England would not give us that. She has maintained here a dominant oligarchy. Many a farmer could not marry his daughter without asking the agent. If the agent saw a girl nicely dressed, he would often raise her father's rent. The other day one of the Land Commissioners told me he was going to value a farm, and seeing a fine clover field, turned to the farmer, and said : ' Shure, you can't say your land is bad.' He replied : ' Bad luck to that clover field! ' and explained that after he had worked at it a long time and succeeded, the landlady saw it, and made it the standard for the whole farm, raising the rent accordingly."

In the evening at Purtill's store, half a dozen of us sat and smoked our short clay pipes,—Comyn, a farmer ; Egan and O'Connor, shopkeepers ; and Kennedy, the foreman of a quarry.

Egan. " Nothing short of Home Rule will satisfy the Irish people ; but they will accept any Land Bill as an instalment." All agreed.

Comyn. " No matter what the leaders wish, the tenant farmers would accept a Land Purchase Bill as final and give up Home Rule."

Kennedy. " I want whatever Parnell wants, and Dillon —nothing short of that. If I had sufficient force at my back I would clear the whole lot of landlords out of Ireland to-morrow, but that 's impossible. I would be content with nothing short of separation for all the wrongs of the last six centuries,—separation and reparation ; till then I take all our leaders can get. We are as favorably situated as Belgium, with its own king, near

France. Why should n't we have a republic or a king of our own here? I think the majority of the younger men agree with me."

Egan. "If we adopt the action of our leaders now, how can we, as honest men, take Home Rule except as a final settlement?"

O'Connor. "If we cannot get Home Rule now except as a finality, are not we right in pretending? The biggest rogue is the best politician. Take Gladstone. His speeches are inconsistent, and he is our model."

Purtill. "Would the country accept Gladstone's bill as final?"

Omnes. "That is the question."

Purtill. "That would depend on the financial settlement. We pay on whiskey, our national beverage, a tax one third higher than the English pay on an equivalent amount of beer, their national beverage.

Comyn. "There is a great deal of sentiment still against the connection with England, no matter what the financial settlement might be."

Egan. "Seeing that the people are apparently satisfied with what the members are doing, and the members have accepted Gladstone's bill, we should be satisfied with it."

Kennedy. "The best way of getting total separation is to get partial reparation first."

O'Connor. "If I have an account of £60 against a man, I would accept £30, but should be very slow to give him a receipt in full."

Egan. "Suppose the man said, 'Will you take ten shillings in the pound as payment in full?' Ought n't you, on getting the £30, to give him a receipt in full?"

O'Connor. "If the fellow had gone to court with you,

and you knew he had the money, you would be a fool to do so."

I suggested : " Surely the government has done some generous things. Why else should they have passed the last Land Act ? "

O'Connor. " That was in deference to Russell and not to Parnell. There were too many lease-holders in Ulster."

" Where will the Home-Rule Parliament get money ? " asked I.

Purtill. " From the English people."

Fallen (a shopkeeper and farmer, who had just come in). " Even if my wages were less under Home Rule, I should still cry out for it. Our Parliament will have the treasury of the country to start industries with."

When I asked how the condition of the west would be improved, he replied : " It is not with the sea-coast people we have to deal, but with inland men like these here."

" Would you accept a constitution like that of Massachusetts, with clauses against the violation of contracts and taking of private property without compensation ? "

" No ! " he exclaimed. " Can we not pass laws for ourselves, without England saying we must not pass a law in violation of contracts ? "

Fallen then said he would tell me his story if I cared to hear it. This is the story :

" In 1846 my father, with five other promising young men, went up to Dublin to buy a farm offered in the Four Courts. He got it for thirteen shillings an acre, a hundred and fifty Irish acres in County Roscommon. In 1863 William Daniel Kelly, the landlord, being a spendthrift and short of money, raised the rent to a pound an acre. The next year, he inveigled the tenants, under a threat that some Scotchman would come in and turn the whole into sheep-walks, into taking out leases. We had to pay £30 for the lease, which was for thirty-one years, or three lives, at £1 2s. an acre. Up to 1876 we found no difficulty in paying our rent, and my father brought up a large family—ten of us. He built a house and offices, made a boundary fence, or 'mearing,' and drained it. In 1873 I went into ironmongery here and served my five years, being supported by my father. In 1876 my eldest brother emigrated to America, and the next year two sisters. In 1880 an elder brother married and got £150 with his wife. He had his portion of the farm set off to him, sixty acres ; a house was built for him, and he took a mare and foal at £20, two heifers and twenty sheep at £50, a cow at £12, and £30 was allowed for the house. His wife's fortune soon went, and in 1886 he was totally without capital, and was on the eve of eviction for one year's rent. I had saved some money by that time and paid the rent, becoming tenant myself. Last year I paid a second year's rent, partly out of my savings ; and now another is due. How am I to pay it ? It may drive me to desperation—it may drive me to the Devil !

" The farmers are quite willing to have the land ques-tion settled first, but if our necks were in the gallows we would n't rest till we got Home Rule. Even with Home Rule we may never get over our feeling for a separate nationality, but our children may."

A " PLAN OF CAMPAIGN " TOWN.

"Go to Loughrea if you want to study the land ques-tion," said a casual acquaintance at Clifden. " There

the ' Plan ' is in full blast. In 1881 and 1882 the foundation for the agitation was laid in blood. Within a
circuit of six or seven miles there were eight or nine
agrarian murders. At Woodford, on the property of
Lord Clanricarde, who also owns Loughrea, March
twelvemonth, Finley, a process-server, was shot dead in
the wood while cutting timber. He was an old Crimean
soldier, and his widow went down to the village and
cursed the Catholic curate, who was an officer of the
League. The police had to bring a coffin from a distance
of fifteen miles to bury him.

"There were about a dozen evictions near Woodford
about a year ago, and so great was the excitement that
the sub-agent and all the wood-rangers on the estate re-
signed their places simply from fear.

" In the present agitation there have been many murders ; for boycotting proves a very efficient weapon, as
there is a wholesome recollection of the outrages that preceded it. A man who lives in a wild, remote spot in the
country, and gets a letter threatening him with the fate
of Blake or of Finley, if he persists in a certain course,
must be a brave man to hold out."

These remarks I had in mind as I drove to Loughrea,
the town of the " gray lake," through an interesting country, twenty-two miles from Ballinasloe.

The town itself is decayed and wretched. I counted
over twenty ruined houses. Few people were moving in
the streets, the shops looked as though a purchaser was
unknown, and the hotel as though no guest had rung a
bell there for a year. Constables were strolling in twos
and threes wherever one turned. One, a sergeant, spoke
about the outrages :

" Mr. Blake, an agent of Lord Clanricarde, and his

driver, were shot, a short quarter of a mile from town, as they were driving in on a market day.

" Mr. Burke Rihassane, a landlord, near Castle Taylor, and Corporal Wallace who accompanied him, were shot in open daylight, while returning from Gort ' Petty Sessions.'

" Dempsey, for taking an ' evicted ' farm, was shot at Hollypark, on his way to mass, about ten o'clock in the morning.

" Dogherty was murdered for land-grabbing, at night, in the yard of his own house, at Carrigar.

" Sergeant Lintan was shot in Church Lane, nearly opposite the church here, about nine o'clock in the morning, because he was too sharp after the publicans.

" There were several persons tried for these murders, but no evidence could be got, and no one was convicted, except in the case of Dogherty's murder.   Two men were sentenced to be hung for that, but they were remanded and are now in jail."

James Kennedy, who is famous as the first man in the town who paid his money into the " Plan of Campaign " fund, was standing in the doorway of his shop, a spirit grocery, like a sentinel on duty.   " I am standing here," he said, " on the look-out, to give warning in case any one pounces on us.

" Two hours ago, there was a sale of shop goods, across the way, belonging to John Bowese.   He can pay well, but we are all on a general strike.

" Loughrea is in a state of siege.   Sometimes we have three hundred police here, and then they are cut down to forty or fifty.   It was once a prosperous town, before the crops failed and the cattle and sheep died from some kind of disease.   It was a centre of grazing, but that has

been ruined by American competition. Our only industries, are the 'awl' and the 'needle.' Every thing
now is at a deadlock, and I don't believe six houses in
the town are self-supporting, far less making any rent.
The town is in a state of semi-bankruptcy.

" We pay ten shillings in the pound taxes.

" The rental of my house and six acres of land attached
to it, is £27 10s. My license costs £10, and the rates
and taxes for the year are £8 10s. During the eight
months past I have n't made the taxes from my business.
This year my land which I let in conacre did not bring
me in the rent and taxes.

" Last October, Lord Clanricarde offered us twenty
per cent. reduction, but we wanted forty per cent., though
we would probably take thirty per cent. Then we struck
against him completely, and he has not got a penny from
us since except by seizures. We all paid a half year's
rent under the ' Plan of Campaign,' less eight shillings in
the pound. I and a dozen others are fighting the battle
of fifteen hundred tenants. Lord Clanricarde wants to
keep up his rental in order to have a good basis for selling under a Land Purchase Act. He 's a limb of perdi-
tion, seizing and evicting and doing every thing he can
to annoy us. He seems to be entirely callous. There
is no sign of surrender yet on either side.

" Every sod and house in the town belongs to Lord
Clanricarde. This part of his property is worth about
£20,000 a year to him, and we have n't seen a Clanricarde
here since the old marquis died twelve or thirteen years
ago.

" There have been no outrages here since the shooting
of Blake. The outrages then were caused by ' landlordism.' The policeman who was shot was shot for his

officiousness in attending Land-League meetings as a government spy.

"P. Sweeny is president of the 'District Organizing Branch,' which has charge of offiences against the League. How do they punish offenders? By not speaking to them, by not dealing with them, by avoiding them in the market-place, in town and country, and leaving them to the indignity [*sic*] of their neighbors. This has a good deal of effect. At least a couple of tenants have been forced to give up farms they had grabbed.

"Tullahill farm, eighty or ninety acres, was held by a brother of mine, who gave it up because the rent was too high. Another man went in and took it over the heads of the town people, who wanted it for a town park, for the accommodation of milch cows. The new man was of course obnoxious to the people and had to give up the farm, which Lord Clanricarde finally had stocked and kept by the Land Corporation.

"The agent, his bailiffs, and emergency men get no supplies from the neighborhood, and the soldiers have to keep a shop of their own in the barracks."

Land purchase he strongly approved of. "I consider," he said, "the farmers would be willing to buy for any reasonable price."

A more detailed account of the causes of the agitation here was given by the Catholic Administrator, Father Cunningham.

"The trouble has been going on since the Nolan election, about 1876, in the life of the old marquis. The rents were raised then because the tenants would not vote for the landlord's man. Blake was the agent. The times were good, and he put on all the rent he could. Such tenants were the first to go into the land courts;

and then, owing to Lord Clanricarde appealing the cases
and pressing them, they found they could get no justice
from the courts or the landlord, and took to the wild justice of revenge. The other outrages were due to much the
same circumstances.

"In 1879, owing to the famine, the tenants were unable to pay the full rents. The Land League started here
in 1880. In 1881 the Land Act was passed, and great
relief was expected from it ; but those who went into
court then got only about five per cent. reduction, and
that was not enough, though it brought the rents down
to about Griffith's valuation. That valuation, however,
was unusually high on the Clanricarde estate, because in
1858, when it was made, this was a great wheat-growing
country, and wheat was high ; now wheat is very low,
and the wheat lands have been turned into pastures.

"Lord Clanricarde appealed from all the judicial
rents, and that deterred others from going into court.
But after Blake was shot, in 1882 and 1883, there was a
sudden jump in the price of cattle and sheep, and for a
while the rents were pretty fairly paid. When prices fell
again suddenly, the farmers had to sell off stock on a
falling market to meet the rent, and that impoverished
them greatly. Every half year, Joyce, the new agent,
instituted legal proceedings to recover the rent, and that
impoverished the tenants still more, for they had costs
to pay.

"Last August twelvemonth, six tenants were evicted
and some twenty others writted who have not yet been
disturbed. Some of them were only a year and a half
in arrears. Whenever the amount due was over £20,
Lord Clanricarde brought suit in the Superior Court, so
as to carry £10 costs. A company of soldiers and a

number of police were here, and it took weeks to get
into one house.

" In October, last year, Lord Clanricarde offered, without solicitation, a reduction of twenty per cent. to those
agricultural tenants who had holdings under £50 valuation and who had not gone into court.   The tenants rejected the offer, and none has been made since.   A number of them would have accepted if the evicted tenants
were reinstated, but the majority did not think the reduction sufficient, though twenty-five per cent. all round
would have been taken.

" The Plan of Campaign was then adopted.   The shopkeepers, of course could pay, but they said they would
fall in with the rest, as they lived on the people.   Many
of them were writted last Christmas, and within the last
fortnight the new agent has made a number of seizures
of shop goods.

" The government has suppressed the League here, because, I suppose, of the intimidation.   There has been
intimidation, without doubt, but no serious outrages of
late.

" In the end, Lord Clanricarde can get the rent from a
certain number by proceeding as he is doing, but from
more than half he will never be able to get the full rent,
and he won't be able to evict them without a great
scandal.

" Peasant proprietorship must come in time ; I don't
care from which party, but when it does come I think
the people will lose their interest in the Home Rule
movement.

" The leaders use the land question as a lever for
Home Rule, and don't want a settlement ; but if a good
bill were introduced the people would not mind them.

The priests will give sounder advice ; and without any advice at all the farmers will look out for their own interests. Then the same feeling which prompts a man to buy land will make him keep it ; he will be as loath to sell as he now is to give it up to the landlord, and landlordism will not spring up again.

" The landlords are few in number and the tenants many ; so of the two, it is better that the former should suffer ; besides, the ruin of the tenants would not benefit the landlords, for they could not make the land pay without them.

" From Home Rule, impossibilities are expected, and changes that will require vast sums of money. A Home Rule Parliament will have no capital and little credit, and the only means of raising money will be by taxation. What the people expect to do is to tax imports, and they argue that that will both fill the exchequer and encourage native industries. The two objects are probably inconsistent."

On the way back to Ballinasloe I stopped at a village, Kilreegan. An old farmer with white hair talked in a loud, good-natured voice.

" Michael Henry Burke, of Ballydoogan Castle," he shouted, " is the best landlord in Ireland. His father was a good one too, and gave good reductions. We pay a good landlord his rents with satisfaction. He was in Texas for four or five years, and our tongues could not express our gladness to get him home.

" In his father's time, if we wanted some timber, whatever we wanted, he never refused us.

" Lord Clonbrook was very popular, but he evicted a man some days ago, and when some of the tenants asked for a reduction, he evicted them.

" Nineteen, twenty, and thirty pounds I have known added to the rents as costs on Lord Clanricarde's property.

" I am seventy-seven, and the corn-crop is the poorest I ever saw, and the meadowing never was so light. The potatoes are good, but the cabbages have failed. We cannot live by the profits of the land."

Pat Gallagher, a tenant of Lord Wallescourt, was standing by :

"I have seven acres, rented at seven pounds, and am now evicted. The tenants asked for thirty per cent., and only fifteen was offered.

" The locality is not able to pay taxes, much less rent.

" What do I do with my land ? Begorra, I can't tell."

Here a workingman broke in with : " We can't get any work. Half a day, during the harvest, and during the winter nothing but an odd day or two. The farmers are too poor to give us work ; they could n't if they owned their holdings."

GWEEDORE—AN EVICTION.

TWENTY-TWO miles from Letterkenny, in the centre of a wild, desolate region, is a large, square, wooden building, enclosing a broad courtyard—this is the Gweedore Hotel. Behind us, on either side of the long, dreary road stretch hills that seem little more than vast piles of loose stones, variegated with patches of bog and grass, black and green-bronzed over with the fading heather ; the desolation unbroken save when a black-faced sheep peers curiously through the low wire fences that reach from rock to rock, or where a thin blue line of smoke curls from a tiny stone hut nestling by a narrow ribbon of potato ridges in the rare shelter of a wind-driven clump of trees. Before us towers that beautiful mountain Erigal, a pyramid of gleaming limestones ; at our feet are neatly trimmed hedges of purple-crimson fuschias, and, when all is still, to our ears the light wind brings the murmur of the neighboring ocean.

This is the property of Captain Hill, the eldest son of Lord George Hill, who in his day was regarded as a model philanthropic landlord.

"He built the hotel," said a business man, a strong Nationalist, who for fourteen years had been familiar with the place. "He tried to encourage neatness and industry by offering yearly prizes to the tenant who kept the tidiest house or who made the best frieze. He was a constant visitor at the hotel, and took the greatest inter-

est in the property. The great wrong he did was to let
the commonage of the mountains to Scotch graziers,
and then to fine the people for the destruction of the
sheep, which was only in part malicious. Except for
this, there was little difference between Lord George
and his tenantry."

To the loss of their ancient rights of grazing the
people attribute their poverty ; but the graziers are to-
day more hard hit by the fall in prices than any other
class in Ireland, and there must be other causes to account for the unquestionable poverty of the people.
The average size of the holdings is not over four acres,
but thirty years ago these small tenants were fairly well
to do, for Gweedore was famous for its lobsters, which
were exported as far as Paris, and the kelp which
abounded all along the coast was extremely valuable.
Now the lobster fishery is exhausted, and the price of
kelp is low. In such a district the pressure of American
competition is severely felt, for the smallest rent cannot
be paid without ready money, and farm produce is becoming more and more difficult to dispose of at prices
sufficient to meet the cost of carriage to the nearest market. The average rent of a holding is twenty-five shillings a year, but even this cannot be collected without
threats and violence. For this purpose some seventy-
five of the Royal Irish Constabulary have been quartered
for the last month in the garrets of the hotel stables. A
resident magistrate and a stipendiary magistrate are
waiting the directions of the agent, Colonel Dobbing,
and in an angle of the road, anxiously watching the
movements of the police, may be seen the sturdy form of
the parish priest, James McFadden, and beside him in
long cloaks Professor Stuart, M.P., and friends.

Colonel Dobbing was the agent of the late Lord Leitrim, who with his driver and footman was murdered
some years ago. To pacify the tenants he was dismissed
by the present Lord Leitrim, and was recently appointed
agent to Captain Hill. "Father McFadden," said my
informant, "protested against the appointment, and the
tenants refused to have any thing to do with him, though
they were willing to pay their rents to Robertson of the
Hotel, or to Hill himself." Until the present Land Act
comparatively few of the tenants were able to go into
court, because so many of them had sublet. In the
spring, several were evicted and were allowed to return
as caretakers on a promise by the parish priest that they
would either pay or go out quietly in six months. Such
at least is Dobbing's account. "Dobbing," said a visit-
ing priest to me as he offered me a seat on his car,
"Dobbing is a descendant of Heppenstal, the 'walking
gallows,' who in '98 used to hang criminals on his own
neck, he was so tall and strong."

Father McFadden is beloved by the people as much
as Colonel Dobbing is hated. About 1872 he was appointed curate in the Rosses, and won a great reputation
for zeal and benevolence, starting the temperance movement and harmonizing the people. A few years later he
was appointed parish priest of Gweedore, the youngest
priest in the diocese, at a place requiring great energy.

Here he built a parochial schoolhouse and decorated
the church. "A stream passed under the church," said
an enthusiastic admirer, "and a few years ago it was
flooded during service. He had to get up and cling to the
altar, and two persons were drowned. Father McFadden
had a new channel dug for the stream on one side of the
church ; and all these things he did with money collected

outside of the parish.   Almost all the people he has now
got enrolled in a temperance society, and he leads them
and protects them in every thing."

Such are the priest and the agent.   It is perhaps not
surprising that, in the words of a magistrate, "Father
McFadden and Colonel Dobbing are like cat and dog.
Dobbing insists on the tenants paying at least half the
costs of the ejectment proceedings, some thing like £250,
in addition to the rent, and that Father McFadden will
never allow."

Soon the long line of constables, in their blue military
uniforms and forage caps, began to move, headed by the
Stipendiary Magistrate, a mild-mannered gentleman with
but little heart in the work, and Colonel Dobbing with a
rifle on his shoulder, a rigid, uncompromising, pale-faced,
and haughty man.   Two miles from the hotel the police
halted by the roadside, while the agent and the magistrate marched slowly up a sloping field to the door of a
little cottage,—a rude stone hut, with one window,
thatched with "scraws" of sod, green with grass and
weeds.   "Here lives Margaret Doughan," said a voice at
my side.   "The rent is fifteen shillings a year for the
cottage and a patch of land, and she has turf from a bog
and grazing on the hillside free.   The landlord built the
house himself at a cost of seven pounds, and now he is
pulling it down. I used to be bailiff here, but for the
last six years have had no dealings with the people.
When I did I found them the best people in the world."

The agent stepped quickly to the door to demand possession, and at that moment Father McFadden ran up to
him, crying out, "I have a proposal to make."

"Will you pay the cash ?" demanded Colonel Dobbing.
"No !"

"Then go ahead," he shouted to the emergency men.

"I offer two thirds of one year's rent, if all arrears are forgiven!" cried McFadden, in great excitement.

"Mr. McFadden, walk off, sir!" shouted the Colonel, now thoroughly aroused. Four or five rough-looking men seize long iron bars and begin striking at the door. In a few minutes it is torn down and discloses a rough barricade or rather a wall of large, flat stones five feet high, and from behind it a shower of hot water issues in a cloud of steam. Several constables now join in the fray and taking shelter under cover of the wall on each side of the door dart forward from time to time, ducking to avoid the water that jets out in intermittent streams, tug at the stones in the doorway, and finally carry them off in triumph as they are loosened by the continuous blows of the emergency men. At last they leap over the ruins and reappear with the still struggling warriors,—an old woman in a patch-work dress of rags, a boy and a girl, and a neighbor called in to assist in the defence of the homestead. This valiant neighbor is—a sturdy young married woman with an unweaned baby at her breast. The contents of the hut are now removed, one by one,— an old bench, a few pots and pans, and some soiled blankets.

The eviction was scarcely over when up jumped Father McFadden and again confronted Colonel Dobbing, and in an instant it became clear that at the bottom of the difficulty at Gweedore was a personal contest for mastery between these two men, the aristocrat and the peasant, both equally sincere and equally uncompromising.

"I am authorized," said the Champion of the People, "to make a most generous offer. I offer, in the name of Professor Stuart here, two thirds of the whole year's rent of the agricultural holdings on the estate, £600 or £700, if all arrears are wiped off and the same reduction allowed for the future."

"I refuse to allow any interference."

"I am sure," retorted McFadden, not uncourteously, "you cannot arrange the affairs of the estate without my assistance. I represent the people."

"I wish to make this offer," interrupted Professor Stuart, gently, "believing I know the condition of the tenants."

"I don't believe you can," was the reply. "You have got your facts from the camp of the enemy. I will discuss the matter with you at the hotel, but not here, and not until these caretakers have given up possession."

"I want to stop the whole wretched business," said Professor Stuart as he turned away sadly.

The agent and the magistrate then went up the hill to another little hut to demand possession, but, on the priest interfering, it was found that the warrant was directed to a widow who had lately died, instead of to her three daughters, who were now the tenants ; and the magistrate descended to the road in disgust, amid the shouts of the bystanders, and marched the constables quickly back again to the hotel.

One of the officials who had watched the scene throughout, expressed what seemed to be the general opinion : "Any settlement almost would be for the benefit of the landlord : for, in the first place, he will get some money down, and then the combination would be broken, and a great many will pay who dare not do so under the 'Plan of Campaign.' The postmistress here, for example, would be glad to pay, for if she were turned out she would lose her situation."

A neighboring hill-top was black with people, watching our doings, for the priest had forbidden them to come any nearer. A mile from the hotel they met us, a great crowd, clamorous and excited. In a moment the priest stopped his car, and was standing on a low stone wall, with the English visitors beside him. In the hush that followed, Professor Stuart began to speak : "I only wish there were a continuous stream of Englishmen coming here. An eviction in England is merely a house-flitting ; it is not so here. Here you have reclaimed the soil and built your house, and are turned out of the holding you have made productive. In England a farm is let with the house and out-houses already built ; here you make the land itself out of the rock, and when you improve it the landlord raises the rent." (A Catholic curate beside me admitted this was not true now.) "When the English people understand that they will turn out Lord Salisbury and bring in Mr. Gladstone.

"I would suggest that if Colonel Dobbing took a sail to Tory Island to-morrow, and then a few storms arose, no one here would feel any particular pain.

"From seven o'clock we have been making offers and they have been refused. I offered to pay the present year's rent, with certain reductions, if all arrears were wiped out, and the evictions stayed. Many an English landlord would be delighted to-day if he got such an offer. These evictions will sound in the ears of England, and it will be said the landlord had an offer and refused it.

"It is a crime to evict, but it is a bigger crime to send people to the workhouse or make them emigrate. It will be sand in the eyes and vinegar in the mouth of the landlords if you build the evicted tenants houses on the land and keep them there."

"I say," continued Mr. Beal, an unsuccessful candidate for M.P. for St. Pancras, London, "I say that any man who says that Home Rule means Separation, says a black and infamous lie. Is it Home Rule you want or Separation?" (A voice: "Home Rule, not Separation!") "I can now say I have seen Irish Nationalists and they do not want Separation.

"Then, again, the smallest outrage will be magnified a thousand-fold by the jealous lenses of the Tory party, so commit no outrages. Those who have justice on their side need not break the law. Let the Tory government break the law, as they did at Mitchelstown."

Up spoke Mr. S., the secretary of the London Liberal and Radical Union : "I have seen the monstrous inhumanity of your landlords : but the Liberal party has put its hand to the plough, and will not draw it back until Home Rule is won. *I want England also to have Home Rule, and London too.*"

Large raindrops began to fall, and the people were dismissed by Father McFadden. "We are about being evicted by the weather. You will keep the principles you have observed the last few days. It is abominable to have these atrocities carried out in a hidden way, and you are justified in attending them. Three evictions remain in the body of the parish. If they come off we will meet to-morrow without fear of the proclamations, which are not worth the paper they are written on. Be satisfied of this.

"The full rents Captain Hill will never be able to obtain : not even with the English fleet by sea and the army by land. It is impossible. And of the costs he will never get one farthing. We will never do the impossible ; we will never do the unreasonable.

"To-day the agent went up the hill to that hut and was going to pull it down without a legal warrant. That is the sort of man you have to deal with. In our absence he would ride rough-shod over the people."

The rest of the speech was in Irish. The meeting closed with cheers for a constable who, the day before, had refused to obey an order to load.

From Father McFadden some further facts about these evictions were obtained. Margaret Doughan, evicted to-day, had been evicted before, and was in as caretaker. Her rent was twenty-five shillings, and the legal costs were £4 17s. 4d.[1]

Seventy-three tenants had gone into court to get judicial rents fixed. The rents due from sixty-nine of these tenants amounted to £156 4s. 1d., which arrears brought up to £235 4s. 3½d., and the rental fixed by the court was £95 6s.

In the evening a neighboring farmer was talking about a proposal made by Father McFadden to buy the property for ten years' purchase of two thirds of the annual rent. "I would give twelve years' purchase of a fair rent, but not over ten years' purchase of the present rents, which would make our annual payments forty per cent. of what we pay now. I can't make more than that.

"Many of the people, though, will not be satisfied with any thing. They seem to want the landlord to plough the land and pay them for digging the potatoes.

[1] Sheriff's fee when the writ was lodged, . £1 1s. 6d.

Execution fee . . . . . £1.

Costs in court : solicitor's fee . . £2 15s. 10d.

"The cause of the agitation is simply that prices have fallen to half what they were. Five years ago, in 1882, the people would have been glad to give twenty years' purchase of the land, now they would hardly be satisfied with ten.

"Good landlords are treated now no better than the bad, because before the Land Act they all acted as a body, whenever the tenants tried to improve their position, and because since the Land Act, instead of being as kind to their tenants as before, the good landlords have become stubborn and enforced all their legal rights to the utmost, until they have all the tenants set against them.

"The settlement of the land question would not stop the agitation for Home Rule, but it would take the edge off it. One has been the feeder for the other. We are bound up with England, and would be injured by any thing like separation.

"My hopes for the future rest on the fact that the people are gaining so rapidly in intelligence and education, and that the things that in the past caused ill-feeling are disappearing, and will be avoided in the future."

ABOUT FALCARRAGH.

Falcarragh, or Cross Roads, is a little fishing village on the bleak Donegal coast, opposite Tory Island, one long street of two-storied, slated, stone houses. These houses were built twenty years ago, when times were good, and give the place an air of prosperity that is perhaps misleading. So at least Father Stephens seemed to think, the sturdy, athletic young curate, who has since been imprisoned under the "Crimes Act."

"Five or six years ago," he said, " £1,000 a week was

paid in this parish for bog ore. The carters used to spend their money freely, and as many as ten ships at a time were owned here in this one industry. That business has died out.

"The kelp trade also is going. Kelp once fetched £3 a ton, instead of thirty shillings, and now there is only one buyer of kelp here where there used to be three or four.

"The fall in prices has further impoverished us. Half the pigs were driven home again from the last great pig fair, for no money could be got for them. Oats that sold for a shilling a stone are selling now for sixpence.

"All the men here go to Scotland as harvesters, and the price of labor has fallen. The children over ten years of age go out to service to the farmers in the Laggan, the grazing district between Letterkenny, Lifford, and Derry. The children are sent in droves to the spring hiring-fair at Letterkenny, and the farmers, Scotch Presbyterians, examine them as they would animals, and pay for them according to their condition.[1]

"The landlords here were very niggardly. Twenty years ago there was n't a church or a school in the town, for the landlords would n't give us land to build on. Finally one gentleman, Daniel Sweeney, twelve years ago, gave us land for a schoolhouse and a church too, and he was so boycotted by the neighboring gentry that he had to go away.

"The great act of tyranny was the taking of the mountain pastures from the people. They used, from time immemorial, to send their beasts to the mountains; but thirty years ago the landlords combined to take the

---

[1] Such hiring-fairs were once common throughout the country, and even in England. They are simply the survival of an old custom.

mountains from them and let them to Scotch graziers. Many of the sheep disappeared, probably from the severity of the weather, for it is the custom here to winter the sheep in the kitchens. The landlords then applied to the grand juries to have taxes assessed on the county for malicious injury, and thousands of pounds were taken from the poor people, who have not yet recovered.

"We want Home Rule, for that will develop our industries. What is needed is capital. No one will invest now, but as soon as the agitation ceases, as it will under Home Rule, money will come here in abundance."

After service in the beautiful large stone church, I went to the weekly meeting of the National League, in a large barnlike room. Father Stephens presided over an assembly of earnest-looking farmers. Resolutions were adopted sympathizing with the tenantry of Gweedore; and then the good Father urged all present to file without delay notices under the new Land Act, and gave advice to all who asked it, usually farmers served with writs, who did not know what their rights were or what to do.

For a long time we sat and chatted. Said one farmer, like the rest in rough, warm home-spun : "Children from seven to ten years old go to Letterkenny for from sixteen shillings to a pound for the six summer months. There is not a man here who has n't been through this."

"Olphert, the landlord here," chimed in another, "would not give any land for a church, and would n't allow any house in Falcarragh to be used for a school."

"The people here usually wear *lapins*, stockings without soles."

"We have n't any coin at all here most of the time; for six months in the year the only currency is eggs."

George Brewster owns the hotel and several houses. I asked him how Falcarragh came to look so prosperous ? "Why," said he, "some years ago I made as much as £1,200 from the bog ore, which is now all used up. Many of these houses were built then. With few exceptions, however, American or Australian money builds the houses in Ireland. That pine house with the Welsh tiles was built by a man who is indeed a publican, but he got the money to build it from his brother in Australia."

"Ah !" said an old farmer, "a farm by the sea-shore that could pay £25 a few years since cannot make £15 rent now. Flax is £2 1s. a hundredweight. I saw it sold for thirty shillings last Friday in Letterkenny, and in 1860, at Cookstown, I saw seventeen shillings paid for a stone. Corn used to be sixteen shillings a stone ; it is now from four to six shillings. I have two cattle I bought seven months ago for £12, and if any man will give me £10 for them now he can have them, though the six months' grass is worth at least thirty shillings."

The next day muffled horses were being walked up and down the street by diminutive jockeys, and the little town was crowded with excited farmers and fishermen, for it was the day of the autumn horse races. The races were announced to take place in a large level field offered by Mr. Olphert ; but early in the morning the crowds were addressed by Father Stephens and Father McFadden of Gweedore. "The landlords must be boycotted," they shouted ; "the races must be run on the shore, and twenty pounds of the League funds will be given as prizes." The jockeys cursed, but obeyed, and the horses galloped and slipped on the broad, flat sands, where the sea-water lingered in an infinity of pools and runlets, while the people cheered lustily—weather-beaten Tory-

Islanders, farmers in gray home-spun coats, and women with picturesque red shawls and petticoats. In the evening pandemonium reigned, and "poteen."

Such a jolly, stout, rosy-faced fellow was McCarthy, now on his third trip through Donegal this year, a drummer for tea, sugar, drapery, spirits, and cordials, and to crown all, a life insurance agent as well. "I know every man, woman, and child in Donegal," he cried, as he slapped me on the back. "Up with your bag on my car, and off with me to Creeslough." Away we drove, up hill and down, by bleak inlets of the sea and stony valleys, every view dominated by Muckish, that lumbering mountain, with its "pig-shaped back" capped with snow. Hail fell viciously as we passed a great stone workhouse, and reached neat, picturesque Dunfanaghy.

"This country is rich in natural wealth," said the drummer, as he flicked meditatively at the pony's tail. "In Erigal there is indigo, good for making blue-balls and for dyeing the cloth the natives weave. Silver is found there too. In Muckish there is some of the finest flint-glass sand in the world. The gray and red granite there is equal to Aberdeen granite. Only Mr. Olphert's exorbitant demands prevented a London company from building a tramway to get it. How the country would be benefited by granite works, for the pottle needed for the polishing would make a distillery profitable!

"All along the coast is found Carrigan moss, used medicinally, and in Germany turned to account in finishing collars and linen fronts. There is a buyer of the moss in Derrybeg, who ships it to Derry and thence to Germany.

" From the kelp on the shore they make iodine and potash, and the refuse does for manure. The importation of iodine from South America has lowered the price, but it is rising now, as that supply is failing.

" The water power of Donegal is so great, and labor here so cheap, that in the manufacture of flannels and tweeds our people could compete with the world ; and the sea-weed furnishes the finest dyes imaginable.

" The fisheries should be encouraged by loans from the government for the purchase of better gear. The fishermen need smacks to go out to the banks, for, with ordinary boats, they have to run in and leave their nets at the least storm."

We are passing now through the beautiful demesne of Stuart of Ards, seven miles from gate to gate. Magnificent forests of oak and fir fringe the road ; and at every turning one catches a glimpse of many-cornered Muckish or of the glancing waters of Sheep Haven, and the bleak coast beyond ; but every thing has fallen into melancholy ruin : the leaves are ankle-deep in the paths ; gigantic trees lie uprooted by the roadside ; while countless gray rabbits are merrily leaping in the thick brown ferns. Past large farm buildings, a little village in itself, we turn up a steep road towards the tiny village of Creeslough. A keen wind blows tempestuously from the Atlantic as we mount the long flight of wooden steps to the hotel of Edward Lafferty, as he stands expectant, twenty-six stone of good-natured hospitality, by the side of a large fuschia bush still in full bloom.

The drummer and the landlord, who is a farmer as well, talked long and earnestly. " The country is really bankrupt," said McCarthy. " Every one is in debt to the banks.

" The farmers borrowed largely in the good times, and put all the money into the land. Prices have fallen since, and now the largest farm does n't make the interest of the money spent upon it. The merchants for years have been supporting the landlords. Here I know all the debts, and the poorer the country is the deeper it is in debt. Along the coast of Donegal there is not a village where there is not three thousand pounds outstanding, and if the farms were sold the proceeds would not meet the indebtedness.

" Stir-about and potatoes are what the people live on. All they buy from the shopkeepers is tea and drapery. The blue cloth cloaks are, indeed, of West of England manufacture, but the friezes they wear about Gweedore are home-made."

" Yes," said Lafferty, " I agree. There is at least £3,000 out in Creeslough and more in Dunfanaghy. The banks have at last become shy of lending, except on the best security. They pay one and a quarter per cent. on £200, and less on larger deposits, and they charge the people seven per cent. for the use of it."

" It is morally impossible," was their conclusion, " for the land now to support the people living on it. No remission of rent will help that, especially where the people have never depended on the land but on kelp-picking and going out to service. In Gweedore the people are not able to live two months on what they get from the land, and it is the same all along the coast. In Donegal the people will never be able to live unless they get employment, but here are fisheries and water-power. Industries must be encouraged by the government ; and in the greater part of the country no good can be done except by protection duties. The same thing is true of England

and Scotland. The expense of labor has been increasing and the price of the product has been decreasing so fast that protection has become necessary.

"Cattle are not paying. Flax has gone down. The people have fallen back on pigs, and they are very low. Pigs are the last resort, the people's little savings-banks. Oats are 4½*d.* a stone, 7*d.* for the best, and they used to be 16*d.* and 17*d.* Sheep sell fairly. The people cannot pay the shopkeepers, who give them a year or more, while they get only three or four months' grace themselves. The big farmers are losing all the time," continued the drummer ; "the only restraining power at present is the medium-sized farms, what a man can cultivate himself without outside labor."

"How large would that be ? " I enquired.

"A man with two sons and two daughters," replied Lafferty, "could cultivate from ten to twenty acres."

"If we had no rent," he said further, "we might live. A mountain farmer with £4, if the potatoes failed, could buy meal for his pigs and be still a pound to the good ; next year he would have more. Two pounds are a great deal to a poor country farmer. In May such a man can often not get a bit of meal, and an extra pound or two would tide him over till the potatoes came. I believe, in time, things will find their own level. No change of government is necessary, except to one that will develop the industries of the country."

The last thing I heard that night was the voice of Mc-Carthy in the next room shouting : " It was a good thing that Gladstone did not buy out the landlords ; the failure of that bill has been the salvation of the country ! "

The next morning early we started again on our rounds. One view was beautiful exceedingly, where from a high mountain road we looked down on the ancient, weather-stained Castle of Dove, seated on the beach of a winding inlet of the sea, with golden strands jutting by it far into the water, behind it yellowing woods, and in front the bare, gray headland of Derg.

On the hillside an old man was digging potatoes ; we called to him and went into his hut to try to sell him some tea. No sign was on the door, but one of the side rooms was a tiny shop, where eggs, butter, pipes and tobacco were lying promiscuously on dingy shelves. "There is coal in this locality," grumbled our host, "but the landlords won't let it be worked, for they claim the mines and all minerals. They can't open them themselves for three fourths of them are bankrupt. The country won't be opened up till we have Home Rule."

"Lord Leitrim has done some good," suggested the drummer. "He built the houses at Dunfanaghy and Creeslough. He made that fine market-place at Creeslough, and started the steamer from Milltown."

But the farmer was in a pessimistic mood. "The steamer has ruined the country. It has encouraged the farmers to sell very cheap. It has left Milltown without a penny. It takes away the little provision of the people. Many a man who has a market is better wanting it. As to the market-place in Creeslough it has done no good, no one used it, and it was n't opened at all this year.

"There is nothing for the laborers to do. A laboring man in Milltown told me the other day he always got employment till this steamer came.

"What is wanted is employment and opportunity to earn money.

"Things are getting worse every year. Land at the

present time is not worth any rent. Flax is the only thing that sells at all. Potatoes are a good crop, but oats are too low to be worth threshing. For eggs we pay only 8*d.* a dozen, and eggs are depended upon to support the house."

"They are shipped to Glasgow chiefly," suggested the drummer, "for they expect larger eggs in England than we raise. Well," he added, "I never found it so hard to get money. Tea is cheap. Can I do any thing for you?"

"I can get good tea at Milltown for two shillings a pound," was the only answer, but the drummer spread out his little packages of samples on the table, and the farmer's wife began to inspect them minutely, rubbing the little black grains between her palms, and biting and sniffing at them with an air of extreme intelligence.

In the next house we stopped at I listened sympathetically to a long complaint about the rights of the tenants to a strip of salt meadow by the waterside, now claimed by the landlord; and thence we hastened to the house of the parish priest, an elderly gentleman, with the most polished and amiable manners in the world.

"Ten acres," he said, as he poured us out some whiskey, "is the average size of a farm about here, including arable and grazing land, but some have only an acre or an acre and a half to two acres and a half arable land.

"Lord Leitrim is the principal landlord, and the rents are high. I, for one, pay £6 7*s.* for six statute acres on Cochrane's property, and for a farm of eight acres near by a widow pays £8 10*s.* I have a right of commonage of ten or fifteen acres on the mountain, but it would n't pay to put cattle there.

"The rents are often kept up by people who come back

from America and pay three or four times the value of the land for a farm to die on.

" The people raise a little oats, flax, and potatoes. Oats and flax are very low ; flax from here sold a fortnight ago for two shillings and eight pence a stone at Letterkenny. Very few use oatmeal ; they usually get Indian meal, and often feed the pigs on it.   A cow or two is often kept.   Cash is got only from pigs and butter and eggs. A little flannel is woven here, but no tweed. There is some fishing of flat fish, sole, and cod, but only near shore and from ' corraghs,' of which some thirty are owned in the parish.

" My people go out to service, not so much to the Laggan as to Milltown and Rathmelton, but only for the summer months. There is not much suffering here, if you think people who live on dry potatoes don't suffer, for few eat butter except in winter, and meat or fowl only once or twice a year.

" The widow who pays £8 10s. is going into court. The landlord offered to make it £6, but I would n't let her accept it, it was too much ; and yet the land is considered good land.   The rents all along the coast would not have been paid for the last twenty-five years but for American money.

Lord Leitrim's steamer instead of doing harm has been useful to this parish.   We had to go to Milltown, fourteen or fifteen miles off, to get a market ; now we have one at our doors.   A chicken used to sell for twopence, now it brings eightpence.

" A Purchase Bill would help the people, but slowly, for what they need is employment, the encouragement of industries, the opening up of the country.   Whether this would be brought about by Home Rule, I don't know.

There is a sentiment in favor of it, but I have no positive opinion. It may be said that our laws are now made chiefly by Englishmen and Scotchmen."

Many were the anecdotes that my companion poured into my willing ears as we drove rapidly along the darkening roads. These are samples :

" On Rutland Island there used to be, before 1848, a sailors' home, salt-pans, a custom-house, and a town as large as Falcarragh, for a great herring fishery was carried on there, and one could pass from one island to another on the decks of fishing vessels. One year not a fish was to be seen, and now fishermen have to go out to sea, outside of Aran Island, beyond the course of the Anchor Line steamers.

" A Major Barton has a property at Greenfield, in Feenit. The charges on it are so great as to leave him little or no surplus now, and as twenty per cent. reduction will probably be taken off under the new Land Act, he could n't live off the land, though even that reduction will give the tenants little enough. The Major is a magistrate, but he is now starting in the provision and whiskey trade, and I have his opening orders.

" Stuart of Ards used to spend an immense amount of money here, and provided much employment, but later on he got into difficulties, through no fault of his own, and now he has n't been seen in the County Donegal for the last twelve years."

It became necessary to say " Good-bye " to my kind, energetic, intelligent friend. " Remember," he said, "that the farmers cannot be bettered so long as present prices continue, even as peasant proprietors, and the only thing that can improve their condition is a protective tariff, which we cannot get until our laws are made by a Home-Rule Parliament at Dublin."

A MANUFACTURER IN COUNTY TYRONE.

As one travels from Donegal to Belfast, the signs of industry seem to increase with every mile of the way. A little village I came to one evening, that was nothing but a large manufactory ; tidy operatives, cottages clustered round an immense flax-spinning mill. The wealthy owner of the mill is a representative Ulster man ; a devoted Gladstonian in the days of the Reform Bill, and now an ardent Unionist, a practical business man, and successful, though still young.   He began by speaking about Gweedore.

" The average rental there is about twenty-four shillings, and yet Father McFadden has made all this row to get off thirty-three per cent., an average of eight shillings a year.   What good would that do them ?

" ' Compulsory land purchase is necessary,' said a Catholic Divisional Magistrate to me the other day, ' to make the tenants settle down in peace.' Now local guaranties alone can make purchase practicable, for only by some such system will any pressure be put on a man by his neighbors to make him pay his instalments. Suppose that in one electoral division there are ten farmers ; if one of them is a defaulter, his default will raise the amount payable by the rest, and it will be their interest to get in a new and a strong man in his place, instead of boycotting any new-comer.   You suggest that a guaranty involves the existence of a surplus fund ; but there is a surplus fund.   The value of the land is made up of the tenants' interest and the landlords' interest, and both together would be clearly a good security for the latter value alone.   If you say that local boards will often refuse to give any guaranty, and that they cannot be forced to, the answer is simple.   Don't let that particular locality purchase.

"Some of the landlords will suffer, but though in the north they are a superior class, in the south and west they are, many of them, a wretched lot, who have incomes of only three or four hundred pounds, and who think of nothing but amusing themselves.

"The landlords acted patriotically in refusing Gladstone's Purchase Bill. They would n't bring the country to ruin for a sop of that sort. There is plenty of land about here worth twenty-two years' purchase, and most of the land in Ireland is worth ten; but there are little holdings in the west, bog and mountain, that it would be criminal to allow the tenants to buy at any price. Twenty-two years' purchase all round was obviously unjust.

"Even with a peasant proprietary, prosperity is not assured. In Eelgium the most fearful rack-renting exists; very short leases are usual there, and just as soon as a small tenant improves, his rent is raised; but the people don't mind that so much, because the new landlords are of their own class.

"The first thing needed is the opening up of the congested districts. The government must do that, whether it pays or not. The government has been too niggardly, and, as in the Light Railway Act, has always exacted the strongest guaranties from local bodies. In opening up the country, the expense ought not to be charged to the localities immediately benefited.

"The desire the people have for protection is very unfortunate. Ireland is not rich enough to consume its own manufactures; we shall always have to depend on our export trade. Under protection the cost of necessaries will be higher, and so the cost of labor. This is a good climate for manufacturing, from its moisture and even temperature, and labor is very cheap. These are our only advantages. Cheap labor enables us to sell all over Europe, as I do; but if we had protection we could n't compete abroad at all. There is so much competition, as it is, that the greatest patience and perseverance is necessary to make any manufacture successful, but the people talk as though they could jump into manufacturing at one bound.

"As business men, we are here absolutely opposed to Home Rule. The Nationalists may want to encourage my business, but every idea I have of justice, honesty, and liberty is opposed to their practices and principles. Our opinion ought to have weight, for what is the value to a country of a lot of uncultivated, ignorant people in comparison with an educated, industrious, manufacturing class. Gladstone's bill was an absurdity in proposing that we should continue to contribute to the imperial exchequer and yet cease to take any part in imperial affairs. We are determined not to allow ourselves to be separated from England. To my mind the whole thing is now completely over. All, except the most ignorant electors, have learnt that we have made up our minds, and that it is impossible to force a division upon two million of the most industrious and wealthy people in the country. The Irish will never get Home Rule without fighting for it, and they don't dare to fight. I feel sure that Ulster would fight, if a Home-Rule bill were passed, and I would join the Ulster men.

"Local self-government is a different thing, and we believe in it. Questions about railroads and water-supplies, and local or private bills generally should be passed upon by county boards, or by provincial boards sitting in the capital of each province. These boards could not be purely elective at the outset, but should be appointed.

"The misery of the west and south is largely due to its being a Catholic country. I do not venture to have more than half my workmen Catholics; if I had more my mills would soon be closed, for the priests would make us stop work on saints' days, and would insist on all the overseers being Catholics by threatening to strike if we refused. Now we are independent of them. The priests do evil that good may come, and join the League, whose principles they detest, for the sake of keeping their influence. The old Catholic curate here told me he disapproved of the League, and yet now he makes Nationalist speeches in public.

"The linen trade is said to be shaky, but in fact more looms are going in Ireland now than ever before, and there is more demand for labor. It is true that the profits of the capitalists are diminishing, but so long as the labor bills are as they were there is no loss to the community."

CHANCE ACQUAINTANCES AT DUNGANNON.

Dungannon is a well-built, attractive town, the centre of an agricultural district, and on that account deserted and dead-and-alive every day in the week except Thursday, the market day. Then the streets are crowded and the shops thronged. In the large square before the Belfast Bank, the farmers range their carts along the cobble stones that line each side of the road; in temporary booths are displayed apples, butter, eggs, crockery, and plaster images, and the contents of the shops are transferred from windows to stands upon the sidewalk,— drapery, joints of meat, and hardware.

"This town is half Catholic and half Protestant," said a clergyman, "and of the latter half are Presbyterians. The lowest stratum is Catholic, the next, chiefly store-keepers, Presbyterian and Methodist, and the gentry and some of the poorest people are Church of Ireland.

"I consider that Gladstone is a traitor, and in old times would have been hung as one. In the event of Home Rule, however, I don't believe there would be more than a riot in Ulster, and not a very serious riot."

"I would die rather than have Home Rule," exclaimed Mr. Black, the genial proprietor of a comfortable hotel, "yet I don't think there will be a real rising in Ulster; and while many rich men will go away, their places will be taken by Americans with money. The evil, however, of Home Rule will in the long run be greater than the good."

"Where I live," broke in a farmer who was listening, "in twelve townlands there are only forty-eight Catholics. How are we going to have Home Rule there? We won't have it."

"We want Home Rule," replied another farmer, "because prices are so low. The Americans are sending us cheap cattle and grain. We want a tax on those things."

In a cosy room, Hursen, the owner of a spirit grocery and Secretary of the League, a neighboring shopkeeper, and Flanigan, an auctioneer and news agent, discussed freely and at great length the condition and needs of Ireland. This was what was said:

"In County Fermanagh the Catholics slightly preponderate, and we expect soon to return all Nationalist members at the next election. In Dungannon the majority of the tradespeople are Unionists, and the same is true of Cookstown, but at Strabane, the largest town in the county, every member of the town council is a Nationalist.

"Home Rule is needed," said Hursen, "to develop our resources, the woollen trade, the fisheries, our rivers and harbors, our railroads, which should be owned by the government, and our waste lands, which should be reclaimed. We also want a final settlement of the land question, and the establishment of a peasant proprietary.

"It is hard to get finality. Suppose our manufactures increase and laborers multiply; they might be much tempted by the theory of Henry George that Davitt preaches. However, popular as Davitt is, the farmers would drag him off the platform if they half understood his meaning."

I asked if the Nationalists would try to make a good purchase bill successful.

"Many farmers," he replied, "would be contented if the land question were settled, and that is why they won't get it settled till Home Rule and Land Purchase are given us together. Home Rule will never be granted unless it is asked for, and it must be demanded with the same persistency and determination. We are not all farmers, remember, and how about the men who are not farmers, who are the cream of the whole country and the leaders of the movement? They will have to be reckoned with. Parnell owes his great reputation largely to his not having formulated the demands of the Irish people. Look at his position towards the Land Act of 1881. If he had accepted it as final, how could he have demanded a revision of the judicial rents this year? He is quite right in throwing on the other side the task of making any Land Act or Purchase Act successful.

"As to the land, I think we have done very well. We

have certainly a tenure superior to any I know anywhere. I do not look on the landlords as a class better or worse than any other class in the country, but landlordism has become unworkable, and a new system must be devised that will involve fewer interests.

"No settlement of the land question will ever settle me. Every thing we want is given us from fear and not by reason. Catholic Emancipation was to avert civil war. The first Land Act was passed from the fear of Fenianism, and the last one to satisfy the Unionists.

"However, we don't object to England because she governs us badly, but because she governs us at all. My position is that we have only one grievance—the government of Ireland by England. That is the whole trouble. The land laws of this country are indeed vastly better than those of England or of any other country. Even Henry George admits this."

"The land laws good!" shouted Flanigan.

> " 'A decent hat, a wife's new coat or gown
>   For higher rent may mark the farmer down;
>   'Neath your cottage window cease to plant a rose,
>   Lest it may draw the prowling bailiff's nose.
>   Beware of whitewash lest your cottage lie
>   A target for the bullet of his eye.'[1]

"That explains why the tenants do not make out of the land half as much as they should; the fields next the road they never used to cultivate as well as the fields at a distance. The lying and dissimulation that these things caused have not been grown out of yet."

"Not a farmer in Ulster," chimed in our third companion, "is able to pay his rents out of the profits of the farm. The land of Ulster has deteriorated more

[1] William Allingham.

than that of any other province, in consequence of the culture of flax. Flax exhausts the soil; it returns no manure to it, and in the linseed oil extracts a quality that seems impossible to restore. The prosperity of Belfast is momentary and shadowy, based as it is on the flax culture, for every year the flax grows poorer and weaker. They manure and put in potatoes and grass, and cannot repeat the flax with safety for seven years, but even then it never comes up in the same perfection."

"I don't see," said Hursen, "that the contiguity of Ireland to England justifies England in annexing Ireland, any more than the contiguity of England to France would justify France in annexing England. I base the demand for Home Rule on the ground of inalienable right. Our position is that we owe no loyalty to England, but we think the ruin of England would be the ruin of Ireland, and we do not desire separation, because we need England as a market for our goods, and we wish to keep England in all its integrity as a good, big, beneficent neighbor.

"From a military point of view the empire would not be endangered by Home Rule. I believe there is a friendship growing up between the English and the Irish democracies. I cannot imagine that the Irish Parliament would be rich enough to provide defences, forts, guns, navy, commissariat, sufficient to protect itself from surrounding nations. I don't think either we should intrigue with France or any other power. It would n't be safe to rely on French help. When Parnell went to France to enlist the sympathy of Gambetta, he was not received, from fear of international difficulty, it was said, but really, I think, from contempt. I should, too, prefer to live under English than under French rule.

"Resistance by Ulster to Home Rule is absurd. If the Orangemen resisted they would have to beat the rest of Ulster before attacking the other provinces. If the Orangemen cannot beat the Nationalists at the polls, how can they expect to beat them in the field?

"These people, too, are beginning to lose their terror of Home Rule. If it comes they will take advantage of it, just as they took advantage of the Land Act of 1881 after opposing it.

"As to the religious question : the people are leading the priests, not led by them. They are united now. O'Connell never had the priests with him as Parnell has. Some Protestants are with us too. The president of our branch is Moffat, a Protestant who lived long in America.

"About outrages much nonsense is talked. The people should never be held accountable for moonlighting, for the reason that they have not the making of their own laws. What is the use of our trying to rectify the state of society, when we are not paid constables, and when those very acts complained of have been the means of our getting the greatest benefits. If we do not get Home Rule we are prepared to go on with a constant guerilla warfare till the crack of doom."

It is time, perhaps, to listen to a landlord who has property in this county and the neighboring one of Fermanagh. A young man, of an old Protestant Orange family, he was educated abroad and early adopted liberal views, but as soon as the Home Rule Bill was introduced he became an energetic Unionist.

"I have," he said, "a typical Ulster property. The mountains are inhabited by Catholics, and the valleys by Protestants. When a tenant fails in the valley, the ten-

ant right can be sold for what it is worth ; but when you
go up into the hills within reach of the League, a man
who fails and wants to sell insists on being evicted.   He
allows himself to be evicted, and then we let him sell if
he can.   I have a tenant in that mountainous district,
a drunkard, who went about collecting money for the
League.   He did n't pay any rent, so I evicted him, but
reinstated him on account of his old mother.   After a
time I asked him to sell out ; but the people would n't
let him.   I kept him on then as caretaker.   Soon the
Protestant tenants in the neighborhood became tremen-
dously excited about something, and the agent overheard
them saying, 'A nice way to treat decent Protestants
who pay rent !   That Irish Papist blackguard you give
three years to and reinstate him.'   I spoke to the man
and he said, ' Shure, if I did n't tell the people about it, I
could n't get a grazier to put a beast on the land at all.'
I asked the neighbors whether any one would take the
land if we turned the man out, and they all said ' No.'

" Near me there are a lot of small farms of ten or
twenty acres on the slopes of the mountains.   Formerly,
with the help of his sons and with cheap labor, the farmer
reared cows and pigs, made butter, and raised oats
and potatoes, and so paid his rent.   Now labor is dear,
and the young men, after getting a national-school education, go into the constabulary or emigrate ; the farmers
cease to grow potatoes and oats, and the money from
the calves and the butter goes to buy Indian meal, etc.,
for family use.   So things get worse and worse.   The
style of living has changed for the better, perhaps, but
the farmers are very incompetent.   Such incompetency
would be impossible under landlordism with full powers,
and probably under peasant proprietorship.   Even un-

der a peasant proprietary, I do not suppose that evictions will die out wholly, for in some way or other a system will be devised for securing the survival of the fittest
instead of the survival of the unfittest, which is the case
to-day.

" A large majority of the landlords would accept any
reasonable terms of purchase now, and are coming to
favor a purchase scheme more and more. They feel that
their property is being taken from them slice by slice,
and they would rather take an insufficient sum and put
an end to their losses. In Ulster the landlords would
rather have the terms of purchase fixed by private contract, but elsewhere they would welcome a compulsory
system of purchase. The Ulster landlords were opposed
to the Land Acts, because they were getting their rents,
and all the landlords were opposed to a reduction of the
judicial rents, because it was understood when these
rents were first fixed that they were to be a basis for purchase. The outcry against Gladstone's Purchase Bill
was justifiable, because it was associated with his Home
Rule Bill, and the Act would be unworkable under Home
Rule. Under Home Rule local guaranties would be
sure to be repudiated, but they might answer without
Home Rule, as in India.

" There is a conspiracy here amounting to rebellion.
Certain men lead it, whose language shows that they are
animated by hatred of England, and that they are working for what they hope will lead to separation. In speaking to their followers, these Parnellite M.P.'s say that
no limits can be set to the march of the nation. Such
speeches show the insincerity of their guaranties.

" Again, historically, the Irish Parliament of the
eighteenth century proved unworkable ; in eighteen years,

twice coming to loggerheads with the British Parliament, and yet that Parliament was exclusively Protestant and conservative, and now it is proposed to start a Parliament composed of the men most hostile to England.

"I read over Gladstone's bill carefully, and marked sixty-two points over which England and Ireland were bound to come to a violent disagreement within two or three years.

"The Nationalist movement here is a Jacobin movement, and like all such movements must fall into the hands of the extreme party. Compare it with the French revolutionary movement, the analogy is close. The priests will finally split from it, and that will make matters worse.

"The rural population will be inclined to make the best of things at first, but the town Protestants will be hard to reconcile to Home Rule. 'No taxes to support nunneries,' will be the cry, and ultimately, I believe, the north will be arrayed almost solid against the south."

SOME BELFAST MERCHANTS.

"I am a moderate man," said a merchant of great weight and reputation, a director of innumerable companies,—"I am a moderate man, and people like me would see Home Rule come with the utmost reluctance, but would not actually resist till the Irish Parliament had abused its powers.

"Unfair taxation is what we fear. Some Nationalists propose a general poor-rate for the whole of Ireland ; that would be a gross injustice to Belfast, where people have something to lose.

"An Irish Parliament would be likely to resort to protection. If food were taxed, that would press severely

on the artisans ; and if flax were taxed, the manufacturers
would be ruined, for we import flax from Holland, Belgium, and Russia.

"The Belfast Chamber of Commerce, on April 22,
1886, unanimously adopted a resolution deploring the introduction of the Home Rule Bill, at a meeting expressly
called 'to consider the proposals now placed before Parliament by Mr. Gladstone.' The sudden fall in the price
of all stocks while that bill was pending shows how serious
is our dread of Home Rule.

"Private bill legislation in Ireland is necessary, and
the establishment of local county boards. Indeed, most
moderate men would be willing to accept a Home Rule
measure, provided that the executive were responsible
only to the Imperial Parliament, and the police and the
judges were appointed from London and not from Dublin. The police in Belfast used to be appointed by the
town commissioners, but during the riots the force was
found to be so partisan that a change was necessary, and
Belfast is now policed by a detachment of the Royal
Irish Constabulary, under the command of a town inspector. So if the judges or the police were appointed
by the Parnellites, they would lose their impartiality.

"The views of the mercantile community are expressed by the *Northern Whig,* which as early as 1881
suggested the separation of Ulster. 'We want no separation ; but should such a question ever be discussed,
Ulster as a province, with Belfast as its capital, would
have as much right to claim separation from the other
provinces of Ireland as the latter have to ask for separation from the other portions of the United Kingdom ; for
it would only be by such separation, and the maintenance, so far as she is concerned, of the Union with

Great Britain, that the present manufacturing and commercial position of Ulster could be maintained.'¹

" The League has recently tried to prove that Ulster is poorer than either Leinster or Munster, but the fact is not so. The railway companies, the banks, and the Inland Revenue Department all pay their income taxes and duties to the government in Dublin. All the passenger duty of the Great Northern Railroad Company was paid in Dublin, even before the road was built so far. For all that, Dublin gets the credit. So when a merchant in Belfast exports a hundred cases of linen to New York *via* Liverpool, those goods are credited to Liverpool. In this way the error has become possible.

" There is supposed to be about £100,000,000 invested in the flax and linen trade in Ulster. Some of the companies are shaky, but such is not the case with the generality of them."

At the Merchants' Exchange there are some six hundred members, of whom probably not over twenty-five are Catholics. The brief remarks elicited from one merchant after another were much the same : " In 1884 the Bank of Ireland stock was 342, in 1886, 249, and now it has only recovered to 288. What does that prove?" " We grow one million pounds worth of flax ; a duty of ten per cent. would ruin all the mills in Ireland and turn the trade over to the Germans and French." "If you will tell me what legislation would be done by a Home-Rule Parliament, I will tell you how it would affect business. We do not believe it would legislate wisely."

One gentleman, often referred to as the leading Unionist in Belfast, spoke at some length.

" A Home Ruler would make out some case for Home

¹ January 1, 1881.

Rule if he could mention things we want that Parliament cannot or will not give us. We have no special grievances here.

"Agricultural depression is everywhere ; the depreciation of land is as great in England as in Ireland. The question of the rent is rather a small matter. Twenty-five years ago an acre of land in Ireland would probably have produced from £8 to £10 worth of gross produce. The value of that produce has depreciated about twenty-five per cent., so that a farm of a hundred acres would now make £600 instead of £800. The average rent was 25*s.* per acre, and the average reduction 6*s.* or £30 on the hundred acres. The cost of labor is, however, a third or half as much greater than it used to be. Omit the rent altogether and you would not put the farmer back where he was twenty-five years ago. There are 200,000 tenants who pay rent of less than £4 a year, that means that there are a million people who cannot make their living out of the land. They used to go to England to harvest, but the introduction of machinery has largely decreased the demand for them. The stir of capital is necessary, and agitation and the impoverishment of the landlords have done them great injury.

"Till within the last fifteen years the peasants were in a condition of serfdom, afraid of their landlords, whom they always approached as a debtor would his creditor, making a poor mouth. Their votes were their landlords, until the Ballot Act. Since then they have obtained secrecy of voting and an independent interest in their holdings ; but as yet not half a generation has been born under the new conditions, and the people are now led blindly either by the priests or the agitators. Is it not a risky experiment to entrust the government to the hands

of these people, who have never cast a responsible vote in
their lives or not till very recently ? In England you
have urban and rural constituencies nearly equally divided. You have artisans and mechanics and a great
body of professional men. In Ireland the urban constit-
tuencies are in the proportion of one to sixteen, and
there is no middle class except the small country shopkeeper and the merchants to be found in a city like Belfast. The whole idea of the bulk of the voters since
1870 has been to hit the landlords and get something
from them. Can they be trusted now to decide wisely
difficult economical questions ? Yet the Irish are very
able and have a genius for politics, and but for the legislation since 1870 I should be a strong Nationalist now.

" The first legislation of an Irish Parliament would be
apt to be dangerous. Protection is the panacea the Nationalists advance, and that would be fatal to us. The
Irish are not accustomed to factory life, and are fond of
feasts and holidays ; they would try to foster industries
under unprofitable conditions, and would throw the burden of the experiment on communities like this.

" There is almost a certainty that an Irish Parliament
would change the national-school system and make it
part of the machinery of the Catholic Church. The influence of men like Davitt and Parnell is the only coun-
terpoise to the influence of the clergy. The leading politicians may be free from bigotry, but not the ignorant
masses who elect them. That is true of the south and
the west, while in the north the only politics and pretty
much the only religion of the masses is hatred of the
Pope.

" The National feeling is chiefly fed by Catholicism.
The Catholics don't intermarry with the Protestants, they

don't live together, nor even dance together. No race feeling could be half so strong. Any legislation in the interest of the Catholics would cause riots in Belfast. Who would put the riots down? The police? They eat the police alive in Belfast. The military? I know many officers who would throw up their commissions sooner than interfere ; and how long would the English people tolerate the shooting down of loyal Protestants by the British army at the command of the National League? It would n't be a question of shooting a few rioters, but of suppressing the whole country-side, with the clergy at the head of their congregations.

"There is no good in giving Home Rule unless the measure is thoroughgoing ; a system of local boards would be useless, because the membership would not give sufficient dignity and responsibility to attract competent men.

"Representation in the imperial Parliament would be absurd, because Irishmen would then be interfering in English and Scotch affairs, which could not possibly be separated from imperial affairs as Parliament is now constituted. Home Rule for Ireland must then be correlated with Home Rule for England and Scotland. This would mean a complete change of the constitution, and a senate of some sort would be necessary in which members from each country could meet on the same footing. If the Irish Parliament, for instance, passed a law of doubtful constitutionality, could it be abrogated by the Parliament of Great Britain, in which we are not represented?

"When you begin to cut up the country and establish separate local parliaments, where are you to stop? With Wales and Scotland, England and Ireland? Will you separate the north of England from the south? Are you going to upset the whole cart, the government of some forty million people, for the sake of three million Home Rulers in Ireland ?

" There are certain reforms we do need. Our executive and administrative departments are all inspired from Dublin Castle, and that means a very narrow clique, traditionally opposed to the real sentiments of the great body of the people. Every poor-law inspector, every stipendiary magistrate, is appointed by the Castle, and that is the secret of the hatred of the government in Ireland. It is not a question of parliamentary government. That could n't be successful so long as the two opposing parties are fighting so bitterly, for agitation would continue, and extremists on each side would keep the ear of the people.

" We Presbyterians object to this centralization as much as the Catholics do ; we are out in the cold as much as they are, and as things settle down will work with them for changes.

" I would recommend that the executive consult with the Nationalist leaders as to the appointment of magistrates. The private-bill legislation for Ireland might also be entrusted to the Irish members sitting at Dublin, as a committee of the House. If this were done, the members would soon be weeded out. Most of them now are regular adventurers, and under Home Rule they would be our masters. What we need is to be able to test and increase the ability and honesty of these men without throwing our whole constitution out of joint. I should like to see Healy made Attorney-General ; it would make a much better man of him.

" I think the notion of ' a separate Ulster' is totally wrong, but I am sure the north of Ireland would not at present obtain justice from a legislature at Dublin. In sympathy, connections, and interests the bulk of the Protestant north are more closely allied with England and Scotland than with the rest of Ireland. As to the lower agricultural population, ninety-nine out of a hundred would want a separate Ulster if Home Rule is to be given at all, and they had to make their election ; but they are not willing to adopt that policy yet ; they don't want to remove the block they now are to Home Rule. Many people believe that as a separate province the future of Ulster would be made, for the best people in the south say they would come here. I think it a miserable alternative, for it would create a constant source of trouble, a regular sore. There would be competition between the legislatures inside and out of the pale for the interests of particular classes. I am opposed to it also in sentiment, for I prefer to be an Irishman than an Ulsterman. We are a desperately bigoted people, politically and religiously, Presbyterians, Methodists, Churchmen, and Catholics.

"At present I think that Irish affairs can be managed as well at Westminster, or through Westminster, as by a Parliament at Dublin. In time the people may grow out of their present state of demoralization ; the National movement has changed enormously from the time of the Fenians, and the alliance between the Liberals and the Nationalists will modify it still more, for the Liberals will not stand outrages, and don't sympathize with extreme views. In time the legislative benefits of the last few years will begin to show some results, and the farmers, as they become proprietors, will become conserva tive. After a while a better set of politicians will, I hope, come to the front. In five or six years then there may well be less danger in Home Rule, but no special benefit."

"A friend of mine," said a flax manufacturer, as he drew his chair up to the table in the club, "tried to start a mill near Cork. The difficulty he found sprang from religious interference. The parish priest made him take on an incompetent foreman he had dismissed, and soon there was not a foreman or overseer under his control. The result was a bad failure. Even when the men don't care about sectarian questions, the women do, and the priests work on their husbands and sons through them.

"We have had no advantage over the rest of Ireland, but rather every disadvantage. The climate is better in the south ; and we, too, have neither coal nor iron.

"Peasant proprietorship will do one good thing. It will clear out a whole lot of incompetent men. Moreover, there will then be nothing to agitate about. It will not, however, bring the millennium. The few shillings a year saved will not enable the smaller men to live here, and they will have to emigrate."

Another manufacturer, not in the linen trade, but still one of the most successful citizens of Belfast, represented conservative Presbyterian opinions :

"The Protestant Home Rulers are people who would not be considered by anybody, and for the most part are not Protestants at all but deists and infidels.

"There are some 220,000 people in Belfast, of whom 70,000 are Catholics, and they are the hewers of wood and drawers of water, and would never have been introduced into the city except from the demand for mill hands. Nine tenths of the public-houses are kept by Catholics, while the vast majority of the large wholesale merchants are Protestants.

"The Nationalist success is the first result of the extension of the suffrage to small tenants.

"Agriculture to be profitable needs to be conducted on a large scale, and this is impossible with such small holdings. Till we get the population down to three millions we shall never come to any good. How can five or six people live on a five-acre farm? It is necessary to find something else for them to do. Why does n't Parnell take up some of these questions, for most of the existing misery has nothing whatever to do with the want of Home Rule? Why, too, have the National Leaguers never paid a poor man's rent out of their American money? The other day a friend of mine was obliged to evict a tenant because he had been in possession without paying rent for eleven years, and eviction was the only means by which my friend could retain his title.

"The poverty of the landlords has already ruined many trades. From ten to twenty years ago half our trade in Ireland was in stable fittings and such goods that the landlords can no longer afford to buy. I calculate, too, that some £500,000 has been lost to this country by the boycotting of hunting.

"The people have lost more in morality since 1880, than they have gained by the reductions of the rent. It is, too, the payments to one another for tenant right, and not the payments to the landlords of rent, that have ruined so many farmers. I know many a man who has gone into debt for the purchase money of a tenant right.

"The Catholics complain of not being given political offices, but out of ten thousand people you will scarcely find six Catholics fit to administer out-door relief or to sit on the local boards.

"We are satisfied in Belfast fairly well with things as

they are. We want quietness; we don't want any radical change. Many things have contributed to our success: that we can get coal as cheaply as on the Clyde, that our taxes are low, the houses cheaper and more commodious, and that men can live better here for the same money than elsewhere. Here is my list of local taxes, so much in the pound of my real-estate valuation : 'Poor-rate, 1*s.* 8*d.* ; borough rate, 3*d.* ; general purpose rate, 2*s.* 6*d.* ; park rate (a special temporary charge), 3*d.*' This is far less than taxes in Dublin.

"Home Rule, we believe, would absolutely ruin our trade. The linen trade of course could not be moved, but the ship-building would go. Harland himself has said he would not stay, and he employs over six thousand men. We do most of our business in England and Scotland and only one tenth is in Ireland. We, and others like us, would go out of business. The whiskey trade will go. John Brown, worth about £200,000, said that if Home Rule came he would close up his works and go to England. The banking system is altogether English, and the banks will be ruined. One of the first things a Home-Rule Parliament will do will be to establish a national bank, whose notes will be issued or guaranteed by the Irish government, and that will destroy the issue business of the other banks. The process of transferring the business houses from Belfast will be slow but inevitable.

"Although I don't want Home Rule, I think the passing of the Act of Union was bad for Ireland, because it created a great inducement to absenteeism, and the best class of people got into the habit of going to London.

"Again, we don't want to have to go to England in order to get a new bridge built here. The grand jury system should be elective, so that we could control our own taxes and expenses. Primary education should be compulsory.

"Call at the Clerk's office and note the number of illiterate voters in Belfast at the last election. There are nearly four times as many illiterates in the district that returned Mr. Sexton, the Nationalist, as in any other." [1]

An enthusiastic young man, a ship-broker, carried me off one afternoon to the office of the only linen firm of which the members were Catholics. A shrewd-looking, gray-headed gentleman turned round in his chair to greet us.

"I am not a politician, as my brother is," he explained. "I had a strong fit of political enthusiasm in 1848, and that exhausted all I had in me. Since then I 've been merely a spectator.

"The Protestants would be greatly indignant if we had Home Rule, but I don't think they would do more than grumble, and they will probably take every advantage that Home Rule offers. They are opposed to it not as business men but as politicians, they don't want to lose their political ascendancy. We have been for a long time carrying them on our backs, or rather they have been riding on our backs, and don't want to dismount. The Ulster Protestants raise all this clamor, because they want something given to stop their mouths."

[1] The figures are :

Division.	No. Illiterate.	Vote Cast.	Elected.
East Division	228	6292	Cobain
West Division	944	7559	Sexton
North Division	125	5254	Ewart
South Division	153	5199	Johnson

" There is n't one Catholic in the Harbor Board or in their employment, except two brokers," interrupted the young man.

" Protection," continued the old gentleman," is probably impossible ; because if agricultural products are taxed, the working-men will complain, and if manufactured articles are taxed, the farmers will complain. Two or three years ago there was a good deal of talk about Fair Trade, but it seems to have died out. If I thought protection would come with Home Rule, I would vote against Home Rule.

" I don't suppose we shall get any great benefit from Home Rule in Belfast in my day. Indeed, the saving of expense in sending our private bills to London to be passed, is the only immediate benefit I think of."

" No, no," cried out our companion. " These men are the descendants of colonists, and still consider themselves as colonists, living off the country but caring little for it. Won't it be a benefit to make them care for it ?

" Again, the encouragement of our resources would be a great boon. There are mountains in Antrim and Down full of iron ore, and £2,000 would be enough to make experiments and start mauufactories. Then our people might make the iron plates for the Belfast shipyards. So with coal, there is plenty of it about Dungannon in Tyrone, and Ballycastle in Antrim. The English government does make various loans to Ireland, but many of them are jobs, and very little of the money reaches its destination.

" Again, we want Catholic education. The books issued by the Board of Intermediate Education, though half the Board are Catholic, contain frequently matter insulting to Catholics. I would n't have a child of mine contaminated by reading them. The national-school books are freer from this fault, but I would n't have my children brought up without perpetual religious instruction. The government is dead to every thing Irish. The gist of the matter is that we live here and wish to prosper, and we think we can manage our own business best."

" The question of religion has nothing to do with it," said the merchant. " If the priests had their way there would n't be Home Rule here for two hundred years."

" That 's the truest thing you 've said this evening," replied the young fellow; "and I will say this, that if you could secure to Ulster influence in the Dublin Parliament, Ulster would go for Home Rule to-morrow."

" They would go like sheep, even the educated classes," continued the merchant.

"Would you trust the present M.P.'s ?" I asked.

" I would n't trust them farther than I could see them," cried the older man, "but no more I would any politician."

" If we sent the English over eighty-five apostles," shouted the younger man, " they would find names of abuse to fling at them, and some would stick. These men are unimpeachable and irreproachable, and we should all feel extreme gratitude to them."

" I don't feel a particle," said the other, "but it makes little difference what they are or what their motives are, if they get us benefits. I would take a good thing even from the Old Scratch."

" An Ulster Parliament seems to me such an idiotic idea that no one out of a lunatic asylum could believe in it. What is Ulster that she should have a separate Parliament ? Statistics prepared by the League

show that Ulster is less wealthy than any province except Connaught. Belfast is prosperous, but largely by
accident. It is on the Marquis of Donegal's property ;
and his debts were so great that he was glad to give
blank leases for almost any thing. Lisbourne was not so
fortunate, and the Richardsons, the linen merchants,
tried in vain to get satisfactory leases there and had to
go to Newry where they have built a village."

I walked home to take tea with " the firm," and on the
way the conversation was continued. The land question
came up.

"There is no man," said the merchant, "with an
article to sell, who will not try to get the best price for it.
The landlords have not been so much to blame after
all. So eager for land are the people, that they even
borrow money from the banks at twelve per cent. to buy
a neighbor's tenant right. It will not be more than two
generations after a peasant proprietary is established
before a new class of landlords arise.

" I have always believed that a man should stick to his
bargains about land as about any thing else ; that he
should be allowed to make his own bargains ; that land
is a commodity like other things, and that if a man
could n't pay for it he should leave it. But the last Land
Act has changed my mind. The government has decided
that land is different from any other commodity ; the
rents are now fixed by the courts and not by the parties ;
and free sale of the tenant right is allowed, which operates to impose on the land an additional rent. The
present system won't work ; and the old system is declared to be false. The only way I see out of the mud-
dle is the nationalization of the land."

I mentioned the difficulty in the way of Home Rule,

that if the Irish M.P's. remain in Parliament they will be acting on questions of purely English concern, while if they are excluded from Parliament, the Irish people will be taxed by a body in which they are not represented, and will be subordinated to a policy purely alien.

"What is workable for Canada," was the reply, "might do here."

"I think now," he went on, "of some further advantages of Home Rule. You can bring goods from Leeds to Athlone for less than you can take them there from Belfast. An Irish Parliament might superintend the management of the Irish railroads."

After tea the other member of the firm, the politician, the leader of the Nationalists in Belfast, took up the tale.

"Home Rule," he declared, "would be an enormous benefit. Here are 70,000 Catholics in Belfast without any influence in the city government. It is true that the Catholics control no considerable industries, except that of mineral water, but man for man in Ulster I think their accumulated wealth would equal that of the Protestants. Statistics are hard to get, but during the twenty-five years of the administration of the late Catholic Archbishop of Down and Connor, his parishioners contributed over half a million pounds towards church buildings, schools, convents, and colleges. There is one Catholic spinning-mill in Ulster, that of William Ross, who got into the trade by accident. Not a Catholic could become a manager of a spinning-mill here. Hughes, the great baker in Belfast, a Catholic, tried in vain to get his three sons into the mills. The Catholics have been pushing lately in the tobacco trade and the jewelry trade. Brown is the chief Catholic jeweller, and Leahy, Kelly, & Leahy is a great Catholic tobacco firm. Until a few years ago no prominent shopkeeper was a Catholic outside of the public-house business. Now most of the hotels are kept by Catholics,—the Royal, the Prince of Wales, the Linen Hall, the Donegal, and the Union ; this began, perhaps, as an extension of the publican trade.

"It would add strength to the commerce of Belfast if Catholics had a fair share in it.

"There was no Catholic organization here till 1885. If we were organized properly we could upset the corporation of Belfast, but we don't wish to do so, for we are peacefully disposed and want only a fair share in the distribution of power.

"That the Nationalists when they get into power will act patriotically, without religious prejudice, is shown by the conduct of Sexton in Parliament. Sexton has brought in a bill to equalize the municipal with the parliamentary franchise, though this change will enfranchise more of the Orange than of the Catholic democracy. The town council has been promoting a main drainage bill authorizing them to borrow nearly a quarter of a million pounds. Sexton has had the bill postponed on the ground that the council now is a mere clique and not representative, though the new council is just as certain to be wholly Protestant. Harland and Wolff's men struck some time ago for weekly wages, which had been usual till recently. Sexton, accordingly, had tacked on to Bradlaugh's 'Truck Bill' a clause to give weekly payments in Ireland, except in piece-work. Yet these Island men, as they are called, are the most bigoted Orangemen and stir up all the riots against the Catholics. Sexton has also brought in a local bankruptcy bill, to establish courts in Belfast, Limerick, and Cork.

"Sexton, the first Catholic M.P. for Belfast, and the

only active M.P. we have had, is a living proof that we
don't want to set up a counter ascendancy to the
Protestants.

"There will be no successful rebellion in Ulster, for
in 1881 forty-nine per cent. of the population were Catholics, and now the Catholics must be equal or more than
equal to the Protestants.   What rioting there might be
would be easily checked by the police.   There would
have been none in 1886 if the police had been energetic.
The riots began on the 4th of June, and continued intermittently till the end of September.   Only about thirty
persons were reported killed in that four months' fighting.   As to what the police could have done, see in the
parliamentary report[1] how Sergeant Carey with only
nine truncheon men drove a mob of a thousand men
down Stanhope Street, and up and down Porter's Hill.
'If every one had done so,' said Sir John Charles Day,
the President of the Commission, "these riots would have
ended long ago.'   Was Carey promoted?   Not he; he
was sent out of Belfast as too good a man for this place.

"Our day is near at hand, for as Gladstone showed
lately a change of only six per cent. will put the Conservatives out and the Liberals in."

"Will not taxes be higher under Home Rule," I asked,
"and the credit of the country less?"

"As to money," he replied, "we have plenty of
money, thirty-two millions of Irish money are invested in
England.   Our payments to England will be less under
any rational scheme, for, as Sir Charles G. Duffy pointed
out, we are paying nearly seven million pounds a year
towards the interest on the national debt, instead of

[1] Belfast Riots Commission, 1886, Minutes of Evidence, pp.
538, 539.

£3,500,000. So far as I can see, I agree thoroughly with his idea of a constitution for Ireland.[1] I think too that we should be more than just to the Protestant minority, and allow them more than their full representation.

" The existence of Orangeism and Masonry here has helped to destroy the linen trade. The merchants buy and sell not on commercial principles, but for the benefit of their brotherhood. The system of limited liability companies has increased this cliquishness.

" So much money was made in linen during the American civil war, that mills were built in excessive numbers. Every small shopkeeper put his mite into the trade. The result of this over-production is that a large number of the spinning-mills are now insolvent. The Northern Spinning Company is in process of liquidation. The Ulster Spinning Company, with one twelfth of all the spindles in Ulster, some 60,000, had to reorganize a short time ago.

" The large spinning concerns are largely carried on with deposits lent them for specified times by the farmers and the Catholics who have no opportunity of using their money in starting business of their own. The York Street Flax Spinning Company, Limited, had, for instance, half a million on deposit, over and above its capital, on which it pays five per cent. A business managed

---

[1] Sir Charles G. Duffy proposed a Parliament, with the same powers as the Canadian and Australian legislatures, of two houses. The Lower House to consist of 105 members, three members being elected by each of thirty-five constituencies, no elector voting for more than two candidates. The Senate to consist of 54 members, appointed in the Constitution, but to be elective after ten years. A court of three judges is to be appointed to act as interpreters of the Act of Constitution ; and the judiciary at large to be appointed.

in such a way, even though the deposit receipts circulate as bank notes, must always be liable to be shaken.

Mr. James Canning, Mr. Oldham of Dublin, and Michael Davitt, with the Protestant Home Rule Asssociation, are trying to extend the cultivation of flax outside of Ulster. Our object is to reform abuses in the trade, not to attack the trade itself.

"Revolutionary methods are now discredited. Davitt tried to draw a red herring across the Nationalist movement by introducing Henry George's theory of nationalization of the land, but he will not be allowed to interfere with the business now in hand. All the old Fenian movement is dead now. Mr. James O'Kelly, an out and outer, who would be as willing as any one to head a force in arms, now admits that the English democracy is heart and soul with us, and he and Tim Healey are honest converts to the ' New Departure.' "

Another business man, interested chiefly in the Stock Exchange, has the advantage of being a foreigner by birth, though he has lived in Belfast for the last twenty-six years. "Unless England," he said, "sends an army here to enforce obedience to a Dublin Parliament, I don't believe that Ulstermen will pay taxes or submit to it in any way. What interest has England in establishing a hostile government at its back door?

" The welcome paid here to Chamberlain was general and not merely Orange. At the great banquet in his honor, out of the four hundred guests probably not five were Orangemen. The middle and the upper classes here are not Orange.

"The banks here are very prosperous, chiefly because they have a small paid up capital and get large deposits from the farmers who have nothing else to do with their

money and are contented with about one per cent. for it.
The Ulster Bank pays eighteen per cent., the Belfast
Banking Co., twenty, and the Northern, twelve per cent."

The views of a couple of commercial travellers may
well close this brief sketch of the sentiments of the business men of Belfast.

"Here," said Mr. S., in the commission trade in Donegal Street, who has travelled through "every village in
Ireland,"—" here in Ulster we have nine counties as prosperous as any in the land. We are an energetic, honest
race, very different from the south of Ireland people.
The successful Irishmen in America are chiefly of Irish-
Scotch descent. The southern Irish are born politicians and form a clique in every city, but they are not
capable of self-government. The reason is that they belong to a system, semi-religious and semi-political. Here
we are as free as any where under the sun, but the Catholic Irish have a different idea of liberty. See how they
assaulted the English in Boston at their celebration of the
Queen's Jubilee. They want no one to be free except as
they dictate. The farmers, too, on the hills and mountains are very ignorant and brutal. They have no sympathy with manufactures. Now that they have the suffrage, Home Rule would give us over into their hands.

"The people of Belfast simply want to be let alone.
They think they are doing as well as any people in the
world. We are always on the job, and make bargains
without telling lies. We want peace and quiet, and very
much object to getting hurt, but when put on our mettle
we don't give in easy. We have never been conquered,
and never will be. I am not an Orangeman, but I am
the kind of stuff Orangemen are made of.

"I am not rigidly conservative. I was a member of

the Land League till the Land Acts were passed, but this talk of nationality I don't believe in. I cannot look on myself as hemmed into a little place like Ireland. I want to be world-wide. Though born in Ireland and of Irish parents, I can go to any colony to-morrow and find myself still in my own country as an Englishman."

"I have been all over Ulster," said another commercial traveller. "The farmers want the land cheap ; that's the peg the whole National question hangs on ; settle that and all is settled. The farmers are chiefly Presbyterians, and all agree on this.

"The people are very selfish and there has been an immense amount of land grabbing. A farmer will often have, say £100 in the bank at £1 a year interest. He cannot use the money profitably in any occupation except farming, but there is a farm next door which he can work without much increase in his expenses. The landlord often in the past would say to his tenant : ' Here 's a man who wants the farm and offers more rent than you are paying ; you must pay the increased rent or go.' In many parts of the country the landlords are mean and with but little sense of honor, and if it were not for the boycotting the rack-renting would have been extreme."

SOME BELFAST PROFESSIONAL MEN.

The great majority of professional men in Belfast are Protestants and Unionists, but an able statement of the Nationalist position was made to me by Mr. Andrew Mc-Erlean, a gray-haired solicitor.

"In the time of James I. the Irish were driven to the mountains' sides and the waters' edges, and the whole country was planted with Protestants, chiefly lowland Scotch. Gradually, as the rents were raised, the Scotch retired and were succeeded by the Irish, who would pay any rent. For centuries the Catholics have been suppressed. Even now, from the appointment of a street scavenger to the purchase of a horse, religion is brought in. There is only one Catholic in any public board in Belfast, and he is on the water board. There is not a Catholic official in County Antrim, and in the rest of Ulster the only Catholic officials I can think of are one in County Down, and the Clerk of Newry. Not one of the forty Town Counsellors of Belfast is a Catholic, and not one is a Liberal, except two who were elected by Conservative votes and who were more Tory than the Tories. The foremen and managers of all the mills are Protestants, and in the banks every man is a Protestant.

"In 1870, Professor Galbraith, John Martin, and A. M. Sullivan established a branch of the Home Rule Association in Londonderry. At the election that year I was Joe Biggar's canvassing agent, and Joe Biggar polled 89 votes for Home Rule. Now the seed sown by Galbraith has brought forth fruit, and Justin McCarthy is one of the M.P.'s for Derry, Sexton one of the M.P.'s for Belfast, and Ulster is represented by seventeen Nationalists to sixteen Unionists. Such is the progress of Home Rule in Protestant Ulster.

"The landlords can no longer keep the white slaves they did, and are making a desperate struggle. Wherever you go—if you go where Stanley is, and where he is no one knows—if you want to kick up a row you kick over the idols of the people. That is what the landlords do with the Orangemen. There is scarcely a parish or town land in Ulster without an Orange Hall, for which the landlord has given the land and a subscription. There the Orangemen hold their tea-parties, and the landlord

or his head bailiff presides   A year ago they were calling John Morley an emissary of the Pope, and Gladstone,
Antichrist.   All this is done to preserve the privileges of
a few landlords and their friends.   Deprive politics of
the religious element and there would not be the smallest
opposition to Home Rule.

" The talk about civil war is nonsense.   The moment
you place her Majesty's troops before the Orangemen,
they will retire ; they are valiant only against the Pope.
Is Belfast, with the counties of Armagh and Antrim,
going to make a revolution ?   One third of Belfast is for
Home Rule, and a great part of Armagh and Antrim.
Scotland won't interfere, for the Scotch are Nationalists
at heart and will get Home Rule themselves in a few
years.   The Nationalists won't want to fight, for they
are getting all they want without fighting.   It will never
be left to the people on each side of the Boyne to fight
the question out.   Home Rule, if it is granted, will have
the sanction of an Act of Parliament and will be enforced
by the imperial army.

" Moreover, the Protestants are as good Irishmen as
the Catholics.   The last struggle we had for freedom was
in '98, and that was exclusively a Presbyterian movement.   Wolf Tone, who founded the United Irishmen,
was an Ulster Protestant, and so was Henry Joy
M'Cracken, who was executed in Belfast.   The leaders
of the movement of 1848 also came from Ulster—Charles
Duffy, John Martin, and John Mitchel.

" In a plebescite, even among the Protestants, I don't
believe the majority for Orangeism would be large.
Many of the best men in the town are strong Home
Rulers, but not openly, for fear it would interfere with
their business.   A number of linen concerns have gone

to the wall lately. Foreign competition is driving the trade out of the country. If it was n't for the banks the linen trade would cease to exist. The merchants are in the hands of the banks, and the banks are in the hands of the Orangemen. The least movement would shake the merchants, and that is the real reason why they want to keep the present régime.

"Religious persecution under Home Rule would be impossible. Here are three or four million Catholics within a few miles of thirty or forty million Protestants. There are enough Protestants here to keep the Catholics very well employed till the arrival of steamers with the English army, and the army ought to come if ever such a diabolical thought entered the minds of the Irish people.

"In the Home Rule Parliament I don't expect to see a single national body. It will certainly contain a progressive party and a whig or conservative party, and they will keep each other in order.

"The arguments of the opposition are hearthstone arguments—arguments true only in Ulster,—not principles that will sway mankind."

A gentleman of a different profession, who has gained, though a Catholic, a distinguished social position, is a pronounced Home Ruler, and his opinion on the land question seemed of special significance : "The Land Acts were absolutely necessary. It is essential to the prosperity, of a country that the people should have an interest in making improvements. The provisions of the Land Act of 1881 were approved by John Stuart Mill.

"Suppose two men take two adjoining farms, thirty acres each, at £1 an acre. A keeps the land in the same state of cultivation in which he took it, and at the end of twenty years he is paying the same rent and neither better nor worse off. B thoroughly drains the land and generally improves it, and at the end of twenty years his rent is doubled. What has B taken from the landlord that A did not take? For what is the extra payment exacted of B? Simply for the labor of B. Such additional rent is a tax on industry.

"In the matter of land purchase the imperial Parliament might fairly vote some substantial relief to the landlords. They might give them ten or twelve million pounds, as was done at the time of Church Disestablishment, when the government added some twelve per cent. to the purchase money of the life interests of the clergy."

Let us take now the point of view of a master in one of the higher educational institutions of Belfast, an Irishman of experience and keen observation.

"In County Down," he began, "which I know well, every shilling of capital expended in putting the land in a workable condition has been paid by the tenant. In England the reverse is the case. Even if the English landlord charges the tenant interest on the capital invested in improvements, while in Ireland some compensation is made to the tenant through the rents being on the average much lower than on similar farms in England, the fact remains that the English tenant is chargeable with the interest only while he is in occupation, while the Irish tenant, on the other hand, so soon as he ceases to be occupier, until lately lost all the capital he had invested.

"Now the tenant has absolute security for his improvements, but it will take a generation more to remove the feelings and habits that the old system developed.

"All interest in Home Rule will certainly die out in the north, when once the land question is settled. The only settlement possible is by establishing a peasant proprietory. In Seeley's 'Life of Stein' there is some account of how this was done in Germany.

"At the same time something needs to be done for the landlords. As the government is diminishing their income, it ought to relieve them to a corresponding degree from the burden of family charges and mortgages. Interference with family charges is generally approved of, but mortgages are said to be on a different basis. Money was borrowed and spent, it is said ; it ought then to be returned without regard to the depreciation of the security. But would not this plan be equitable ? Suppose a capitalist twenty years ago lent £10,000 on the security of an estate, for which he gets five per cent. Why did he get five per cent. from the landlord when he could have got only three and a quarter per cent. from the government ? Because the land was considered a less secure investment than consols. The two investments were equivalent. Now if you give the mortgagee consols sufficient to yield him the same income that his capital would have produced at the time of the mortgage if invested in consols, surely you have met the sentimental objection to any interference with mortgages.

"Antrim, Down, Derry, Tyrone, and Armagh, are the strong Protestant counties, and they are the flax-producing and the linen-manufacturing counties The nearer you get to Belfast, the more exclusively Protestant the country is. If the land question were settled, I believe that only West Tyrone, South Down, and perhaps South Armagh would return, even for a time, Nationalist members.

"Under the national-school system here, the government goes so far as to provide for religious instruction, with the simple proviso that it shall be so given as to avoid annoyance to the minority. Yet what did Archbishop Walsh say the other day when he addressed four thousand school children near Dublin? He said the Catholics wanted freedom of education in Ireland. I asked a Catholic inspector of schools what this meant. He said : ' The freedom we want is, first, to get a government grant without being obliged to adopt the Board school-books ; secondly, to have religious instruction unlimited as to time and place ; and thirdly, to have the right to exhibit Catholic emblems in the school-rooms at all times.' Now, such freedom of education as the Catholics want would mean in all parts of the country where the Protestants are in a minority, either no school, or a separate Protestant school, or only Catholic schools ; in other words, a choice for the Protestants between ignorance, inferior schools, or proselytizing schools.

"University education is made the subject of another grievance. The Catholics think the government ought to lend or give money to found a Catholic university, to be in the hands of the hierarchy. Is there any country where that would be allowed?

"Religious sects here have all perfect liberty to establish sectarian schools ; but why should the government do so?

"Under a Home Rule Parliament this would unquestionably be done, and we in Ulster would have to bear half the expense.

"For the time being political excitement has thrown Catholic bigotry into the background. But the bigotry exists notwithstanding. In South Down, for instance, if Home Rule were granted, the people would relapse into complete subserviency to the priests ; and it would probably be the same throughout Ireland.

"At Richhill the Orangemen were actually drilling during the pendency of the Home Rule Bill. The Orangemen are chiefly laborers and artisans. Half the conservatives are opposed to Orangeism, and the higher up you go in the social scale the fewer Orangemen you find. Three quarters of the Presbyterian clergy are, or rather were, Liberals, while two thirds of the Episcopalian clergy are in sympathy with Orangeism. In North, South, and East Belfast the Orangemen control the elections, without regard to the Tories.

"There will, I think, be fighting under Home Rule. There will be riots first, then repression, and then great popular excitement and a general rising. The beginning of the riots here last year was significant, one Catholic workman at the Queen's Island yards saying to another, a Protestant : ' Ah, it will soon be so that none of your kind will be able to earn a loaf of bread in the country.' During the riots the police were regarded by the Orangemen much as they now are by the Nationalists. They were called then, ' the foreign police,' ' the French police,' ' Morley's murderers,' as they are called now ' Bloody Balfour's myrmidons.'

"Where you have a large dissenting minority, both sides are always intensely bigoted. In France and Belgium the Protestants are comparatively few in number and much scattered, so there is little danger of intolerance or persecution. A central, controlling, impartial government like that of the imperial Parliament is far more likely to hold the scales of justice even between two such bigoted factions than any local body."

The editor of the principal Unionist paper may finally be quoted, as a practical and clever man of affairs who is most competent to define the position of his party.

"The majority of the farmers in Ulster," he said deliberately, "are opposed to Home Rule, but the temptation is strong, and there is danger that if the Unionists do not offer them something of material benefit they will vote against them at the next election. As yet there are not a thousand Protestant votes in the north for the Nationalists, and this shows how wonderfully they have resisted the enormous bribes they have been offered.

"The landlords have been extreme even in Ulster, and have offset the benefit of free sale by raising the rents. But there are many districts where there is no margin for rent at all, not through any fault of the landlords, but on account of the extreme prolificacy and the uneconomical habits of the people. Those who shout most for Home Rule would be no better off if they got it, for they have not the enterprise and the capital necessary to raise them above a hand-to-mouth existence.

"The present Nationalist leaders are smart, clever dogs, but without any experience in affairs of government ; most of them are good as destructive politicians but would not be likely to succeed as constructive statesmen. William O'Brien, for instance, is one of the few thoroughly honest Nationalists, and he is fanatically honest ; but he is a dreamy, poetical fellow who, if he sees poverty anywhere, assumes it to be the fault of either the government or the landlords.

"If we had Home Rule to-morrow, I should expect the situation would be trying enough for the period of my lifetime. I don't fear there would be much robbery or shooting : but however fairly a Parliament at Dublin might govern, you could n't get an Orangeman of the extreme Protestant party to believe it, and there would be endless turmoil. As a result, the credit of the country would suffer. It would, however, be humanly impossible that a Dublin Parliament should be perfectly fair. There has been too much bitterness in this agitation for the people to become quickly just and wise. There would be, first of all, a clean sweep of all the officials. That would not promote efficiency in the public service. A Dublin Parliament would be sure to affect Ulster injuriously. For one thing, there would probably be a national poor-rate instead of the existing local poor-rates, and prudent Ulster would have to pay for the improvidence of Kerry and Clare, as well as of Donegal and Cavan.

"What would be necessary to make Home Rule in any way successful would be the existence of trained men to draw upon for officials. If we began with an elective council, a grand jury for each county or province, with full control over local affairs, in ten or twenty years we should have some trained men who had had some responsibility, and then if they wished to come together they could do so with comparatively little danger. In Scotland the people would go in for Home Rule simply because it would bring certain practical advantages ; but here they would rather have Home Rule with greater misery than prosperity without it. It is a question here of sentiment rather than of self-interest.

"Self-interest requires certain changes. Whigs and Tories have been equally short-sighted in not appointing local boards to act on the spot upon local questions. This is a real grievance. The last local Police Act, for instance, cost us probably about £10,000.

"I am a Presbyterian of Scotch descent, but I don't

believe that Home Rule would be as bad as many think, though I am certain that it would be so bad that I would rather be for a long time in some other country.

"As to resistance to Home Rule. There is this difference between the northern and the southern Irish : In the south they blacken their faces and fight at night ; but here they fight in the open, and face to face. I am not an Orangeman, but it is true that individuality here is stronger than anywhere else in Ireland. I don't believe there is the organization among the Orangemen that was reported, but if they did turn out they would cause a riot very different from the riots last year, when the police only had to do with isolated and usually unarmed crowds. The Orangemen have no good leader. The two members for Belfast are not competent to lead an army of chickens, much less to head a revolt. There will be nothing like civil war, but merely very serious rioting. In the last riots I saw men marching in the streets of a class far superior to any I expected to see there, and I was amazed at the sympathy shown them by the better citizens."

SOME COUNTRY NATIONALISTS.

I met him in the train as he was returning from the great fair of Ballinasloe. He was a burly, rough, amiable man, and was soon chatting confidentially. "I live," he said, "two miles from Dundalk. My farm is near the sea, and the soil is so light that we always have a hard time if we don't get rain in June. There are only about twenty tenants on the estate, which belongs to the Rev. Sir Cavendish Foster. He lives in England, and we seldom see him, but both the landlord and his agent have always been kind and indulgent, never pressing us, and they have made many improvements, giving us timber and slates when we built, and iron gates for our fields, and sharing in the expense of draining.

"All the landlords about us have been giving reductions for the last three years. Last Christmas we asked for a reduction of 30 per cent. on the half year's rent then due, but it was refused so we none of us paid any rent till June, when the landlord gave in. My tenancy is one from year to year, and I have not yet gone into the land courts, but I intend to go now.

"My rent is very high—£2 5s. for the arable land per Irish acre. I raise chiefly corn and turnips on half the farm, and graze the other half. The oat crop this year is almost a total failure. The turnip crop is a third of the average. Hay is about half. For cattle there is scarcely any price to be got.

"There will be no peace, I think, till the landlords are bought out, but I would give them fair compensation. A land-purchase bill would be very good if it allowed the tenants to buy at about sixteen years' purchase of the reduced rents. We offered to purchase our farms, but the landlord would n't sell.

"I am a Catholic and believe in Home Rule. There are many reforms necessary. The Lord-Lieutenant nominates three men for high sheriff of each county, and they decide among themselves who shall accept. The high sheriff then has the appointment of the grand jurors. In County Lowth the Catholics are to the Protestants in the proportion of four to one, and yet this summer there was only one Catholic on the grand jury. The grand jury levies the county cess, and appoints all the cess collectors and the jail officials. The levy is often excessive. I pay, for instance, £29 a year in county cess, and only

£6 or £7 in poor-rates, which are levied by the Unions.
Retiring county officials are paid extravagant pensions,
almost equal to their salaries, and these take some
£3,000 a year out of the county cess.

"The magistrates are appointed by the Lord-Lieutenant. They are apt to be extremely unpopular, and
many of them own no property and are totally incompetent.

"For awhile Home Rule appointments might be made
for partisan purposes, in a spirit of tit for tat, but that
would right itself in time. As to local appointment of
the police, which some Nationalists urge, I don't believe
in that at all. They would favor their neighbors. The
police should always be appointed by the central
authority.

"The grand-jury system, then, should be replaced by
elective boards, and the government should be decentral-
ized. But we want Home Rule above all, because it is
our right. Canada has Home Rule, and why should n't
we have it ?

"The danger of rash legislation under Home Rule is
exaggerated. The farmers on the whole are exceedingly
conservative ; and I believe that if we had Home Rule
to-morrow Parnell would lead a strong conservative wing.
I think, too, that if the land question were settled, the
farmers would be unlikely to agitate for any thing else,
even for Home Rule. They are exceedingly selfish.
They are even opposed to the building of these laborers'
cottages. They would become as conservative then as
now they are the reverse.

"As to the Protestants not wanting Home Rule : the
Presbyterians about me are as thick as bats ; they don't
dare to vote or to go to meetings of the League ; but yet

they are very willing to accept all that the Catholics can get for them."

At Cavan I left my new acquaintance, to spend a day in that old-fashioned, badly paved, dirty little town. The chief public building is an enormous jail with walls like the walls of a fortress. The old waiter at the hotel spoke mournfully of the good old days when landlords were rich and spent their money freely, but the secretary of the League, McFinley, in his spirit-grocery, seemed unusually full of hope and determination.

"We are all Home Rulers here," said he. "At the last election, in December, 1885, I was agent for Biggar, who stood against Saunderson, the best landlord and largest employer of labor in the neighborhood, and Biggar had a majority of 6,564 out of a total electorate of 10,000.

"One of the absurd anomalies of our government is that the county cess, over ten shillings in the pound, is levied by the grand jury, in which the farmers are absolutely unrepresented."

"Might not that be changed without a revolution in the form of government?" I asked.

"Certainly," he answered; "but the people think it best to concentrate their exertions on one reform once for all, instead of having year by year to push for little reforms, one by one.

"The general belief is that a Home Rule Parliament would be sufficiently conservative to deal with perfect justice with the land question. The influence of the Catholic clergy is conservative and all-powerful.

"The present land system must be done away with. The land this season has not produced any rent, and for the last two seasons we believe it has been paid out of the capital. Every effort has been made to meet the landlords.

" The increase of deposits in the banks does n't prove that the people are prospering ; the money would have been invested in the land instead if the farmers had been prosperous.

" Have not transactions in land been discouraged ? Certainly. Why not ? A high price paid for the tenant right, the result of competition, might have led the land-lord to think his rents were fair, however excessive they might be.

" Land purchase, even, is not all that is needed. There are any number of holdings in County Cavan of five or six acres each. The League programme is, in such cases, to transfer a number of the tenants to land now uncultivated, and to throw two or more of these little plots together to make one holding of a profitable size.

" Would I deprive the landlords of their demesne lands ? Certainly. If one of these swell landlords wants to keep a park, or a cover, or a pleasure-ground, as he is diverting the land from the use Providence de-signed it for—the support of the human race,—he ought to pay for it a tax equal to the rent that average tenants would pay for it. One individual ought not to have a thousand or five thousand acres within his demesne walls, while thousands outside are starving for want of it. These and other similar questions should be left to the collective wisdom of the country to settle, though perhaps some of the suffering farmers may be rather severe. This will, possibly, drive the landlords away, but there are already any number of residences vacant throughout the country, for the Land Acts have whittled down the rents so much that the landlords could n't keep their places up. There were two tobacco factories here :

one, kept by a local landlord, was closed a year or two ago ; and the other, kept by Mr. Kennedy, was transferred to Dublin.

" Under Home Rule, there will have to be local control of the police. It is their interest now to make themselves as unpleasant as possible. So if there is a street row anywhere the people side against the police, or at least are indifferent. Mrs. Curtin of Mollahiffe might be unsafe if the police were appointed by her neighbors, but why deprive thirty-one counties of a right, because in the thirty-second it might be abused ?

" Now policemen and detectives are often the heads of local secret societies, paid by the secret-service fund. They often push on the more hot-headed young men to commit outrages. The Sunday after the Crimes Act was passed, last spring, a meeting of the secret societies was held near Cavan at three o'clock in the morning ; and before six, full particulars, with the names of all the people present, were lodged in the police head-quarters.

" As to the Fenians, many of them are good men and the people owe much to them. When there was nothing like law between landlord and tenant, the dread of the Ribbonman's bullet or of a Fenian rising kept many a landlord's conscience open to the law of God. Now, however, all are blended with the Nationalists.

" It is an herculean task in one year to settle the friction of centuries. If Mr. Gladstone's bill had been passed as it was, there would have been amendments needed within three years ; and what is wanted is a final settlement.

" Parnell, at the beginning of the movement, ordered us to seize the Municipal Boards and Boards of Guardians, and now the people have done so and become educated by the responsibility. Delay has been a good thing for us, and will secure a more satisfactory bill in the end. Tim Healey, the Irish platform orator, and Tim Healey, the Attorney-General, would be very different people.

"Many of the Unions have been mismanaged, and that is used as an argument against Home Rule. But the reverse is often the case. At Old Castle, in County Meath, less than twenty people received relief under the Conservatives, and now the Nationalist Board is giving out-door relief to over three hundred without any increase in the rates. The only thing the Nationalist Boards have done has been, where an unjust landlord has evicted a number of people and made paupers of them, to give them one or two pounds each a week, half of which the landlord pays ; and this is only fair, since the landlord has made them paupers.

"In this county, the Catholics are nearly three quarters of the whole people, and outside of the landlords and their immediate dependents, not five per cent. are opposed to Home Rule. Lough, a leading Protestant merchant here, is openly with us, and many others are so in secret. You must not confound Protestantism with Orangeism, for Orangeism is to Protestantism much what Fenianism is to Catholicism."

A few miles farther on was Clones, a fairly prosperous town, with several streets straggling down the slope of a high hill surmounted by a large Catholic church. As in other country towns no business seems to be done except on the weekly fair day, when the farmers throng the narrow little streets, and are succeeded the next morning by a troop of commercial travellers eager to fill their orders while the money is in the till. The people seemed peaceful and contented, perhaps for the reasons suggested by T. Coffey, a leading publican and farmer. "Sir Thomas B. Leonard," he explained, "my landlord, has sold the whole of his agricultural property here to the tenants, at from eighteen to twenty years' purchase. I bought at the lowest price of any, seventeen and a half years' purchase, and while I used to pay £16 a year rent I am now purchasing by yearly payments of £11 for forty-nine years.

"The landlords about here are good and have had no trouble with their tenants, though we are all Home Rulers. There is neither religious excitement nor boycotting here, and the people generally would buy if the landlords would sell."

SOME ORANGEMEN.

The Orange Society, though comparatively modern, has its roots in the seventeenth century. The siege of Derry was early celebrated by local feasts and processions. In 1688 a secret society was formed among the adherents of William of Orange, in the army on Hounslow Heath, and was perpetuated as a semi-military association in County Antrim. For a century afterwards the Protestants of the north were perpetually alarmed by fears of risings among the Catholics, who had been dispossessed of their ancient properties ; both parties organized intermittently, and in 1795 a riot, grandiloquently called the Battle of the Diamond, took place between the rival secret societies—the Defenders, who raided Protestant farmers for arms, and the Peep-of-Day Boys, who used to get up early to recapture them. The outrages that followed were so alarming that the more respectable Protestants began to organize semi-vigilance societies after the fashion of Masonic lodges, calling themselves Orange Boys ; and three years later, when the Nationalist feeling revived under the influence of the French Revolution, and the Presbyterians of the north united with the Defenders of the south in the highly centralized association of the United Irishmen, the Orange lodges were merged into the Orange Association. " We associate," ran the preamble of the old constitution, " to the utmost of our power to support and defend his Majesty George the Third, the Constitution, the Laws of the Country, and the succession to the Throne in his Majesty's illustrious house, being Protestants ; for the defence of our persons and properties and to maintain the peace of our country ; and for these purposes we will be at all times ready to assist the civil and military powers in the just and lawful discharge of their duty. . . . We further declare that we are exclusively a Protestant Association ; yet detesting as we do any intolerant spirit, we solemnly pledge ourselves to each other, that we will not persecute or upbraid any person on account of his religious opinions."[1]

During the Revolution of 1798 the Orangemen performed important military and police service. Two years later they were generally opposed to the Union with England, from a fear of Catholic Emancipation and the consequent downfall of the Protestant ascendancy. During the reign of William IV. the society was the subject of a parliamentary investigation, and the oaths were subsequently modified. When the disestablishment of the Irish Church was proposed by Mr. Gladstone, the most violent and revolutionary language was used by the Orange leaders, and in 1886, during the pendency of the Home Rule Bill, the Orangemen began to

[1] Published for the use of Orangemen only, 1799.

drill nightly in Belfast, at Rich Hill, and at Armagh. The speeches delivered at the opening of the Ballynapage Orange Hall in Belfast this last autumn, to an immense and enthusiastic audience, show the high-water mark of Orange feeling at the present moment. "We do desire," said Colonel Saunderson, M.P., "to perpetuate memories of the past, which we believe reflect the glory of the race to which we belong and the religion which we profess, but we do not do it with the unchristian purpose of perpetuating discord and hatred in this our country, . . . but we do it that we may teach our children, as we have learned ourselves, that if a day should ever come when we are to be confronted by a similar danger and a similar foe we are ready to perform the same deeds again. . . . We require now an organization more than ever we did yet. Our opponents are organizing, and therefore I impress upon you and, through you, upon all my Orange brethren who may read these words that I employ, that no effort should be spared, and no stone should be left unturned, to make the Orangemen of Ulster prepared to meet a day of danger, and it may be a day of battle." [1]

The opinions of Orangemen when taken alone are perhaps more temperate than such words would imply.

"The great objection we in Ulster have to Home Rule," said a landlord, one of the recognized leaders of the Orangemen, "is that we have inherited certain rights as British citizens, and we believe these rights will not be secure under a Dublin Parliament. We do not believe that the men who have come to the front in the National movement are people from whom we could expect fair, sound, and reasonable legislation.

"Parnell is a conservative Nationalist ; but can Parnell

[1] *Belfast Newsletter*, October 18, 1887.

lead his party? The people will insist on returning their own favorites.   No guaranties would be of any value; the Irish-Americans are at the back of the Irish in Ireland, and they are parties to no guaranties.

"The recent Land Acts have been unjust, not because they have made our property worthless, but because they have deprived us, without compensation, of proprietary rights which many of us bought not many years ago with hard cash.   If such things are done in the green tree, what will be done in the dry?

"Again, prejudices, religious and social, are so violent here that no Irish Parliament could be impartial.   I know, on good authority, that, four or five years ago, a priest in County Down said from the altar: 'The time will come when there will be not a landlord nor a Protestant in Ireland.'

"The present local boards are mere jobs, and a Home Rule Parliament would be of a similar character.

"All English laws are based on the theory that the majority of the people will obey and enforce them. Here the reverse is true.   The people disobey the laws and do every thing to hinder their execution.   The juries, who should be merely judges of the fact, make themselves interpreters of the laws.   In such a state of society of what good would be any constitutional limitations?

"Some people suggest that Ireland be given a constitution like that of Massachusetts, with the imperial rights enforced by federal courts.   But such a system has been successful in America only because the United States are composed of so many States that the interest of no one State preponderates.   We are a small country next a very much larger and richer one, so that there can be no balance between the two.

"It has been suggested that Ulster be given its own Home Rule legislature. The feeling about that suggestion in Ulster is creditable. The people believe they would do very well as Ulstermen, but they don't want to cut themselves off from the large loyalist minority in the rest of Ireland, who would then be left at the mercy of the majority.

"We are loyal to the laws of England ; if England chooses to transfer us to the control of a Parliament at Dublin, we shall owe that Parliament no allegiance, for allegiance cannot be transferred, and we shall not obey it. Such is the simple position of the Orangemen, and I suppose there are over a hundred thousand of us in Ulster.

"If we refused to obey or pay taxes to a Dublin government, it could n't force us to, for it would not have the control of the police, and half the military would side with us. The Unionists would begin to drill, and would have in the Orangemen the nucleus of an army. In the Belfast riots, it was the street boys and not the Orangemen who fought, and more serious riots have happened in the past, when the Queen's Island men have turned out in force with their riveting hammers to strike and their bolts to throw. In the case of such a rising as Home Rule would occasion, the movement would be taken up by the leaders and would go from the top to the bottom of society."

Portadown is a smoky, bustling manufacturing town, the centre of an intensely Orange district. There is not even a branch of the National League in the place. The Orange Hall is a simple stone building, but the number of lodges that meet there regularly or occasionally is enormous. In Portadown itself there are thirty-three lodges, and within a radius of a little over nine miles there are one hundred and fifty-seven more—thirty-four in Lurgan, twenty-nine in Killylea, twenty-two in Tanderagee, eleven in Richhill, twenty-seven in Legoniel, eleven in Gilford, and twenty-three in Armagh. The attitude of the Orangemen is that of stubborn, but rather gloomy, determination. "I don't know how we can prevent Home Rule, but I do say this, that we will not have it." This was the deliberate statement of one of the Town Commissioners, and the feeling of Portadown could not possibly be expressed with more precision in a hundred pages. Those Protestants who are not Orange are even more pessimistic still. "People like me," a substantial shopkeeper remarked, "will quietly slip away; and those who stay, will never be at peace. I have seen them chasing the police here like goats before them."

It is the fear of unjust treatment by the Catholics and not any theory or sentiment for the Union that arrays the Orangemen against Home Rule. One who protested most loudly that the Irish flag was blue, not green, and that "the Church of Ireland" was properly termed the Catholic Church, since it dated from apostolic times and had never protested against any thing, confessed that what Ireland most needed was "education—education to prepare the people for Home Rule."

"We are partners in a mill near here," said one of two table companions at Larne, where I was waiting the sailing of my steamer. "We began as common mill hands, and gradually saved money till we were able to set up a bleachery of our own. We have won prosperity by our industry, and don't wish to help support these Nationalists in a Dublin Parliament or in new political offices.

The south of Ireland people are lazy and thriftless. We won't have Home Rule."

"We don't believe we should get fair play from a Home Rule Parliament. With only sixteen members out of eighty-nine or more, we should be completely swamped. We will fight first.

" If we believed that our interests as British citizens would be secure, we should not of course object to Home Rule ; but, as it is, we are a divided people, and oil and water would mix better than we do.

" During the riots the manager of a flax company near here was attacked by some hundreds of his hands, simply because he was a Protestant, though a good and generous man, and we had to organize parties to sit up with guns in our hands to guard him at night.

"Well, we can hold our own against the Nationalists, and we will fight, if need be, to keep our liberty."

CONCLUSION.

THE reader has been listening to many voices ; much of what they say is contradictory ; and not a single word, perhaps, is beyond question wholly impartial and unpartisan ; but in spite of the confusion some facts seem to be definite and undeniable.

From a distance the various classes in Ireland seem separated one from another by wide gulfs of feeling and interest. Close at hand they are seen to contain within themselves every variety of opinion, to be all sincerely in love with Ireland, and all dissatisfied with the present system of government. In the event of " Home Rule " there is no danger of actual civil war, and a Dublin Parliament, so long as it holds the scales of justice even, will be criticised and ridiculed but not forcibly resisted. No general exodus of the merchants is expected. Except under compulsion a merchant does not go out of business, and with the exception of a few distilleries and iron manufactories about Belfast there is little business now transacted in Ireland that could be transferred to another country. The landlords also will remain for the most part, if they can. Only those will leave the country who are driven by poverty or persecution to live or to earn a living in a more business-like or tolerant community. Home Rule, if it does come, will be given a fair trial even by those who are hopeless of its success.

The poverty is unquestionably extreme ; the proportion of paupers to the population is from three to four times greater than in England ; not only do the farmers generally complain of failing crops and falling prices, but the shopkeepers and commercial travellers, usually a conservative class, are also in despair ; the landlords, who were once large employers of labor are becoming bankrupt, and the laborers who used to depend upon them can find no work. It is true that the drink bill of Ireland is enormous, and that the deposits in Irish banks were never larger than to-day, but drunkenness is as often the consequence as the cause of misery, and in prosperous times a deposit yielding one per cent. is not a popular investment. Irish poverty, when it is not laid to the account of the government, is attributed to American competition in grain and flour, a sufficient cause and a true one.

The general desire for Home Rule is, it would seem, a natural result of the general poverty. The most pronounced Nationalists do not rest their claims on purely sentimental grounds, but argue that one nation cannot govern another nation well, and then point to the distress of the farmers, the incessant emigration, the absence of manufactories. The farmers and the priests, who usually belong to the farming class, believe in Home Rule, because they think it will mean the purchase by the tenants of their holdings at a minimum price, and protective duties on American grain and English manufactures. In Galway the shopkeepers and fishermen expect a Dublin Parliament to build a railroad to Clifden, piers along the coast, and boats for those who need them. In Donegal the farmers look for a redistribution of land now occupied by landlords or graziers, and a rapid development of the resources of the country. In Athlone and Kilkenny vast industrial schools are expected to train the people in manufacturing processes under government supervision. In many places the railroads are complained of, and it is suggested that they should be controlled by an Irish government. The people, in a word, are Home Rulers, because they wish to see Ireland prosper and to share in her prosperity. The only means suggested to this end are the reduction of taxation and the creation of industries more profitable than agriculture, and these benefits they think will come only under Home Rule.

A few fanatics there are who would prefer Home Rule and greater poverty to a continuance of the Union and less poverty, but they are clearly in a minority. In private and serious conversation a priest, a farmer, a shopkeeper, or a laborer invariably denounces the government for some particular grievance that seems to him preventable and that touches his own pocket or the pockets of his neighbors. In these primitive instincts an Irishman is not unlike other people, and of this human tendency, that in the course of time is sure to influence conduct, many of the more radical agitators are unquestionably afraid. It is significant that in Donegal, in Tyrone, and elsewhere, local leaders admit that the farmers would lose interest in Home Rule if the land question were settled, and that in Ballinasloe and Cork it is noticed that the laborers are satisfied where they have employment.

Certain grievances are admitted to exist by men of all shades of political opinion : the amount of the law costs in proceedings in the land courts, which often equals or exceeds the amount of the reductions granted ; the absence of local authority to incorporate companies for purposes of local improvement, to run tramways, build bridges, or to furnish towns with gas or water-works ; the non-representative character of the grand juries ; the excessive centralization of the government, which keeps it wholly uninfluenced by Irish popular opinion, which fills too frequently important offices with men unknown or without reputation or even hated in Ireland, and which affords Irish Nationalists of ability and political influence no opportunity to acquire that sense of responsibility which can be given only by administrative experience.

The recent Land Acts are certainly so revolutionary in character that they would be held unconstitutional in any State in this country, but as yet they have not been given a fair trial by the people. Free sale of the tenant right, and purchase under the various acts of the landlord's interest, have been generally discouraged by the Nationalist leaders. Farms have been boycotted often for the most trivial reasons : the spite or greed of a neighbor, the political opinions of the tenant, the discharge or hiring of a laborer. Throughout the country are to be seen fields black with rag-weeds, or white with thistles. In such conditions farming can be successful only by accident. The reopening of judicial leases, however equitable in principle, has had the effect of finally stopping any improvements by either landlord or tenant, and of encouraging the tenants to regard any land act, however advantageous to them, as a temporary makeshift, certain if disregarded to give place to something better. Such tactics are abhorrent to the survivors of the movement of 1848, and to the priests of the older generation ; but they, or the sentiments that inspire them, are prevalent throughout Ireland.

Among the Catholics at the present time there is little

apparent religious intolerance. In the south and south-west there are not a few Protestants holding elective offices in Catholic communities, and I did not hear a word in Ireland spoken by a Catholic against a Protestant, as such. In Connemara and Donegal some feeling had been plainly excited among the Catholics by attempts at proselytizing. In the north and in Dublin shopkeepers and others were full of fear of Catholic aggression, and in the south ignorant Protestant laborers and intelligent Protestant landlords were as one in believing that murder and outrage would be the result of Catholic supremacy. Such alarm seems unfounded; but one danger exists, and that a grave one—the opposition of the Catholics to any but a Catholic system of education. "There," said Archbishop Walsh, pointing to four thousand children of the Christian Brother Schools, "there is the protest of the Catholic people of Dublin against the maintenance in this Catholic country of a system of education in which religion is shut out from the opportunity of exercising with unrestrained freedom her legitimate influence in the education of the young." As the freedom that is desired is the repeal of the "conscience clause," forbidding religious instruction and the exhibition of emblems, except at certain hours, it would seem that in the matter of education the religious line is sharply drawn.

"Home Rule," a Parliament at Dublin, with exclusive control of all Irish matters, is proposed as a means for restoring prosperity to Ireland. This it is expected to do by settling the land question, by fostering domestic industries through protection or a system of loans and bounties, by founding technical schools, by reducing taxation, and by restoring law and order.

The " Land Question " would severely tax the skill of a body of men with little knowledge of political economy. Mr. Michael Davitt and many other Nationalists would approach the subject with confidence, but few landlords would trust themselves willingly to their tender mercies. A just price is seldom paid by a purchaser who can fix his own terms and enforce their acceptance. Even leading Nationalists see the danger and impolicy of such a course. " There can be no doubt," Mr. Timothy Harrington wrote me, " as to the eagerness of the Irish Nationalist party to have the land question settled by the imperial Parliament, and settled as early as possible. We are all extremely anxious that a question calculated to excite so much feeling and bring so many opposing interests into collision should not be left to be settled in the early and therefore trying days of a new legislature. No sincere Irishman could honestly entertain any other opinion." Such is well known not to be the opinion of Mr. Michael Davitt, and these notes would seem to show that many of the local leaders would not consider favorably any land legislation proposed by the imperial government. It is also clear that Irish statesmen are now confronted by a very pretty dilemma. The land question should be settled before Home Rule is established, and yet no guaranty for the purchase money is suggested by the Nationalists, except a guaranty by a Home Rule Parliament. The creation of a peasant proprietary is, moreover, not the work of a year, nor even of a few years, and is apparently impossible, except under the continuous supervision of a strongly centralized and stable government.

" Protection " is an article of faith in the economical creed of the great majority of Irishmen. The farmers look to protective duties on cereals and cattle to restore the prices of the last decade ; the shopkeepers and many landlords share the hopes of the farmers, in whose prosperity or poverty they are partners ; and everybody in Ireland believes that Irish manufactures cannot be established without protection against the manufactured goods of England and the Continent,—everybody, that is, with the significant exception of the only successful manufacturers, the Ulster linen manufacturers, and the owners of the woollen and tweed mills of West Meath. The protective system is now on its defence in the United States, and the chief argument of its defenders is that our home market is more valuable than the foreign market, and at all costs must be retained. This argument does not apply to Ireland ; England and the Continent are the chief markets for Irish linen, America is the chief market for Irish woollen goods. For manufactures of a high grade there is no demand in poverty-stricken Ireland ; for manufactures of a low grade even the demand is restricted to the necessaries of life. If any manufactures cannot be profitably conducted in Ireland without "protection," it is because those manufactures cannot be profitably sold at the same price as similar articles of foreign make. If any manufactures shall be profitably conducted in Ireland with "protection," it will be because those articles are bought at greater cost than similar articles now are by the consumers, the Irish people. The farmers and laborers who cannot pay their shop bills now will not be benefited by an increase in such bills in future. But the farmers will be recompensed by the higher price of agricultural products. They may be, and in that case the bills of all other men in Ireland will be still further increased by

the amount of the farmers' extra profits ; while the graziers certainly will be ruined by a duty on live stock, for
their market is England and the prices in the English
market will not be affected by "protection" in Ireland,
which can raise the cost of beef and mutton to the inhabitants of Ireland but to no one else. "Protection," then,
may not affect for the worse the Irish farmers, but it will
starve the laborers unless the manufacturers can afford
to pay higher wages than are paid at present. This they
cannot do without raising proportionally the prices of
their goods. The foreign market will then be finally
lost, and those manufactures only will survive in Ireland
that are needed to supply the home market. Less money
and goods, instead of more, will flow into Ireland from
without, and the only effect of "protection" in the course
of time will have been a redistribution of Irish property
among Irishmen in Ireland.

"The bounty system," which some regard more favorably than protection, is identical with it in principle, and
produces, though more rapidly, similar results. The
system, with regard to beet-root sugar, has been recently
discussed in Europe and seems now utterly discredited.
It would in Ireland require an immediate increase in
taxation, an increase less indirect than that exacted by
protection, and on that account it is less likely to com-
mend itself to an Irish Parliament.

Loans to fishermen for boats and schooners and nets,
grants for piers and harbors, for prizes and exhibitions,
for railroads to open up the country, for experiments and
surveys to discover mines and quarries, for founding industrial schools and colleges,—such expenses cannot
easily be incurred by the most patriotic representatives
of people on the verge of bankruptcy.

Taxation, even though lightened by a great reduction in the cost of police, of which a part is now borne by the imperial exchequer, is not likely to be materially reduced for many years after the peaceful establishment of " Home Rule." If it is accompanied or preceded by the creation of a peasant proprietary, and the claims of the landlords have not been completely extinguished, the national guaranty of the purchase money or of interest upon it must seriously impair the credit of the Irish government. Expenses for bounties, grants, and loans will have to be met by borrowing at high interest or by direct imposts ; in either case the people must pay. In certain respects the government of Ireland will cost more than it does now. The members of the Irish Parliament will certainly have to be paid salaries from the Irish treasury ; several new offices must be created ; and if any large measures of a socialistic character are undertaken by the government, such as the nationalization of the land, or the management of the railroads, the number of officials and the amount of public salaries must be increased very considerably.

One difficulty, then, in determining the question of Home Rule that cannot be called theoretical, is the fact that it is doubtful whether " Home Rule " would restore prosperity to Ireland, even if the Dublin Parliament were to do all that the people expect of it ; while it is certain that any practical pecuniary benefit would be long delayed. The faith that the Irish people have had in the power of the imperial government to create poverty or wealth by legislation, to change the laws of nature by Act of Parliament has been transferred to an imaginary Home Rule government. No change of government can effect a change in the tendencies of natural processes, whether they are called economic laws, physical laws, or the laws of God. If all the land in Ireland were to-morrow divided equally among all the Irish tenant farmers, it could raise the standard of living in Ireland only for a few years. In no country, in no county or town in any country, can the standard of living be permanently raised, or the population increase and maintain the same standard, without "the development there of some industry, the discovery of some local springs of industry, a new appreciation of previously unrecognized facilities for the application of more efficient processes of labor."[1] So long as agriculture continues to be the chief industry of Ireland, no legislation can improve the condition of its people and save them from the fate which between 1880 and 1883 drove from Norway, that land of peasant proprietors, one twentieth of its inhabitants. The one practical benefit of Home Rule, if wisely administered, will be the restoration of law and order, until such time as recurring poverty shall reproduce the elements of disorder and lawlessness.

The more or less theoretical difficulties or dilemmas in the way of Home Rule are many and serious. Of the various nationalities inhabiting the British Islands the population and wealth of England is so much the largest and the greatest that a federal union between them, a union that recognizes the equal claim of each nationality, as in the United States Senate, is preposterous. The interests of England must prevail in all questions in which those interests are involved, for the same reason that the interests of New York would prevail in the federal government if the United States consisted only of New York, New Jersey, and Rhode Island. No sys-

[1] Mr. L. Courtney in *The Nineteenth Century*.

tem of Home Rule would be practicable, therefore, that gives an Irish government any control of the excise; and yet it is for that purpose that the Irish mainly desire Home Rule.

The analogy of Canada and Australia does not apply to the case of Ireland. The secession of Canada or its cession to the United States at some future period is contemplated with complacency by many English statesmen, as is the independence of Australia by Mr. Labouchère. That the cession of Ireland to France, or its independence, would be ruinous to England until the advent of the age of universal peace, proves conclusively the inaccuracy of such an analogy. The integrity of Ireland is essential to the independent power of England in a sense in which the integrity of no other territory is essential to it. The union between the two islands must therefore be peculiarly close, and the links must be forged of something less brittle and more material than sentiment. Any local government, then, accorded to Ireland must possess only strictly defined and delegated powers, and the imperial Parliament or some other central body must retain the authority and the means to enforce any measure judged necessary for the general safety.

Certain principles of justice, impartially enforced by law, are recognized as conditions of modern civilization. Intercourse between England and Ireland would be hindered, just men without reason would be sacrificed, and the public conscience would be outraged, if laws subversive of such principles were suffered to be enacted in Ireland. The power of a Home Rule Parliament should then be still further restricted by constitutional provisions in the nature of a bill of rights prohibiting legislation in violation of contracts, taking private prop-

erty for public use without compensation, imposing un-
equal or unjust taxation, or discriminating against any
individual or class. A court, appointed by the central
authority, should then be established, to go on circuit
throughout Ireland and adjudicate all causes involving
constitutional questions, or questions touching imperial
or other reserved rights. Such a Parliament, it is worth
observing, would be unable to enact laws similar to the
Land Acts.

The grant to Ireland of a Home Rule Parliament,
however constituted, and with powers however limited,
involves a complete revolution in the system of government in Great Britain. Parliament now is the autocratic
committee of a highly centralized democracy, with unlimited and undefined powers. The local affairs of Ireland cannot be removed from the discretionary interference of Parliament without limiting the powers of
Parliament. Is such limitation possible? It may be
suspected that a Home Rule Parliament, so long as the
government of Great Britain remains otherwise unchanged, will and can exist only during good behavior,
at the pleasure of the capricious British democracy.

If the consideration of Home Rule is postponed till
after the settlement of the land question, it is likely that
many years will pass before an Irish Parliament sits in
Dublin. In the meantime, if Irish discontent is to be
allayed, certain changes should be made in the management of Irish affairs and at once. The grand-jury system is obsolescent, and grand juries should be made
elective, or should be superseded by representative bodies
with more varied powers. It is, moreover, absurd that
the promoters of schemes of purely local improvement
should have to apply to Westminster for incorporation.

These, and all the more obvious Irish grievances, would be removed by an extension to Ireland of the Local Government Bill, now under discussion in Parliament. By that bill county councils are to be elected by the ratepayers for three years, to add to themselves one fourth their own number from the ratepayers to sit for six years. They are to exercise "the existing administrative powers of the justices in respect of county rates and financial business, county buildings, county bridges, the provision and management of the county lunatic asylums, the establishment and maintenance of reformatory and industrial schools, the granting of licences for music and dancing, the granting of licences for the sale of intoxicating liquors." They are to have "the control and maintenance of all main highways, the power of making all provisional orders under the Pier and Harbor Acts, the Tramways Act, the Electric Lighting Act, and the Gas and Water-works Facilities Acts as regards companies"; and a variety of other powers not of a judicial character may be transferred to them by the government of the day by a mere Order in Council, subject to no control except Parliament and the common law. The powers specified are so extensive as to make the office of County Councillor one of sufficient dignity, responsibility, and experience to attract men of ability ; and if a salary were attached to the office, as it should be in Ireland, it would be the means of turning many a brilliant demagogue into a useful public servant. Some abuses and jobs might be perpetrated in the beginning ; but the people would soon learn by experience that few luxuries are so expensive as abuses and jobs in the granting of public franchises or the expenditure of the public money.

In the matter of the appointment of judicial officers in Ireland, it would be wise for the government to consult with the Nationalist Members of Parliament, and whenever possible to adopt their suggestions. It is not always easy for a man of legal training to decide a question of law on grounds purely sentimental, and a few gross miscarriages of justice might yet be counterbalanced by an increased respect for law among the people. All public offices should of course be filled by Irishmen, and Irishmen not specially connected with Dublin Castle.

Finally, with generosity and discretion the government should promote works of public improvement in Ireland ; loans should be granted for the extension of railroads in Connaught, for the building of piers, for the purchase of boats and nets for fishermen,—and the liability for such loans should not fall only on the districts chiefly benefited. In every way technical education should be fostered ; and primary education should be made compulsory, even though it have to be largely sectarian and Catholic.

As the farmers become occupiers, as the laborers find employment, as the people by controlling their own local affairs learn to blame themselves rather than the English government for local discomforts, the number of Irishmen in Ireland will increase who will be perfectly contented with a measure of Home Rule far less sweeping than that proposed by Mr. Gladstone, and at the same time they will become more and more competent to operate with benefit to themselves and without injury to others any measure of Home Rule that shall be granted.

www.ingramcontent.com/pod-product-compliance
Lightning Source LLC
Chambersburg PA
CBHW060535030726
47498CB00004B/1209